MIGHT AND MAJESTY

BAPTISM BY FIRE

SEAN MITCHELL

MAPS ILLUSTRATED BY
AMELIA LANGFORD

DEDICATION

Dedicated to my mother who gave me a passion for writing
And to my father who gave me a passion for fantasy

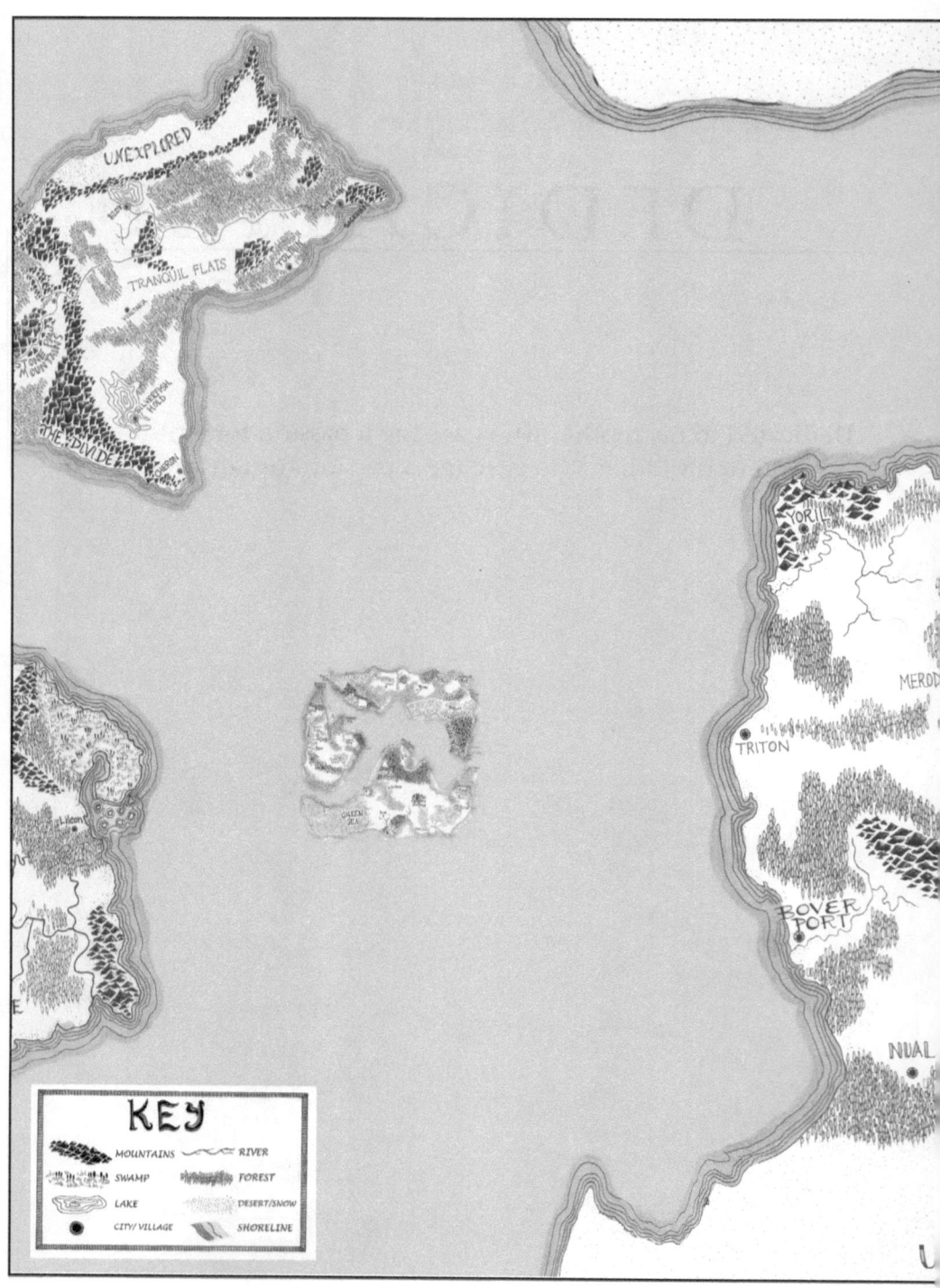

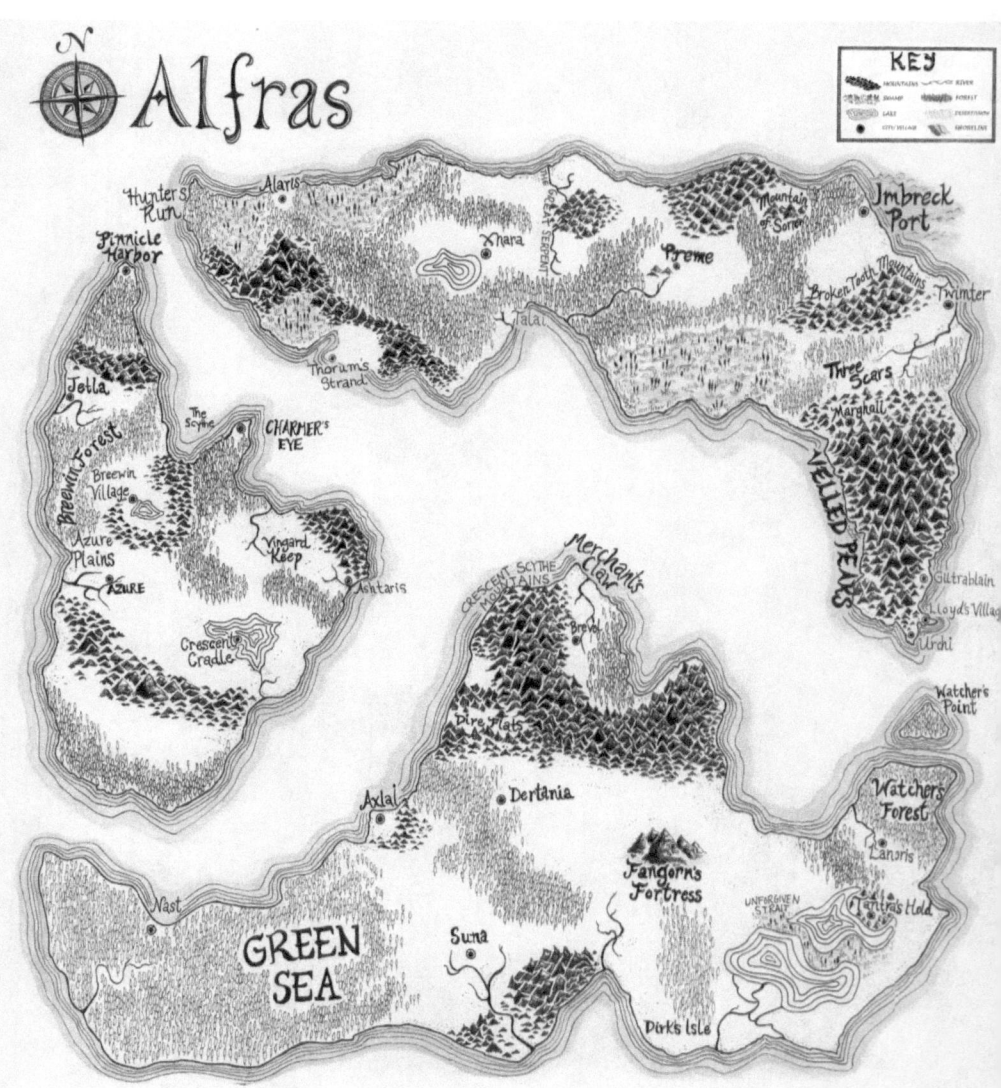

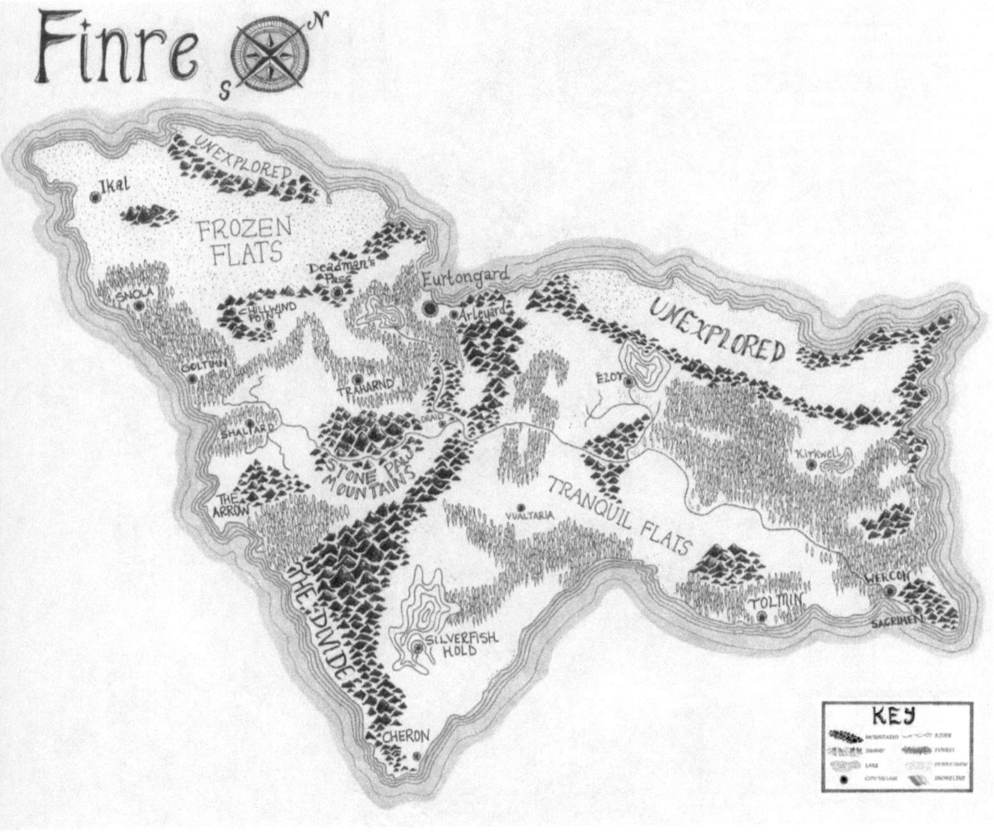
Finre
N
S
UNEXPLORED
Ikal
FROZEN FLATS
Deadman's Pass
Eurtongard
SNOLA
CHILLWIND POINT
Arleyard
UNEXPLORED
TRAHARND
EZOY
SHALTARD
STONE PAW MOUNTAINS
Kirkwell
THE ARROW
TRANQUIL FLATS
VUALTARIA
THE DIVIDE
SILVERFISH HOLD
TOLMIN
WERCON
SACRIMEN
CHERON
KEY

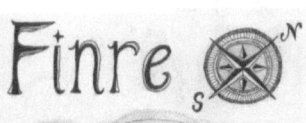

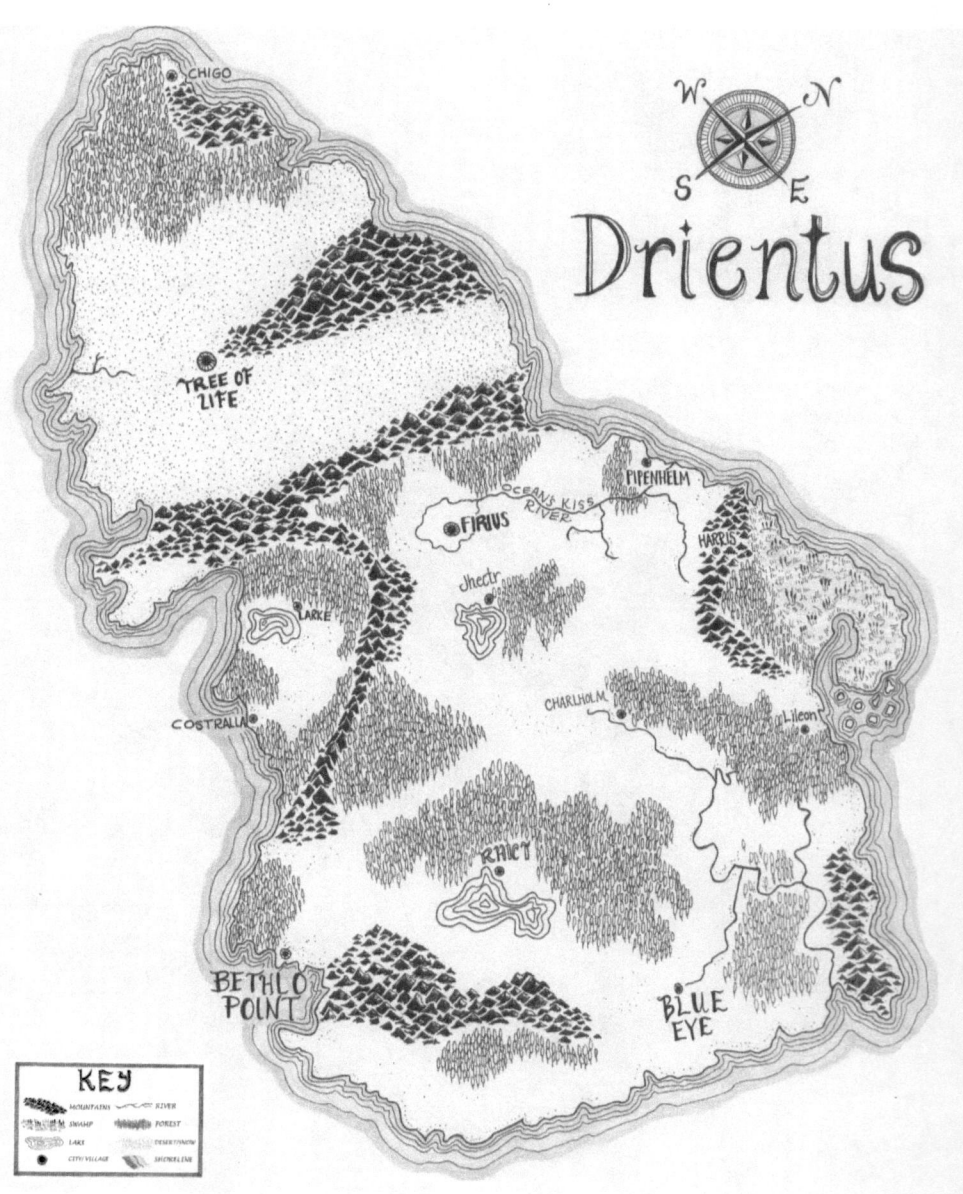

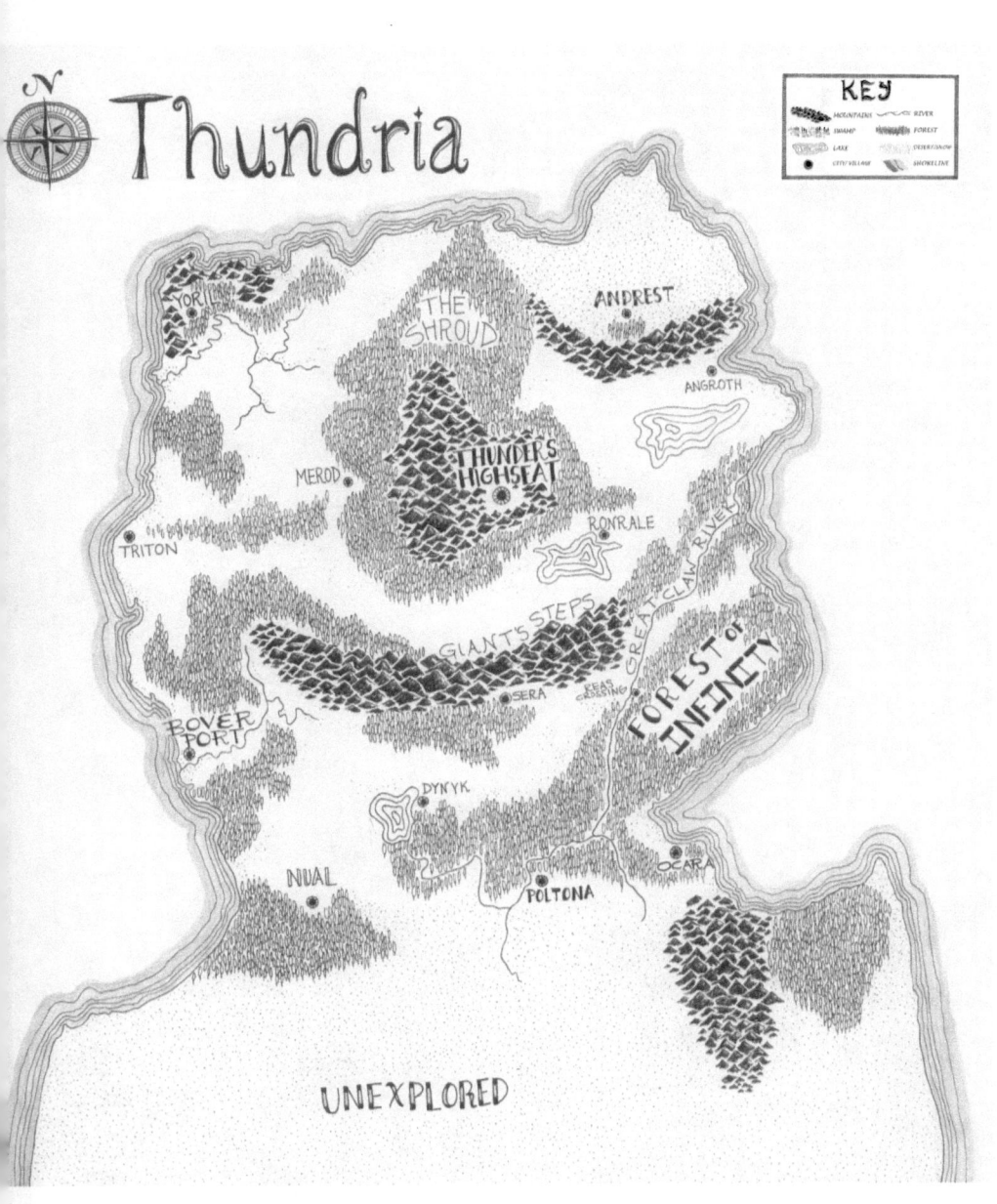

PROLOGUE

Before life and being, before light and dark, before peace and chaos, there were Two. The great God and Goddess of old times dwelled in the kingdom of the divine, where they were forever enthralled by their love for each other. The God was a strong, valiant entity with limitless ambition, while the Goddess was an angel with a heart of gold and the unique, nurturing care only a mother could hold. After eons of passion, the Two sought to create life in honor of their love. They created the planet as a canvas for their undying affection. Upon this sapphire of blue they painted the lands with their fiery, fearless ardor, and life began.

By their hands, a great island emerged from the restless oceans that blanketed the world. This raw earth was sculpted like clay until the Two were satisfied with their landscape. Once the tranquil world was made and filled with wild creatures, the Two created a race to rule above all else. They created the angels. These winged creatures of both voice and thought were brought to the land and cradled in their infancy. By their Father's might, they grew in great number and created a civilization, while by their Mother's majesty, they were given control of the natural world around them. Over countless generations the winged ones learned to harness their powers and command their natural surroundings by channeling the life energy from their holy parents into their surroundings. For a millennium angels were the only beings to populate the land–until a new race began to emerge.

Over many generations, some angels began to have children who were not born with wings. These creations were unknown even to the Two. This new race could not control the elements, and over time the creatures crafted a crude language of their own. These anomalies, which came to be known as humans, proved to be more physically fit than the angels and were admired for their determination and willpower. The Divine Two watched in silence as these creations began to multiply and walk side by side with the angels. Even though their hands had not directly created the humans, the Two loved them all the same.

Across the lands stood three massive pillars that stretched high into the infinite heavens. These pillars of shining gold and flawless marble held up the everlasting kingdom of the dead, and through them the people found eternal peace. The pillars served as bridges between the tranquility of life and the sanctuary of death. Through them the dead never bid the living farewell, for all that left the world would forever be in contact with those who remained. The power of the pillars was harnessed by the peaceful folk of the lands, and through these structures they found that nearly anything was achievable. Those with the greatest power and dedication could unleash the full power of the pillars and reap their wonderful rewards. These few, sacred individuals manipulated time itself in minute ways by using the pillars as anchors for their magic. A field of seeds could grow into a vast crop in a day, and people lived well beyond their natural years as a sacred few harnessed the time-altering qualities of the pillars. For thousands of generations, peace reigned and there was no name for evil, until one fateful day.

He emerged from the deepest crevice in the darkest valley of the ocean. His was an evil beyond words, and through him the world would burn.

An unknown force unleashed sin upon the pure world and brought newfound pain to the innocent hearts of all who opposed him. Using dark magic unknown to even the God and Goddess, he summoned seven stone giants of pure wrath to bring ruin to the lands. The beast commanded legions of horrific creatures to follow his giants and swept over the utopia as the night sweeps over day. The Divine Two named him Gulinthor, the harbinger of darkness.

From the start of his campaign, the goal of this sinister entity was clear. The beast sent his armies to the pillars so that he could harness their power for himself. The God and Goddess used all their strength to destroy the army of malice at his command, but despite their best efforts, they could not shake the foundation of Gulinthor's dominance. Using his near-divine strength, Gulinthor created bestial soldiers who found glee through primal malice and cruelty. Using his army of unholy might, he wrought unspeakable evil upon all. Battles between the creations of the holy Two and the evil from the depths of the planet raged for many years, but as time wore on it became clear that the humans and angels had no chance against the power of Gulinthor. The dark one continued his slaughter of the innocent children born from the Two, without relent. Finally, as he approached the final pillar he had yet to claim, his ultimate goal just within his reach, the God and Goddess wept in despair. It was in this final hour of defeat that the unthinkable happened. The very tears that dropped from the Divine Two flooded the earth and eliminated all life, both dark and light.

After four days of sorrow, the God and Goddess looked at their pale blue sapphire of a planet with bloodshot eyes. The land they had created was submerged beneath the salty oceans and no sign of good or evil could be found. The Two desperately searched for any sign of life on the blue tapestry, but to no avail. After many long days they had lost all hope of finding their creations, until they saw a young human boy and a young angelic girl in two woven baskets, tossing among the waves. The children screamed as waves threatened to capsize their baskets, and in this moment the Divine Two gave up their greatest gift for their children.

A dark cloud of grief swept over the God's heart, yet the silver lining of this cloud was coated with hope for a better future for his remaining children. Using the last of his powers, the God created a third race of life to save the children. This was a race of raw, scaled creatures that could breathe both air and water. He created two of these sentient beings and called them "lizards." Upon breathing their first breaths of life, the lizards grabbed the two baskets and stabilized them so that they would not capsize amid the violent sea. Once the God realized his creations were in safe hands, he let out his final gasp and plummeted to the earth.

The Goddess brought rocks up from the depths of the ocean to form a new body of land that would serve as a home for the four survivors. The land was massive, but not stable, and the Goddess' last regret was not being able to make the land secure. She fell from the heavens as the land she created began to crack and splinter. Once the Two crashed into the rolling waves, the heavens crumbled, and the three pillars sank deep beneath the dark waters. Their divine utopia had fallen, but the memories of such a grand place became forever imprinted upon the four survivors.

With no guidance and only their will to survive, the four beings settled on the land and began to multiply. Through them, the four races of the world emerged: humans, angels, a mix between the two that became known as half-humans, and lizards. These four races began to populate the planet with a swiftness that none could have anticipated. As decades turned to centuries and centuries turned to millennia, the story of the Divine Two continued to be passed down through the generations; yet over time, the story became obscured. Fact became legend, and legend became myth as the world continued to spin.

Countless millennia after Gulinthor's rise, the temples that once served as places of reverence for the Divine Two had long since been torn down, despite the fact that some still gave thanks to the fallen Two for their sacrifice. Mordikai thought of all this and more as he sat atop his throne in the icy domain of his forefathers. The two-legged walkers of the world dared not traverse here, for their kind feared Mordikai's clansmen with a brutal passion. Mordikai surveyed his kingdom of frost as he continued to ponder.

As the Divine Two slowly faded from the forefront their creations' minds, a fifth race made itself known. Mordikai's ancestors were not a friendly people, but rather, they were regarded as beasts to be both respected and feared. Ever since the cataclysm brought by Gulinthor, the dragon folk had detached themselves from the world of men, lizards, and angels. The people rarely spoke of them, and when they did they uttered words of dread and derision through tight, quivering lips. Mordikai knew his race was feared long before his time, but as the tide of darkness crept toward the four civilized kingdoms of the world, he knew the true destiny of his people would be revealed. Mordikai stretched his wings wide and shivered as he began to think of how the two-legged ones had conquered the natural world.

The landmass created by the Goddess that scores of creations called home continued to split into many islands, which drifted apart from one another as time crept by. Organized life claimed these landmasses and brought banner and steel upon them. Three islands separated by a thin stretch of ocean in the western sea came to be known as the Alfras Islands. These lands were blessed with bountiful woodlands and an abundance of sustenance in their waters. No formal monarchy ruled them.

Mostly lizards and humans inhabited the continent far to the northwest of Alfras. All of the land was covered in frost except for a grand peninsula on the southwestern tip, which was laden with forests that endured the never-ending brittle cold. This land had once been unforgiving to all who dared trespass it, yet in time, lizards and men learned how to tame the elements. The inhabitants discovered great ores beneath the land and were quick to create mines and towns scattered across the environment. The land became known as Finre, and her capitol of Eurtongard stood as a testament to the will of man and lizard alike to survive in even the harshest of lands.

Across a strait of rough waters to the southwest of Finre sat the continent of Drientus. This land was blessed with rich soil and a long, pristine river that stretched to the heart of the country. Humans and some lizards scattered across the unstinted land, and at its heart sat the capitol on an island that lay in the middle of a great lake just south of the merciless desert. The capitol, Firius, was built around the dormant volcano at the middle of the massive island. Though their nation was strong, these people never sought to do harm to others due to a long line of benevolent kings.

If one were to follow the setting sun from Drientus, one would behold the biggest continent of them all. The people called the land Thundria, and all the races of the world shared it. Abundant plains existed throughout the land, yet if one were to progress into the deep reaches of the south along the continent, one would find oneself at the unforgiving southern pole of the planet. At the center of this great land the people had constructed a massive capitol wrought in iron and magma, which all referred to as Thunder's Highseat.

The ever changing and growing land experienced many generations of peace until the king of the Thundrians wrought an ancient evil upon the world. He sought to raise the pillars from their eternal resting place using unspeakable dark arts so he could acquire their mythical, infinite powers. He slaughtered the people of the planet and forced countless lives into slavery as his evil began to envelop every free corner of the world. His plan seemed impenetrable, until one day he was met with an army of all races, including Mordikai's dragonkin, who vowed to end his reign of terror in the name of peace and justice.

Two hundred fifty years ago Mordikai followed a great general into many vicious battles across the entire world. Countless lives were snuffed from existence, and before the final battle was over, the dark king channeled the power of Gulinthor into himself to bring ruin to his foes. The final battle raged with a terrible fervor like none other until, in the final hour when victory seemed most imminent to the forces of light, Gulinthor made his presence known. The incarnation of evil itself tore through the battlefield until it came upon the leader of the rebellion force. The rebel leader's name was Lloyd, an angelic savior and a king among kings. By his hand, he stopped the wretched madness and brought independence and order to the lands once again before vanishing in a holy light along with his three most trusted companions. He was never seen again.

To this day, the people of Thundria hate the young general Lloyd, who killed their dark king, for in their eyes the king had been a God who would lead his people into a new era of power and prestige. The rest of the world frowned upon Thundria for this notion, and since the great conflict, tensions between Thundria and her neighbors have only heightened.

Two hundred and fifty years have passed since Thundria's terrible war engulfed the world in fire. For all that time, Mordikai has watched the world change into the fragile thing it is now. He diligently awaits the day when the thin glass pane of stability finally shatters. Soon the world will crumble, for it has been prophesized to him by an old friend that he has missed for many human generations. Not nineteen years ago it reached his old ears that the world was once again graced with this friend's presence.

Now, as the tides of darkness slowly encroach upon his home, Mordikai flies forth with several faithful companions who have prepared for this moment since they last fought alongside the two-legged races of the world, over two centuries ago. Despite all his preparation, the fate of this world resides within the young one's hands, and his hands alone. Mordikai knows that as darkness sweeps over the free lands, only Lloyd can save the world from fire and destruction.

CHAPTER 1

As the waves gently caressed the side of my small fishing vessel I looked to the sky and let out a sigh. The vast blue canvas above me was dotted with white patches of rolling clouds. The warmth of the sun seeped into my skin and caused me to yawn as the grip on my fishing pole loosened. Rays of sunlight danced across the ever-moving ocean around the numerous miniscule boats about mine. Today, the blinding ruby high above was unusually scorching. Normally, in the eleventh month of the year the sun hid behind a blanket of clouds, yet today it shone with an unconventional radiance. My bones ached and my skin went numb as I turned my longing gaze to the not-so-distant shore of my homeland, Alfras. On this day the great island I had called home for all my life could be seen in its full splendor. Luscious green foliage dotted the edge of a dense tropical forest that stood against a shore filled with fine sand. As my eyes followed the sand to the north, I soon beheld the cliff face that stood against the crushing power of the ocean. My eyes lingered on the waves that violently smashed against the rock just as they had for all the long years of my life. The top of this rocky mass had given birth to my small village comprised of simple fishermen. As my back ached and I let out a yawn, my sole desire was to return from the sea to my refuge on land.

My only escape from the unyielding sun was the occasional cool breeze that swept across the tumbling ocean. The gentle wind wisped across the ocean spray and met the side of my small vessel, rocking it gently atop the waves. The boat I sat in was just shorter than the length of two men and bobbed back and forth in a fashion that could easily lull me to sleep. A thin layer of stagnant salt water resided at the base of my feet and lapped against the two oars that had been placed in the boat early in the morning. The water reeked of salt to such an extent that my nostrils curled as I took in the sea-stained air.

"Lloyd! You've got one!" came the voice of the man who shared my boat. His sharp and commanding tone slammed me back into consciousness.

I quickly looked at my pole as it nearly flew out of my slack hands, and I shot back into reality. My grip tightened, and a bead of sweat crawled down my neck as I struggled to bring in the foolish creature that had fallen for my trap. The water violently thrashed, and I yanked the pole back with all my might. Despite all my effort, I could not seem to bring the beast aboard. I could bring in most creatures that took my bait, but this one put up a fight the likes of which I was unaccustomed to. In an attempt to behold my foe, I briefly glanced over the edge of the boat to witness a murky shadow plant itself firmly on top of the sand bar not far below me. Try as I might, the veiled silhouette would not breach the surface and accept its fate.

"Come on, son! We can get this one!" shouted my father as I continued to struggle.

After another quick moment, my father took matters into his own hands and snatched my fishing pole, which was on the verge of breaking. My aged father tightened his grip on the pole, and in one magnificent sweep brought the thrashing creature to the surface world. With a mighty heave, my father dropped it to the bottom of the boat before letting out a raspy groan. I looked to my foe and instantly recognized it as a good-sized crawler. I had never liked crawlers; they were disgusting creatures, but were considered a great meal in my village. Their six muscular, beige-colored legs held up their flat bodies, which gave way to two massive claws. The crawlers' eyes were the most repulsive features of their small bodies, for they seemed to emerge directly from holes on their rounded, armor-plated bodies. These eyes were planted on twisting stalks that darted about once the creature was on the surface.

"Nearly an arm's length," my father commented as he wiped his damp brow with his hand. He looked down at the crawler as it squirmed around the boat and tried to snap at him in a hopeless attempt at survival. Without hesitation, my father brandished a small dirk that he carried by his side. His eyes looked to the shimmering blade before they fell upon me. I did not meet his gaze and instead lowered my eyes. After letting out a dissatisfied sigh, my father stabbed the animal in between the eyes in one masterful motion that was backed by years of experience. I watched as a murky, puss-like blood emerged from the hole my father had created in the carapace. I hated the fact that after nineteen years of life I still found these small creatures disturbing, and I could only watch in silent horror as the creature began to die. The foul meal stopped moving and its legs gave out, causing it to fall backward onto the floor of the boat with a heavy clunk.

"Is that one an arm's length, Kiordiam?" a man yelled from another boat in the area. This man had rowed his boat over to our vessel during the fight, but I had not noticed him due to my frantic struggle.

"Yes, friend! First one this month!" replied my father with pride. There were at least seven other boats in our vicinity, as this was the best place to hunt crawlers on the southern tip of the island. The man nodded at my father before turning to his own son to make a declaration about how well my father and I worked together. Upon hearing this, my father did not meet my longing gaze. Rather, he turned to the crawler with a frown painted across his worn features. The man who had beckoned us rowed his canoe away without another word. Once again I found myself alone with my father.

"That was good, son... that was good," started my superior before he looked me straight in the eye. "You just have to pay attention next time. You wouldn't want one this big to get away."

In a dull tone, I simply said, "Yes sir."

For nearly the past decade I had been fishing with my father, and each day I found myself loathing the activity even more than the previous day. In my village it was the responsibility—no, the duty—of a male to provide for his family, and ever since I had turned ten I'd had to join my father in his hunts at sea. Our village had followed the tradition of men catching food and women preparing it for many generations, but I didn't care about hunting crawlers on the reef. The last thing I wanted to do with my time was sit in a boat all day and roast under the sun. My father had been doing this for thirty-five years, as was clearly evident due to his thick, leatherlike skin. My flesh still remained rather fair despite a decade of work, but I knew that if I continued to fish into my later years, I too would soon have skin that resembled a tanned hide. This fate was one I never wished to achieve.

"Soon the sun will dip below the horizon. Let us row in before darkness reaches these waters," my father declared with a strained smile stretched across his face. He grabbed an oar with his one good hand and waited for me to take the second. My father had lost his left hand when he was twenty-eight while hunting crawlers on this very reef. When he had stabbed his grand catch all those years ago, he hadn't completely killed the crawler. Because of his mistake, he had lost his left arm to the creature's razor-sharp claws as he had rowed back to shore. This story brought me misery as I thought of the dangers in my future, so I extinguished it from my mind and turned to the shore. I grabbed my oar and dipped it into the salty water, which was dusted with amber rays of the setting sun. My father and I remained silent as we made our way to the golden, sun-drenched beach. Once aground I beached the boat as my father walked up the dirt path toward the top of the cliff with our catch in hand.

"Dinner will be ready once night falls. Don't be late, son," he said with no change to his stonelike face. I watched him walk up the path that led through the woods, and once I was sure that he was gone, I walked down the beach until I came to a small hut nestled against the side of the high cliff. The old, battered hut had been deserted for generations, and to my knowledge, no one in the village ever entered it. I once asked my father about the history of the home, and he claimed a foolish man had built it as his own. Both the house and the man had swept away in a great tsunami many years before. No one in the village ever bothered with this place, so I had decided to make it my own. I entered the decrepit ruins of the home that once was and looked around as the ever-flowing tide graced my ears.

Inside, the smell of mildew filled the air. I slowly walked over broken floorboards that squeaked and rattled with my every step. Against the house's eastern wall stood an old bookshelf that I slowly pushed aside, revealing a small room where I kept my secret treasure. Once I entered the room, which was mostly intact, I couldn't help but stare in awe at my prize. It gleamed as the setting sun shone on it through one of the many holes in the old thatch roof. The treasure, which I visited weekly, had washed up on the island's shore during a tsunami four years ago. I had found it at the young age of fifteen, and from the second I laid eyes on it, I had known I could not let it go.

I grabbed the sword's hilt and gently took it from two wooden spokes that were affixed in the wall. As I gazed out at the ocean through the many holes in the eastern wall, I swung the sword around for several seconds, then jumped into the air and stabbed a wall. Planting my foot against the wall, I used a great deal of my strength to pull the blade out of the wood. Once the sword was tight in my grasp I arced it around my frame, then skillfully planted it into the ground. I smiled and pulled it out of the floor after a moment of admiration, then looked out the broken south wall of the hut and made sure no one was watching me practice.

Becoming a swordsman in the Alfrasian militia had been a dream of mine since I had been a child. When I was young, soldiers came through my village for a festival after the men of the village had killed a small pod of whales in the deep ocean. The colossal yet benign creatures not only fed many people, but valuable pieces of them were traded with the Thundrian Empire to the east for a great sum of money that was divided among the people in the village. That night, the soldiers in the festival displayed their skills by sparring with each other before a massive fire. I watched them spar in wonder, and from that day forward I swore to myself that someday I would be the one wielding the sword before awestruck children.

After practicing with my sword for a brief while, I walked out of the hut and knelt on the sand. I took off the cloth headband I had been wearing that day and soaked it in an incoming wave, then gently patted my forehead as I gazed out at the ocean with my tarnished sword beside me. Soon dinner would be prepared, so I returned my blade to its resting place and prepared to go home. The hill my father had taken earlier began to dim as half of the sun vanished below the horizon, so I hastened my steps as I began my ascent.

After a short run through the woods, my village came into sight. The village was rather small and sat on the southern tip of an island that stretched for over four hundred miles to the north and seven hundred miles to the northwest. Huts dotted the top of a smooth plateau that overlooked the seemingly infinite ocean.

My village was almost devoid of life on this night, for most families confined themselves within their respective huts at this hour. As I walked through the village, I occasionally glanced in the doorways of the huts I passed. Nearly every family I caught sight of was devouring various sea creatures that the men had caught earlier in the day.

Soon I found myself standing before the battered hut that had served as my shelter through many storms and tsunamis. I entered to see my family sitting down at the table in the small kitchen to my left. Our hut was simple like all the others, yet it had one luxury many wished they could build. A second story sat above the first, accessed by a simple ladder. This upper area was a welcome comfort whenever I sought to escape those around me. The first floor was large by most standards, and it had three rooms. To the left of the main room were a simple kitchen and eating area, which were warm due to a billowing fire within the fireplace; to the right was a small washroom. On the second level, a single small niche contained three beds. My aching bones nearly brought me to the ladder, but my stomach growled a deep, booming rumble, so I turned back to the kitchen. As I approached the table in the kitchen, I noticed that the burning candle in the center of the table was almost spent.

"Lloyd, you're late again. You know we can't eat without you here," my mother softly chided as she stood up. "You can't keep coming in late and expecting us to wait for you."

She was a very loving woman, like most angels were. It was rare that an angel and a human married, yet this very occurrence was what had brought me into this world. The one unfortunate side effect of being the child of an angel and a human was that I would forever be known as a half-human. This brand had been imprinted upon me due to the fact that my back had neither smooth skin nor wings. Instead, two small, bare stubs of bone and flesh protruded from my upper back. These diminutive and inconvenient stumps irritated me to no end and oftentimes I tried to hide them, but it was never to any avail.

My brother and sister, Arthur and Daria, chuckled to each other after my mother's reproach. Arthur and Daria had been born eleven years earlier, both on the same date, and shared a great resemblance to each other. Unlike me, their stubs grew into long and beautiful white wings that sparkled in the fleeting sunlight. They could fly a little, but were not yet fully fledged. They had not yet learned of the responsibilities that an adult had to face on the island, and still spent their days running about the village laughing and playing with other carefree children.

"Well, Yuri," remarked my father as he looked to his wife, "at least he's here now."

My father raised a wooden utensil and looked to the little ones with a grin before he told the children to eat up. He took a bite of the crawler and, with a stuffed mouth, declared, "Yuri, you know that crawler I brought in today? Our boy caught that one!"

A strained smile appeared across his face as I sat down at the table and took a bite of the eel my father had caught the day before. The eel had been steamed and was very chewy. It slid down my throat and caused me to grimace.

"By himself?" Yuri asked with a warm smile directed at me.

My father hesitated before adding, "Well, he lured the crawler to his pole, but he didn't have the strength to pull it onto the boat." He took another bite of the crawler, then turned to me and remarked, "One day you'll be able to lure and catch one by yourself Lloyd, just wait."

I nodded and ate my dinner as I held back a cringe that ran through my spine. The thought of fishing for years weighed heavily about my mind. I watched in silence as my father conversed with my mother right before my siblings passively shut me out of their conversation. I constantly felt like I was the odd one out at the table, as the two pairs would talk to each other while ignoring me. Even in the rare circumstance that we had one of our neighbors over, they rarely paid me any mind. Our village was populated with dozens of steadfast workers, but I was the only one of my age, and a half-human, so I kept to myself, mostly. I finished my dinner quickly and ascended to the second floor to watch the infinite number of stars twinkle in the night sky outside the window above my bed. During this time, I dreamed of leaving the island. I felt as if my life was one tedious routine that could only be escaped in the world of dreams that I soon entered.

I woke up the next morning as my father tapped my feet with his hands.

"Get up, we have to go out early today," he said as he tapped me again. I moaned and turned over on my small bed and felt the thin wool blanket entrap me once again. He continued to pat my feet, yet I would not budge. This was one of my least favorite ways to be woken up.

"I have to talk to you about something important, Lloyd Kiordiam Shoresquatter," he added in a stern tone.

Whenever that man called me by my full name it was because I was either in trouble or about to be asked a great favor. I had never been fond of the last name taken up by my family generations ago, when they had left Thundria to settle on Alfras. It was said the man and wife who were my long-dead ancestors had spent more time building houses ashore than fishing for food. The name Shoresquatter was used to describe them and their descendants and, despite my distaste for the name, I did not mind it so much as to complain about it to my father.

Hearing my full name caused my weariness to vanish in an instant. Without a second thought I rolled over and sat on the side of the bed. My father glanced over his shoulder at my two siblings, who were still sleeping in their bunk bed on the opposite side of the room, and whispered, "Meet me outside."

Still in my dirtied and salty clothes from the day before, I stood up and watched him exit the room. My skin felt greasy and soiled as I stripped off the garments. I ran my fingers through my tangled dark hair, which fell just under the tops of my shoulders, before stretching my arms high into the air. With a yawn, I turned to my bed and reached under it to where my clothing lay. Before putting my light tan tunic on, I patted it down and watched as rogue specks of dust danced into the air. I pulled a pair of rag-gedy pants up to my waist and then turned to face my bed. A belt lay lodged between the blanket and the wooden frame of the bed, and I quickly yanked it out from its resting position and secured it around my pants. I did not wish to keep my father waiting, so I hastily pulled a dark crimson cloak out from under the bed and fastened the tip around my neck before slipping on my boots. I ran my hand over the light stubble that crowned my chin and grew below my nose, then decided to forgo cutting the hair for another few days. Once I was ready to meet my father, I descended the ladder to the first floor and walked outside to see him sitting with his back against the hut. Without saying a word, I sat next to him and looked out at the morning sky.

"Lloyd, you know the season to trade is almost upon us, and I must get our goods to Thundria," he said. I shook my head in dis-belief for a second. I had completely forgotten about my father leaving to go about his business overseas. My father routinely left home and ventured to the east during this time of year to sell various amenities to Thundrians. He and many other farmers and fishers from other villages paid for safe passage on massive trade vessels that safely took them to our eastern neighbors. After realizing that the time for my father's departure was near, I sim-ply nodded my head.

"Well, Lloyd, you know I'm getting older, and I know you're becoming a man, and a man must provide for his family," he continued.

This same speech had been given to me many times before. My father would tell me to stay behind and care for the family in his absence, just as he had every year since my tenth name day.

"Yes, I know father," I murmured as I looked out to the ocean. The morning sun skimmed over the low, rolling waves as they continually drifted to and fro. The few clouds that rolled by cast light shadows down upon the sand of the beach, which almost shimmered when shadows did not beset it.

"You are nineteen years of age and the time for you to dis-cover the workings of this world is now," said my father in a stern voice. "I want you to go to Thundria in my place."

I jerked my head to the man who had clearly lost his senses.

"Are you sure?" I asked him in an instant. I hoped that he would not take back anything he had said, yet in the moment I was forced to ask this question out of sheer disbelief.

My father looked to me with a smile as he stood up and offered his hand. I took it, and he quickly pulled me to my feet. He gently placed his scarred and aged hand on my shoulder.

"I know that you long for adventure," he declared as my eyes widened. "I know of how you lust for action. I have seen the sword."

I did not know what to say to my father, who was all but comforting on most other days. Instead of clear words escaping my breath, the simple stutters of a child reached my father's ears. He raised his hand for silence before he continued with a slight laugh.

"That old, shabby shell of a house isn't exactly the best place to hide something of such value," he remarked before walking around the edge of our hut. He was out of sight for only a brief moment before he reappeared with an unexpected gift in his hand.

"Any good sword needs a fine scabbard, my son." He slowly brought the blade I had been practicing with before me, encased in a sheath. I had kept the blade exposed, for I did not know how to obtain a scabbard, but my sword would be naked no longer. I took it from him in an instant. My eyes scanned the basic yet finely crafted sheath as if it were the greatest treasure in all the lands. Without hesitation, I released my sword from its resting place and held it before me. My father had obviously shined the blade, for it glistened in its full glory.

"How did you know about this?" I asked.

He seemed quite different from his normal self, and his reply came swiftly as a smile stretched across his slack face. "Believe it or not, I too was once your age," he said. "I once held your same longing for travel, yet by my father's commands I would not see distant lands until the age of twenty-five. For many years I resented him for imprisoning me on this island, and I will not have you hold the same disposition toward me."

This moment was a type that my father and I rarely experienced together. For a fleeting instant he and I saw eye to eye. Yet the moment was ephemeral, for he wasted no time in giving me instructions.

"Do you know how to use the blade?" he asked.

"I've trained with it every week for a long while now," I said. "I know its balance well enough."

"But you do not know combat," replied my father. "When you get back from your journey, allow me to teach you how to strike against a man. In the meantime, keep your blade sheathed unless you mean to use it and don't draw attention to your weapon."

I nodded before he turned to the southwest for a moment. After a distant stare, he continued.

"Once you reach the port city you will have to find a friend of mine. There is a human there who has been my friend for many years. You can find him at the southern docks. He's just over six feet tall, and rather hefty. His name is Mithias, and he will be the captain of the ship that will take you over the sea to the port of Triton. His fees have been paid and he has sworn an oath to protect you until you are returned to me."

My gaze became distant and my breath wore thin as I uttered, "Are you sure I can handle this?"

"I would not entrust you with such a task otherwise. Just remember, a fat man with dark hair named Mithias will take you on board his ship to the eastern port city of Triton on the continent of Thundria. You need not worry about your safety while you are in his care. He is an old friend," my father confidently replied.

"Mithias, Triton, Thundria," I repeated this several times to myself under my breath so I would remember, and then I found myself displaying a rather unusual grin to my father. He soon gave me more instructions.

"I loaded up the wagon with some of our finest catches. Mithias shall take care of getting the best deals on these goods in the city, but you should be there to see how he works. Take the wagon into town after bidding your mother and siblings farewell," he concluded in his usual gnarled voice before he turned toward the shore where he would spend the rest of his day. Without so much as a glance back my way, he added, "I'll see you in a month."

"Father!" I yelled after he was several paces away from me. He turned, and in a voice that was just above a whisper, I muttered, "Thank you."

The wise old man nodded at me with the slightest hint of a smile across his face before continuing on his journey toward our boat.

Before I could leave I knew that I would have to bid my family a fond farewell. With light steps I made my way up to the second floor where both my siblings and my mother still slept. I went to the bunk my siblings shared and woke them both up gently. The two were quite grumpy in the morning and were quick to question my action. To my surprise, they were not taken aback by news of my leaving. In their groggy state, they waved me off after declaring that our father had told them of my trip many days ago. Their response was disappointing, yet my mood drastically changed, for as I turned to my mother's bed I beheld a welcome sight. My mother had heard my words directed at my sleepy siblings and quickly awakened.

Without a single yawn or blink of a heavy eyelid my mother asked, "Shall you make off before long?"

"I plan to immediately," I replied as I approached her. My mother looked at me with a frown as she stood up and raised her head to meet my eyes.

"I do not like the idea of sending my eldest son across the sea. There are dangers beyond the horizon that I don't believe you are ready for," she murmured. I was about to speak up, but my mother added a final declaration that brought a smile to my face. "But you are slowly becoming a man. I cannot cradle you forever."

I said nothing and instead gave my mother a tight hug that she desperately clung to before I attempted to pull myself away. Once I had released her from my grasp, I said, "I shall be back before long."

"Make haste on your journey, Lloyd," replied my mother in a soft but firm tone before sitting back on her bed. "Your father is getting old and his ignorance of his physical limits will best him if you do not return to his side out among the waves. He needs you more than you know."

12

"Yes ma'am," I calmly replied before backing away from her. I wanted to believe her, but my father's stern disposition was a constant reminder that I was more of a hindrance than a help while fishing. Regardless, I had a task to perform, so I put thoughts of fishing behind me. I said no more to my family, for the duty at hand lingered about my mind as I exited my house and turned my frame to the simple wooden wagon my father had presented to me.

I jumped on the wagon, and soon one of the four horses my village owned began to pull me down the winding path toward the port city of Urchi. As I left, I glanced down the coast at my distant destination. In this early hour I noticed that the community was beginning to stir with life. Though they appeared as only specs against a green and gray gradient, people of all shapes and sizes exited their houses and began their business in the morning sun. My home upon an outstretching cliff soon became the backdrop for my journey toward Urchi.

The road that led to the city was a short one that dipped into the tropical forest and looped around to the north side of the city. I did not push the steed granted to me too hard, for the horse's innocent nature made it nearly impossible for me to treat the creature with anything but compassion. The horse maintained a steady trot as the sun slowly drifted higher into the sky. The garron moved so slowly that I thought I could easily match its speed on foot. I arrived in the city when the day was still in its infancy, no more than an hour after I had left my village.

Before me was the greatest sight in my world: buildings made of stone that were twice—or even three times—the size of my hut extended to the sky. The streets were paved with cobblestone, and hundreds of people rushed about the city performing their daily routines. The incoherent buzz of the crowd echoed against my ears with such fervor that I found myself longing for the sound of waves gently stroking the shoreline. I made my way past the crowds and soon found myself at a large pavilion surrounded by gardens and populated by crowds of all races.

A sizeable fountain could be seen at the center of the town square. Children laughed and danced about the cascading falls as adults went about their business in the pavilion. Some conversed with smiles under the sunlight while others talked of business and production. I followed a tightly-packed path around the fountain and guided the horse south of the town square until I came upon several rows of docks that shot out above the sea. On the sides and at the ends of the docks were ships that had amazed me every year I came to the town to see my father off. In my mind, these ships that had as many as a dozen sails stood as a testament to the power and ingenuity of people. Whenever I had visited the city as a child, it was these Alfrasian ships that had caught my imagination and made me long for adventure more than anything else.

As I looked for a man that matched my father's description, I maneuvered my wagon through ragtag groups of ruffians who eyed me suspiciously in a manner that made me very uncomfortable. As I continued to travel down the dock, a single grand boat caught my eyes and held them amid the foreign sights around me. It was a magnificent vessel with three masts, each of which held many sails. The wood was fine on the hull, and from where I stood I could see a massive wheel perched atop the upper deck. The deck eventually gave way to a set of stairs near the front of the bow that led to a raised platform, where two sailors stood and conversed loudly. Beneath the boisterous sailors, my eyes fixed on a carved mermaid gracing the front of the bow. She had long, flowing red hair that wrapped around the front of the bow, and on her face one could see the slightest hint of a smile and a wink. My admiration of the ship was cut short when I remembered I had to meet Mithias. I looked to a group of heavily built men who maneuvered my wagon near a ramp that led to the deck of the boat and hopped down.

I stepped onto the planks of the dock and watched several hefty men remove crates from a large stack. They hauled them onto the boat's deck and then stowed them behind two doors opposite the bow. The men then emerged and repeated this routine once again, frowning all the while. I approached the group of robust men, and the thick stench of sweat on morning dew rushed inside my nostrils. I stood silent for a moment until I adjusted to the raw stench.

"Excuse me," I said after none of them broke their routine to notice me. None of them cared to stop, so I repeated myself, but no one listened. I saw a man picking up a small crate and grabbed his shoulder in an attempt to get a response.

"Excuse me," I began in soft voice.

"Aye!" He yelled as he dropped the small crate. I jolted back before he barked, "Ya can't sneak up on a man like that, kid!"

"I'm sorry!" I nervously replied. The hefty man looked like he could crush me with ease, but he merely shrugged his shoulders and turned back to the crate he had been carrying before speaking once more.

"Eh it's okay, crate's fine," he responded as he picked up the crate again. "What do you need, kid?"

"I'm looking for a man named Mithias," I said with wavering confidence.

"My father, Kiordiam, has sent me to the port city of Triton on the Thundrian shore so I can trade my wares. He told me a man named Mithias had been paid to ensure me safe passage."

"Aye," he said slyly, "and what's this Mithias character look like?"

"Well," I started as I scratched my head and thought of the description my father had given me. As my father's words came back to my mind, I hesitantly stated, "He's a human, has dark hair, and is rather... fat."

The man let out a loud laugh and put down the small crate. He promptly placed his hands on his hips before exclaiming, "That Kiordiam, he taunts my weight to no end!"

"Oh!" I felt heat rush to my face. This man could end me with a single punch and I had just insulted his figure without realizing it. He had a short brown beard that connected with an untamed mustache that was as dark as his furrowed brow. His short dark hair was tarnished with salt from the glancing sea breeze, and his deep eyes looked as if they had beheld a hundred wonders and then some. This man was not so much fat as he was physically huge. He was over six feet tall, yet his structure was that of a grand fighter. The man looked quite older than I, but younger than my father. Not unlike my father, his face was worn from years of being on the ocean, and with every facial expression the man produced it seemed that parts of his skin cracked and splintered. His stature scared me, and the fact that I had just insulted him to his face did not bode well with my gut.

"You're Mithias!" I yelled in surprise. "I'm sorry, sir... I just was told—"

"It's fine, boy!" he nearly yelled as he dropped his hands to his sides. He let out another hearty laugh, then declared, "I am Mithias, and you must be Lloyd! Like the hero of old times, right?"

Had I not been so afraid of this man, I would have sighed. I'd heard that remark countless times in my life, and I would have expressed disdain for the statement had I not just insulted the man. I did my best to smile as I stated, "Yes, like the hero."

"All right lad, it's good to meet you. Your father has spoken highly of you before our meeting," Mithias calmly said as he handed the crate he was carrying to a deck hand and wiped his hands on his dirty clothing. He wore a simple captain's outfit that was blue, wet, and worn from his time on the high seas. It looked as if he hadn't changed in days, and the long gray-blue coat that draped down his entire body was clearly falling apart.

"Really?" I asked in disbelief as I thought of my father praising me. My father wasn't the type of person who would talk highly about me to anyone. My eyes glanced toward my sword for a moment and I tried to think of a time before this morning that my father had been so warm to me. Nothing came to mind.

"Yes, he says you're a young man of strength and courage, which is good, because you'll need both on this journey. Tell me, son, have you ever crossed the ocean before?" He turned to the tumbling waves.

"No, this will be my first voyage." I responded in full honesty as I kept my eyes trained on Mithias. The rugged man gazed at the sea with a fondness sparkling in his eyes before these words escaped my breath. Once I made my declaration, the man's gaze shot from the ocean to mine as he spoke.

"First?" Mithias barked. I nodded, and he let out another hearty laugh at the notion. "Kiordiam never told me that! Kid, you're in for hell, then. The first time across the sea is always the worst."

"Why's that?" I asked in a wavering tone.

Mithias' smile slowly turned to a frown as he watched the rolling waves. This man's grimace was not one anyone would ever want to see, for with it came an air of derision that swept into one's consciousness. It was the type of expression that could remove the joy from a whole room.

"The sea is unforgiving," he said as his eyes turned to the ocean once again. "Monsters, pirates, it's all terrible... I nearly lost my life to a leviathan when I was just about your age."

He continued to look at the sea as the wind tossed his hair about.

"Leviathan?" I asked. I had heard of these horrid creatures taking down ships in the seas one would find if one followed the setting sun, yet never had I heard tales of the beasts residing in the eastern seas.

"Don't be surprised if you see one of them on our way over there," Mithias said with a deep gaze about him. "Dreadful creatures, they are; smart, too. Some say them sea snakes stretch for miles, but I'll tell ya different. It's not their length that scares ya, it's their jaws. A leviathan could swallow ya whole and not ever notice." He paused for a moment before asking, "Kinda makes you feel a bit small, doesn't it?"

I responded by nervously swallowing a wad of spit as Mithais continued to look out at sea.

After staring away for a few seconds, Mithias turned to me and firmly declared, "But don't worry, kid, the next four weeks won't be that bad, and chances are we won't cross paths with any monsters. Just don't eat what you can't stand to look at, and if you vomit, do so over the side of the ship."

Nightmarish images of the leviathan filled my head before Mithias added, "Bring that wagon up the ramp there. We're setting off soon."

I walked back to the wagon's seat and carefully maneuvered the horse up a wide ramp onto the ship. Once on board, I commissioned several other reluctant men to help me push the wagon against the side of the craft and tie it down with a net and two long pieces of rope. Afterward, I led the horse back down the gangplank and soon saw Mithias sitting on a barrel.

"What about the horse?" I asked him as I stroked the gentle gelding's flowing mane.

"A city guard will take it to the stables and keep it there until we return," he replied.

I had never heard of this practice, yet I swiftly followed Mithias' next order.

"Tie it to the post," he commanded. I did as he said, then turned around and noticed what he was doing while he sat. He had a long axe that was half as high as I was tall. The great and powerful man was sharpening it with a grinding stone as he sat on the barrel. As I glanced to Mithias, I noticed a great concentration about the man's face as he smoothed out every fine contortion along the blade's edge. I then looked at the axe itself and noticed ornate details carved into the long handle. Around various leaves carved into the handle were the words "Honor in Tradition, Tradition in Honor."

He must have noticed me admiring it, for he asked, "Pretty nice, huh?"

"Yes," I said as I watched him continue his diligent work.

"Stole it off one of the dogs that invaded my village," he remarked without taking his eyes off the steel.

The only word that escaped my breath after this declaration was, "Why?"

Mithias slowly rose to his feet and turned toward the ocean once more. He slung his axe over his shoulder. "That is a story for fonder ears on another day."

Mithias soon turned back toward me with a distant gaze in his twinkling eyes.

"You know, your father was the first person on this island to put his trust in me. I made my first money from him and was able to start a fine life here. For that I owe him many things." He leaned his axe against a pole and placed his hand on my shoulder before continuing. "This'll be a fine voyage. Don't worry."

I smiled and said, "Thank you, Mithias."

After a friendly moment, he bellowed, "Well enough of that! Let me show you to your quarters!"

The bulky man grabbed his weapon, then ascended the plank connecting his vessel to the dock. I followed him up the length of timber with my scabbard in one hand and my basket of clothes in the other. Once on the ship, I watched as several crew members continued to rush about, performing their duties tirelessly under the scorching sun. Through the overwhelming commotion I saw Mithias walk below deck so I quickly scurried behind him.

Once below deck I found myself in a long corridor lit only by the light coming in through the small window in the door I just opened. I saw Mithias disappear into a door at the end of the hallway, so I walked up to it, but before I even had a chance to enter, the door swung open and he declared, "Sorry, kid, only the captain is allowed in the captain's quarters; you have to sleep elsewhere."

I turned to my left to see a damp, open room with many hammocks swinging about. Several dirtied and stagnant men slept on them, and in an instant I turned back to Mithias with discontent all about me. The man was quick to pick up on my disdain.

"The son of Kiordiam Shoresquatter does not have to sleep with the thugs that service this vessel," he said with a grin. "Take the quarters to your right. It should prove to be more to your liking."

He slammed the door shut, and soon the familiar scent of my father's pipe leaf emanated from the captain's quarters as I turned to my right and opened the door. The room was dank and contained nothing but a cracked bed and a moldy sea chest. I unloaded my clothing into the chest, laid on the damp bed, and looked about for any form of entertainment whatsoever. My eyes soon laid themselves upon a dusty old book entitled, "Lloyd's Plight," which was wedged between the mattress and the wall.

Just by reading the title I knew it was about the great historic hero. I stood and swiftly put the book out of sight. The story of the angelic leader Lloyd and how he had defeated evil had long been a part of my life, due, in part, to my name. Whenever people met me and discovered my name, they felt compelled to explain the story of the great hero and how their great-great-great-great-great-great-great-grandfathers had fought beside him or something along those lines. Enduring those dull conversations was a chore, and I did not want to spend my time reading a book full of imaginings that had been thrust upon me as a child. As I lay on the bed, my eyelids began to fall and my ears heard the men on deck scuttling about. Although I had awoken only several hours earlier, it felt as if my eyelids were weighted. The obnoxious dripping from some unknown source of water and the minute squeaks and squeals from bands of mice annoyed my senses as I lay in bed, yet once my eyelids clasped together I quickly entered a serene world of dreams.

CHAPTER 2

I awoke to loud pounding on my door. Without thinking about my actions I rolled over and raced to the noise, but before I could open the door a voice echoed in the hallway.

"You okay in there?" came a voice from outside. I had made a loud thump as I jumped out of bed.

"Yes," I said as I poked my head out of the doorway. "Just taking a nap."

My eyes felt heavy and my sight dimmed as a grizzly seadog watched me.

"Mithias wants you to come on deck," the man said over his shoulder as he turned and left me. I had slept in the tunic from earlier in the day, yet my sweat and movement had not tarnished it. With my cloak now wrinkled from my slumber I chose to put it into the lone chest in my room, then I stumbled out the door and made my way toward the deck. The boards swayed under my feet as I slowly walked forward, and it took me a moment to adjust to them.

Once outside, I saw many men working around the ship under the setting sun. Several were tying down lines or swabbing the deck while one was at the wheel making sure we continued on a steady course eastward. I scanned the deck for Mithias but could not see the large man anywhere.

"Up here, Lloyd!" The voice came from above me, as if one of the seabirds circling the ship had called my name.

I looked up and saw Mithias in the crow's nest and yawned. I didn't want to climb up the ladder after just waking up, but

Mithias continued to hail me until I waved him off and grabbed a rung on the rope ladder. I slowly climbed the loose ladder as the setting sun shimmered against the gentle waves. The ladder was tall, but heights had never scared me, and before I knew it I had arrived at the top of the ship.

"Thought you might want to see this," Mithias said as he pointed out to sea. Off in the distance I saw gigantic dark objects breach the water's surface, then moan and shoot water high into the air. After they did this, they slammed into the calm currents and caused crests of water to form. The strange dark objects looked to be the size of trade ships, yet they remained distant.

"What are those?" I asked as the sounds from these strange things continued to reach me.

Mithias said nothing and handed me a long wooden object with glass at one end. I was confused and simply looked at it in my hands.

Mithias laughed at my confusion. "It's a spyglass, boy. Point the big end at the objects and put your eye up to the small end."

I looked to the man as if he were crazy, but did as he said after he repeated his request. Suddenly the objects became huge in my sight. I stumbled backward and nearly dropped the spyglass in shock. Mithias cursed as he grabbed the spyglass from me and yelled, "Damn it, lad, this cost me a lot of money! Be careful with it."

"The objects were right in front of me!" I yelled back at him as I rose to my feet.

"This device makes things from afar seem near," he replied as he shook his head. As he gave me back the strange instrument, he added, "You are in no danger."

I hesitated, then pointed the end of the spyglass toward the objects and slowly put my eye up to the small end. The dark, distant, objects became vibrant sea creatures that seemed to dance above the water and sing as they penetrated the surface.

"Are those whales?" I asked as I continued to stare through the spyglass.

"Big ones," Mithias replied in a soft voice as he looked to the creatures with a knowledgeable gaze. I continued to look at them as Mithias said, "You don't see those from the island, do ya lad?"

"Not when they are alive, at least," I said as I continued to watch the creatures. As I looked on, I noticed that they gradually stopped breaching the surface of the murky waters. I continued to watch as the creatures became shadowed objects amid the dim ocean. The small shadows slowly became larger and larger as I watched them through the spyglass.

"I think they're coming this way," I noted as I continued to gaze at the strange creatures through the spyglass.

"Oh?" said Mithias, before adverting his attention to the creatures once again. "Let them come. They will do no harm unless provoked."

I took the spyglass away from my eyes and watched as the dark shadows came to the port side of the boat. I had not realized how big the creatures were until they were right before me. The boat, which was as long as the buildings of Urchi were tall, looked miniscule in comparison to these gentle giants. I counted four whales as they passed under the ship, each one larger than the last. The final creature had an oval shadow with a grand fin behind it and was nearly three times the size of the already massive ship. They swam under the vessel and came back to the surface once they were far past the starboard side. After they had gone under the hull of the ship, they no longer moaned their strange yet almost melodic song. The four whales had converged beneath our vessel and swam under it together, but once they were past it they separated.

"Why are they going their separate ways?" I asked.

"If I know anything about these creatures, it's that they travel together," said Mithias. "Something we cannot see or cannot understand has broken them apart now, but surely they will find each other again."

As I continued looking at the distant shadows, Mithias said, "We're going to have supper soon. Meet me in the dining hall."

He took his spyglass back, then made his way down the ladder and onto the deck where he promptly disappeared into the interior of the ship. Before following the captain, I stood in the crow's nest and looked out at the calm sea. By turning around completely, I realized that there was no sign of land in sight. This realization struck fear into my soul, for the vast ocean seemed barren and frightening. The ocean had been a part of my life since childhood, but I had never ventured so far into her that I could not see the shores of my island. I no longer wanted to look out to sea, for my stomach began to churn, so I scurried down the ladder and onto the deck, where I noticed several deck hands entering the double doors that led to the inner workings of the ship. I followed them down a dark passageway until we descended a small spiral staircase that led farther into the ship's hull. By following the men, I soon arrived in a small dining hall that contained a single table and many chairs.

Laid out on the table were foods of all kinds that had only one thing in common: they all looked disgusting. Whether I looked at rotten fruit or undercooked meat, my stomach violently growled and it felt as though an egg were in my throat. I sat down near Mithias and did my best to eat just enough food to tide over my hunger. The men did not address me as I nibbled on my meal like a child. Rather, they talked to their captain, shared stories of adventures, and wove tales of promiscuous women. I enjoyed the company of the sailors, whose names I was starting to learn through their conversations, but I did not dare to speak. Once I had finished my meal I promptly took my leave of the men, who did not seem to notice my disappearance. Once I was alone again, I meandered around the boat until late in the night when my eyes began to weigh down. I made my way to my personal quarters and soon fell into the sweet embrace of sleep.

For the next ten days, all went well. Every day I awoke at dawn and headed to the deck, where several crew members taught me about the workings of my temporary home. In an attempt to make the sparse food more editable, I worked as a cook for the crew when I wasn't tending to various odd jobs around the ship. Over time I was praised for my excellence in the kitchen and slowly but surely I learned the names of all those onboard. The crew eventually accepted me into their ranks as I helped throughout the day, and soon a unique feeling of brotherhood came over me. In a very short time, the ship hands seemed like family, and I felt as though I was the newest, youngest member of this band. They were welcoming and warm despite their tough appearances, and in the night I found myself longing to remain in their ranks even after my journey was complete.

The eleventh day started off like any other. I awoke at dawn and decided to watch the sun breach the ocean in the morning. The sunrise above the ocean was a sight I had respected since I was a young child, yet despite its repetition, it never ceased to amaze me. Once half of the orb of fire sat above the horizon, I began my work with the crew until the mighty sphere of flame was high above our vessel. When the afternoon came about, I realized the sun was blazing with a fierceness I had yet to experience on this trip, so I asked a deckhand named Persius if I could take my leave. After some lighthearted banter, he released me of my duties for the day. With my newfound freedom I chose to escape the scorching heat and return to my cabin, where I could nap before I had to begin preparing the evening meal. After my short rest, I emerged on deck, but the usual playful and prank-filled atmosphere had been replaced by one of urgency and darkness as distant clouds rolled toward us.

"What is it, Mithias?" yelled one of the men from the deck. I followed the man's gaze to the crow's nest where Mithias stood. The hefty captain looked eastward for a moment before he jumped onto the rope ladder and slid down to the deck. A circle of crew members had formed around the ladder's base, and once he landed Mithias glanced through his ranks. He soon spoke, and in an attempt to hear better, I moved into the crowd of sailors and made my way to the inner part of their circle.

"The storm is heading westward," said Mithias with a frown upon his sunburned face. "The skies grow dark, and soon bolts of lightning will rain down upon the sea all around us."

The crew fell silent at the news, and several men scanned the skies to the east. From what I could see, the sky above the eastern horizon was dark and threatening. Voluminous clouds moved swiftly into the oncoming wind, and any man could easily tell they would bring rough seas with them. Just then a bolt of lightning smashed into the ocean, and soon the distinct crack of thunder followed. One of the crew members, whose name was Guinth, stepped forward.

"Captain, those clouds beckon us to our demise," he began in a loyal but stern tone. "What should we do?"

Mithias was silent as another man spoke.

"This vessel might be able to weather the storm. We could continue forward through the wind and rain."

Mithias was quick to reply, "The might of the heavens would prove too much for even the greatest vessel on this day. We must get away from here."

"And where would we go?" asked Guinth. "The storm before us blankets the sky as snow blankets the untouched plains of northern Finre."

Some men began to bicker about a course of action, but none could be decided. Mithias listened to all the ideas thrown at him, such as attempting to outrun the storm or turning hard to the north with hopes of dodging it, but he did not praise any. After all the ideas had been voiced, he walked toward the southern edge of the boat and looked out to the sea with dismay. A grand sigh the likes of which I had not heard the man release escaped his lungs before he raised his gaze.

"We could go to the island," he softly stated as he gazed across the ocean.

"What island?" asked another man in confusion. The entire lot of sailors seemed to have no idea what he was talking about.

Mithias turned toward the lot of us. "There is an island due south of our position with an inlet that would be perfect for us to set anchor in. Within the safety of the inlet, we could easily ride out the storm."

"A brilliant idea," said a man who went by the name of Cain. "Let us depart for her shore immediately."

"There's one thing, Cain," Mithias said with a distant look in his eyes. "Angels reside there."

"Angels?" asked Guinth. "On an island? I thought most of them were scattered about the four continents."

"These are the only angels I have ever known to live on an island," Mithias said. "I ventured onto their land once for aid and supplies after being attacked by a sea creature many years ago. By their grace I received aid, but their rigid tradition cast me from their home. Like most angelic tribes, they seek seclusion, and they threatened to kill me and my former crew if we ever returned. None of the men I worked with on that voyage ever spoke of the island again, but I'm sure they remembered it all the same, for the threat of death from the angelic tribe was no jest."

The crew was silent as it took in this information. The sails pulsated against the sea breeze that drew us ever closer to the storm. Rogue lightning strikes slammed into the sea like great war machines slamming into a castle. After a barrage of lightning struck the ocean, Guinth declared, "Well, it seems we have no choice."

"I will only go to the island if all agree upon this course of action," stated Mithias. "If a single man objects, we will sail into the storm and attempt to brave it. If the air is silent, we shall sail toward the angelic island."

In my eleven days at sea, I had learned that Mithias was unlike any ordinary, distant, and militaristic captain. The crew members helped their superior make all his important decisions, and it was not uncommon for the great man to seek advice from any able-bodied brother.

No one voiced disdain for Mithias' plan, so the captain declared, "So we steal our fate from the hands of nature and put it in the lap of the angels. Let it be done, then. We go south."

All the men hurried to their posts and prepared the ship for its new route. I continued to watch Mithias as he walked up to me and placed his hand on my shoulder before climbing the ladder to the crow's nest once again.

Rain began to relentlessly pummel our ship as we headed south. The mighty vessel rocked violently from side to side, and countless times I thought it would sink. The hull warped and moaned but not once did it splinter. After nearly two hours of wind and rain on the edge of the storm, the island came into sight. The inlet Mithias had spoken of lay before us, and it was clear that if we could navigate the ship through the narrow passage to the small body of water we would find calm seas. Mithias himself expertly maneuvered the vessel through a coral-laden stretch of water that separated us from the dot of land. It took every ounce of the man's focus to take the ship through the treacherous passage, but soon our boat had braved the horror and we found ourselves in an inlet. Once in the calmer body of water, the crew took down the sails dropped anchor into the ocean depths as the storm continued to move above us.

I stood on the deck in silence and looked out over the island with many deckhands beside me. The trees were being whipped about as if the Two themselves blew against them, and the air twisted like a serpent around its prey. As I continued to watch the tropical forest, I witnessed a tree smashing to the ground from the violent winds. The rain was harsh and my clothing was heavy and cold, yet I remained on deck, strangely fixated by my ominous surroundings.

The crew members moved about me as they continued to prepare the ship for the storm, yet my eyes remained transfixed on the tree line. Something about the trees seemed bizarre, yet try as I might, I could not pinpoint the awkward presence that caused the muscles in my legs to weaken. Suddenly I felt a light object land on my cold, damp head. I snatched the weightless and soggy object and brought it before my eyes. In my hand was a single white feather that was unnaturally large. The damp feather was crumpled and soaking wet as I examined it while none paid any mind to me. Just then I heard thunder crack in the distance and I looked up to see where the feather might have come from. My surroundings were illuminated for a single moment, and in that moment I beheld a horrific sight.

Above me, along the ropes and lines and in the crow's nest, were nearly two dozen angels. Each one was cloaked in garb as dark as the night. I could only behold them when a flash of lightning emanated from the shadowed sky. When the lightning struck, I noticed that each held a taunt bow, pointed toward my company and I. Before I could turn to another crew member, a greater flash of lightning caused a blinding white light to temporarily fall over my eyes. When the flash receded I felt the distinct touch of cold steel at my neck, and as I lowered my eyes I saw an angel standing in front of me with his curved blade to my throat.

Fear overtook me. I was unable to move, and the cloaked figure said nothing as his blade graced my flesh. Instead of speaking, the angel stared at me with deep blue eyes that shone like fine crystals even in the black of night. I scanned the area while remaining still and quickly realized that the other members of the crew and Mithias were all being restrained with steel to their necks as well. From the corner of my left eye, I saw Mithias raise his hands into the air as the angel who stood before him held his silver knife to my burly friend's throat.

"What brings pirates to this island?" demanded the angel whose knife was pressed against Mithias' throat.

"We are not pirates," Mithias responded in a surprisingly calm and collected fashion. The angels did not waver as rain continued to assault us all.

"Can you prove this?" the angel asked, still holding the blade to Mithias' neck.

"We are simply a trade vessel," replied my captain as distinct rivulets of water made their way down his face. "If you check below deck you will find shipments of fish and Alfrasian trinkets."

The angel looked at him, then at the crew, then back at Mithias. He kept his dagger raised and looked over to the angels next to him.

"Kiltion and Albatra, check on this," he demanded. Two angels hustled through the doors. The angel turned back to Mithias and promptly ordered him to sit down.

Mithias did as he was told, and then the rest of us were ordered to our knees. Soon the two angels who had been sent through the double doors emerged on deck and spoke to the angel who held Mithias hostage. They spoke in a tongue I had not heard in a long time. It was one my mother had once attempted to teach me, but my stubbornness as a child had caused her to cease her lessons. The two angels conversed in their own dialect for several moments before they ordered us to our feet.

"It seems your story checks out," the angel informed Mithias, motioning with the hilt of his dagger. The angel lowered his blade to his side as he said, "but that does not explain why you are here."

"We sought refuge from the storm in this inlet so that we may live to continue our journey east. Once the wind and rain recede we shall leave," replied Mithias as he slowly stood. The angel looked into Mithias' steady, dark eyes, then sheathed his blade after glancing at his own comrades.

"Very well," the angel stated in a commanding voice. The rest of the angels who had boarded the ship sheathed their weapons as the angel said, "If you are to stay on this island, you must stay under the watchful eye of my people."

Before any further declaration could be made, another angel approached and, in an angelic tongue, beckoned the one who had spoken to Mithias. The two angels spoke in their native tongue while glancing at Mithias and his crew with sharp gazes. They seemed to be arguing in harsh, foreboding tones. Mithias could not keep silent while such gazes fell his way.

"Is there a problem?" Mithias asked.

The angel shook his head, then replied in a low voice, "You must come with us now."

Many angels fluttered away to the trees on the shore before the one who had once held a blade to Mithias' neck demanded that we take a rowboat to shore. We rowed in the wild currents, and some of the crew nervously whispered words of ill will toward the angels until we reached the coast, where our captors were waiting for us. The angels came down from the trees, encircled us without hesitation, and began to lead us forward through the woods. The two angels that led us forward were the only ones to keep their eyes off us, for the rest of the twenty-some angels stood armed and ready for any sort of attack by Mithias or the crew. I attempted to talk to Mithias several times during the trek, yet each time I spoke, my tongue was silenced by an angel in the pack. Soon we came to a clearing of bizarre homes. Each wooden house had been built around a thick tree. Most of these buildings were only two or three stories tall, but there were some that stretched as tall as the very tree they encased. The wooden roof of each residence was slanted at a great angle around the tree trunk. As the rain continued to batter these homes, great falls of water cascaded from the planked roofs to the ground in small, circular basins that surrounded the trees like moats.

"Once the storm ends I will come for you," the head angel said after ceasing his stride. The angel pointed to a three-story home built around a massive tree trunk before he yelled over the rain, "Take up residence in there until the weather subsides. When the skies are clear you will be summoned."

"Summoned for what?" asked an edgy crew member.

The head angel turned his eyes to the unsteady man. "Your judgment."

Before we could say anything else, the angel whipped around and walked back through the woods. Our lot was hustled through two doors and thrust into a large room void of rain and mud.

The ornate circular hall we stood in was nothing short of astounding. The planking that lined the interior was riddled with verdant green vines, and these thick vines had given birth to numerous leaves that dotted the walls and the massive dark tree trunk before us. I glanced to the door from whence we came and noticed that four angelic guards were stationed just outside the residence, so I continued forward. The pine flooring made loud creaks as we stepped across it toward a lone old angel who stood with his back to the bark of the trunk.

"You must be the pirates," he stated as he slowly walked toward us. Once he stood before us, the old angel pushed on his cane and propped himself up so that he could look at the lot of us.

"I haven't seen humans in quite some time," he added in low moan.

"We seek to weather the storm," stated Mithias from where he stood at the head of the pack.

"Yes, yes... I have been told this," replied the old angel with an innocent smile. "Word travels on the winds here, you know. If someone needs to tell someone something, they need not wait long!"

"So it seems," Mithias responded with little interest. "But how exactly do you expect to hold us here?"

The old man wasn't taken aback in the slightest and simply smiled before declaring, "I know little of humans, but surely you hold some intelligence. Steadfast guards have eyes all over this island. If you or your crew attempts to escape they will not hesitate to do what they must to keep this place safe."

"Detained by damned angels," muttered Mithias under his breath. The old angel either didn't hear him or paid his comment no mind, for he reached for a lone candle that sat on a side table next to a comfortable-looking chair. Once the old one held the tamed flame in his hand, he slowly walked to a grand, curved set of stairs that stretched along the trunk. He stood at the base of the steps, opened his left arm, and made a swift motion.

"Come, you can stay upstairs," he said. I followed his slow ascent, with Mithias' men right behind me. Once on the second level of the house, the old angel sat on a bench beside the stairs and said, "My family used to live here with me, but they have all since gone."

The angel let out a soft sigh before adding, "Too many are drawn to the cities these days, and now I have many empty rooms. Choose whichever you will; there are seven on this floor and four on the next."

Before walking into one of the rooms, Mithias scoffed at the old angel, who looked as if he could drop dead at any moment. The other men soon scattered to their desired rooms and I did the same, walking into a room with a lavishly carved wooden bed against the wall. Facing the bed was a bookshelf full of books with titles written in the unfamiliar angelic language, and in front of the bookshelf was a small table with three chairs positioned around it. The slant of the roof cut the ceiling in a way that made the outer wall only come up to my chest, but toward the doorway the ceiling was twice my height. A welcoming fireplace against the room's far wall pulled me toward it, yet once I was upon it I found that the wood was damp. I could not light a fire, so I sat on the bed and looked out a small window to my right. My cloak felt heavy and cold, so I wrapped my sword in it and placed them both at the bedside. As I watched the rain wisp about outside my window, I pondered why Mithias had not been killed for his unorthodox return to the island. Perhaps the angels were not as tough as we thought, or maybe they had simply forgotten his face. I could not draw any conclusion at the moment, but the words of the angel who had led us to the house brought fear to my consciousness. I chose to rummage through the bookshelf as the rain continued to batter the roof above me. My eyes could not read the angelic text in the books I flipped through, yet in these tomes I came across images that any man could cherish. I flipped through the pages as if I were reading picture books for hours until the pounding rain turned to a gentle drizzle. As I looked out the window to the village that began to team with life once more, I knew whatever judgment the angels had in store for my lot was near.

CHAPTER 3

"Get up, kid! We're meeting the leader in a few moments," ordered Mithias as he barged into my room. "The chief wants to see us in his grand oak. Given the circumstances, you'd do best to not keep him waiting."

The great man slammed the door shut and I sprang out of bed. As I went to pick up my sword from its resting place I looked out the window and saw a pleasant sight. Angels of all shapes and sizes walked about the dew-laden earth and went about their business as minute drops of water left from the great storm fell from the canopy of leaves above. Some angels walked deep into the woods, while children pranced about a dim fire that had recently been lit at the center of the muddy village. These children reminded me of my siblings back home, and for the first time in many days I found myself longing to return to them. The idea that I might not return home entered my mind, but I was quick to shake my head and rid myself of such a thought. The angels were not happy, but I could not see myself being detained on the island, or worse. Once I was ready to go, I emerged outside in the evening light that soaked the leaves and began to dry the wet ground.

Outside, I was not met with the beauty I had observed from my window earlier. The angels who had previously moved about without a care stopped to stare at me as I clumsily made my way through their village. The children's laughter died and they ran from my sight upon their mothers' commands until not a single smile could be seen in the clearing where I stood. Dark whispers bounced about the population, who made me feel exceedingly unwelcome in their exotic world. As I wandered through the village I came upon the most prevalent tree, and once I reached it I was stunned by its glory.

As I stood before the colossal old willow, my mouth fell. The leaves gently glistened in the light of the setting sun and looked like glass as they shimmered all about me. Soon I approached the two guards who stood before a grand doorway that was carved into the very trunk of the tree. They took one look at me and opened the beautifully carved doors without hesitation. When I stepped inside I saw Mithias and all the others standing in front of a wooden throne where an old and sickly-looking angel sat. The throne was ornately carved and made of birch wood, and the smell of fresh flowers pricked my nose once the room surrounded me. The walls themselves were lined with every color of flower imaginable, and as the sun shone in through holes in the wooden trunk it looked as if the flowers were moving ever so slightly. These beautiful elements of nature were arranged so that waves of color seemed to roll on the wood of the tree. My eyes looked to these beautiful walls as I approached the motley crew before me. As I got close to Mithias and the others, the angel on the throne became more than a distant blur.

The pale angel had flowing white hair that rolled down his back. His eyes were as blue and deep as the most pristine waters in all the lands, yet his face was terribly aged. Cracks and crevices adorned his ghostly face, which frowned at me as I approached. This angel looked even older than the one at the house we had sheltered in, but despite his old age he seemed to have an intimidating presence about him. There was something about his lifeless blue eyes that seemed to penetrate my mind, and this made me advert my eyes from his.

"About time, Lloyd," Mithias irritably whispered once I arrived by his side. I was about to speak when the old angel told me to kneel.

I knelt down before the angel and peered through my thick hair to see him gaze at me with a grimace. With a voice that was more of a moan than anything else, the angel told us to rise.

"Now that all are present, I shall talk with you, Mithias," the old angel said as he leaned forward in his chair and clasped his hands together.

"There is not much to discuss," stated my companion. "My crew was in danger of being killed by the ocean's might, and I did what any captain would do in the situation."

"You aren't just any captain," said the old angel before Mithias could say anything else. "You are the only captain who has trespassed on my sacred land twice now."

A smirk stretched across Mithias' plump face. "I was wondering if your people would remember me. For a moment, I thought your old age had finally taken a toll on your memory."

"You insult me even now?" asked the old one as he stood. "By all that is holy, I should kill you for your transgressions!"

Numerous guards in the room slowly encircled us with weapons drawn at these words.

"We had no choice in coming here," shot back Mithias. The angels stood ready for any order as the captain added, "I did what was best for my crew, just as you would for your clan. Their safety is my prime concern, and I will not let wild winds or secluded angels threaten them."

For a moment I feared a fight as the angels encroached upon us. Each one awaited an order from the old angel, but any such order was cut short before their leader could speak. The sound of the two grand oaken doors slamming open caused all to look toward the entrance and abandon the fight. Against the beams of light stood an angel who looked to be about my age holding a slightly older angel in his arms. Both angels' clothes were tarnished with bright red blood that dripped onto the ground as the conscious angel advanced. His approach was slow and cumbersome, for he coughed and struggled to maintain his balance. As several angelic guards went to help him I noticed his right wing was severely cut and covered with a bloody sheet of cloth.

"Chief Shamayim," yelled the standing angel who held the other in his arms. His voice resounded all about the chamber due to the urgency within it.

The chief quickly stood up despite his old age and bellowed, "What has happened?"

The guards who still surrounded us lowered their weapons as the wounded angel rushed past us still holding his comrade.

"Ships to the east, they sacked our fishing vessels. I flew back with my brother." The angel gasped for air after uttering these words and was able to regain his breath a moment later.

"What of our fishers?" the leader asked.

The angel quickly nodded his head and replied, "All fled to the village before more damage could be inflicted, but my brother fell victim to the enemy archers."

"Pirates?" ask the chief angel as his wrinkled hands balled into fists.

"No," the angel responded. He placed the unconscious angel in his arms on the ground and motioned to the guards to get medical attention. As the guards lifted him I saw two thick arrows lodged in his left wing. The limping angel watched as they took his brother out of the room, then he reached into a woven bag that was dangling from his waist. He pulled out a small arrowhead and dropped it on the ground. The arrowhead was made like any ordinary projectile of the sort, but the tip was painted black at the point and bright red on the edges.

"These are Thundrian arrows," the angel stated in disgust as he brought his eyes up to the old chief.

The revered angel stared at the projectile, then slowly walked over to it. He picked it up and turned it in the shining light, then dropped it to the ground.

"How many ships did they have?" the angel chief asked.

"Their fleet blankets the seas," the angel said with a quiver in his voice. "They probably number in the hundreds, if not thousands. Their wide ranks stretched to the very edge of the horizon."

"Why are they here?" the chief asked in an urgent tone.

"I do not know, but rogue parties have landed on the eastern shore. They travel fast and with great resolve," the angel replied.

At this, I heard the crew member Guinth whisper that our vessel was on the eastern side of the island. For a brief moment the angelic leader glanced toward Mithias' lot, then he turned back to the bearer of the terrible news and stated, "Tell the people to head for the western shore. We must leave."

"To where?" asked the angel.

"Alfras. We shall seek shelter on her peaceful shores. Rogue traders from our clan have never been denied access to the port town of Urchi. I'm sure they will allow us to seek refuge there."

I snapped to attention at the mention of my home island, and visions of my family seaped into my consciousness.

The old angel walked over to the two guards who stood strong at his door and told them in a deep voice, "Gather the family and make haste toward the western shore. Tell them to leave all but the necessities behind. We sail for the islands of Alfras so that we may gather information as to why this would happen."

The two guards nodded and darted off to opposite ends of the town yelling something in the tongue of angels. Before we could say anything the old angel rushed before Mithias and shouted, "Have you brought this pain upon my people?"

"This was not my doing," said Mithias in an irritated tone.

The chief stared at him for several moments, then shook his head and shouted for more angels to enter the room. Nearly a dozen fully armed angels rushed into the room at his request and were quick to surround us.

"I speak the truth!" yelled Mithias as the guards advanced upon us. Not a single hint of desperation could be heard about his voice as he added, "My allegiance is to the sea and my men, nothing more!"

The old angel shook his head as an angel with skin as black as night appeared from the shadows behind him. The angel looked over the lot before turning to his leader and suggesting, "Now is not the time to deal with this rabble. Let us take them aboard our ships and seal their fates once our people are safe."

The chief scanned Mithias slowly before he reluctantly nodded his head and let out a slight sigh.

"My shadow is right," said the aged leader, glancing at the dark-skinned angel behind him. "Take them to the western shore. They shall remain in our company until we reach Alfras. Once we find the motives behind these attacks, their fates will be sealed."

"What of my ship?" demanded Mithias.

The old angel was quick to reply, "You heard the angel. The eastern side of the island is being overrun. You are welcome to try to get your ship back if you think you can take on a Thundrian fleet."

Mithias was silent for a moment as all eyes turned toward him. After a moment of thought, he huffed and said, "Once you realize this was not my doing, I demand to be taken back to this island so that I may sail away from your company once again."

"And if the Thundrians destroy your ship?" asked the old angel.

Mithias glanced away for a moment before saying, "They would surely not destroy a simple trading vessel, though I fear for the wares onboard. Regardless, if I am proven innocent, I demand that I be freed from this wretched island."

"A fair bargain if you prove to be trustworthy," said the old angel, "but know this, Mithias: your crimes against my people will not go unpunished once the imminent threat is dealt with."

After saying those words, the old leader turned to the shadowed angel behind him and nodded his head. The dark angel then approached our company and led us outside, where we beheld a chaotic sight. We watched as angels of all ages rushed through the woods to the west with nothing but items of food in their arms and the clothes on their backs. The dark-skinned angel paid no mind to this and quickly turned to Mithias.

"Follow me swiftly, human," he said.

"Our steps will echo yours," replied Mithias.

The dark-skinned angel darted into the underbrush at an unbelievable speed. Our lot followed him through the woods as fast as we could, but it seemed even with our speed we could barely keep pace with him. Within minutes we arrived at the beach and noticed several ships nestled on the sand.

They were small ships compared to the trade vessel we had arrived on; each only had a single grand sail. The sail on each of the four ships was large and blue with a white wing painted onto it. The strange thing to me was that these vessels sat on the sand and faced the ocean, yet they were far too massive for any man to push them from their resting places. They had even been put on the beach backward, with the sterns embedded in the sand, which made no sense to me.

"How do we get these off the beach?" shouted Mithias. "They're too big!"

"Patience, human," the angel replied before he flew up onto one of the ships. Once on board, he dropped a rope ladder down the side and yelled, "Climb the ladder!"

Without hesitation, I scuttled up it with Mithias' crew right behind me. Once on board the ship, I saw nothing unusual about it, yet I had little time to contemplate my surroundings with such panic all around me. Mithias was the last to come up the ladder, for his girth slowed him down. Just as he came aboard I turned to see a swarm of angels exit the forest like wasps from a hive. They ran toward the boats and took flight onto the decks once they reached the beach. Dozens, then hundreds, of angels emerged from the trees. Through all these unfamiliar faces I noticed the chief, Shamayim, fly up onto the deck of the ship we stood on. After several moments of angels scurrying about, Shamayim raised his voice above the commotion.

"Make haste, my followers! We must fly away, but we will return!" he yelled from his boat. Nothing special happened at his word, so I turned to behold a strange sight. All the angels who had emerged from the dense wood had gathered in circles on their respective ships.

"What are they doing?" I asked Mithias as I kept my gaze on the angels.

Before he could answer, the angels closed their eyes and let out a melodic tone. Their chorus sang a long, steady note that echoed throughout the island and seemed to stretch both far and wide. Just as quickly as they had begun their wail, they ended it. All was silent for just a single second until I felt a violent shaking beneath my feet. I struggled to make my way to the stern amid the violent rocking, and once I had reached my destination I held onto the vessel with all my might and looked at the beach, which shifted as if it were about to swallow us whole. The sands opened up and water from the ocean quickly flooded the newly formed basin under each vessel, caused by a powerful sort of magic that I had never beheld before. It was an amazing sight, but I noticed that the sails were not moving in the wind, for the wind was against us.

"Look!" yelled an angelic child from our boat. He pointed to the north, where we saw several battleships coming around a jagged cliff and into our view. Mithias picked up his axe in both hands and looked onward as the fast-moving ships rushed toward us at an alarming speed. Several angels joined him on the starboard side of the ship to watch as a mass of ships with crimson sails made their way toward us. I was not so focused on the immediate threat, for I had turned to see two angels drawing something on the wooden deck with blue and white chalk. The image was that of a jagged blue circle surrounding several white lines. As the last line of the circle was completed I felt another shaking deep below me. I heard the unique sound of rushing water against a wooden hull. The vessel lurched forward and I watched as the sails caught a great gust wind that seemed to be blown from the Divine Two themselves. Despite the fact that the Thundrians were quickly approaching, the angelic villagers did not panic. Instead, most looked over the vessel's railing, so I decided to do the same despite my anxiety.

I ran to the side of the boat and looked down to see the waves brushing against the stern, slowly pushing it into the ocean. The sails burst into action as a powerful gust of wind swept in from the east and propelled us to the west at such a speed that I was nearly knocked off my feet. The two angels who had made the chalk circle stood on the stern of the ship and watched with satisfaction as we fled from the enemy ships. The enemy ships encircled the island like a pack of wolves encircling a wounded doe, yet we were soon on our way to safety. Angelic guards made sure that all individuals were accounted for as Shamayim made his way toward Mithias' tightly-packed company.

"It seems that our situation has changed," he stated with a stern gaze as he wiped a bead of sweat from the folds in his brow. He turned to look at the other three angelic ships for a moment before returning his gaze to Mithias and me.

"You and your company could have fled to your ship and returned to the Thundrians," said the old angel as the sun beat down upon the frantic and confused angels on deck. His brow tightened. "Why did you not return to the force you brought to my land?"

My fear-stricken tongue conjured no words, yet Mithias was quick to reply.

"You still think we brought that force upon you?" asked Mithias, with anger laced about his voice.

"For six hundred years we've only had eight visitors," said the old angel, who advanced toward Mithias as he spoke. All on deck watched. "Five of those were scouting vessels for violent forces, and only twice before have we had to flee to our safe haven in Alfras."

Mithias' anger could not be quelled. "The odds may not be in my favor, then, but let me tell you: despite my deepest wishes, I did not bring this violence to your land."

One of Mithias' crew members, who went by the name Knoll, grabbed his captain's shoulder.

"Please, captain, your words reflect us all," he whispered.

A smirk appeared across the old angel's face as he leaned into Mithias and declared, "You'd do best to listen to your inferior. He knows that if I am displeased with you, I could have your whole crew tossed overboard."

Mithias lurched toward the chief, but two angels who held weapons restrained the man. This action caused many of Mithias' crew members to draw their weapons and ready themselves for a fight, but as I looked about them it was clear to me that the angels aboard our ship outnumbered us nearly ten to one. The confrontation between the old angel and Mithias had brought all who found themselves on deck over to watch the tense moment unfold. Every adult and child on board was ready to react to the seemingly unavoidable fight that had lingered about us since we had met the old angel, yet there was no violence. Instead, there was silence for a single short moment as all eyes looked on, but that silence was quickly broken.

"Stop this nonsense!" yelled a female voice from the crowd. I turned to look at the source of this voice and saw an angelic girl. She looked as if she was about my age and stood just barely shorter than I. Her skin was white, but not pale, and she carried a head full of long blonde hair that flowed down her back like a gentle brook through a mountain pass. Her hair graced two pristine white wings that were at least five feet in length. She had cerulean eyes that sparkled in the light and showed a look of concern for my company as soon as I beheld her. Her presence itself held a majesty that brought the eyes of all those around her to her body. Her thin white robe nearly grazed the floor she walked toward the conflict. Her eyes met Shamayim's as she positioned herself at his side.

"We are not savages, father," she stated as she placed her hand on his left arm. Her voice was soft and thin, yet direct, and as it graced my ears a smile panned across my face. She glanced at our lot before she added, "You and your company may stay aboard this ship so long as your weapons are not drawn."

Her thin, catlike eyes turned back to her father briefly as she said, "Your fate will be decided when we act upon facts rather than tradition and superstition."

Mixed low-voiced reactions could be heard from the surrounding crowd as I asked, "So we will not be harmed?"

The radiant angel before me turned away from her father. "At our speed we shall reach the Alfrasian shore in roughly ten days. There we shall gain information as to why we have been attacked. Once the facts our set straight your fate shall be decided."

I nodded to the young angel as Mithias shook the two guards off him. Upon discovering that he would be allowed to keep his life for another week or so, he put his axe away. The displeased captain began to make his way to the bow as all the angels in his path parted before him so as not to touch him. I followed Mithias as our crew members sheathed their weapons and watched their leader walk away.

Mithias did not look at me once he reached the bow. Instead, he stated, "Savages, every last one of them."

"Why did the Thundrians come toward the angelic island?" I asked, choosing to ignore his comment. "Aren't angels peaceful folk who live in seclusion?"

"Peaceful?" asked Mithias, "That's debatable, yet most angels stay within their clans' territories. But make no mistake, if it were up to their chief, Shamayim, we'd all be dead right now."

I held a very different view of the winged folks due to my experience with my mother and siblings, but I chose not to prod Mithias further. Instead, I asked, "What will become of your ship?"

Mithias glanced down at me with an air of rage about his figure as he declared, "One thing at a time, Lloyd, one thing at a time."

Mithias soon turned around to the crowd of angels that our crew members as if they were plagued with some terrible disease. The great man was quick to lower his voice and state, "Be wary of these winged folk, Lloyd. Theirs is a tradition of superstition that holds its roots across many generations."

With my only ally on board enthralled in mistrust, I turned back to the crowd of angels in an attempt to see the female who had brought me salvation, but she could not be found in the sea of skin and feathers. I believed that no angel met my eyes as I scanned over the crowd, until the girl who had quelled the chief came into view. She looked deeply at me as I scanned her suspiciously through the crowd. Her stare pierced my soul and caused my spine to tingle with a strange sensation, but just as my eyes met with hers, she hastily turned her head and retreated among the sea of angels. As the fluttering in my heart subsided, I turned away from her and looked out to the west in desperation as I realized that I had failed my father. Losing a whole season's catch would make the winter harsh and probably cause my family to never let me leave my home again. As the ship headed back toward Alfras, I dreaded the punishment my family would give me if I was lucky enough to escape the angels' judgment.

CHAPTER 4

In the nine days that passed at sea I hardly spoke to any angel, yet I still learned a great deal about them through observation. They were an amazing race of people, much different from the few angels who shared my island. These angels used magic constantly and had a great grasp of their powers. If we were hungry, an angel conjured food for us. If we were thirsty, water was conjured by a child who couldn't have been more than eight years of age. Several children chose to talk to me against their parents' wishes, and through them I learned that this remote tribe considered itself to be "pure angels." When I asked them what this meant, they simply stated that they could harness the power of nature much better than city angels due to the fact that they had not integrated into the kingdoms of lizards and human. Their magical potency amazed me as much as their dazzling flight. Whenever an angel flew, he or she seemed to flow with the wind instead of cut through it like our ship. These angels were unlike any I had ever encountered on my island, and every day they stunned me in some new way.

The trip was mostly spent in silence, except for the fourth day. As I stood on deck awaiting the sight of my homeland with both anticipation and dread, I thought back to that day. On that day, I awoke early in the morning and walked onto the deck. A few angels stood on deck looking over the port side of the ship in silence. I chose to join their ranks, and once I did I beheld a sad sight.

Bobbing in the water was the gutted carcass of a whale. It had obviously been killed by a land dweller, for its body was adorned with spear holes. Much of the whale's meat that could have been eaten was now rotten, for the remains of the creature's body were not stripped clean. Strangely, an old woman in the group took me aside and spoke to me in a soft voice.

"Our people greatly value the lives of those in nature." Her eyes turned to the whale. "It is said in our clan there are two great sins one can commit. One is for an angel to kill an animal without having the intention of consuming it and using all its body has to offer."

She was silent for a moment, so in a low voice I asked, "And what is the second?"

The old woman looked to the horizon, which was tinted with a warm shade of orange, and tenderly said, "To kill any of the four races that rule this world."

This was surprising to me since my life had been threatened by an angel just days before, so I asked the elder why the angels threatened my life and the lives of Mithias' crew. Her response silenced me for the rest of the morning.

"If one is to kill a man, for whatever reason, he is allowing an evil into his heart the likes of which will never be quelled in this life or the next," she began as she turned to me with an empty gaze. "Our leader and his guards would risk letting this darkness enter their hearts in order to protect us."

Her words faded from my mind as a voice echoed through the air. I heard an angel yell something in his native language, and all eyes turned to the bow. Excitement and fear grew in my heart as I turned to the distant shore of Alfras that was no more than a hazy stretch of earth. For many days I had anxiously awaited this sight, for it brought salvation from the angels whom Mithias cursed daily, yet when I returned home so soon without any money, I was sure that my father would berate me or even cast me out of his home. I had failed him, and I feared his reprisal more than I feared the angels around me.

I rushed to the front of the boat, ready to see my land again. The tropical trees gracing the walls of the port city Urchi would be swaying gently in the sea breeze. The people of the city would be going about their day collecting foods and trading with one another.

Each man would be searching the city for an honest coin. If I were to escape my captors and run to my village, I would behold its full glory in low afternoon. The boats of my people would be scattered on the sea, and the numerous huts would be filled with maidens going about their chores. I wanted to go home once again, and after this ordeal, part of me never wanted to return to the outside world and all its chaos ever again. I stared at the horizon as I began to make out the details of the city with hope in my heart.

Yet my eyes did not behold the city that I had known. The images that flooded my mind instantly dissipated as I beheld an entirely different picture.

Thick smoke rose from the shore of my island. As we sailed toward the city, an eastern wind brought the smoke to our boats. It was thick, and soot fell upon my clothes like snow. Several angels chanted a few words, and our vessel began to split the smoke in two as it rushed through the waters toward the docks that had once harbored the magnificent vessels I had seen when I first met Mithias. All that remained of the once-glorious vessels were splintered and broken remains that floated about the sea and rolled with the tide. I ran to the side of the boat to get a better view of the city.

It was ablaze with a violent flame. A bright gold color gave way to thick black smoke that was pushed out to sea by the winds from the west. In a frantic action fueled by adrenaline alone I ran through the stunned crowds on deck and climbed to the crow's nest, where I could catch a better view of the city.

Between the orange flames and black smoke I could barely make out the inhabitants of the city. Burnt and charred bodies were scattered through blood-soaked streets that were licked by fire and covered in ash. The crimson tinted tide was littered with hundreds of fish that lay dead on the disheveled sand. My knees buckled, and I soon found myself slumped against the barrier wall around the crow's nest.

"What horrors have descended upon this place?" asked Herman, another of Mithias' deckhands, who suddenly appeared on the rope ladder beside the crow's nest.

I violently coughed as our ship entered the thick cloud of smoke that drifted above the waves. I coughed in an attempt to breath but my coughing only made breathing more difficult. Herman made his way down the ladder, and I was quick to follow in shocked stupor once I had caught my breath. Once I reached the deck I found that the boat was in dock, so I jumped off the side, rolled as I hit the dock, and bolted down the planking. Mithias beckoned me back to the ship with great fervor, but to no avail.

I rushed toward the town, fueled by a sort of madness I had never known. The bodies, the blood, the flames—it was all so inhuman to me as I thrust myself into the horror. The pungent stench of death emanated from the burning pitch that fell around me. I beheld terrible, mangled corpses as I rushed between crumbling buildings, coughing all the way. The only sound to be heard in the once-bustling city was the crackle of rising flames inside the broken stone houses. Through this chaos a terrible realization pierced my heart like a dagger. My village was only miles away.

I looked to the northern gate and saw that it was open, so I bolted through it without thinking. My heart raced and sweat poured from my forehead as I ran down the long dirt path through the woods. I recklessly sprinted as thorns and branches tugged at me all the way, as if the natural world itself did not wish for me to continue. I became bloodied and dirty, yet ran faster and faster as my heart beat like a drum. Sweat covered my face and I panted like an animal before I finally beheld my village.

It looked the same. From where I stood I saw no fires or death; all seemed well. I clutched my stomach in pain, clumsily jogged up the path to the center of the village, and leaned on a large log that was positioned next to a fire pit as exhaustion set in on my being. I did not realize that I must have sprinted for over an hour to reach my home, for the adrenaline-fueled jog had seemed to pass by in seconds. I looked toward the fire pit and realized the embers were still glowing; I could tell the fire had recently been put out. After several great breaths I regained my composure and looked around to behold an ominous sight visage. Sharp, fresh ebony-tipped arrows were scattered around me and stuck out from the ground at all angles. I realized that no noise reached my ears. It was almost noon, and by now the women and children of the tribe should have been about the village while the men fished. Commotion should have been all about me, yet the only noise that I could hear was that of the rolling tide crashing into the cliff face. My mind raced as I contemplated all the terrible things that had occurred here. Looking to my left, I could see inside a building, where arrows jutted from the ground as if they had been fired high into the air before reaching their marks. The house's thatched roof showed many holes, and inside I saw a trail of blood flowing out the door. My heart pounded and my knees shook as I focused on my distant hut. Without thinking, I ran to my home and burst through the front door.

Some floorboards were not of their normal hue. Instead, thin splotches of ruby-colored liquid adorned them, slipping through the floorboards and dripping onto the dirt below. It made a curious tapping sound, much like the sound one hears during a gentle rain. As my eyes followed the stains I saw my brother lying in a pool of this crimson. I rushed to him, and as I did I caught sight of the lifeless bodies of my mother and father. I stood before the three of them and all at once my body fell limp. My conscious mind seemed to exit my body, and I dropped to my knees as a cold bolt ran down my spine. Arrows had pierced my family's flesh, and it was clear that they were long gone. I grabbed my brother and began to wail in a voice that would damn the most innocent man. My eyes flooded with tears and I rocked my brother's corpse; his still-warm hand tightly clenched the hand of my mother, who had three arrows protruding from her body. Behind the two of them was my father, who clutched a flimsy short sword in his right hand. His soul had left his body, yet his hand still clung to the instrument he had used to fend off an unknown attacker. Still on my knees, I lowered my brother to the floor and clenched my fists as hard as I could; I did not feel pain as my nails ground into the palms of my hand. Fresh blood emerged from my palms and dripped to the floor, but I paid it no mind. I opened my hands and nearly clawed the side of my own face in agony. In the nineteen years I lived in this place, nothing had given me more pain than seeing my family dead at my knees. I screamed and pounded my fists on the ground until they were bloody and bruised. Tears and sweat soaked my face and my hair fell over my eyes as I stared at their bodies. Every terrible emotion any man had ever felt and ever would feel entered my veins, yet all left me as fast as they arrived as a single noise echoed through my ears. The distinct thump of a shoe connecting with the floorboards caused all my emotions to pause for a single moment.

I jolted up and drew my sword. I heard a scream, then I beheld a little girl before me. I shook my head upon seeing the girl and dropped my sword to the ground as I gazed at her. She looked at me with tears filling her vacant, almost lifeless eyes.

"Daria..." I said as I opened my arms. My kid sister ran into them and slammed her face into my stomach before letting out an ungodly howl. The urge to yell and curse and cry filled my soul, but as I held my sister, I knew I could not do this. I held her tight as I looked down at my family. My blood-soaked palms tainted her dirty dress as she wept and wailed. Before I could take any other action, another thump echoed in the house. This one came from outside my home.

I turned to see a bloodied man standing in my doorway. He wore a leather vest and long dark pants. On his vest, under several splotches of blood, I could see the emblem of Thundria. In his hand he held a long, blood-soaked knife that shimmered in the afternoon light. I stood up and moved my sister behind me as a dark smirk overtook his scared and bloodied face.

The man turned the sharp end of the blade in the direction of my neck. My joints locked as he slowly walked toward me with an awful grin painted across his fat face. I stood like stone as the man thrust the knife toward my gut. As I felt the cold tip of the knife glance my skin, all time stood still for a moment. In this single instant I looked at my foe. Power flowed through my veins, so I grabbed his right arm with my left hand. The tip of the knife had barely scathed me, so I swiftly punched him in his face. The man stumbled back in a daze and dropped his knife as he slammed into the wall. I ran to my attacker, screaming, and leapt at his throat, but he maneuvered his body away from where I was to land and extended his arm. The edge of his arm slammed into my throat and I crashed to the ground. As I gasped for air, the man stood over me, gripped my neck with two massive dirty hands, and squeezed with an intense force as he lifted me. I felt my feet lift off the ground as my eyes bulged. His grip tightened; I choked for air and struggled madly. My sister screamed while my eyes began to feel as though they would pop. A dark, dizzy feeling slowly overtook me as I weakly swatted at the man's pulsing arms. Just as a dark curtain began to creep over my eyes, the man's grip loosened. I felt air escape his lungs and wash against the front of my face. The man released me from his grasp and fell to the ground as I wheezed and clenched my neck. On my knees, I rubbed my throat and looked down to see that an axe had been thrown into his side. My eyes darted to the wielder of the axe in an instant.

Mithias rushed into view and took his axe out of the man, who wailed in agony as he rolled on the floor. My comrade wasted no time and quickly plunged the same axe into the man's chest. My sister stood like a statue as Mithias pulled his bloodied axe from the mutilated corpse of my attacker.

"Are you okay?" he asked as he helped me to my feet. I shook and rubbed my neck until he repeated the question in a louder and more direct voice. I slowly nodded before turning to my sister.

My sister still breathed, yet she didn't seem alive. Her wide eyes had witnessed all the horror that had just befallen my village, and she looked as if she was about to pass out at any moment. She looked at Mithias with motionless, doll-like eyes as she remained frozen. My first words came to me.

"It's okay, he's a friend," I said in a whisper. My heart pounded and tears seemed so close, yet in the presence of my sibling I held them back.

She held onto me as Mithias walked over to the bodies of my family. He looked at each of them and let out a short sigh. Mithias went to each member of my family and closed their eyelids as my sister and I watched in silence.

"I'm so sorry," Mithias said as he shifted his gaze from the dead to the living. He glanced at my father in particular before adding, "Your father did not deserve to meet such an end. This shouldn't have happened."

"Mithias," I said in nearly a whisper as I buried my emotions, "What has happened?"

"Thundrians," he said. "They have attacked the island. We cannot talk now, for Thundrian troops are still scattered around this place."

"But what about my family?" I shot back.

"Kid, they're dead," uttered Mithias. "There's nothing we can do for them."

"We must take them with us! They require a burial!" I heard myself shout.

"We cannot take them," replied Mithias as he began to make his way toward the door.

"We must!" I screamed. I bolted forward and tightly grabbed onto Mithias' coat. My sister began to cry again as I looked him in the eye. My comrade looked down at my hand and then to my eyes before gently taking my arm and pushing it away from him. Mithias looked me dead in the eyes as he placed both his hands on my shoulders and declared, "Kiordiam was a good friend of mine, and on my honor I pledged an oath to him. So long as you are away from home, I am to protect you, and now that you have no home and Kiodiam is dead, my oath is bound to me. By my honor I am your guardian so long as you journey. So as your protector, believe me when I say, if we linger any longer then we shall join your family in the afterlife."

I looked back at my sister and took a deep breath after a swell of silence washed over me. With great hesitation, I grabbed my sister's hand and began to lead her out of the house. I stole one last glance at my fallen family as my sister began to weep once again, yet I could not keep my eyes on them for long. Time stood still as pain struck me like an ice-cold dagger that carved the image before me into my consciousness. The excruciating moment seemed to last forever, but once it had passed I found myself longing for it again. Yet it was all over, and I had to follow Mithias.

When I exited the house, I looked toward the ocean, where I beheld the ship I had called home for the last nine days. Before me was the leader of the angels and around him there were four guards. Mithias approached Shamayim and spoke the first words he had spoken to the old angel in many days.

"His family is dead," declared Mithias in a soft voice. "Had I not entered his home in time, he would also have been slaughtered at the foot of a Thundrian who now lies in a pool of his own blood."

"Thank the Two that we arrived here when we did," said Shamayim before turning to me. His tight brow softened and his eyes shook as he beheld me in all my pain. His lips parted and it looked as if he were about to utter some word of wisdom but he did not have the chance to speak.

"Where shall we go now?" Mithias asked, clearly assuming that we would stay with the angels.

The old angel let out a sigh. "Given your past transgressions against my kind I had planned on leaving you here, but in the face of such horrors I cannot do so. We must travel north to the continent of Finre, where we can seek shelter in the sacred land. It is there that we shall stop our fleeing and learn of our foe."

"You would take us there?" asked Mithias, who appeared perplexed by the old angel's change of heart.

Shamayim slowly nodded his head as he turned his eyes to my sister and me. He spoke with soft words that cooled my burning heart.

"I cannot leave these two here," stated the angel before turning to Mithias and adding, "and despite the fact that you trespassed on my land, you have killed a man who fought under the flag that seeks to end me. It seems that our fates are intertwined."

This acceptance did not mean much to me in the moment. I thought deeply about my family and all the inhabitants of Alfras as I squeezed my sister's hand tightly and asked, "What of the other islands to the south and west?"

"I can only assume troops have attacked those as well," said the old angel as his guards scanned the area for any hostile activity. "My scouts report flames rising in the northern skies of this island. It's a day's journey to sail to the southern Alfrasian island. If their forces truly blanketed the sea as my scouts have said, then they are probably crawling all over Alfras."

"The soldier I killed was no stranger to the sea," Mithias said. His voice was not haughty and proud, as I had suspected it would be. Rather, it was monotonic and lifeless. "His skin was like leather, as if he had been baking under the sun on the deck of a ship for many days."

The old angel thought for a moment, then said in a far-off voice, "They beat us here."

"Of what do you speak?" Asked Mithias in a heartbeat.

The old angel took a deep breath as he pieced together all he knew. "The Thundrians who attacked my island, they must have reached Alfras before us. There's no way such devastation could be unleashed by anything less than the fleet we fled from."

"Impossible," Mithias said. "Your people propelled the boats at speeds no human or lizard could achieve on these waters. None could have passed us!" He paused for a moment as the old angel stared him down. Soon, Mithias whispered the word, "Unless...."

"Unless they had angels with them who had a far greater grasp of magic than we do," the old chief said. As he said this, two well-armed men bearing the mark of Thundria emerged from the trees. The two looked surprise to see us standing in the village and turned to the woods to flee, but their efforts were in vain. Two angelic guards took out their bows and swiftly shot them in their vitals. The men fell to the ground and entered the next life within seconds.

"We must head back to the ships; it is too dangerous here," barked Shamayim as he stretched his wings. "My guards shall carry you to the ship."

"But what of the people to the north?" I yelled before the angel completely turned away.

"The northern villages may already be gone, Lloyd," Mithias stated.

"Thundrian troops might not have reached each village yet. We could save them!"

"We cannot take that chance," said Shamayim. "My men could die and—"

Before he could continue I let go of my sister's hand and lurched forward, bringing my face just a few inches from his, and in a voice more mature than I knew I held, I declared, "My family has just been butchered. If we have the chance to save any more innocents, then we will. You say you care for your people?"

The angel was silent.

"Well, I care for mine, and I will not go with you unless you guarantee that we go to the northern village of Giltrablain and try to save them from the terrible fate that has befallen me!" I shouted.

After a moment of silence, the elder angel let out a solemn sigh and replied, "You hold true to your people, young one. Very well. Once the other three ships in our fleet sail to my position we will sail along the coast of this island and stop to evacuate your town of Giltrablain. So long as my people are not put in danger, we will do as you wish."

"I see only one vessel out at sea," I said, turning to Shamayim. "Where have your other ships gone?"

Mithias chimed in, "The other three unloaded at the port. Angels scour the city for any who still live. The only reason we're here is because I assumed that you rushed home."

"So you came for me?" I asked Mithias.

Shamayim said, "Mithias and his crew gave us little choice, yet now is not the time to discuss this. We must regroup with the fleet. Come, let my winged guards take you back to our vessel."

I nodded and turned to my sister, who had heard the entire conversation. An angel quickly approached and scooped her into his arms and flew for the coast. Soon, another angel grabbed my arms and took flight toward the boat with the utmost speed. As we flew, I could see two angels struggling to lift Mithias off the ground among the barren village. They eventually succeeded, and we flew back to the ship with great speed. As I left my tattered house behind, I bid it one final farewell that was filled with hate for the Thundrian Empire. Soon I was placed upon the deck of the ship that was to be my new home. My hate stewed until the other three ships of the angelic fleet arrived from the south. Once they arrived, a young angel landed upon our vessel and spoke to his chief.

"My liege," the angel said as he approached Shamayim, "we found no innocents alive, but did come upon a Thundrian whom we have taken prisoner. We believe he is one of the troops who did this to the island."

"Interrogate him, find out why this has happened," said the elder. "Continue our course north around the coast of this island."

"Should we not sail away from this place?" the angel asked.

The chief shook his head and replied, "No, Grinra. There is a village near the coast to the north. We head there to aid the people."

"Can we fight off the Thundrians?" another angel asked from the small crowd that had gathered around us.

The old angel lost himself in thought, until I said, "If we know more about our enemy then we can better prepare for the encounter. We could ask the prisoner how many there are."

The old leader nodded his head before saying, "You and Mithias shall take care of that. Find out why Thundria has attacked and how many have come with him."

"And then what do we do with the worm?" Mithias added, unsatisfied with what the chief had declared. The angel knew Mithias desired blood, but shook his head once again. "No blood shall be shed on my ship."

"If I may," started Mithias after a moment, "Lloyd's entire village has been killed by these people. Would you rob him of his vengeance?"

The elder was quick to shake his head at this notion.

"Your kind knows nothing of death, human," he declared. "Those who harm others let a darkness seep into their very souls. If his blade cuts the prisoner he will allow his heart to be cut a thousand times over."

Shamayim glanced my way as he added, "I would not let a youth damn himself."

"My path is my own," I said in a voice that drew all attention to me. "Let me get information from the prisoner and do with him what I will."

Shamayim was silent for a moment before Mithias declared, "The boy is just. He will get the information you need."

"Very well, then," the elder angel said after a moment of silent contemplation. "But know this, young Lloyd: the man in our hold is a human being just like you. He has hopes and dreams and fears all the same. Harm him and you will only mar your mind with a terrible bloodlust."

My mind was enveloped in passion and hate, so I did not heed his words. Instead, I simply asked the elder angel where the prisoner had been taken as I felt my eyes blaze. The angel warned me against any violence once more, then gave me directions to find the prisoner below deck.

I left Daria in the care of the angels and pushed open the double doors that led below deck. My force caused the doors to slam into the wooden wall and make a loud thud that echoed across the air. Once in the hallway, I burst through the second door on my left with great speed and fervor. Inside the dank room, I beheld a middle-aged man who was bound and gagged. His arms and legs were tied together, respectively, and his face was sweaty and worn. He had long, ginger-tinted hair and an eye patch over his left eye. The angels had stripped him of his armor, and now he wore nothing but simple rags. I drew my sword at the sight of him, yet he showed no fear.

He began to chuckle, and I screamed at him in furious rage. For reasons I will never know, the man attempted to speak, so I untied the rag around his mouth. I had to know what he would say.

"They send a child to kill me?" he asked around bits of laughter. "The angels are weaker than we expected!"

I raised my sword to his neck and his eyes widened, yet he still remained calm.

"Why is my island ablaze? Why are you here?" I shouted as the steel tip of my sword bored ever so slightly into the man's neck.

He looked at the sword, then back at me with a sneer.

"You don't have the guts," he said with a smile.

I did not hesitate to prove him wrong. Using the sharp tip of my sword, I cut a swift mark on his cheek, causing blood to slowly drip to the floor. The man cursed as I put the sword back under his neck.

"We came for the pillar!" he yelled as his eyes buldged. The mocking smile he once held was gone now, and sweat began to form on his brow.

"What pillar?" I yelled back.

"One of the three, from the days of old, you know of the stories, do you not?"

"What do you speak of?" I asked in a calmer voice as I retracted my blade.

"It is said in the old days, three pillars of unimaginable power led to the kingdom of the divine. They now lie beneath the earth, and my king claims that he who raises them shall govern the heavens and the planet."

"Lies!" I screamed as I marked his other cheek. The idea that an army could cause such destruction based on an old tale that I had learned as a child caused a white-hot rage to rise deep within me. My hand shook as I aimed my quivering blade at the man's neck.

"I speak the truth, boy!" he screamed.

"How many of you are there?"

"We are twenty thousand strong on this island; we have forty thousand more troops between the other two islands of Alfras."

"What of your soldiers? Tell me about them," I demanded with a steadier hand.

"All races are among our ranks. Humans, lizards, and angels, we have them all. I was in charge of sacking minor villages on this island with archers. We took out three to the north of Urchi."

I gripped my blade tightly and lowered it to his chest, as if to thrust it through his stomach.

"You will kill me for telling you what I know?" he whimpered in disbelief. I held the sword at his stomach as he continued to speak. "Please, boy," he yelled. "I have a family back in Thundria!"

"Should you be so lucky!" I screamed as I dropped the sword to my side.

"What do you mean?" the man hesitantly inquired. His brow was drenched in sweat and his eyes madly darted about as I approached him.

"You were the one who led forces into my village!" I yelled at the top of my lungs. "You were the one who ordered the archers to fire upon innocent men, women, and children! You were the one who took my family from me!"

My body pulsated as wrath overtook me, and without full control, I began to pummel the man madly with my fists. Blood poured out of his nose and mouth after several blows, yet I continued. At first, the man tried to writhe away from me or plead for his life, but after a handful of blows his words became muffled by the blood that poured down his face. My punches left him battered to the point where his face looked nearly inhuman. He gasped for air and coughed up profuse amounts of blood. Using my sword, I cut the ties that bound him and dragged his limp body out of the room and onto the deck.

There, angels gasped at the sight they beheld, but I did not waver. I dragged the man to the edge of the ship, then propped him up on his knees before slamming his head into the wooden railing. A terrible splintering noise echoed from the man's skull, and the angels looked on in horror. I jerked the man to his knees once more, and to my surprise he still remained conscious. Under the beating sun, the mangled excuse for a face looked at me with blood spilling over it, and I heard him beg for mercy in a low whimper. Through his eyes I saw one who sought to escape from my grasp, yet unfortunately for him, he would not live to see tomorrow's dawn. Without a second thought I shoved the man over the railing and cast his body to the merciless waves. He was quick to sink beneath the waves and paint the waters around him scarlet. I felt no remorse. I felt no pain. I simply turned around to see a group of angels gathered around me with wide eyes and fear about them. All except the bravest of guards backed away from me in fear.

"Clean things up in there," I calmly said to them as I put my sword in its scabbard. My eyes scanned the crowd for a familiar face, and to my surprise I beheld Daria amid the angels. I walked toward my sister and attempted to hold her, yet as I extended my arms she darted away from me and vanished below deck. I looked toward the doors she had disappeared through in dismay, but before I could give chase to her, Shamayim and Mithias approached me from the crowd.

"I see you decided to take his life," the old angel muttered in disappointment as he glanced at the bloodstains upon his deck.

I stared beyond the angel with eyes that held a pain that could not be quelled. Without saying another word, I disappeared into the ship's hold and walked into an empty room, where I sat and sharpened my blade to such a fine tip that the slightest glance from it would cause my finger to bleed. I stayed in that room for many hours before I was summoned on deck, and when I made my way topside I looked at the western shore, where I beheld a dreadful sight.

An orange blaze steadily rose from the shell of the city Giltrablain and sparkled as darkness overcame the day. On deck,

Mithias stood next to Shamayim. I walked through a crowd of angels that parted as I took each step. Once I arrived at the railing, Shamayim addressed me.

"We cannot help this place now," declared the wise angel after he let out a deep sigh.

I said nothing, but Mithias would not be silent at the notion. The great man turned to Shamayim and asked, "We have come all this way, can we not search for any survivors?"

As I turned to Mithias I noticed that all four ships of the angelic fleet were still together. Because of this fact, Shamayim's next words held more truth to them.

After slowly shaking his head, the old angel stated, "I cannot risk exposing my whole village to the forces that caused such destruction."

Strangely enough, Mithias said nothing as he looked at the other ships in our fleet. His eyes then skimmed over the burning village before he looked back at Shamayim. He simply said, "I understand."

It felt strange to hear Mithias agree with the old angel, but as I looked at the burning city I knew that Shamayim's words were true. Ours was a small force that did not have a great capacity to fight. When I came upon this realization, I spoke for the first time since I had taken another man's life.

"Where will we go now?"

The old angel looked across the bow of the ship before speaking.

"We shall head to Finre," he declared as he trained his eyes on the northern horizon. "Our angelic sanctuary of Sacrimen will serve as a safe haven during this time."

"What will you do there?" asked Mithias.

Shamayim turned his gaze to the portly man and replied, "A wise old angel resides there with his village. I shall inform them of these tragic events and a course of action shall be determined."

Mithias was strangely hesitant before he slowly asked, "Then we shall join you?"

Shamayim softly said, "It is clear by the actions of you and your crew that you did not unleash such chaos. Though we have our differences, I cannot leave you on this island to die by such a force."

The giant man thanked Shamayim before I did the same in a soft, empty voice. The voyage to the north would take many weeks, and eventually the legendary cold frost of Finre would coat our ship like a thin blanket. Knowing that my sister and I were safe, I disappeared below deck once more to sharpen my blade in solitude, yet once I arrived in my room, a rush of pain hit me. The faces of my fallen family became more than images in my mind as I stood in the small room. The room began to spin and the walls seemed as if they were going to close in around me. Pain and sorrow ravaged my broken mind in a way I had never thought possible. My hands trembled and my body shook uncontrollably as sweat began to pour down my face. Everything was too much for me in that single moment, so I threw myself to the floor, where I wept like a child.

CHAPTER 5

For a lone long week at sea, dark thoughts the likes of which I had never encountered plagued my mind. I spent days locked away in my room, where I contemplated the horrific events that had taken place back home. Evil thoughts of how I would slay all those who claimed allegiance to Thundria seeped into my mind, yet I could not let others see my true feelings, for I had to maintain a guise of integrity around my only surviving family. As the days wore on, my sister became closer to me than ever before. She constantly sought my company despite my public murder, but something always seemed amiss whenever she was around. She looked at me in a different light, so I tried to mask my darkness around her in hopes of her warming up to me again. Yet once the sun set, the girl distanced herself from me and found rest in her own quarters for reasons she would never disclose. It was in the darkness of night that I allowed myself the liberty to hate my unknown enemy. Not a day went by that I did not resent those who had taken my home, yet after a week of solitude I began to walk about the decks once again. The angels soon put me to work on the ship and I happily obliged so that my mind would not be idle. Through my work I became known less as a threat and more as the half-human I was. There were those who continued to look at me with cautious stares, yet those who worked by my side grew to appreciate my presence.

With my home gone, my sister became my prime concern, even above revenge, for she was my last link to my fallen family. I knew I had to protect her against the force that had destroyed all we loved. Questions about this force still lingered around the cloud of contempt that poisoned my mind. Why had Thundria invaded and slaughtered the innocents? The man I had killed talked of raising the legendary pillars, yet my rage in the moment had not allowed me to question him further. Deep down I wished I had gotten more information from the man before ending his life so abruptly.

Killing the man who had wronged me ate away at my conscience like a caterpillar devouring a leaf. Despite my best efforts, the longing, desperate eyes of that man stared into my very soul whenever my eyelids grew heavy. His eyes had begged for mercy, and that haunted my dreams constantly. Oftentimes I attempted to escape these nightmares by meandering about the deck of the ship late at night.

On the twelfth night of the five-week voyage, I found myself enveloped in one such nightmare. I awoke from the terrifying vision and turned to my door, where a dim light shone under the crack of the barrier. On this night, my ears caught a thumping alongside the sound of the waves. These soft thuds echoed outside my door for a moment before the light under the entry was blocked by a shadow. The soft pounding began to fade away and as the shadow moved past the light. I did not wish to close my eyes and enter a terrible dreamscape once more, so I decided to go onto the deck in hopes of finding the source of the noise. I soon emerged on deck into cold night air, which grew more frigid with each passing day.

From the light of the two moons I saw a lone figure standing at the edge of the ship. This silhouette was no taller than I and had long wings that were stretched out into immaculate crescent tools of flight. They shone as the light from the dual moons gently caressed them. I cautiously approached the mysterious figure, then slowly extended my hand so I could tap the angel on the shoulder. Suddenly, the silhouette whipped around, grabbed me, and twisted my arm behind my back.

"Are you friend or foe?" the figure whispered in my ear from behind me.

"Your chief has not yet decided that," I said. The figure loosened his grip, then pushed me away. I spun around and quickly realized that, despite his strength, the figure was not a man. In the light of the moons I could see a glimpse of the figure's face and saw that a female angel stood before me. In an instant, a smile emerged on her familiar face and she burst into quiet laughter as I stared at her. Her behavior did not seem right in the tense situation.

"Why do you laugh so?" I asked the angel, who looked very familiar.

Her laugh slowed and died before she replied, "You're still so tense! Can you not take a little joke?"

It was in this moment that I realized who I was talking to. "You were the one who saved us from Shamayim's wrath!" I exclaimed.

Her smile widened and she replied, "I'm glad you remember."

I had many questions for this angel, but none could be voiced before she asked a question that struck a painful chord in my heart.

"I have heard some things on my ship," she began as she glanced at one of the three other vessels in our fleet. "Many speak of a half-human boy who violently killed a man who begged for mercy."

I did not hesitate to harshly declare, "That man killed all who I knew and loved."

"So I have heard," she stated as she leaned against the railing. "None have ever spilled blood aboard this vessel—"

"And I pray that none will ever have to again," I replied as the massive moons illuminated the sea all around us. All was silent for a strange moment until she said words that no angels had said to me yet.

"Well, if it means anything, I am so sorry for your loss," she said softly as her eyes met mine.

These words came from a soul I did not know; yet, for some reason, they made me feel rejuvenated, almost like a new man. With these words came a newfound sense of acceptance that I longed to hold. The next words I spoke seemed to not be my own.

"Hate and murder will not bring them back," I said as painful realization washed over me. "I should not have harmed that man."

"Though my clan would scorn you, I will not," she said as her gaze came to mine. "I do not know what I would do if I lost my clan along with my home. My brothers and sisters may look to you with dark gazes, yet I do not stand by them on that account."

With a worn smile on her face, she extended her hand and said, "My name is Ariel."

Without hesitation, I firmly grasped her hand and shook it while presenting my name to her. "What is your sanctuary like?"

"Beautiful," said Ariel as she turned her eyes to the dark sea. "It is called Sacrimen, and by all accounts it is a lovely refuge away from the chaos of the world. I'm sure you'll discover that it is a pleasant place."

The comforting words of this kind angel were very welcome during my dark time, but I had to ask her one question.

"Why have I not seen you aboard this ship aside from when you quelled Shamayim?" I asked.

Her gaze was set on one of the other vessels in our small fleet as she replied, "I spend much of my time tending to the young who accompany our fleet on another ship. They have never set foot on a ship before, and the rolling waves often cause them to fall ill. On the request of my father, I help them through it."

She turned to me with a smile as she asked, "What exactly brought you to my island in the first place?"

For some reason, I began to tell her everything. She seemed warm and trusting, unlike all the other angels who maintained residence on the ship. Ariel was engaging and kindly asked me questions about my homeland. She apologized for my losses and expressed grief for the fallen whom she would never know. She had an air of empathy about her, and it was this feeling that caused me to babble for many hours. Once I finished my tale, she had only one thing to say.

"You've come quite a way," she concluded.

"I must find out why Alfras was attacked," I was quick to declare.

She replied, "That is just, for the ones who have fallen must be accounted for."

"Thank you," I said hesitantly, after stealing a glance at her beauty once more. Simply put, she was beaming as she stood under the light of the two moons. Her cascading, silky hair flowed past crisp, bronzed shoulders that were exposed. The silken robe she wore was cut at the shoulders and stretched down to her ankles, and it almost looked like a sort of wedding dress. She had eyes of the deepest blue, and a warm smile that stretched across plump lips. Even in my pained state, I could not keep my eyes off her as we spoke. We stood in silence for a moment before I asked a question that had lingered about my mind for quite some time.

"When you saved us," I began softly, "Why were your words able to calm Shamayim's anger when he wished to harm my kind?"

The angel turned back to the gently rolling wave. "I am his only child, and as much as he wishes to deny me, he cannot say no to his one and only."

All her features looked flawless and beautiful, unlike Shamayim, whose skin looked like leather. Ariel's hair was thick and flowing, unlike her father's coarse, thin strands. This girl was far too kind to be of his blood, so without thinking, I asked, "He is your true father?"

After speaking I realized that this question might strike a negative chord with Ariel, yet as she turned to me she smiled and remarked, "You are quite astute."

I continued to watch her as she said, "No, Shamayim is not my real father. My parents hailed from a different angelic clan that sought shelter on my home island long ago. It is said that my parents' clan was nearly slaughtered by the hands of men."

"Why would humans do that?" I asked the angel.

She looked out to the dark horizon and stated, "All races of this world seem bent on destruction for one reason or another. A powerful band of barbarians brought my original clan to its knees. Had it not been for the intervention of Shamayim and his clan, I would surely be dead now."

"So he was able to save your village?"

Ariel shook her head. "He could only save three members of my clan, which formerly numbered in the hundreds. An elderly couple and myself were taken to his island where we received a warm welcome. I was too young to remember them, but the elderly couple soon passed away after our arrival, so Shamayim took me in as his own daughter. The rest is history."

"It is good that you have a family," I remarked in an attempt to lighten the serious situation.

Ariel smiled and turned to me with an unexpected response. "If you can call Shamayim that," she replied, with a strange distance about her. "I love the old man with all my heart, but his duties as a leader take him away from his duties as a father."

"Yet he is there for you," I began as sorrow enveloped my heart once more. I thought of those I had lost and gazed out to sea, yet I was not alone on this evening. Soon the smooth, fair hand of the angel graced my shoulder.

"You are not alone, Lloyd," she said. "Mithias and his crew love you like a brother."

I remained silent as the angel's eyes met mine and she declared, "You seem to be a good person. Though my clan may contest, I am here for you if you ever need someone to talk to."

My heart still longed for the family that I would never be reunited with, yet this girl's compassion brought me back to my usual self for the first time in many days. My soul lifted and I thanked her for her words before going back below deck. That night, my mind was not marred with terrible nightmares of death and destruction.

For the next two days I got to know Ariel, and she came to tell me a great deal about her life in her native land. As the next weeks unfolded, the angel and I grew closer with each passing day.

It was the fifth week of travel to the northern lands when I finally heard an angel announce to all that land was in sight off the tip of the bow. The weather was more frigid than anything I had ever experienced. As I walked to the bow, I ran my hand along one of the ship's railings, only to discover that it was coated in a thin layer of frost that stung when my hand touched it. I released my grip on the railing and stepped next to Ariel as I beheld a most foreboding sight on the horizon.

As I looked on my destination I could see cold, deep, blue water washing up onto gray sand. Against the sand were ridged cliffs coated in ice. The cliffs were adorned with deep, foreboding caves that wore many icicles on their entrances. I looked onto the shore with a heavy heart, for the cold weather was a new thing to me. The hairs on my back and legs rose, and I instinctively began to rub my hands together as the boat continued toward the small beach that lay between two cliff faces.

"We are to traverse a deep network of caves before arriving at the hidden city of Sacrimen," stated Ariel as she took place beside me. "Though the angelic clans of the world may not be united, my kind has put aside any grievances with one another and sought refuge here for generations. I'm afraid your friends should not expect a warm welcome, for the native leader of this place has a heart that is colder than this weather."

I nodded before letting out a slight sigh. The last thing I needed was for someone to treat me with disrespect at a time like this. I longed for someone to tell me things would be okay, and that over time I would find peace. The only person who had spoken any words of comfort to me in recent days had been Ariel, yet even words from my new friend could not completely heal my broken heart, which tore evermore with each palpitation.

The four boats carefully maneuvered between jagged rocks in the water leading toward the shore. As we went by the rocks I could see that some stretched high into the sky like shark's teeth as we passed them. We came dangerously close to some of the towering rocks as we maneuvered toward the shore, but never once did we hit one. The boats eventually made it to shore safely, and everyone was upon the sand in due time. I had the clothes on my back and my sword in its sheath and not another thing to my name as I stepped onto the continent Finre for the first time. I had only taken a handful of steps before I heard a familiar voice.

"Lloyd!" yelled my sister from a group of humans and angels around her. Daria ran toward me and stood at my side for warmth and protection from the crowd. She grasped onto me tightly, and as she did this I looked down to her with a strained smile. My sister bent her pristine wings inward as she looked up at me and smiled. Daria's seclusion onboard the ship had constantly worried me, so one day not too long ago I had asked Ariel to lend an ear to her. As fate would have it, Daria warmed up to Ariel rather quickly. My new angelic friend seemed to be the only one who could get my sister to talk, so I was relieved when I saw her approach me from the crowd. Behind Ariel stood Mithias and his crew, who cautiously observed the commotion about the crowd. I was about to speak to Ariel until I heard Shamayim's voice rise above the crowd.

"Stay your tongues, my friends!" he yelled over the worried conversations of all others. Shamayim stood on a large rock as he surveyed the audience and ran his left hand over his balding head.

"We are to travel deep underground through way of a cliffside cave," he said. "There, we will find a safety in the ancient sanctuary of Sacrimen. Stay close and stay quiet, for those who meddle with the deep do not live to speak of it." There were whispers of fear and the possibility of death until the chief angel silenced the people. "Give the angelic guards around you your trust, and in return they shall give you their protection."

Low laughter from Mithias' men brought on a curse from the captain himself, which could be heard about the beach. The chief of the angels' ears perked up, and he swiftly hopped off the rock and walked through the crowd until he stood in front of Mithias. His face only met Mithias' chest, but his words were above anything Mithias could handle.

"Mind yourself, captain," he said as his eyes penetrated Mithias'. "Though I have granted you life, the guardians who protect this sanctuary may deem you unworthy of entry. If that be the case, then even I can't diffuse their wrath."

The crowd grew silent at this remark and watched Mithias for his response. The burly captain let out a great breath of air and straightened himself to the angel, but he said nothing. Deep down I think he feared the chief angel's power and wisdom, yet his stone cold face did not show it. The old angel was at least one hundred, or maybe even two hundred years old, and in the moment I believed that Mithias knew that with the angel's age came a great deal of wisdom and experience. I suspected it was this idea that caused the man to withhold any foul retort.

"Come!" the chief angel announced as he began to ascend the cliff face by way of a narrow stone ridge. The icy ridge wrapped around the cliff until it met a landing before the mouth of one of the many dark caves. The old angel did not hesitate to lead the line of refuges into the darkness of the cave. Once inside this darkness, he uttered words in a tongue that I could not recognize, and a small light illuminated the space about him. Several other angels whispered the same words with the same results, and clusters of people drew themselves toward the light. The old angel continued to hobble through the cave with all of us trailing him in silence. As the darkness crept about us I felt my little sister grasp my hand and squeeze it tightly. I picked her up and held her in my arms as we continued to shuffle forward. Ariel soon came toward me with an orb of light about her.

"Is she okay?" Ariel whispered as she glanced at my sister.

"She's a little scared," I responded as my sister turned her gaze to Ariel.

Ariel smiled and said to her, "Don't worry, Daria, my light shall keep us safe."

My sister managed to smile at this before burying her head in my breast once more. Before continuing, I smiled at Ariel and mouthed the words, "Thank you."

Daria continued to shield herself from the darkness as I looked at the light that glowed all about Ariel.

"How do you do that?" I whispered so that my voice would not echo about the cavern.

She turned to me with the slightest hint of a smile and said, "It is magic. My people know how to control nature and, in this case, bring the remnants of light from the shore with us so that all can see."

I stood close to Ariel as I continued to walk, and looked behind me to see the line of people continuing to enter the cave. Mithias and his men held up the rear and lit torches as they entered, making sure they did not come too close to the angels.

The small opening of the cave led to a grand hall that began to echo with the footsteps of hundreds. After progressing along a narrow platform that led us above a shimmering pool of water, our group came to a staircase carved from the very earth. These earthen steps were so narrow that we could only descend them in pairs. I made sure to stay close to Ariel so my sister would not lose her sense of security as we began our descent through the narrow passage. The stone steps echoed in the darkness as individuals paired off and continued down the steps. After several minutes of following these steps down into the earth, we emerged into a grand open area. Stalactites and stalagmites were scattered everywhere, and the sound of water dripping down from the ceiling into small pools could be heard. Everything outside of the small globe of light cast by the angels was black, but as my eyes adjusted to the darkness I began to see that the cavern stretched for an unfathomable distance before me. Broken corridors and aged passages were all around us, yet the line of angels and humans followed Shamayim's steps without wavering.

We progressed in the dark and remained silent for what seemed like an eternity. The trip continued on this way for a great deal of time, until the angel in front of me stopped. I was confused and peered beyond him to see that the line had ceased its journey. I heard a whisper making its way down the line, and eventually the angel in front of me turned to Ariel and said, "Silence is required to ensure our safety from this point on. Tell those behind you."

Ariel did as he said and the whisper continued down the line until it could no longer be heard bouncing off the cave walls. Just as the last whisper dissipated into the air, our line began to move again, only now our pace had slowed and people looked all about them as they shuffled through the menacing network of passages.

Within minutes of the line moving, I noticed two interlocking steel rods embedded into the rock in the cave ground. On them was some sort of language I had never seen before, but it was obvious these served as warnings, for atop each rod sat a dirtied old skull. My eyes followed each cross down to behold bunches of skulls dangling from either side of the simple structures. I quickly held my sister tightly to me so she would not see and turned to Ariel in confusion.

"This is not the doing of my people, but of the guardians," she whispered in the faintest voice. "Stay close, Lloyd. The guardians will not hesitate to harm anyone without wings."

After those brief words Ariel refused to speak anymore as the line trudged forward. One minute passed, and there was nothing. Two minutes, three minutes, even four minutes passed and things were fine. Then, in the fifth minute, I saw two glints against the darkness. I quickly fixed my gaze upon the sparkles and saw that they were of a bright gold color. The pair of golden globes came and went, appearing in different places each time they reappeared. It did not take long for me to discover that they were pairs of stoic, almost lifeless eyes watching our advance. These eyes belonged to some unknown creature that I could not see against the darkness. I tapped my hand against Ariel's shoulder and frantically nodded my head toward the glints in the dark. She opened her mouth and the softest whisper made its way to my ears.

"Guardians. Made long ago to protect this place from the horrors of the cave and outsiders. If someone with a black heart enters the cave, they will strike them down. The skulls of the unworthy serve to ward off curious adventurers."

I shrugged my shoulders and mouthed the word "why?" then she whispered again, "Angels who journey here seek protection from the outside world and those who inhabit it."

Suddenly, the guardians made an ungodly hissing sound, the likes of which curdled my blood and caused me to nearly scream. Ariel clamped a hand over her mouth, and the entire line stopped for a moment as the golden eyes of these veiled creatures darted all about us. I stood like a statue as pairs of golden lights danced all about us. I felt a warm, moist feeling on my neck as two golden lights appeared right next to me, yet I held my ground and held my sister even tighter. The hairs on my neck stood erect as a terrible stench entered my nostrils. The foul air from one of the creatures engulfed me for several moments before ceasing. The lights soon continued on their way, and after a moment the guardians ceased their spine-tingling hiss.

Our pace quickened as the guardians continued to move all about us. They kept their distance from us, but oftentimes their giant illuminated eyes scuttled across the distant ceiling above our line or darted besides us. In the handful of minutes that passed I never did get a good look at them, but one thing was for certain: these creatures brought a fear into my heart that I wished to expel with all my might. The minutes spent with the guardians all about us seemed to drag on for hours, but finally a spark of hope shone against our line.

Tendrils of light that seemed to come from the sun began to illuminate the cavern, and the eyes of the guardians slowly vanished behind us. This light slowly entered the cavern, but within seconds it spread all around us. The line of angels and men about me began to dissipate into a bright, open cavern. My eyes quickly adjusted to the light, and my mouth gaped in awe at what I saw once I entered the holy sanctum.

It seemed to be something out of a dream. I began to feel a familiar soft, spongy substance beneath my feet. Below me was short, tamed green grass that stretched across the large, open clearing. The colossal circular clearing we had come into must have been at least a mile long, yet as soon as I entered it my eyes fell upon a single predominant stalactite that stretched downward from the distant roof of the clearing, until the tip was just a few feet from the ground. The thick stalactite shone with a beautiful white light that resembled something more of glass or crystal than of rock. The light from this stalactite lit the entire open area and made the environment around me shine as if it were exposed to the magnificent sun itself.

The walls of the clearing had intricately-made stairs carved into them that led to multileveled walkways. These walkways spiraled around the edge of the grand clearing and stretched as high as my eyes could see. If one were to walk along these natural stairs one would come upon a plethora of doors that were scattered in the cave wall itself. Against these same walls were simple windows carved through the rock, and the stalactite brightly illuminated the inside of each residence.

A winding pathway was laid out before me that led to the seemingly divine crystal at the center of the utopia. Once the path met the crystal, it circled around and branched off to the many different stairways that were cut from the cave walls. When my eyes fell down to ground level I beheld colossal oak and maple trees scattered among the grass between flowers and the path. As we continued to move forward, I began to see angels moving all around us. When these inhabitants caught sight of my lot they stopped their business and stared. Dark whispers accompanied these unwelcome stares, yet I paid no mind to them, for my ears caught another sound.

I heard rushing water very close to my left and saw a grand sight. Angels gathering water surrounded a waterfall that ran into a basin. Numerous waterfalls shot out of the cave walls and cascaded into stone basins all about the chamber and the familer sound of rushing water was quite pleasant to me. The waterfall I looked to seemed pristine, and sparkles of light danced against the clear falling water. I observed a small rainbow, which appeared against the water as children splashed about numerous puddles that had formed around the basin. Angels of all shapes and sizes carried jars of water away from the waterfall. These containers of water were sprinkled about gardens and under trees in a very delicate fashion. It was clear by the untouched beauty of this oasis that neither human hands nor lizard claws had tamed it.

"This is not right," I heard Ariel whisper under her breath as we continued on the path. She cautiously eyed the multitude of angels about us as our line continued down the stone pathway.

"What's wrong?" I asked in my momentary lapse of reality.

"This sanctuary has long been nearly uninhabited," she said. "The angelic clans united after the great hero's triumph over Thundria two hundred years ago, yet old ties have long since dissolved. This sanctuary is available to any clan that wishes to use it, but not since before my time has it been so populated. The high angel Retrius resides over less than one hundred angels here. By clan law, none should disturb him unless the most dire of circumstances comes about."

As I walked forward it was clear that there were hundreds, perhaps thousands of angels all about the colossal interior. After walking around the monolithic stalactite we came to a staircase of only four stairs. This natural ascension led to a marble building that was carved into the face of a deep cave. Upon the columns of this building I beheld masterfully cut etchings of the natural world. Above the thick columns, a pediment could be seen. This archway had many carvings of great angels that overlooked the utopia at all times. Though I wished to observe my surroundings more, I could not, for Shamayim was quick to act.

The elder angel pushed open a pair of massive marble doors that were engraved with scenes of angelic history. These doors gave way to a circular room illuminated by many light-blue torches. The torches stretched about an ovular area that contained several doors around its sides. I paid no mind to the small doors, for in the center of this room was a circular table roughly the size of my hut on Alfras. In the center of the table was a large podium, where a single angel stood. To my surprise, there were many angels sitting around the table, all whom turned toward Shamayim as he entered. In the chamber I could hear the distinct sound of rushing water, and as my eyes followed the noise I noticed many small waterfalls pouring into a moat that encircled the entire room. While I marveled at the building a voice rose through the air.

"Retrius!" Shamayim exclaimed as he took a bow before the lone angel who stood at the central podium.

Our lot of hundreds discovered that they could not all enter the room, so many huddled outside the structure and attempted to peer inside. I was lucky enough to enter the structure with Ariel by my side, but against the angels I stood out like a sore thumb. The angels with us were strong and wore beautiful clothing of silk and decorated armor of gold and silver. Meanwhile, Mithias, his crew, and I all wore rags.

"Shamayim? Is that you?" asked the old angel as he leaned on the podium and looked the chief in the eyes. "By the Two, who is with you? Have you brought humans to our sanctuary?"

The old angel who leaned on the podium stuttered to get his last words out as he squinted at the lot before him.

"We must talk," responded Shamayim as all eyes turned to him. "A grave danger has befallen us and as fate would have it, these humans are now in our company."

"You know it is forbidden to bring their kind in to this place!" the angel on the podium yelled as he pointed toward Mithias and me.

"This is no time to bicker about tradition," Shamayim responded. "Thundrians attacked my island and have ravaged the free lands of Alfras. We are lucky to have survived their raid."

"Your island, too?" an angel sitting before the circular table asked as he stood. "I did not know."

Retrius looked at Mithias as he said, "These humans must be from Alfras. Is that true?"

Shamayim replied, "They were aboard a trade vessel and came upon us before Thundrian ships made their way to my lands. They have broken many of our traditions and under most circumstances radical action would be taken, but they are refugees, and I do not plan on slaughtering those who seek shelter from the same force that battered my people."

There was silence for a moment before Shamayim turned toward the angel who had spoken at the table and asked, "You say 'your island, too?' Is something amiss with the other clans?"

Retrius answered before the angel at the table could reply. "You have been gone from this place for far too long, Shamayim. Many of us have."

The angel at the podium glanced at his winged brothers throughout the room before adding, "Many clans have come here with similar reports of Thundrian aggression. A clan from northern Alfras arrived just four days ago with reports of genocide and devastation."

Hearing these words paired with the name of my home pained me, but I remained silent as Shamayim desperately asked, "What are we to do?"

"Angels from the world over are making their way to this place with that same question," began the angel from his podium. "I can sense that more clans from Alfras are still approaching, so we shall wait for them."

Shamayim was clearly displeased with this, for his tongue would not remain still and his formalities began to wear thin.

"If I may, Retrius," he began, "should we not hold council as soon as possible? The Thundrian force is swift and strong; it is not in our best interest to wait for every last clan if we have a majority here."

"Not all traditions shall be broken on this day," shot back Retrius as he glanced toward my lot with a scowl. The whole room seemed to grow darker, as if a cloud were passing over the crystal's light, as he added, "Though we have not held council between the clans for many years, we will not disregard those who are absent. We shall wait for a week before beginning deliberation."

Defeated, Shamayim slowly nodded his head and said nothing more, but I could not be so silent.

"But we do not have the time," I said. For a moment I did not realize I had voiced my thoughts until the whole room turned upon me. I looked at the frightening masses with quivering eyes as Retrius spoke.

"And just who are you, boy?" he demanded.

"Lloyd Shoresquatter of Alfras, son of Kiordiam, sir," I began as I slowly stepped forward. Though my hands quivered, my voice remained still as I added, "I stand by Shamayim's side not by choice, for my family has been slain by the Thundrian Empire."

I glanced at my sister and held her hand before saying, "The Thundrians are ruthless and bring their blades down upon women and children without hesitation. They slaughtered my village except for my sister and me. The young one by my side had to witness these atrocities and bears a heavy burden every day. With every moment you waste, more innocents are in danger. Will you not act on their behalf and save them from the same fate as my sister and I?"

Retrius was silent for a moment, and I thought him enraged until his eyes met my sister's. His brow softened and his eyes grew deep at the sight of her.

"A child so young had to endure such hardships," he began as he took a step down from the podium. He crossed a narrow moat that surrounded his stand and made his way before my sister and me. He placed his hand upon my sister's head for a moment before stating, "Yet she remains unscathed. Her resilience is shocking to say the least, for she has to go against her natural urge to break down like the weak human she is."

"Enough of this," interjected Mithias. "We have experienced the same horrors as you angelic folk. Because of this we should be welcome here like the rest."

"And who are you?" asked the angel in a shrill voice.

"Mithias Landrunner," said Mithias. "I was the one who saved this boy and his kid sister. Had it not been for my presence, they would be dead."

Retrius nodded and turned back to Daria.

"These times are dire, and many seek security..." he began. "Though humans are not welcome here, we shall not eject them to the unforgiving snowscape."

"And what of the meeting?" I asked as I held my sister's hand.

Retrius looked back at my sister before slowly declaring, "I too have a sister, and when we were young a storm nearly swept her away from me. The fear of seeing my own blood stand before the reaper was beyond words. It was unlike any fear I had ever felt, and I would not wish that upon anyone." He made his way back to his podium. "You hold a wisdom and compassion past your age, Lloyd, son of Kiordiam. We will wait for one more day before deciding upon a course of action."

He looked over the multitude of winged angels that sat around the table behind him as he proclaimed, "If any object to my declaration, speak now or hold your tongue forevermore."

Not a single voice could be heard.

"Then it is settled," he murmured before turning back to Shamayim's lot. He glanced toward Mithias' crew as he added, "Shamayim, it will be your duty to accommodate these wayward souls."

Shamayim was quick to order several of his angels to Mithias' crew. Ariel took her place beside me and firmly declared that she could show my sister and me to our own quarters. Soon the three of us emerged on the verdant lawn outside as crowds of angels flooded out of the chamber. Ariel was quick to lead us up a set of natural stairs near the council chamber. I held my sister and followed Ariel closely as we ascended three flights of stairs, all while the inhabitants of the utopia went about their day. We passed many identical doors until Ariel stopped before one and knocked on it four times. When there was no answer, she slowly pushed it open.

Inside, we beheld a small and cozy room. The walls were solid rock and smooth all the way from the ceiling to the wood floor below me. The floor lay atop the cave foundation, and as I stepped inside a deep echo could be heard with each of my footsteps. A large wooden armoire was on one wall, and opposite from it were two simple wooden beds. Once inside the small room, my sister made her way to one of the beds and stretched out.

"You and your sister can rest here until you are summoned again," said Ariel as she shut the door behind us. "If you require anything during your stay, do not hesitate to leave this room and ask Shamayim or myself for help."

"Thank you, Ariel," I said with a smile. She smiled back, so I asked, "How could all of this have been made?"

She let out a short laugh and declared, "When you control magic, you can do great things."

Her answer did not satisfy my curious mind. "But how could all this life have been created so far underground?"

Ariel made her way to the cave wall, which she looked at for a moment as she ran her hand over the smooth rock face.

"It has been a long time since someone has asked me about our magic," she began as she slowly moved her hand down the rock before turning toward me. Her next words were soft and captivated both my sister and me.

"We do not create life. We merely redirect it. The water that you have noticed flowing around here comes from the ocean and is purified by the aura of the crystal. The grass that grows so plentifully? It has been brought from the ground using no seeds, yet it grows because of the magical aura cast by the grand crystal."

"And how was that aura made?" I asked as Ariel stepped toward me.

She shrugged. "No one knows. It has been here as long as we have. It is said that angels found the massive crystal which hangs down from the roof of this grand opening long ago. The crystal possessed a sporadic, uncontrollable magic that was channeled by my kind. Through the collective work of nearly every angelic clan, this safe haven was made hundreds of years ago."

"Yet the ties between your clans have since dissolved," I remarked.

Ariel did not meet my eyes. "Our clans were united after the great uprising led by the hero for whom you are named against the Thundrian Empire so long ago, yet that time has passed. The slow decay of time has led the clans to become distant, and our ancient alliance has since dissolved. All has been well since just after the rebellion against the Thundrians, yet now I fear that if we are not united we shall fall." There was a brief silence before

Ariel remarked, "But I will stave off that fear for the day. I shall take quarters on this floor, so I'm just three doors down if you need me."

I nodded and was about to speak until I heard Mithias' voice boom, "This is my room?"

Ariel looked distressed as she turned away from me and opened the door that we had entered just a moment ago. She quietly walked outside with Daria and me trailing her every cautious step into the light. Once we exited the room, we beheld Mithias shouting at a guard just two doors down.

"You expect a man of my bulk to find peace in this room?" Mithias yelled as he raised his hands to the startled angelic guard. Mithias noticed my presence and quickly turned to me. As he hobbled toward me, he boomed, "Ah! Ah, Lloyd! Have you seen these rooms? They are made for puny angels, not a real man!"

I sighed, then asked him, "Why are you so dissatisfied?"

He yelled back at me in my face, "I merely want a room in which I can fit! A man of my girth needs large and comfortable surroundings."

I shook my head and grabbed the man's shoulder. I brought his head close to my ear as I whispered, "Please, let's not cause trouble here. Half the people of this place can probably hear you complain."

Mithias was about to open his mouth until I whispered, "My father entrusted my safety to you, and you claimed that the angels would not hesitate to kill us. So I ask you, are you upholding your vow to him by causing such a ruckus?"

He looked at me, then back at Ariel as a grimace emerged on his face. For a moment, the grown man looked like an upset child who had lost his greatest toy due to his own incompetence. With this childlike portrait upon his face, he stomped off, past the small worried guard, and into his room. Mithias slammed the door behind him, and through the door I could hear him moan and complain at every minute detail of the room.

"Must he always cause trouble?" Ariel asked me before I could apologize for my compatriot's actions.

"He can be quite..." I paused, trying to think of a word to describe Mithias. None came to mind, and I ended my sentence there. Ariel laughed and turned to walk away, yet I wanted to continue our talk.

"Ariel!" I called back to her. "What am I to do until the meeting?"

She turned back to me and walked toward me with a smile.

"The crystal shall dim as the curtain of ebony falls over the skies far above ground. Sleep will overtake your weary bones as the magic from the crystal temporarily rests."

Ariel smiled and was about to walk off before I asked one final question.

"When shall we eat tonight?"

With a grin still across her flawless face, the angel simply asked, "Have you not noticed yet?"

"Noticed what?" I asked.

"You will not grow hungry in this place, Lloyd," she said before she turned from me. I thought of the last time I had eaten and realized that it had not been for nearly seven hours. After going without food for such a length I would normally grow weary and hungry, yet as I stood on the rock platform I did not feel the slightest hint of hunger. The angel continued to walk away from me, but I wished to know why I felt no hunger.

"Why don't I require sustenance?" I yelled to her as she continued on her way.

Without even turning to look at me, the angel yelled back, "It's just another wonder of the crystal!"

I sighed then turned back to my room to see my sister standing right beside me. She looked up at me with baggy eyes and a fading smile as she yawned.

"I'm sleepy," she stated after her brief moan.

"Go rest," I said as I stood in the doorway. "Tomorrow will be a long day."

Daria was not content with drifting into sleep without my assistance, so per her request, I followed her to her bed and tucked her in.

Once my sister was under the warm sheepskin blankets, she requested that I tell her a story, so in an instant I made one up. I spoke of a valiant knight who fought a shadowed beast that plagued his homeland. I spoke well of the knight and told my sister of beautiful lands beyond the ocean where the knight made his residence. I never did tell her if the knight defeated the shadow that rose against him, for she fell asleep before my conclusion. Once she was in her own world of dreams and magic, I left the room and stood on the threshold of my door. From this place I observed my dazzling surroundings.

I looked at the crystal that hung in the center of the colossal place with disbelief. Its light had dimmed since I had first entered, yet it still glowed with a ginger radiance that mirrored that of the sun in the evening. The fields of vibrant green grass stretched all about the circular enclosure before me, and the residents slowly began to make their ways to their respective shelters. Each blade of grass shimmered in the crystal's continual luminosity with such magnificence that for a moment I believed the grass was laden with dew. My head tilted up so that I could behold the stories of platforms that led to small rooms where angels took residence during these uncertain times. I looked at angels who spoke on the lawn or under trees as the crystal grew dimmer and dimmer with each passing minute. By the time all was dark, I had made my way to my comfortable bed and drifted into the temporary reality that was sleep.

CHAPTER 6

Across the world, a woman clothed in blood-red armor walked to the edge of a ship that had braved the violent wind and rain for many days. The vessel was gigantic by any standards and was constructed from dark strips of sturdy pine. This woman's crimson armor was made from the strongest dragon scales in the world, and as lightning struck in the distance it illuminated the Thundrian soldiers standing in formation around her. Under the ominous overcast sky, the waves tossed and turned with great force, yet the mighty vessel did not waver amid the turmoil.

"This is the place?" she asked a small soldier who stood next to her.

"Yes, Admiral," he responded as he pointed to the water. "Our king gave us coordinates for this exact spot. We're directly in the center of the three islands of Alfras."

The female solider took off her spiked helmet to reveal a sinful smile. Her short platinum hair hardly fluttered in the wind, and out of her ruby red lips came a dark voice.

"The mages are prepared?"

"They stand ready at the bow," responded the same solider as he motioned to a group of hooded angels that stood on the bow.

"Tell them to begin," she declared in a hollow voice as she crossed her arms and turned to the ocean.

The ghostly man quickly nodded and stated, "At once, ma'am."

He ran to the bow of the ship and began to converse with a group of angels who stood there. Not long after he arrived at their side. the covered angels began to chant in an ancient and nearly forgotten tongue. An unholy, dark echo that few had ever heard in all the history of the world came from their chorus and drifted on the winds that swirled about them. The winds began to whip and circle the boat as their chant grew louder and louder with each passing moment. The very planet began to shake, yet not a single individual on the boat felt shock or fear. They stood fast with mad anticipation in their hearts.

Finally, after a gripping moment of expectation, a ripple came in the distant waves. The ripple parted the ocean itself and grew with unnatural resolve. It evolved into a multitude of colossal waves that threatened to swamp the ship and all the soldiers who dwelled on it. The crew and soldiers aboard ship cautiously watched from behind their helms a sight that would be engraved into their minds forever. As the colossal waves poured out from the ocean, water rushed out in all directions with tremendous speed. A particularly monolithic wave met the boat and swamped the deck, knocking several soldiers into the unforgiving waves.

Several others attempted to grab ropes to help their comrades, but the blonde woman shouted, "Leave them! It is working!"

As terrible rain began to batter the crew, the angels at the bow continued their chant. The waves grew even bigger, stretching high into the air and blotting out the clouds as they rose above the ship and threatened to sink it. Several angels began to shout different magical words, and a translucent golden bubble encircled the boat. Waves slammed into this golden globe but harmlessly rolled off it and the ship remained safe. The globe became encased in waters that violently shot up from the sea, but the ship remained stable. The dark chant grew louder as the waves increased and seemed to penetrate the very heavens themselves. Just as the waves became largest, the angels quieted their chant and everything stopped. The waves ceased rolling and calmed themselves as the column of water that had rushed to the sky fell to the sea with an unbelievable force.

"Why do you stop?" the woman yelled at the angels. She was about to approach them and scorn the lot, but she soon realized that her task had been completed. Her eyes sparkled as she raised her head and beheld the holy artifact that stretched through the sky. It had been done, and now the woman knew she was one step closer to completing her duty for the nation she had sworn to serve. Her ruby lips thinned outward into a smile as the artifact her lord had sought for so long stood before her. The testament to supremacy itself was right before her, and she knew that soon all the power of the world would fall into the hands of her lord.

* * *

I jolted back to consciousness in a sweat as a great light shone into the room. After sitting up on my bed, I looked over to see Daria still fast asleep in the embrace of her peaceful dreams. Being as quiet as I could possibly be, I emerged from the room to discover that the safe haven was once again bustling with activity. Angels were up and about, making their way around the beautiful environment as they went about their duties. I looked down at a winding path to see that one of Mithias' crew members was sitting on the grass. I had worked with the man, who went by the name Tibet, aboard Mithias' ship and was about to walk down to the grass to converse with him when I felt a hand land on my shoulder. I turned to see a young angelic guard staring me down.

"Your presence is requested in the great chamber," he said in a monotone voice.

"Where is that?" I asked.

The angel pointed across the field toward the building I had entered just the day before. The enormous building that was adorned with graphic images of battle seemed like a small dot in the distance from where I stood, but nevertheless I spoke to the angel with confidence.

"I shall be there as soon as possible," I responded with a nod. He turned and began to walk down the stairs toward the lawn as I turned back toward my quarters. I entered the room and stood by my sister's bed as she slept. I thought about waking her for a moment, but as I looked down at her peaceful slumber I could not bring myself to thrust her back into our terrible reality.

I exited my room and hoped she dreamt of harmonious times that would someday return.

Once on the lawn I followed the path down to the marble building. As I walked down the path I nodded and smiled at each angel I passed, but despite my kindness few smiles were thrown my way. Once I arrived at the immense building I opened one of the doors and stepped inside. I could see many angels of all shapes and sizes sitting around the grand circular table. I noticed that Ariel was sitting next to Shamayim so I walked toward her and took a seat on a flimsy stool that was set beside Shamayim's stone seat. Before I turned to Ariel I looked to my right, where a powerful and foreboding angel sat. A smile emerged on my lips as I looked at him, but he did not return my kind gesture. The angel sneered at me, so I quickly looked away from him and over to Ariel, who smirked upon witnessing the exchange. Shamayim sat between Ariel and I, but that did not stop me from speaking to my friend.

I leaned forward on the table and turned to Ariel as I asked, "Why have I been summoned here?"

Ariel leaned close to her father as she spoke over the commotion of the room.

"These matters involve all the races of the world," began the beautiful angel. "I would suspect that Retrius would like one of your kind to weigh in on the discussion."

"Me?" I asked in disbelief. "Since when have the angels wished to hear from me?"

Shamayim turned to me and quickly interjected, "Since my clan chose to spare you due to reasons the council does not understand. They want to know what is so special about you."

"Why me?" I asked. "Why not Mithias?"

"His nature is too unruly," began the chief as Ariel leaned back in her chair. "Retrius wants human representation here, but I don't want an aggressive outbreak, so you have been summoned to listen to our debate."

The angel, Retrius, soon entered the room through the grand doorway and approached the central stand. This angel took the podium and looked at the circle of angels who were so busy bickering that they hardly noticed his approach. Retrius did not speak until the room was his. Once all eyes were upon him and all lips were sealed shut, he spoke.

"Friends of old, allies of a time long past," he began in a stately tone, "we begin our debate in this most hallowed hall during a dark hour."

After nods of agreement, he continued.

"The islands of Alfras and the northeastern reaches of Finre have fallen to the unrelenting forces of Thundria. This force of unholy accord brings suffering to all unfortunate enough to cross paths with their blades. Their lust for blood will consume all who dare stand before them. Their actions have harmed many, and today we shall collectively decide how to move forward."

A young angel opposite the table from me stood up and declared, "I am Heirold, leader of the northern frost clan. I was in the Finrean capitol when news of an attack reached her king's ears. The gluttonous king of men and scaled folk fears the long arm of Thundria so he writes these attacks off as marauding bandits that will tire of their slaughter. When it was relayed to me that the attackers bore the Thundrian flag, the king refused to wage war on the Thundrians."

"But Alfras and Finre have long since been allies!" another angel yelled from across the table. "In the war for independence hundreds of years ago, Alfrasian forces fought alongside the people of Finre under the command of the lizard king Wallace! How could the king decide this in the face of such historical conquests?"

"I am only telling you what I have heard in the capitol," the first angel responded in a calm tone. "He seeks to protect his kingdom."

"He seeks to protect himself," shot back another angel. "It is common knowledge among the Finrean clans that the king of this barren continent cares only for himself." The angel then looked at the one known as Heirold and snapped, "You have been warned not to communicate with the nobility of this land. Your request for assistance has fallen as deaf ears. Does this not show us that the Finrean king truly cares not for the angelic tribes?"

Bickering between angels of the table rose up slowly, but soon it became uncontrollable. Some praised the words of the king while others called him a tyrant and a coward. Two sides were instantly separated as those of one belief argued with those of another. I turned to Ariel in desperation, but she only lowered her eyes at my glance. It was clear to me that she did not wish for the argument. Retrius quickly raised his hand and called for silence once again. The angels eventually heeded his order and the room became manageable once more.

"We cannot go against the will of the king," started Retrius in an exasperated tone. "We do not fall under his banner or have his support. If we were to act against Thundria without the aid of Finre, we would be decimated."

"So you're saying we should let the forces of Thundria march onto our lands and slaughter our people?" yelled the massive angel next to me as he stood up.

"Our people are safe here," a much smaller angel calmly stated from across the table. "We could remain in this place until the conflict blows over."

After a rousing chorus of cheers and jeers, Shamayim stood up and surveyed the angels before speaking wise words.

"My friends, even if Thundria does not come here, we simply cannot overlook what they have done. My people were able to flee our island without loss, but in the night I convened with chiefs and kings in this council. Many were not so fortunate." Shamayim glanced around the room at his angelic brethren as he spoke. "Minilayim, you told me today that half your clan was slaughtered by the Thundrians, and Espus, you watched as the Thundrians slaughtered women and children without hesitation."

The angel looked down at me as he placed a cold hand on my shoulder. After letting out a slight sigh he stated, "Yet our remorse is not confined. This lad is named Lloyd. He left his family to trade goods with Thundria, but during a storm he was forced to seek shelter on my island. The Thundrian forces attacked my island and he and his captain could have been left to die or flee with us. It was in that moment that I chose to keep the humans alive with hopes that perhaps they were working with the enemy. If this were the truth, we would have a goldmine of information about the Thundrian empire, but as fate would have it, young Lloyd here is a friend. We were heading for this lad's homeland,

and when we came upon the ruin of his village I knew that he did not swear allegiance to the Thundrians."

"And how can you be so sure, Shamayim?" asked the burly angel to my right as he cautiously examined me.

Shamayim could not look me in the eyes as he uttered, "When we arrived at Alfras he returned to his home to discover that his mother, father, and young brother of only eleven years had been slain. He wept madly before them before claiming the life of the Thundrian who had wronged him. Trust me when I say his sorrow could not be false."

The chamber was silent at this news, and for a moment many angels looked at me in a different light. I felt my cheeks grow hot with embarrassment at the attention, so I averted my eyes and looked at the floor. Most gave me gazes of pity that did not falter until Shamayim added, "He managed to save his sister with the help of his captain, but he has lost all else. My companions, heed my words: these are not isolated incidents. Thundria is spreading her borders for reasons unknown, and if we do not stand against their might they shall snuff the life out of everything they cross."

Silence shrouded the room for a moment before an angel stated in a low voice, "It is not guaranteed, Shamayim."

"The evidence is obvious, and their crimes cannot go unpunished," Shamayim responded. He looked at the angel who had spoken and added, "The king of Finre must know that the angelic clans will not stand by and watch Thundria slaughter all they come across."

"But he was firm in his wish to avoid war," the angel who had convened with the king of Finre responded as he leaned forward in his chair. "Besides, our clans have not united for generations. What's to say the king would believe our words?"

Shamayim sighed. "We have no guarantee that he will, but we must try! Or would you suggest we sit in this cave as the lands are scorched by the Thundrian flame?"

Bickering once again arose among the angels of the table. Retrius tried to silence them, but despite all his best efforts, the lot continued to squabble like children. All around us was chaos and I noticed Ariel looking at me in desperation. The shouts from the angels echoed about the room and formed a single mass of irritating noise that could only be quelled by a louder voice. I, the only half-human in the room, conjured such a voice.

"Stop!" I shouted above them in a voice only a human could muster. Some stopped bickering and turned toward me while others continued their bickering in hushed voices. I repeated myself several more times until the room was mine.

"What if the king were to hear my story?" I asked no one in particular.

All were silent as Shamayim closed his eyes and drew out a long breath.

"An angel coming from an unknown tribe holds little favor in the court of the Finrean King, but I know that Alfras did no wrong to Thundria. If a resident of Alfras tells the king of Finre this, perhaps he will be more inclined to take some course of action. For all we know, he may not know of the attacks on Alfras. Perhaps my voice could sway him," I said in a less than confident voice. No one spoke, and I felt idiotic as I stood there. I scanned the room. "I am a burden upon your people as it is. Let me go speak to the king and tell him that the angelic clans want answers for their loss. Let me tell him that your people demand action against the Thundrian Empire. If I relay the message you will get justice, but if I die in the cold wastes, you lose nothing."

There was silence all about me.

"Though your death would not burden my kind, I cannot let you blindly wander into the hostile wastes," Retrius declared. "If some winged man in this room would guide you on your journey, then I would allow it."

Eyes shifted about the room instantly as each soul awaited the voice of one brave enough to speak up, but no such voice arose in the confines of the room. Many eyes fell upon the largest and strongest angels in the room, but the bravest voice eventually came from the most unlikely of places.

"I shall go with him," declared Ariel with confidence as she stood.

"Hold your tongue, daughter!" Shamayim yelled as he took a stand. "I will not put you in the face of danger!"

Before any other angel could speak, the two doors burst open with a massive bang. Mithias confidentially strode between them and bellowed, "I shall protect the boy and Ariel from the dangers of this land!"

"You were not invited to this meeting!" Retrius yelled in disgust and astonishment. "How did you get past the guards?"

"No angel can hold back the will of a man!" he replied with a hearty laugh as he continued his stride. Mithias approached both Ariel and me, and he added, "I swore an oath to the boy's late father that I would protect him. Wherever he goes, I go."

None had time to speak before Shamayim yelled, "This is insanity!" The angel had stood from his seat and looked at Mithias, who now stood between Ariel and me with a hand on each of our shoulders. With desperation in his eyes he turned to Retrius and said, "We cannot be so rash! The debates have only just begun."

"Shamayim," Retrius began with a low tone, "you know I never question your judgment, but under the circumstances voiced at this council it would seem we have little time to deliberate. I think we have no choice but to let them go, seeing as they are the only three brave enough to take on the task. As they travel the harsh lands we will continue our talks on what exactly we should do under any given circumstance, but until we hear from the Finrean king, or one who holds such authority, we can do nothing."

Retrius looked about his council with deep eyes that seemed to beg for assistance, but no one spoke up.

The angel gave his council a disgusted look before declaring, "So this is what the council has become: a mass of angels who speak of change but are not willing to lift a single finger to help the world. Now we must entrust our fates to outsiders."

"But, Retrius—" Shamayim started.

Before he could continue, Retrius cut in. "We have no choice but to let them go. Would you have me hold them here against their own wills and the will of the council?"

Shamayim began to stutter as he attempted to counter his old friend, but it was to no avail. After trying to spit out several words, he turned to his daughter with watery eyes. He looked at her with a longing gaze, as if to beg her to stay, but he said nothing. Retrius then turned to our lot and spoke. "You will need a guide."

All the angels were silent. I did not know why they would not offer their help. Those who were too old to travel had a clear reason to stay silent, but near the old were those who looked more fit and able for this task than I. They wanted to save their kingdom, yet in the face of action the angels were quiet. We stood there waiting for an offer until Retrius realized that none would present themselves as a guide. He scowled and whispered loudly enough so that I could hear, "Is there no courage left in our divine race? Are all winged folk good for only bickering?"

Knowing that he was defeated, Shamayim uttered, "There is a village to the northwest, past the mountains called Wercon. Lizards have set up a flourishing society there and their kind knows the land well. If you venture to their haven, you'll find a guide."

"He's right," Ariel said. "I know the way from my cartography studies as a child. The lizards there are a peaceful and friendly folk who will surely help us."

In one final act of desperation Shamayim turned toward the other angels and asked, "Is this truly the will of the council? To send children to do our bidding?"

Eyes shifted, but not a single voice could be heard until Shamayim asked, "Does no man object to this mad notion?"

Silence.

"So it is decided," Retrius declared. "You shall venture to the village of Wercon."

"And what will you do while we are on this journey?" asked Ariel with a bit of defiance to her tone.

Retrius replied, "We shall survive and wait for your return. Our kind is safe and ready for war if the king wills it. Until he calls upon us, we shall remain here and take in any other clans that may reach us. The clans shall continue to deliberate and formulate strategies for any event that could arise."

Ariel nodded. Retrius added, "Find a guide among the lizards in Wercon and head to the capitol of this great land."

"Wait a minute," Mithias said in a serious tone as a grave realization hit him like a brick. "What of my crew?"

Without hesitation, Retrius replied, "If you travel with such a large pack you will surely be slowed as the weakest members begin to break by the frost. We will provide for your underlings while you are gone."

This notion caused an uproar in the chamber so great that it could only be silenced after Retrius had yelled at the members several times.

"We cannot simply release these people to the harsh environment when their kind shows more initiative than any of you!" he shouted. "Despite tradition, we shall care for them, and if any object to that, they can leave!"

Muttering came from all corners of the chamber, but no angel spoke against Retrius, so I voiced a concern.

"I assume my sister will stay here too?" I asked Retrius. He nodded swiftly.

"I would like to see her before I leave," I said in a calm voice as my heart began to grow sore with each beat. Retrius nodded, then clapped his hands twice. There was silence, so Retrius clapped two more times and once again nothing in the room changed.

Speaking to himself, the angel asked, "What has become of the two outside?"

At this notion Mithias couldn't help but smirk as he declared, "I told them to take a break so that I might weigh in on this meeting."

"They were told to guard this place on their very honor!" exclaimed an anonymous angel from the table. "Why would they leave?"

With a smirk still painted across his face, Mithias casually proclaimed, "I can be a very persuasive man."

Retrius sighed, then turned to Shamayim. "Would you bring this boy's sister to the western exit of Sacrimen?"

Shamayim objected. "I would like to see my daughter off before she is taken away from me."

"And you will," said Retrius without hesitation. "Her company will meet you and the boy's sister at the western exit of this sanctuary."

Shamayim turned and reluctantly shuffled out of the room, clearly distraught, but no one seemed to notice, for Retrius' next words were more important than his whole speech.

"It seems that our isolation is coming to an end," he declared in a soft voice. "Supplies shall be brought to the western staircase to the three of you. Ariel knows the way to Wercon. Follow her steps closely through the treacherous mountains."

"I think we can handle it," Mithias said.

Retrius sighed at the man's quick words, then concluded his time with us by making a declaration that reached every ear in the chamber.

"These are dark times," he began as every eye set upon him. "But it is in the darkest night that the dimmest lights shine brightest. I pray that the cowardice of this council will not doom these three brave souls."

Without another word, he exited the podium and made his way out through the large double doors with several angels trailing behind. We followed.

Once outside the doors, Ariel was quick to turn to Mithias and ask, "So you were listening in on us the whole time?"

The burly man took this as a compliment and replied, "Your guards were skittish from the moment I entered their sightlines."

"I'm surprised a man who carries himself so proudly would reduce himself to spying on a meeting just to satisfy a childlike curiosity," Ariel stated as a grin turned at the corner of her mouth.

Mithias barked back, "I have an oath to Lloyd's father, angel. You'd do best not to question my actions in fulfilling it."

Ariel shrugged as she continued down the path, and Mithias growled in disdain. Surprisingly, the man remained silent as we slowly trailed behind Ariel all the way to the western wall of the cave, where we saw a grand valley that led farther into darkness. This darkness looked cold and foreboding, but before it stood Daria, the last warm and loving member of my family. She approached me clutching a long wrapped object in her hands, and tears soon filled her eyes.

A single tear began to stream down her pristine cheek as she said, "They say that you are to leave us, brother. Is this true?"

As I looked down at my sister I couldn't help but feel my heart plummet. Her innocent gaze nearly pierced my soul and brought about painful memories the likes of which I wished to seal away forever. Without thinking twice, I picked her up and held her tightly in my arms. She looked at me with deep blue eyes that sparkled from light that the grand crystal reflected against her tears. I spoke softly after wiping away the few tears that had begun their journey down her cheek.

"I must leave so that you and everyone here can be safe," I stated softly. My words brought pain to her, so I held her close as continued. "I will return. Ariel and Mithias will accompany me, and the two of them will be sure to bring me back."

Daria's damp face turned to Mithias and Ariel who, for the first time since they had met, agreed on something. Both nodded.

"Lloyd will return soon," Ariel said with a smile as she approached me with Mithias in tow. "Our journey will not take longer than a few months at the most."

Mithias, who rarely showed sympathy, looked at the little girl with a slight smile. As he spoke, it seemed to be that even his barricaded heart couldn't help but feel sympathy for the distraught girl.

"The angel and I shall keep your brother safe," he declared firmly.

No words could ever make my sister feel secure, but for the moment her tears seemed to cease. Upon her request, I put her down and watched as she raised the covered object to me. She requested that I take it, and when I opened it I discovered my blade firmly clasped in its sheath. I thanked Daria for bringing it, just as Shamayim appeared behind her. The old angel seemed displeased with what he saw.

"I do not support this," he began in a sullen tone as I buckled my sheath to my waist. "If I were but a century younger I would lead you, but my body now confines me."

A sigh escaped him after a fit of coughing. Then, he added, "Yet, I cannot argue with the logic of Retrius."

Ariel smiled at her father, who refused to return her expression as he approached the girl. Shamayim opened his arms wide and embraced his loving daughter for a long moment.

Before the two released their embrace, Ariel declared, "I am in the company of fighters who will keep me out of harm's way."

Shamayim turned his gaze to Mithias and me. "Watch after her at all costs."

"Ariel is in safe hands," began the man who had previously expressed only disregard for the old angel before him, before I could speak. With a welcoming smile—which had yet to be seen by the angels—painted across his plump face, he added, "We will take care of her."

The old angel hesitantly nodded as he handed a backpack over to Ariel. Shamayim ordered us to open the pack, and on top of rations and supplies were three thick fur coats that would protect us from the cold. As we donned the cloaks, Shamayim explained that the rations would last us until we reached the lizard-run town of Wercon. Mithias agreed to take the backpack over his shoulders, and with a few final, painful goodbyes, our lot left the sanctuary. I watched as both Shamayim and my sister turned and made their way down the stone path. Daria's steps were short and she was clearly upset, but in that moment Shamayim did something that assured me my sister would be in safe hands. He clasped his old, frail hand around my sister's hand and smiled at her as he led her away from us. I knew she would be okay in the sanctuary, but I did not know if I would be fine. A deep and terrible longing tugged me back toward the sanctuary as I turned to the dark passageway, but try I as I might, I could not bring myself to follow it. I could not bring myself to turn back toward my sister as I entered the creeping darkness before me. Instead, I put one foot in front of the other and began to travel once again.

CHAPTER 7

As I stepped into the obsidian darkness with Ariel and Mithias by my side, I was disoriented for a moment. The absence of light in the crevice was astonishing, and I found that I could not even see my hand before my own face. Ariel led the way, shining her magic light before us, yet even then the surroundings seemed menacing. The warmth from the crystallized stalactite soon faded and eventually a cold wind took its place in the narrow passage. The passage took many twists and turns, but luckily for us the naturally-formed stairs led us away from any guardians who may have lurked in the depths. Within an hour we arrived at the surface, which was just as bleak as the path we took to the surface. An overcast sky rained snowflakes upon us all, and within an instant the cold chill of the rushing wind caused my hairs to stand. The gray sky matched the dismal surroundings, and it looked as if a blank canvas had been laid out all around us. The cave we had just exited put us on a ledge on the side of a great mountain that stood before another such peak in the distance. Ariel paused on this ledge before turning back to us.

"There is an old temple on the top of the mountain across the ice," she declared as she pointed to the west. "If we hurry, we can reach that place by nightfall tomorrow. From there we will come upon the plains that will lead us to Wercon."

Mithias and I followed Ariel silently as she walked a narrow path that led us down the mountain. The path was anything but safe, for with each step we took, a small piece of the mountain came with us. Loose rocks fell from their resting places and disappeared behind the thick fog that separated the mountaintops from the ground. This treacherous walk, mixed with the constant snow, caused our steps to be slow and careful. It took four hours before we stood upon a thick sheet of ice that stretched to a distant mountain range. A thick fog set in all around us, and I could hardly see more than an arm's length in front of me as I struggled to stand. Once we found our footing on the slippery plain, Ariel turned back to us and spoke words of warning.

"Be wary on the ice." She turned to Mithias as she cracked a grin and remarked, "We must travel on it all day, and if too much weight is put on one place, it will break."

"Are you trying to say something, angel?" Mithias barked back at her. Ariel smiled but said nothing and continued to walk on as the snow fell faster. A deep wind whipped against me, and I could feel the skin on my face tearing ever so slightly as minis-cule shards of ice smashed against it. We traversed the barren stretch of ice until dusk, when the fog before us lifted enough that the distant mountains could be seen. The fog crept behind us, obscuring our traversed path as we continued on. The moun-tains were still a far way away when Ariel stopped her stride and turned her head to the north. I nearly bumped into her when she stopped.

"Why have you halted your advance?" I asked. When I stopped, the cold seemed to seep through my layers and my arms began to shake.

The angel quieted my response as she cupped her hand to her right ear. The light from the setting sun continued to sub-side. She closed her eyes for a moment and Mithias and I looked at her in confusion.

Then I heard it.

A distance crashing sound slowly entered my ears and grew louder with each passing second. I listened closely and clearly heard a sound that resembled glass shattering. Unlike a glass object shattering, though, this sound was constant and only grew as I continued to listen. Mithias and I both turned our heads around toward the source of the irritating sound, but we could see nothing through the dense fog and wisping snow behind us. The crashing sound grew louder and louder with each moment until it was so loud it seemed as if it were right on top of us. Ariel whipped her head around as she yelled a single word that brought me to a sprint in an instant: "Run!"

The instant this word left her mouth, Ariel turned from Mithias and me and frantically dashed away at a speed faster than her frozen wings could ever carry her. Without wasting a single moment, Mithias and I gave haste to our steps as the shattering noise behind us grew.

The wind battered my face and my lungs felt as if they were about to rip open as I struggled to keep up with the angel who ran with extraordinary speed. My legs screamed as I ran with all my might against the cold wind on the slippery ice. The crashing grew louder and louder as we ran, so midstride I chose to turn around and view the source of this ear-shattering sound. What I beheld was a sight that would bring fear to the most hardened of men.

The crashing sound was actually the ice behind me breaking. This ice did not naturally break, though, for through the fog I soon beheld the force that rushed at us. A dark gray fin that was as tall as three men and as thick as one shot through the air. This shining yet grainy fin moved with great speed toward us as we sprinted across the ice. As the fin cut through the thick ice, not a single mark or slash could be seen upon it. The fin moved forward with a speed unmatched by any animal I had ever encountered, so my steps grew faster and faster.

I followed Mithias who followed Ariel as the fin continued to pursue us. Without saying a word I continued to glance back at the fin, which was closer to me each time I turned. The fog seemed to part as the fin rushed toward me, and it did not take me long to realize that it would be upon us soon. The ice met a towering wall of rock no more than one hundred steps before us, and I believed that surely if we made it off the icy surface the monster that chased us would be unable to claim his meal, yet the fin seemed to be gaining on us. Luckily, I was not the only member of my party to realize this.

Ariel stopped running in an instant and turned around to Mithias and me. The girl watched as the large man slid to a stop right before her. Mithias was irate as he screamed at the angel as to why she had stopped, but Ariel only spoke in her native tongue as the man wailed. Paying no mind to him, the angel opened both her arms, and I slid into her right arm. She grabbed Mithias in her left as she continued the strange chant. Her long, pristine wings, which were coated in a thin layer of ice, began to flap with great fervor as we all watched the fin rush toward us. It grew closer and closer as seconds passed by in flashes. All the while, the angel flapped her frost-laden wings with all her might as Mithias roared and I gritted my teeth. Just as the fin was close enough for me to see large scars on it, a strange translucent orb of sorts enveloped the three of us. In an instant, the amber sphere around us lifted us up above the fin just moments before we collided with the colossal anomaly. I thought we were safe, but then the unthinkable happened.

From the veiled depths lurched the frame of the gigantic creature. I saw rows upon rows of man-sized teeth rush toward the translucent golden orb that flew away at a great speed. Ice cracked for miles as if it were glass, and rocks tumbled down from the mountain we sought. Ice-cold water slammed against all our surroundings, and for a brief moment I caught a glimpse of what the beast truly was.

The monster was not unlike a deep-sea shark the oldest fishers in my village discussed. Men far past their prime spoke of adventures out to the deep sea, where they had beheld all manner of beasts, including the fabled "gray pearl of the sea." These beasts could be as long as a whole village and would rip ships in half with a single bite. Their gray skin was like steel, and from their backs shot three massive fins that could kill a man upon impact. Gills each the size of a doorway led to the monster's massive head, which always wore an expression of rage. It was said that these enormous beasts could eat a whale whole, and as I fearfully looked down to the teeth rushing toward us, I did not doubt these stories. For a split second, we slipped into the edge of the beast's mouth and I believed I would meet my end. The teeth began to close in on us like a serrated boar trap snapping around the leg of its victim, and my body quaked more than it ever had before. In this moment, Ariel let out a great heave and the orb that carried us shot out of the brute's mouth. The jaws of the monolithic gray pearl snapped shut just on the edge of the orb, not an arm's length away from my legs. The beast, now nearly airborne, was forced back to the water as we shot toward the western cliff. The monster fell below us and sank into the abysmal depths from whence it came.

I couldn't bring myself to say anything as the orb moved to the west. We shot toward a sheer cliff face on the eastern side of the massive mountains as the monster continued to descend into the black, murky waters below the broken ice. I panted in exhaustion, too tired to talk as the smoky orb dissipated into thin air once the three of us were safely on a stone ledge. Just as fast as we had nearly met our end, we had avoided it, and now the three of us breathed deeply as we sat on the ledge that overlooked the icy plains we had just crossed. Mithias and I peered over the ledge in an attempt to catch a glimpse of the creature that had split the ice behind us, but all we could see in the water was a massive ovular shadow making its way back down to the lowest depths of the frozen lake. As we examined the monstrosity, Ariel lay behind us, sucking in air.

Just after the unknown beast disappeared into the veiled depths, Mithias yelled, "What in the name of all that is holy was that creature?"

I had no answer for him, but in between pants the angel slowly responded, "A beast of the northern seas."

Mithias whipped around to her and bellowed, "Why didn't you tell us about such beasts?"

When Mithias asked this question, we both beheld Ariel for the first time since the orb had disappeared. The angel lay upon the dry surface of the small crevice and gasped for air. She looked up at Mithias with glistening eyes that held a plea so pure not even he could deny it. In an instant, Mithias and I were beside the angel.

Her face was pale and her hands shook as she desperately asked, "Can we rest?"

Mithias, still clearly as shaken as Ariel and I, nodded his head. I solemnly replied, "Of course."

It was only then that I realized how cold I had become. The anxious sweat that enveloped me steamed away into nothingness and I began to shiver as my newly damp clothes clung to my body. Mithias slowly took off his backpack and opened it before the three of us.

He pulled out three blankets, two logs, and three odd-looking sandwiches. After wrapping myself in a blanket I looked to the food. The sandwiches oozed with a strange yellow paste that lay between each piece of bread. Mithias slowly raised the top slice of bread before closely examining the strange honey-like substance. After a moment of inspection Mithias put the top slice of bread back down to the bottom and lowered his brow.

"What is this?" Mithias asked as he looked at the sandwich in his hand.

"A great treat among my people," Ariel responded as she arched her frame up and slowly reached for the sandwich in Mithias' hand. Her breath was still bated and her body continued to quiver as she grasped the sandwich. She took a bite of it and, after swallowing, declared, "These can only be made in the sanctuary from which we came."

"Well it looks like an ordinary sandwich to me," replied Mithias as he eyed his.

I didn't have to think twice about taking one of the sandwiches, for the cold environment was taking a great toll on my health. My body had never experienced a cold spell like this, so once my frozen fingers raised the sandwich to my blistered lips I took a large bite without hesitation. I felt the exotic and warm pastelike substance all about my mouth as I chewed. The sticky yellow goo did not stay in my mouth for long because my hunger caused me to swallow the bite in an instant. To my surprise, the golden slime warmed my insides and almost instantaneously brought power to my muscles. My bones felt as if they were being warmed by a dancing blaze, so I smiled as I held the sandwich.

"It's good," I remarked with a smile as I bit another chunk out of the unusual meal.

Mithias hesitantly took a bite, but after a quick moment his eyes lit up and he began to devour the sandwich like an animal. He gorged on the simple meal in a flash, and once he was done his wild eyes lit up. Ariel and I casually continued our first sandwiches as he dug around the bag and eventually turned it upside down to see no more sandwiches fall out.

Amid her own strained laughter, Ariel said, "These will last us until we reach Wercon!."

"What?" bellowed Mithias before he looked at the crumbs on the ground. The man eyed this suspiciously before he looked up at Ariel, who was still laughing.

"Is this funny to you?" asked Mithias. His question only brought the angel to more laughs, so he declared, "We're going to starve!"

The angel quelled her chuckling and asked, "Do you know what you just ate, Mithias?"

"Of course," he responded with confidence. "A single sandwich served to me by a nation of winged souls that can survive on mere snacks. I am a man, and as such I require great sustenance!"

"Let me tell you something," she started in a more serious tone as she took another bite from the sandwich and sat up. "These meals were made in the sanctuary. The grand crystal there provides all with nourishment. The people, the plants, everything revels in the crystal's seemingly holy power. The food you ate was harvested and prepared in the light of the crystal, so it, too, holds this power. After that short meal, your stomach will be full for days. Neither hunger nor thirst shall torment you as we continue."

He shook his head, so Ariel assured him, "We won't have to eat for days."

"That can't be true," Mithias remarked as he put his hand to his stomach.

I didn't believe her either until I realized the hunger pains I had felt just moments ago had vanished. My stomach felt full and supple despite the fact that I had eaten a single sandwich. I felt energy flowing through my veins, and for the first time that day I didn't feel cold.

"I can feel it working," I stated as I felt my stomach and smiled. Once my hand was against my stomach I could feel a slight rumbling on my hand. Pops could soon be felt in my belly as if water were boiling inside of me.

"I feel it too," Mithias reluctantly added with a smile that a man could only get after a great meal. He turned to Ariel and said, "Though your people hold little favor in my heart, I must admit that you know your way around a filling meal!"

Ariel let out a slight smile that Mithias seemed to believe was lighthearted, but I could clearly identify the disappointment in Ariel's expression. Deep down, I think the girl wanted Mithias to like her and her people, but if a meal like that could not change his way of thinking, I did not know what could. I couldn't understand why Mithias held disdain toward her race, but now was not the time or the place to question such blind contempt. Ariel walked over to a small log on the ground and asked Mithias to cut it. I watched as he cut through the center of the log with great speed and precision behind his strike. Ariel then placed half of the log horizontally on the floor of the small landing we sat on.

The angel raised her hand to the log and closed her eyes. Mithias and I soon felt warmth about the angel, and soon this warmth collected itself in a sole location in the angel's smooth hand. A small globe of wild flame appeared for a single moment before it shot toward the log. Once the globe of flame hit the log, the wood caught fire and provided warmth for all of us.

"This wood is made from one of the trees in Sacrimen," began Ariel as she lowered her hand and turned toward us both. "It will burn into the early morning and provide us warmth for the night."

Mithias had many questions about magic for Ariel as I huddled close to the flame. Along with explaining the basics of magic and how it connected one to the natural environment, Ariel added that her skill was laughable compared to the other mages in her clan. As the sun continued to set she explained that she was a novice in the magical arts and the spell that saved the three of us from the unknown creature of the depths had taken a great deal of energy from her. She further stated that had the sandwiches we ate not been exposed to the great crystal of Sacrimen, she would still be on the verge of passing out. Mithias made rude comments throughout the conversation, but his interest in the magical arts and Ariel's people seemed genuine for a handful of fleeting moments. As I fell asleep, I hoped that Mithias would learn to treat Ariel with the respect she deserved.

The next day Mithias woke me up as light began to enter the land, and I could see a thin coat of snow draped across his rugged mustache and beard. I sat up to see Ariel packing up what few supplies we had. I smiled as I approached her and promptly passed the backpack to Mithias. Ariel then hesitantly looked over the ledge upon which we had spent the night. Just below our ledge we could see a simple path that led through the mountain jutting from the side of the rock, so without wasting any time, she began to climb down. The three of us descended a small rock wall, and then found ourselves on an old, snow-covered path that led up to the peak of the mountain.

We began our ascent in silence, for the cold winds had not wavered in the night. However, we moved faster than we had the day before. Our strides were quick, and because of this we reached the mountain's peak just before the sun was at high noon.

The snowy peak contained a flat area, where we stopped to survey our environment. I turned around in a full circle so I could take in all the awe and the glory around me. The snow and fog from the day before had ceased, and now I could clearly behold the gray, washed-out surroundings. Ariel stood beside me and gazed at the surroundings with a smile.

"It's unbelievable isn't it?" she said as she gazed out across the tundra. Mithias meddled about away from us as she added, "All this, created by Two."

I nodded at her notion before adding, "I only wish they had made it a little warmer here. Perhaps then my lungs would not feel as if they were about to rupture."

Ariel smiled. "These lands are barren, but not impossible to traverse."

Mithias soon spoke over both of us, insisting that we continue on our way. The descent down the mountain proved far less tiring than the ascent. We easily made it by midafternoon.

Once on the ground a vast tundra was laid out before us. The icy wasteland gave way to another line of peaks that seemed to be miles away. Upon reaching the ice, Mithias was quick to ask a question that was at the forefront of my mind.

"Do any beasts lurk below this ice?"

Ariel shook her head. "What we encountered was a rogue circumstance. By all accords, we shall be safe during this passage."

Mithias readjusted the backpack and stepped onto the ice as he remarked, "If we are to encounter another beast the likes of which rushes us at a speed we cannot match, I swear I'll curse all the lands until I pass out from exhaustion."

Ariel was quick to add, "Behind those mountains we shall find a nicer environment, one where the ice is not so abundant. We will travel on solid ground once more."

"Then?" Mithias asked as my spirits sank at the thought of more hiking.

"Then we cross the plains for another day. Wercon will appear shortly after we enter a dense wood on the edge of the verdant plains."

I shook my head and said, "Those are the best words I've heard in a long time," as we set out across the ice.

The three of us smiled together for the first time since beginning our journey from the sanctuary. All the while we kept a keen eye and open ear to our surroundings so that we might pick up on any beast that sought to devour us.

Once we reached the second mountain range I looked up to see that it seemed higher than the first. We still had several hours of daylight left, but my muscles longed for rest. My heart sank, but sure enough, Ariel's words brought my spirits back to where they belonged.

"This will be easy," she said as she pointed to steps carved into the side of the mountain. They were worn and smooth but better than having to climb up the mountain unassisted.

"Why are there steps here?" I asked.

The angel began the first step of the long ascent as she replied, "It is said that long ago the angels of Finre sought to create a place where they could worship close to the heavens. They found this peak and built a temple atop it. Many sought to worship the Divine Two there, so they built great stairs leading all the way to the peak."

"I suppose this was before the flood?" I asked Ariel. Since the revitalization of mankind after the great flood, few had sought to worship the Divine Two in houses of the holy due to the fact that the majority of men and lizards did not worship them. I was an exception to that standard, for every night I thanked them for their sacrifice in some hope that they heard, but I often believed my words could only be heard by the gentle breeze of the night.

Ariel nodded her head. "The temple has long since been destroyed by the elements, and all that reminds is a small area where the children were said to have worshipped. We shall stay there for the evening."

Our journey took hours, but through the entire process I beheld the environment with a new light. Being half-angelic myself, I often looked to the clouds and wondered what life would be like if I could soar between them. I had never thought that I would breach the clouds, but I did just that after a great deal of travel. I did what no man from Alfras had ever done: I broke through the clouds and rose above them despite the fact that I had no wings of my own. We reached the peak on the eve of the day, and as I gazed at the night sky, which was dotted with rogue lights and graced by the two moons, I thought of those I had lost. The first moon looked about the size of a large apple, but the second was much more foreboding. At all times of the night and even during most days, this moon could be seen watching over the lands. If I held a balled fist half an arms length away from my face all but the feint edges of the moon could be seen. The surface of this moon was cracked and dark, and at night it looked like a glowing sphere of infected skin that had long since stopped festering. As I gazed at this moon, a terrible, relentless pain throbbed from within the deepest confines of my chest, but exhaustion soon set in to my bones.

At the mountain's peak was the remnant of a small stone building that was shaped like an octagon. All that was left of this once-great temple were a base of stone and several scattered columns that were battered and broken. As I gazed at the sky, Ariel was quick to start a roaring fire at the center of the octagon. The fire crackled under the night sky, and soon Mithias was asleep and Ariel was once again at my side. The angel joined me in my stargazing, and I felt my cheeks go red. I remained silent for a while, but she could not hold her tongue at this great place.

"The Divine Two once resided in the very heavens just above us," she remarked as rogue stars twinkled against their blank canvas. "To think, mortals could once come so close to the Divine Two."

I shook my head. "It's a shame that they are now dead."

This notion seemed to distress Ariel, for she instantly asked me what I meant by my words. I was quick to remind her of how the Divine Two had fallen to the planet as the last of their powers escaped them. The angel looked at me as if I were a fool.

"Just because the Two fell, you think them to be dead?" she asked.

I slowly nodded.

"It is said that in the ancient times, when the Two lived in heaven, the angels were able to use magic by tapping into their very life blood," she said as she looked at the sky. "Combined with the power of the natural world all about us, they were able to harness the elements and use them like never before."

"What does that have to do with the Two being alive?"

The angel did not hesitate to explain her reasoning. "The Divine Two did fall to the lands." She placed her hand on a stone column. "Yet they must still live within the earth, for if they were dead, how would we harness magic? Without their power, angels could not use magic."

I could not reply, so Ariel added, "We only catch a glimpse of truth in this lifetime, Lloyd. True understanding will only besiege us once we leave this world and enter the divine utopia where we shall live forever in peace."

"It is said that the divine utopia crumbled when the pillars could no longer support it," I said, remembering what my parents had taught me long ago.

Ariel did not meet my eyes. She gazed at the heavens intently as she said, "I know of that notion. Most believe it, but I cannot bring myself to believe it true. Our time on this verdant land of chaos is so short, surely there must be something beyond the stars. Surely there must be some place we can go after our time here is done. If the Two are truly alive,

I believe that perhaps some remnant of their eternal paradise remains."

I wrapped my mind around this thought for a moment. The idea that the Two Creators were all about us was quite comforting, and Ariel's idea about the utopia still being a safe haven for the dead was quite unlike what I had been taught. My father had taught me what most humans were told, that the Divine Two were dead and when we died we simply perished. I hated that theory and sometimes wondered why my mother never spoke of angelic theories on the divine. I had one more question regarding the matter before weariness overtook me for the night.

I looked at Ariel. "I have been told not to worship the Two, for they have fallen. My father taught me to simply hold thanks for them every night. Are you telling me that I should continue to worship them?"

Ariel placed her delicate hand on the snow. "My people worship the earth beneath us, for we believe that the power of the Two flows through this land."

She was silent for a moment until her eyes met mine and she said, "I will not tell you what to worship, I will only impart upon you knowledge. Let us cease this discussion, for on the morn we must begin another day of hard travel."

Ariel's idea on the state of divine affairs was quite comforting, and as I lay under my blanket that night I thought about her words. For the first time in my life I chose to pray to the land. I could not feel any special presence while I prayed, yet before shutting my eyes I saw Ariel doing the same. Her figure knelt at the edge of our camp and she prayed for much longer than I. Before drifting off to sleep, I thought of her steadfast dedication to the holy Two and how serene she looked under the light of the two moons.

The next morning I was first to exit slumber. As my eyes peeled open I looked to the dying flame that separated Mithias and Ariel. An all too familiar cold wind struck me with great force once I stood and made my way to the edge of the mountain. I turned my gaze to the west to get a good look at the path before us. The sea of clouds that separated the heavens from the earth had lifted, and I could clearly see a long plain of snow and distant trees that separated my company from our goal. Ariel and Mithias soon woke up and were more than eager to get off the mountain. The three of us made our way down the mountain, and after quite some time we reached the plains once again. We began to walk to the west down a simple dirt patch that was visible through the thawing snow. The rest of the day was spent following this path until the moons began to rise in the sky. The woods had surrounded us for only an hour once darkness set in upon the land.

"Curse all things!" spat Ariel in the midnight air. "The town can't be more than an hour's hike from here, but the cold heart of darkness will soon seep into this land. I can feel air flowing from the east as we speak."

"Let's set up camp here. I'm still not the least bit hungry," I responded from behind Ariel as I placed my hand on her shoulder. "It would be foolish to risk freezing to death."

"In a handful of miles we shall find an inn where we could stay," Mithias declared as he turned around to the both of us. I took my hand off Ariel's shoulder and stood next to her as he added, "A warm bed inside a comfortable house would be a change of things."

"Death would also be a change of things," I sternly responded. "Let us not risk our lives for something as trivial as a warm bed."

"Your cunning avails you Lloyd," Mithias said as he stepped toward me with a grin. "Kiordiam would be proud of such wit."

I didn't know what to say, for the pain of hearing my father's name still brought a tinge of unease in my heart. Mithias soon declared, "All right, then. We shall rest here."

The three of us set up a fire using the remaining log, and it shone brightly through the dark night. Mithias soon complained about a lack of warmth, so he disappeared into the woods north of the path. Ariel and I lightly conversed until he returned with dried twigs and branches. The man fed them to the fire and ignited a blaze that would last all through the night thanks to Ariel's magic. The three of us held our hands close to the bonfire and talked until a sound echoed against the flames. The sound grew and became recognizable as hooves slamming into the solid earth.

The sound was coming down the road, and approaching fast. The three of us turned to see a lone horseman galloping down the path. Against the rider's illuminated torch we saw a blue flag with a grand white claw on it. I was about to extinguish our fire and hide until Ariel spoke.

"He bears the royal flag of Wercon," Ariel said after Mithias took out his axe. As the horse continued down the path, Ariel raised her hand into the air. She could clearly be seen by the fire as she yelled, "Hail, rider of Wercon!"

The rider did not stop. He continued down the road at the same speed and careened toward us. The closer he came toward our lot the more I dreaded this rider. Mithias took his place in the center of the dirt path and drew his weapon as the rider pushed his steed forward. Ariel yelled to the rider once again, but his gallop did not stop. Hooves clapped louder and louder against the worn path as the cloaked rider galloped toward us with a mad resolve. Just as the rider was within feet of us, Ariel yelled a single angelic word that boomed above all else.

An unnatural green light illuminated the area around us in the blink of an eye. The horse reared up in fear, but the shadowed rider skillfully controlled the animal so that it did not kick him off. In the light I noticed that the rider was a lizard who wore a dark green cloak. His horse wildly bucked but the rider was able to steady him.

"Who are you?" he yelled after he had strung an arrow in a bow that he held in his left hand. The arrow had been strung so fast that my eyes had not seen it reach the bowstring. The tip of the arrow was pointed straight at Ariel, who spoke with a swift tongue in the face of such danger.

"We are travelers seeking passage to the capitol. We seek the king's audience."

"What business do you have with the king of Finre?" the lizard barked as he continued to hold his arrow taunt.

"Our business is our own," Ariel said as she stood her ground in the face of death. I took a place next to her, with Mithias right behind me as we prepared for the worst.

"Why should I trust you?" spat the cloaked lizard as he moved the tip of his arrow toward Mithias, then me. "Why should I trust any of you?"

Ariel looked back at the two of us, at a loss for words, and stood like a statue until I stepped toward to the lizard and firmly declared, "We have a message for the king that could save many lives. For every moment you hinder us, the land gets closer to a terrible end. We have been instructed to find a guide in Wercon so that our passage to the capitol is swift and steady."

As soon as I said the word Wercon, the lizard's scaled face changed. His face was amazing, truly something out of a myth. He had an oblong mouth with sharp teeth lining the inside. His eyes were positioned toward the front of his head, but they were as black as night and within them I could see the reflection of the torchlight. Just above his mouth were two small, flaring nostrils. From what I could see, his arms were lined with the same olive-colored scales that marked his face. The lizard retracted his bow and placed his arrow back in its quiver. As he did this I noticed that, like all other lizards, this lizard only had a three-fingered claw. His fingers were arranged much like mine, but it was as if the middle and pointer finger were bound together, and the ring finger and pinky were also bound together. The third finger acted like a thumb and was slightly larger than the others. Each finger had a small and dirtied nail on top. All in all, he looked to be just older than Ariel and I, but younger than Mithias. His vibrant scales glistened against the green light.

"It may displease you to hear that Wercon has been deci-mated," he uttered with contempt in his eyes. "The town has been engulfed in fire and is all but burnt to the ground."

"What?" yelled Ariel. Mithias and I did not believe our ears as the Ariel asked, "How? By whom?"

Before the lizard spoke, I knew what he would say. There was only one nation that could bring violence to this place.

"Thundrians," he declared as he shifted in his saddle.

"We're too late," Mithias muttered under his breath.

Ariel asked, "How long ago did this happen?"

"They attacked from the north at dusk. They cut through our ranks like a swift breeze through fields of grass." There was a pause as his gaze became distant. "These soldiers—they were unlike anything I had ever seen."

Curiosity overtook Mithias. "What do you mean?"

The lizard shook his head before hesitantly stating, "They were larger than most men and looked like something out of a nightmare. When I beheld them I thought I had drifted into some hellish spell, for as they rushed into Wercon like savages, I beheld them in full." All of us hung on the lizard's words. We said nothing as he took a breath before continuing, "These beasts had the heads of wolves, and the bodies of beasts that stood like you or I. Their mangled flesh was unnatural and their strength was imbued with some dark essence that I can't quite describe. In their presence, my men felt a true and lasting fear."

A nightmarish image of such a beast instantly entered the darkest recess of my mind as Ariel asked, "Are you sure that is what you saw?"

The lizard nodded his head. "They came upon my castle with a speed and power that I could hardly believe even as it occurred right before my eyes."

"Your castle?" asked Mithias, who took several steps toward the lizard's horse. "Do you lead the people of Wercon?"

At this notion the lizard shook his head. "My father does, but at this time I do not know if he still walks among the living."

I asked the lizard to explain his words.

He jumped to the ground as he spoke in a muddled and downtrodden voice. "My name is Theron, I am the prince of Wercon, heir to my father's throne."

After his declaration, Ariel quickly bowed before him. Mithias and I stood with dumbfounded expressions on our faces, for we did not see fit to bow before this stranger. Ariel began to speak in a more refined manner as she politely asked, "What has happened, prince?"

Theron cut his hand through the air. "Please, now is not the time for formalities." He paused for a moment. "The dark force came upon my village without warning. They herded us through the trees and killed any and all that they could find. Women, children; all fell to the blades of these beasts."

The lizard had a distant look in his eyes as he continued, "I fought off all I could until the captain of the royal guard ordered my family to escape the village. Through the chaos of battle I lost both my parents."

"So why do you ride away from the fray?" Mithias asked him in a bitter tone.

"The enemy was unlike anything I had ever seen," he responded as he glanced at the three of us. "It took the blows from three of our soldiers to take down just one of theirs. Their relentless slaughter of my people was unimaginable. Under the notion that the bloodline had to survive, the captain of the guard ordered my family away. I retreated as fast as I could, but when I turned to see my parents, they were not there."

Mithias' voice was laden with disgust as he asked, "So you do not know if your parents are alive or dead?"

The lizard lowered his head when he picked up on Mithias' harsh tone. He stuttered and spoke slowly. "I wish to see them again. I wish to save all in my village."

Mithias reared up his axe as he yelled, "Then let us go there now!"

Instantly, Ariel shot back, "Are you insane? He claims that the beasts have overrun his city. What can the three of us do?"

"I have bested my fair share of men over the years. Let me lead our group into the castle and I will kill any Thundrians that stand in our way," Mithias said.

I shook my head. "If what Theron says is true, these are no mere men. These beasts sound like nothing we have ever encountered before." I turned toward the lizard. Perhaps you should guide us away from here."

Theron was quick to reply, "No, your companion is right... I could not live with myself if I did not know the fate of my family. In the haze of battle I only thought to preserve myself, but now that I am on the road alone, I know what I must do. I cannot leave my village without my parents."

"Then what would you have us do?" asked Ariel. "You say the Thundrians are strong and in great number, so how can we reach your parents without losing our lives?"

116

The lizard looked at the three of us with desperation. "There may be a way for us to enter the castle, and if the three of you were in my ranks, perhaps we could live to see tomorrow's dawn," he said nervously. Mithias prompted him to explain so the lizard timidly continued. "There is a passage that can be accessed from outside the city walls. If we enter it we can travel to the castle and see if there are any survivors."

Upon hearing this, Mithias asked, "Well, why haven't you done this yet?"

Theron shied back from the man. "I am just one lizard! If but one soldier caught sight of me I would perish!"

Mithias frowned at Theron. "Well, lad, your lack of heroism is laughable."

"Do not speak to him in such ways," yelled Ariel as the lizard turned his gaze to the ground. She was quick to add, "He may have lost his family, and he is right to flee if his is the last royal blood of Wercon."

The conversation was going nowhere fast, and I knew that with every passing second Wercon was being ravaged by the forces that threatened her. I spoke my mind so that we could all move forward.

"Enough of this idle chatter," I declared before the forked tongues of my allies could continue to wave. This caused all eyes to fall upon me. "Regardless of our path, we cannot sit by as such devastation unfolds. We must help Theron find his parents."

Ariel agreed. Mithias stated, "The Two know that he'll need help."

The timid lizard lowered his eyes at this statement. Theron hesitantly thanked us for our offer before mounting his horse once again. The cold air set in and my bones shook as we proceeded through the darkness toward our goal. After some travel, the dark sky was stained with bright orange and a searing heat began to blast our bodies. As we crept closer to the light I beheld its terrible maker. A broken stone wall encircled a village that contained homes made from thick and sturdy logs. From where we stood I could see a distant castle with burning banners similar to the one held by Theron. A blaze could be seen at several houses, and through the massive open gate in the distance I clearly saw silhouettes of soldiers moving about the wreckage and flames.

We quickly moved out of sight of any who rummaged about the flames and rubble and hustled around the western wall of the city, where we came upon a peculiar boulder that sat against the wall. After dismounting his worn steed, Theron walked to the boulder and lightly tapped it four times. After he did this, a human-sized rectangular piece of the stone slid into the rock to reveal a deep, dark pit in the ground. A lone worn ladder was the means by which Theron began to descend into this pit. The lizard beckoned us to follow him. After a short descent through darkness that stank of mildew and rot, we came to a narrow hallway illuminated by dying torchlight. I could see that the passageway stretched for a great distance before ending at an old, rusted staircase. Before continuing, Theron turned to the three of us and whispered, "Hold your tongues, my allies; the beasts that bear the mark of Thundria roam just above us, and if they catch the slightest hint of an intruder our lives are as good as spent."

With bated breath and light steps, I followed Theron and Ariel and Mithias crept behind me. As we walked toward the staircase at the end of the tunnel the distinct sound of scattered screams could be heard through the ground above. These random screams were muffled by the amount of earth between my ears are their makers, yet they still made me cringe. Once our group had reached the stairs, the terrible sound of desperate cries could no longer be heard, and my heart slowed its incessant pounding.

Theron ascended the narrow staircase very slowly and I, along with my other two companions, followed him closely. Our steps were light, for each small step could be heard against the decrepit staircase. Once at the top of the stairs Theron slowly cracked open a small hatch in the tunnel's ceiling, and after a tense moment of surveillance, the lizard quietly made his way into a room where the rest of us soon joined him. We found ourselves in a storeroom with barrels and crates stacked up against the walls. A single torch burned dimly and illuminated a door at the end of the room.

"All right," Theron whispered as he turned to the three of us. "Stay quiet and tread lightly. Our foes must not take note of our presence."

The lot of us nodded in agreement and followed the lizard out the door and into a hallway. Many doors lined the grand interior, but the lizard led us down the hall to a spiral staircase. We ascended the stairs in silence until we found ourselves in a massive hall. The most notable feature of the area was a pair of enormous double doors next to the stairs we had just climbed. Theron crept toward these double doors, which looked as if they were made for a giant, and peered through one of many holes in them.

"There are two in the throne room," he whispered as he looked through the opening. The lizard turned back to us in desperation and motioned for me to peer through the cracks. I silently did as I was told and beheld two massive soldiers who were covered from head to toe in thick crimson armor. The only thing that looked out of the ordinary was that their helmets looked as if they had been fashioned for a massive dog head, for a steel section of the helm stretched out as if it were protecting a snout. I could not see all the bestial features described to me earlier, so little fear was about my voice as I whispered, "We will fell them."

Theron hesitantly nodded as he readied his bow and moved away from the doors. Once all of us had slowly drawn our weapons, the lizard slammed his back against the door and burst into the room. Theron let loose an arrow upon one soldier, who was struck before he could even turn around. The soldier let out an animal-like growl as he looked down at the arrow protruding from his arm. A thick, tarlike blood seeped from the wound and onto the floor. With his ally by his side, the beast rushed toward my company with a speed unprecedented to any man. Theron shot another arrow at this beast, but the beast did not waver. Soon he was upon Mithias, but the man did not fear the creature. Mithias swept his axe under the beast's legs before slamming cold steel into the soldier's breast. As he did this, Ariel and I dealt with the second soldier. Before he reached me, Ariel shot a bolt of energy from her palms that caused the creature's flesh to sear. His pain was evident by his howls, and as he writhed in agony I thrust my sword into his chest. The soldiers lay on the floor for only a moment before a thick, black fluid began to ooze from their wounds. They looked more like animals than humans as the last light of life left their eyes.

"What is this?" asked Ariel as she took a step forward and placed her finger upon the blood that spilled onto the carpet. The substance seemed to slowly crawl about her fingers as if it were alive, and only when the angel wiped it on the ground did it bubble and steam.

"They are not natural creations like you or I," said Theron as he surveyed the room. "See for yourself."

Mithias then slowly lifted the helmet off of one of our attackers to reveal a horrid sight. Though the soldier had the body of a man, his head was that of a wild dog. Thick hair that was slowly being tainted by a coat of vile blood covered his entire head. Massive yellow teeth filled his mouth. These sharp teeth were those of an animal, and it looked as if they could rip through flesh or bone. The pupils of these creatures were massive, nearly the size of olives, and as they stared blankly toward the ceiling I could not look to them, for even in death their eyes seemed to penetrate my soul. I averted my gaze from the terrible sight as Theron declared, "We are lucky none heard their screams. Let us not linger."

Theron led us through a door at the back of the hall to a room with massive stone columns rising to a ceiling made of glass that revealed a thick cloud of smoke. On the glass ceiling were intricate designs of nature's beauty, yet the glass was cracked and shattered at certain areas so I could not behold the magnificent work of art that it once had been. After quickly taking in my surroundings I heard Theron state, "My father is not here; I shall search the king's quarters. Stay here and secure the hall."

Mithias and Ariel obeyed the lizard, but for some reason I didn't want Theron to go alone. Something deep in my very soul caused me to followed his steps. As the lizard left the room through a small side door, I quietly trailed him without any of my companions noticing. I followed him down a short hall before we arrived at our destination.

The room was bare and not a single friend nor foe stirred within its walls. A library with a fireplace was before us, but the blaze that once had danced within its confines was dead. Between two bookshelves I could see a pair of short marble stairs leading up to a red bed that contrasted with the ornate floors and stone walls. All seemed well until my eyes fell upon the bed of the king and queen, where the very sight Theron must have most dreaded was laid out before him. Having experienced my loss on Alfras, I knew that sight before us would forever change him.

Upon the bed lay two corpses that were covered in nothing but a thin sheet. As my eyes drew themselves toward the corpses I noticed that upon the floor was a trail of dark red-green blood leading up the short marble stairs to the bed. Theron darted up the stairs to the bed and grasped the sheet with his worn claws. He began to tremble uncontrollably and ripped the layer of sheet away. I watched in terrible silence as the fabric flew across the room. I could see that Theron's hands had become stained with the same blood that led up the stairs.

"No," he uttered as his tears cascaded from his eyes. The lizard quickly turned his head and vomited onto the floor, staining the blood with his previous meals in the process. A strong stench rose about the room, and I rushed to the lizard. When I came upon the bed I, too, nearly heaved.

Upon the bed lay a large lizard man next to a petite lizard woman. They had both been stripped of their clothing and were a pale tint of green. The man had been, for lack of a more humane word, gutted, and his insides were spread around the bed. My eyes sought refuge from the horror, so they turned to the female lizard, yet her corpse only brought me more pain.

The lizard woman had died with an expression of unexplainable horror. As my eyes followed the line of her head down to her shoulders I realized that the two were no longer attached. The woman had been beheaded and her body lay in a crumpled ball at the end of the bed. Upon the belly of each royal was the mark of Thundria. It had been engraved upon their rotting flesh, and upon viewing it I gagged.

Theron screamed and pounded the bed like an animal. His eyes grew wide and his mouth began to foam as if he were a rabid dog. This scream could be heard throughout the town and it swiftly carried itself across the ocean and the mountaintops. I clenched my ears so not to hear the primal wail, yet it still crept through my fingers and into my skull as the grieving lizard smashed his hands into the ground. He did this until his hands were bloodied and battered, yet his blows did not cease. Even when his body shook with fatigue, he continued.

The lizard smashed his hands onto the wooden bedposts, splintering them, and began to walk around in circles while cradling his head in hands. Through his hands I heard sobs and screams and ramblings in a language I did not recognize, all while his face became covered in his own blood. Through the lizard's rage I knew that I had to conceal the bodies, so as Theron stomped about I slowly raised the covers over both corpses. The lizard continued his screams until Mithias darted into the room.

"Your screams have brought enemies upon us!" declared Mithias in a tone that was at the peak of a whisper.

The lizard continued to circle around the room, screaming and sobbing. Mithias looked at me.

"His family is dead," I softly stated as the lizard panted and sobbed.

"And we will be too if we do not leave!" yelled the man. "We must flee!"

I looked at Theron and discovered that logic had fled his mind. The prince continued his fit of rage, so I grabbed his shoulders to shake him out of his daze. The lizard tried to shake me free and even hit me across the cheek as I held him steady. My cheek throbbed and I had had enough.

"Theron!" I screamed in his face. He continued to struggle until I yelled, "We must leave or we shall meet the same fate as your family! Would they want you to lie rotting beside them as well?"

Theron slowly stopped then and breathed heavily as he glanced toward the bed, then back at me. He looked around as if he had just come out of a daze, and then turned to Mithias. As he began to talk he nodded and I released him from my grasp.

"I cannot let this stand," he said in between deep breaths. "I must avenge the deaths that have unfolded today. I will gut the dogs that are responsible for this."

"Not here. Not now," said Mithias.

Theron fell silent. He was deep in thought despite the fact that soldiers rushed toward our location. I approached him from behind and grabbed his right shoulder with my right hand. From behind his back, I said, "Theron, come with us."

"What?" he asked as he spun around.

"The three in my group, we all seek an audience with the king of this land to tell him of Thundria's uprising. We need a guide to get us to the king's quarters so that the same terrible fate that befell this place does not envelop this land," I quickly replied.

Theron looked at me with pulsing, glazed eyes before glancing at the two bodies under the covers of the bed. The lizard returned his gaze to mine as he proclaimed, "If we can leave this place, then I will travel with you, but I fear our time in this world ends now."

I looked at Mithias in desperation and the man was quick to reassure me.

"We can kill enough to get out of here," he said confidentially as he readied his axe. "We will live."

Theron timidly nodded. "There is an old outpost just west of here. If we can fight our way past the beasts in this city, we can acquire canoes and use them to travel to the capitol."

Mithias nodded and asked, "Then what are we waiting for?"

The lizard led the two of us back to the room where Ariel stood. The angel had sealed the two double doors shut with some sort of binding magic that she struggled to maintain as she waved her hands at the doors. The doors shook with a great pounding force every passing moment, and Ariel looked as if she were about to pass out. With few words, Theron stated that if we could get out the two large double doors then we could make our way to the courtyard with relative ease. He declared that stables sat on the edge of the vast courtyard, and if we were lucky we could secure passage away from the chaos. The doors shook violently as we readied our weapons for a terrible fight, but Ariel knew we could not survive through brute force alone. She had a plan.

Suddenly, Ariel took her arms down, and the white sheet of light that braced the doors fell. In an instant the two doors splintered and burst to reveal dozens of inhuman soldiers. Before I could get a good look at any of them, Ariel shouted for us to close our eyes. I did so immediately. Through my eyelids I beheld a fiery light as my ears heard numerous screams. Ariel grabbed my hand after the light subsided and led me toward the force before us. I was half blind from the strange light, and the environment around me looked very bright, as if the sun drenched it in the afternoon. Despite this hindrance, I could see that I was being led past the soldiers who wished to end us. Each one was on the ground clutching eyes that flowed with countless tears. My vision returned to me when I was being led down a hall by Ariel. I turned my head to see Mithias and Theron keeping step, so my fears about their well-being were instantly quelled. We rushed down the hall and emerged outside to see flames and soot all around us. Heavily armored soldiers rushed toward us as Theron darted toward two horses that were frantically neighing beside a burning stable. The lizard mounted a bucking horse and instantly controlled it, then Mithias hopped onto the back of the animal. The wild stallion I climbed onto clamored for a moment before Theron spoke to it in a language I did not recognize. After his words were spoken, the horse's eyes became benign once more and he allowed Ariel to quickly mount up. Once we were all on our steeds, Theron cut loose the reins and allowed the animals to bound past all opposition before us. We darted through the flames and wreckage of the city all while being bombarded with arrows from the Thundrian beasts for one brief moment of terror before we emerged on the southern wall. Theron rounded his horse toward the west and galloped ahead of Ariel and me. I followed his horse for a long moment before my surroundings began to change.

As we continued west, all became quiet. No screams could be heard in the streets, no clashing steel, just the sound of rising flame. The city that had been Theron's home for his entire life was being burned to the ground as we galloped away from it. Despite the lizard's best intentions, he could do nothing but listen to the inferno as he pushed his horse onward to the west. None of us knew how many had died in those walls, but one thing was sure: there was never a battle at Wercon. Instead, there was a massacre.

CHAPTER 8

Amid the fire and the flames, a lone lizard walked. No other being in the land was as massive as he, for he stood as tall as two men. His hands were the size of most men's faces, and his eyes were bulging and bloodshot. From his head shot six horns that spanned at least two feet in length. Each one was polished to a fine point and could be seen protruding from his helmet. As he walked, his pristine armor gleamed as if it were kissed by the sun. His helm was imposing, and from it sprung two iron horns that resembled those of a ram. Intricate swirls of gold and diamond flowed around the helm and encircled two small slits that revealed his glowing crimson eyes. His helmet gave way to armor covered in gold and diamond swirls that flowed across his entire suit. The only part of his body the suit did not cover was his back where his tail stretched out. His tail was long and scarred from many battles through the years.

In his right arm he carried a magnificent blade. It was thick and at least as long as most spears. Unlike his pristine armor, the sword was stained with blood and worn from recent battle. The hilt bore a diamond that was shaped to the mark of Thundria.

The gigantic lizard ducked his head to walk through an archway that used to hold two large wooden doors. The doors had since burnt to cinders, and as the lizard entered the room he looked around. He noticed several of his inhuman soldiers dragging a beaten and battered man before them who cursed and clamored as he was dragged. Once the lizard's eyes met with the man in front of him, the man attempted to squirm away, but his efforts were for naught.

"Human," came a voice from behind the large helm that shrouded the lizard's face. His voice was deep and gnarled as if his throat were lined with thorns. "We have killed many, but one royal cannot be found. Tell me, where is your prince? Where is the last of the royal bloodline?"

"Go to hell, foul beast," spat back the wounded soldier. One of the soldiers immediately punched him in the face, and blood shot from the injured man's broken nose.

"Do not kill him; he will be useful," the shrouded lizard demanded in a cool tone.

Once again the man spat back a curse at the lizard. One of the soldiers holding him down was about to strike him again, but the massive lizard lifted his great sword and cut through the beast's belly, instantly tearing him in two. The injured prisoner looked at the fallen beast with wide eyes while the terrifying lizard removed his helmet and placed it on the ground beside the bloodied mess he had created.

His face was scarred and broken from ages of battle. His nose was flattened and as he spoke his lips gave way to sharp yellow teeth. He knelt in front of the prisoner and looked him straight in the eyes as he spoke in a gnarled tone.

"Mind you, soldier, if you reveal the location of the prince, you shall not be damned to the fate as he who nearly struck you a second time."

"Lies!" the broken man yelled.

The lizard of unholy accord showed no signs of malice and shook his head as his deceitful eyes fell upon the scarred and beaten soldier. "Your wounds shall be treated, and great riches shall come upon your name," he said. A smile stretched across his thin face. "I will personally make sure a vessel safely takes you to my kingdom of Thundria, if only you loosen your tongue."

The broken man's eyes darted as he forced himself to contemplate the offer. The lizard remained crouched as he added, "Or I could loosen it for you. So what will it be? Early retirement or death?"

The man's eyes gradually moved up to his enemy. These eyes teared up as the man quivered in fear. His rough lips slowly opened as he asked, "I have this guarantee by your word?"

"By the word of all Thundria," the lizard replied as he wrapped his hand around the man's arm. The lizard could easily crush the man if he wished, but he waited for the man to speak.

The man was lost in silent contemplation for a brief moment as his eyes surveyed the many soldiers. He then turned back to the lizard and in a low voice said, "The prince took a steed to the west."

"Where does he hope to go?" the lizard asked in a low, direct tone.

"That I do not know," he responded in all honesty. "Theron is a ranger, the best I have ever seen. By all accounts he could live in the wilds for months on end, but he is righteous. He will probably seek to tell the king of Finre of this attack, of that I'm sure."

The lizard smiled, then stood up and put his helmet back on. He began to walk away from the man on the ground without saying another word.

"Why do you retreat? What of my riches? My retirement!" yelled the man as the lizard slowly strode away.

Without turning toward the man, the lizard stopped his pace and uttered, "Any man willing to sacrifice his kingdom for gold and freedom shall not find solace under my banner." He turned to a beast to his left and demanded, "Gut him very slowly, and keep him alive. By tomorrow's dawn I want to still hear his screams as this place reeks of his innards."

The man began to shriek and struggle uncontrollably as two guards hauled him off to a room that adjoined the throne room. He wailed a terrible scream that was all too familiar to the malicious lizard. Once the door shut with a loud thump the screams could barely be heard. The lizard turned away from the door and was approached by one of the rogue human soldiers in his company.

"Should we depart, my lord?" asked the soldier, who stood at only half the lizard's height.

"The mantises need rest," responded the dark lizard as he walked out of the arch into the streets, where fires still raged and ash filled the air. "By this time tomorrow they shall be ready to ride."

The lizard glanced toward a stable nearby where his wild steeds screamed. As he looked on, only the shadows of the beasts could be seen against the wall. In the light of the dying flames, the shadows could clearly be seen clawing at each other. As they fought, the ferocious creatures that inhabited the nightmares of countless children produced a sound of genuine sin. The lizard watched the jagged shadows, then smiled under his helm before continuing through the streets. The chaos of the night would soon subside as the sun rose and stained the sky with a crimson aura. The lizard walked away from the pitch and rubble as he prepared to send scouts to track down the one known as Theron.

* * *

As morning began to grace the land I found myself meddling with a stick beside a dying campfire. I glanced to the north, where I beheld the two canoes we had been traveling in for the past week. Both were beached against the rocky shore of the winding river we followed daily. The continent's cold air was still all about us, but it was not so cold for snow to fall from the heavens. I could no longer see my own breath in front of my face. Mithias had told me that as the weather grew warmer my breath would become invisible once more.

The land we traversed was laden with bountiful grooves of trees that bore strange fruit I had never seen before. At night we beached our canoes and lay on the grass under our blankets as we gazed at the gleaming heavens. Every night we were blessed with the dazzling sight of the stars and two moons against their onyx canvas. Under this display of indescribable beauty, Mithias, Ariel, and I would converse. Theron chose to remain silent and distant, and oftentimes he went days without uttering a single word.

We rowed between the plentiful hills that were laden with flowers of gold and white. Plump clouds stretched across the sky as a westward wind pushed us onward. The whole scene laid out around us looked like a finely painted tapestry, and had our duty not called us forward I would have enjoyed relaxing in this place.

Theron and Mithias sat in a canoe within talking distance while Ariel and I paddled our canoe forward. On the eighth day of travel we found ourselves crossing under a small footbridge that spanned the length of the crystal clear waters. As we crossed under the rickety old ropes, Theron spoke up for the first time in a day or so.

"We paddle for at least another four weeks, probably more, before we reach the capitol city," he proclaimed.

"Do we have enough food to last that long?" I asked as I rowed closer to his canoe. The river was quite fertile and we were able to pick fruits from nearby trees to eat along the way, but I did not know if that would sustain us.

"These lands are rich with sustenance," said Theron. "This river shall take us through the heart of its bounty."

His gaze grew distant until Ariel said, "Theron, you've hardly said anything since our departure from Wercon. Are you going to be okay?"

The lizard fell silent, and for a moment all that could be heard was the water splitting before the bows of our canoes. Upon the first day of our journey from Wercon I had told Mithias and Ariel of what I had seen when I followed Theron up the stairs and into the royal chambers. This brought Ariel nearly to tears and tore Mithias into a rage, yet both concealed their true sorrow from our new ally. Instead, they simply offered their best condolences and continued on. I looked up at Theron for a response, but he was silent as his eyes wandered over the lush knolls all about us. After a deep sigh that was clearly filled with a terrible sorrow, he spoke.

"I still draw breath, and that's all that matters," he declared with a slow and wavering voice.

"What's that supposed to mean?" Mithias asked from behind him.

The lizard turned toward the large man, who was stroking his beard. "If I can get my message to the king of Finre, then I will be fine. Give me time."

Despite Theron's words, I did not believe him, for he continued to speak with a distance that he had not held when he had first come upon us in the woods. He had hardly spoken during our journey, and I had never had the chance to rightly tell him about our similar experiences. Now was the time for Theron to discover the event in my life that made us so alike.

"Theron," I started in a low tone as images of my fallen family flooded my mind. "I never told you this, but they murdered my family too. You are not alone in your grief."

He stared at me in disbelief as he uttered, "You seem so content. How can you continue to smile and laugh with such memories?"

After a steady sigh, I replied, "I shall never forget what I saw, but I must go on with my life. Someday I will avenge their deaths and set all things right, but I cannot do that if I show sorrow in every waking moment."

My eyes drew themselves toward Theron's as I added, "With the chance of war looming just over the horizon, we cannot waver. We must be strong, my friend."

Theron looked me square in the eyes for several moments. His eyes seemed to pulsate as his pupils dilated and his eyelids thinned. The lizard searched me as if he wished to find some sort of truth, and then he did something he hadn't done in quite some time. He smiled the slightest hint of a smile and gave me a nod.

"Your words quell my raging spirits, Lloyd. Thank you," he said quietly.

And with that the lizard opened up to all of us and spoke of his brighter days as we spoke of ours. The day went by fast because of our lighthearted conversations, and before we knew it, night had come. After setting up a fire, Mithias and the prince quickly fell asleep, leaving only Ariel and me to gaze at the infinitely beautiful abyss above us.

"It's interesting to have a lizard travel with us," I said.

Ariel was quick to inquire as to what exactly I meant, so I added, "In my village we only had humans and a couple of angels. Never in my life have I gotten to know a lizard."

"I too had never befriended one," said Ariel. "I didn't travel outside the safety of my island more than a handful of times. As such, I saw very few humans and lizards until now, but Theron is a pleasure to know."

I nodded my head in agreement before a grin stretched across my face.

"Now that you have gotten to know a human, what do you think?" I asked with a warm smile.

Ariel returned my smile as she replied, "They're not so bad. One in particular is showing me that their ways can be peaceful."

"Who, Mithias?" I shot back with a smile.

The two of us shared a brief laugh for a moment before silence set in once again. Ariel soon spoke much darker words.

"Though I fear my time with my new friends will be cut short," she proclaimed.

The angel's gaze fell to the ground, so I instantly asked, "What's wrong?"

Her gentle eyes lifted to mine as she spoke words of terrible wisdom. "Back in Wercon, and when we encountered the beast below the ice, I felt fear for the first time in many years. Twice now we have eluded death. I fear that next time we face such madness we will be forced away from this world."

"I too fear our fate," I began with a wavering tone. Ariel still looked distraught, so I was quick to catch her gaze and add, "But together we can survive. This scares us both, so how about we make a deal. I will guard your back so long as you guard mine, all right? Let us look after each other in battle."

A comfortable smile stretched across Ariel's face, and she promptly agreed to my proposal. After that, the two of us soon fell into a deep slumber that was eventually interrupted by the unrelenting light cast down upon us by the morning sun. Our group set out and paddled for the whole day along the blissful river. The gentle flow of the river brought us through beautiful landscapes that slowly became punctuated by massive statues of rock that stretched high into the clouds. Each statue depicted a male or female lizard that stood like a giant on the flat land.

"The great kings of Finre," stated Theron as more of the statues came into our vision across the plains. "By order of the first king who united all the lizards of this land, a statue was built in his honor, and another one was not to be built until his great-grandson came to rule. And so it was that every fourth ruler down the royal line had a statue erected in his or her honor. It has been over three thousand years since the first great king was immortalized. Thus the land now has a plethora of these monuments."

Theron was right, for as my naked eyes scanned the barren landscape I beheld a multitude of colossal monuments. During the next two days of our journey I beheld many statues that stood as a testament to the power of those who resided in this place. Some were worn from weather and several had collapsed long ago and now were just piles of rock in the sea of green, yet all amazed me for their sheer size and splendor. After two days of travel we passed the last of the statues. On the eve of that second day, we stopped and made camp under a massive willow by the river. The sun soon set and we prepared our blankets before the sparkling stars twinkled brightly in the cosmos above us.

As we made a roaring fire using magic and timber, the animals of the night encroached upon us. Their beady eyes shone like stars against the night as they eyed us suspiciously from just outside the ring of light cast by our fire. Most nights we slept with the beasts meandering just outside our line of sight. On this night, however, Theron walked to the edge of the light. We turned to him as he knelt to the ground and began to speak. His tongue was loose and his voice seemed calming, yet he spoke in a language I did not recognize. His voice was melodic but had a primal sting to it that rose my hairs on end. After his speech, howls echoed toward our camp before the creatures of the night scurried away under a veil of darkness.

"In what tongue do you speak?" I asked him from my place by the fireside.

The lizard spoke a few more words before returning to the fireside and taking his place beside me. "It's a language known to the creatures that walk this land."

Mithias eyed him suspiciously and asked, "In all my travels I have never encountered a lizard with such an affinity for animals."

"Can your kind really speak to them?" Ariel asked. She eyed Theron intensely as she added, "I have heard stories of some lizards that could converse with animals, yet never did I believe them to be true."

"It is fact," began Theron as his eyes lay upon the dancing blaze before us. "My kind can communicate in ways no other can. Through our voices, we can talk with the animals, yet few possess this ability. Sadly, these powers are lost to those who do not harness them at a young age."

"So you harnessed these powers long ago?" I asked after a spell of silence.

Theron nodded before declaring, "As a child I read any book I could find. My time was spent constantly studying, and as my youth slipped away from my grasp I found that I had spent more time in the royal library than by my father's side. In the libraries I learned of art, history, and every facet of education known to my people. By the age of seven I had read and mastered all twelve volumes of the animal languages. Though I cannot talk to all animals, many are easy to communicate with after such extensive studies."

"What did you say to them?" asked Ariel. "The animals, I mean."

Theron glanced out to the wilds as he replied, "I have told them that we wish to traverse their lands in peace. We wish them no harm and will keep to ourselves so long as we can take fish from their mighty river and distant game in the north. I told them we wish to hunt in the coming days but we will refrain from killing any of their kin within this stretch of land."

"And they listened to you?" I asked.

"They are wiser than you may believe, Lloyd," began the lizard as he gazed across the distant plains. A smile drifted across his face as he added, "They are both organized and thoughtful. Sometimes I find myself more drawn to animals than to people." Only the crackling fire could be heard for a moment before Theron brought his gaze back to us and added, "The three of you are an exception to my preference."

"But what of their words?" asked Mithias as he toyed with the pebbles at his feet. "What do the animals say to you?"

"Their kind usually communicates through gestures rather than words, much like the ancient people of my race," began

Theron. "Emotions such as anger, or fear, are easy to detect within a creature of the wilds, but only after years of study have I discovered how to truly communicate with their kind by way of voice and minute gestures. All of the native creatures to this land can be understood in time."

"But all must be used," began Ariel. "The meat and skin from these creatures is invaluable to the survival of your people, is it not?"

Theron scoffed at this notion and quickly declared, "The lizards of my colony were not so prone to violence for survival. We took water and fish from the rivers, yes, but the creatures around us were only taken after their natural deaths. I had a pact with the creatures of the woods. They knew my village could hunt them into extinction if we wished, so they chose to leave their dead for us so that we need not kill them in their prime. They mourn their dead as we do, so this was no easy negotiation, but they know as well as any man that a lizard with a longbow can kill any animal. In the end, we formed a strong relationship."

Theron's eyes focused on Ariel as he added, "Angels claim to live in harmony with the land, but they are just as quick as humans to destroy the life on it for their own gain."

Before Mithias could reply with a hotheaded statement I declared, "It is late, my friends. Let us retire and discuss brighter things in the morning."

All agreed, and sleep came swiftly to my company and me. Once day broke we wound down the river peacefully once again. From my seat in the canoe I rowed with the current and watched the shore as my company and I talked all through the day. Occasionally, a pack of wild dogs could be seen running along the shore, licking their chops as they looked at the four of us. They were calmed by Theron and backed away from the water after he spoke to them, and we never feared the wild beasts.

All was well for the next two weeks. The dawn that came on the morn of the fourth week was not unusual, and the four of us entered the canoes with a stockpile of fruit. Within an hour we saw a sight that would mark the end of the first leg of our journey downriver. As the clear stream led us north, the woods that had encircled us for two days slowly began to give way to abundant plains. These plains bloomed with brilliant indigo flowers that led toward the blazing sunrise.

The flower-laden valley grew with each passing hour, and before we knew it our canoes were on their way toward great mountain range that stretched high into the sky. It looked to be nearly twice the size of the one we had traversed to get to Wercon, and its foreboding peaks seemed to loom over us as our canoe slowly made its way through a deep valley. As steep and barren walls of rock surrounded us, Theron spoke in a voice that echoed against our surroundings.

"For more than a week we will find ourselves rowing through these mountains," Theron began as the three of us turned to hear him. "You will find them to be temperate at first, yet as the days wear on they will become plagued with frost and relentless cold wind."

"For over a week we must endure this?" Ariel questioned him as she continued to watch him row. Angels never liked the cold weather. Joints in human legs and arms lock up from the cold; this is common knowledge. But only those who know angels know that their wings lock up in the cold, causing flight to be very difficult and painful. My island was usually quite temperate, but during several winters I could only watch as my mother and siblings moaned in pain while their fragile wings grew stiff.

"It will not be easy," Theron continued as he began to survey the environment. "Each night we hunt, and each day we must drape the blankets on ourselves. Yet there is a good side to this valley."

"What is that?" I asked as I plunged my oar into the water and swiftly pulled it back.

"The currents will pick up," started Theron as he turned forward once again. "Our journey will be swift through this place, and the meat from the creatures of the wild will fill our bellies."

Mithias stopped rowing as he turned to the lizard and asked, "We shall hunt? I thought you respected the creatures of the wood too much to do such a thing?"

Theron nodded his head, not wanting to disagree with the man, but he had to add, "We have left the woods where the animals respect me. Though it pains me to know my arrows shall kill

the species of my friends, we must eat meat. Without such sustenance we will surely perish in the terrible cold. We will make our
kills quickly so not to let the poor beasts suffer."

At that, I leaned back in my canoe and looked at our surroundings. The valley seemed to encroach upon us as we continued down the narrow passage. As the sun began to set, a dark,
cold shadow was cast upon us from the eastern wall of the crevice. We stayed in the valley until the two moons hung high in the
sky and we spotted a location to set up camp on. A small shore
in front of the steep valley walls served as our resting place. That
night we ate the last of our fruit and vowed to hunt before the
next sunset.

Morning's light came speedily, for dreams did not inhabit my
mind. Within minutes our lot was once again in the canoe and
heading farther downstream. Sometime in the day we exited the
valley for a short period of time, and during this time we found
ourselves surrounded by plains that were between two mountains. Theron spotted a wild deer on the riverbank and took it
down with a single arrow. After Mithias had finished congratulat-
ing the lizard on his precise aim, we broke our routine of rowing
all day so that we might cook the creature and eat it. The meat
warmed my stomach and helped me continue on through the
currents that continued to push us forward. That night we ate
the meat from the deer once again and I went to sleep under my
blanket with a full stomach.

As I woke in the morning sunlight I felt a chill in my bones.
Just as Theron had said, the days had been getting colder, and
within another day I found myself shivering in the canoe. The
temperature dropped, and once again we maneuvered down the
river between snaking valleys and snowy plains. With the cold
air setting in we said less and less and I began to observe my
companions. For some reason, my eyes chose to fall upon Ariel
whenever they had the chance.

Her majestic, almost holy, presence was striking and brought
about warm feelings inside me despite the cold weather. I could
never be sure if my other two comrades felt it, but when I was
near her she had a certain nurturing air that set in around the
canoe. Perhaps some sort of enticing bewitchment brought my

eyes to her, but at the moment I did not care, for my weary bones clung to whatever fire they could find. Her presence alone raised my spirits, and in this dark time I did not question it.

On the eve of the fifth week, Mithias was guiding his boat down the river through the valley as Theron slept. I sat behind Ariel and could see frost forming on the edges of her exposed wings in front of me. All was silent as the night descended, for the cold that encroached about us stung like a thousand bees all over my body. Ariel was looking around like a lost animal in the cold weather, shivering all the while.

"Are you cold?" I dumbly asked. Of course she was cold, she was wearing the least amount of clothing and her wings were constantly exposed to an air she had never experienced before. On top of that, the only blankets we had were worn and ridden with holes.

"Yes," she responded through clattering teeth. When she spoke I could see her breath flow away in the wind and dissipate into nothingness. Without thinking, I removed my cloak and placed it over her wings. As the wind hit my exposed arms, they twitched from the immediate shock, but I paid it no mind.

"Are you sure?" she asked me as I delicately laid the cloak upon her wings.

"Yes, take it," I replied with a quivering voice as my arms pulsated with pain. I did my best to hide my pain as she smiled and brought in her wings so that they could hide themselves completely under the cloak. The cloak soon became damp from the melting frost on her wings. I was about to retract my hand when she grabbed my arm.

"Stick close, it will keep us warm," she said without a smile. Ariel leaned back onto my torso and wrapped my arm around her stomach. My hands began to shake madly, but Ariel seemed to pay no mind to this as she leaned against me and pulled my arm closer to her body.

"Body heat," she began as she pulled my arm toward her chest. "The closer we are, the warmer we will become."

The two of us huddled together and my hand slowly stopped quivering. Ariel crossed her arms and leaned against me as she gazed at the distant sky above the steep valley walls. The angel must have been tired, for she slowly drifted off into a deep slumber. She breathed softly as her head graced my breast, and whenever I had to guide the canoe I did so with the utmost care as not to wake her.

Time seemed to stand still as we drifted down the river. Just as my eyes began to grow heavy, Mithias beckoned me. He had set aground on a snowy shore, and I was quick to follow him. He hopped out of his canoe before turning to me with a bashful smile painted across his worn features.

"Don't get too comfortable, lad. We need to set up camp," he remarked with a stupid grin across his face. Upon hearing the man's voice, Theron woke up and slowly stepped out of the boat. Mithias reached into his canoe, where part of the buck's carcass was laid, and pulled it out onto the snow while Theron began to gather the blankets. Ariel continued to sleep all the while.

I looked down at her and whispered in her ear, "We've found a place to sleep for the night."

"I'll start the fire," she said in between yawns as she handed me my cloak. She took several steps away from me before stopping her stride and turning back.

"Thank you for keeping me warm," she said with a kind smile and a nod.

With a confidence I had never known, I simply replied, "Of course."

I dragged the canoe farther onto the shore before joining my three companions at the camp. Ariel started a fire from thin air using her magic, while Theron unfurled our blankets. Mithias came back from a nearby wood soon after this with several thick, sturdy branches we used to cook the deer meat on. The carcass now had little meat on it, so Theron and Mithias agreed to hunt the next morn. The two had become closer through their hunting, and as we set ourselves down at the campfire the lizard and the man sat next to each other. As we began to eat the meat and warm up next to the fire, Mithias spoke in a tone that was unlike our usual lighthearted banter.

"You know," he said as he chewed a large haunch of meat. "I was just thinking."

"That's new," Ariel stated with a smile in between a bite of meat. Mithias paid no mind to her as he continued to inhale his food.

"Once we warn the capitol of the Thundrian forces, what shall we do?" He continued as he chewed. Silence was all about us as we each contemplated the question for the first time since our departure from Wercon.

"If the king holds any sense to him he will declare war," Theron mumbled as dreaded images of battle filled my mind. "If Thundrian forces have taken my home, that means they approach from the east. They will be upon the capitol in the coming weeks."

"That's not a given," I said with hope in my heart.

"Yes it is," Theron quickly snapped back. As he continued speaking, the hope in my heart dimmed. "If you had seen the initial attack at Wercon, you would know. Their bestial army relentlessly moves forward like an unending current and strikes with the force of a blacksmith's hammer on hot steel."

In an attempt to quell Theron I declared, "There's always hope that their forces are rogue."

"Perhaps we will not have to fight," added Ariel. "My father wishes for me to return to the east after we deliver our message. I will need assistance to get home."

"You cannot make it," Theron replied sternly as he gazed to the fire. "The army attacked us from the eastern woods. Their forces are likely scattered through the trees that separate us from the far eastern shore. It would be impossible for one to sneak past their ranks."

Silence lingered in the air for a moment as each one of us waited for reassurance from another in our group. No such words of hope were said, however. Instead, Theron spoke the terrible truth.

"We will have to fight," he declared. With that, our conversation ended for the night as the blaze of the fire drew our attention. We ate without conversation, then swiftly bedded down for the night. As I lay awake I thought of what the future might hold for me.

I hated the idea of battle. I had killed a single man in my entire life, yet the image of his soul haunted me more with every passing day. The man's wild, staring eyes still lingered in the back of my mind and appeared to me when I closed my eyes. This was certainly not a time to think of the fallen, yet his bloodied face that longed for respite haunted me as my eyelids grew heavy. My mind delved deeper into that terrible act as the night flowed on.

Killing a man had been a terrible experience that no one should ever have to face. During the actual kill, fury overtook me and revenge guided my blows, but after all was said and done, I had felt a pain greater than any physical torture would ever cause. Guilt, fear, anger, agony—all of these emotions flowed through me with a force that none could ever comprehend, yet astonishingly enough, they had dampened in my own mind as time continued. These feelings, along with the woe of loosing my home, had been nearly unbearable just after the reality of my crime had sunk in, for they initially plagued me at every waking moment. Yet now, as I lay under the stars, the pain I once felt was reduced to lingering irritation. I did not know whether to praise or condemn the absence of guilt in my heart, and I prayed that once we reached the capital of Finre I would find peace. Deep down, though, I realized that this was nothing but wishful thinking, and for hours I lay awake in agony.

CHAPTER 9

The days in the canoe got colder than ever as we headed north, and at times it amazed me that the water in the rushing river was not frozen over. Upon the thirty-first day of travel from Wercon, the valley faded away and we were graced with a pine forest where each tree was covered in a thick coat of frost that reflected off the crystal clear water. Had the cold not stung me with such fervor, I would have praised the beauty of my surroundings, but as fate would have it I wished to get through this place as fast as possible. During this day a change in our travel came about. Midway through the afternoon, Theron told Mithias to beach the canoe on a nearby shore. The captain did as he was told with Ariel and I following his example. Once ashore, Theron hopped out of the canoe he shared with Mithias and took a deep breath.

"This is it," he declared as he reached into the canoe and took out his bow and quiver. "We will make rest of the journey toward the capitol on foot."

"How long until we reach the city?" Mithias asked as he, too, jumped from the canoe. He steadied himself on the ground and stretched his arms high into the air before swinging his axe from the boat to his shoulder, where it found rest.

"Two days," responded Theron. The lizard began to walk without hesitation into a dense forest that reeked of mildew and decay, and we followed his steps like children following a parent. Thus, for two days we traveled through the woods toward the capitol of Finre. We headed northeast by day and slept in our blankets under the dark canopy of leaves and branches at night. The forest was one that no man should have to traverse, for the night air was filled with unholy sounds from creatures not even Theron could identify. The cold, frost-encrusted woodland stretched for miles upon miles, and finally, after two days of rough travel, the trees slowly gave way to a grand field. Our party smelled foul from the deathly stench of the forest, and our bones were stiff and sore, yet we had arrived. As the last trees vanished behind us, a beacon of light greeted our eyes. The capitol city of Finre was finally in sight, after five long weeks of travel. It gleamed against the snow like a drop of dew in the morning sun and was like no city I had ever seen.

From where we stood on a small hill I could see the general architecture of the city unfold before my eyes. It was built around two mountains that sat adjacent to the sea. Outside of the city gates were many wooden shanties where peasants went about their work. The land was not fertile and warm, so—according to Theron—instead of farming, the men who lived in these shanties made their way toward the woods where they extracted sap from the trees to produce fine syrups to trade. The trees that did not produce quality sap were cut down and the lumber sold while other bands of men hunted for prime game. Others still worked within mines deep below the city, and even at our distance we could hear the sound of quarrymen chipping away at rock. Within the confines of the city, the buildings were made from stone and had curved roofs that were freshly powdered with newly fallen snow.

City streets spiraled around the two unbelievable mountains until they reached flattened peaks atop each mountain. On the top of the southernmost peak was a massive gleaming marble castle that looked down upon the entire city. The castle shone against the clear sun and looked like a candle that lit up the very heavens and earth. On the peak of the northern mountain was a gigantic gold statue. Despite my distance, I could see a marvelous bridge that spanned the length between the castle and statue. I could make out several staircases that led up to this bridge, and small dots traversed them. Mithias handed me the spyglass that he carried on his waist so I could look more closely at the city.

Once I held the spyglass up to my eye, I saw the tarnished golden statue was of the mighty warrior from the days of old for whom I had been named. He stood tall and wore only tattered rags that were made to look like they were stained with blood. Under his right foot was a slain serpent, and his left arm held a sword high into the air. I noticed that he had a scar that stretched from his right temple to his cheek. The scar was the warrior's most notable feature, for it was etched in silver and gleamed in the high afternoon sun. I released my eye from the spyglass and looked at the span of the city once again. It stretched for miles around the mountains, and as I took in all the sights I couldn't help but fall victim to childlike bewilderment. Ariel's voice graced the air.

"The ocean is near," she began as she closed her eyes. "I can hear the waves."

"I guess it's true," Theron responded as he turned toward Ariel. "Angels do have the strongest ears in the land. The ocean is to the northeast, not far outside the city gates.

"Why do they not use it as a port?" I quickly asked as I handed Mithias his spyglass.

"No ship can pass through those waters," Mithias responded as he put away his instrument. "Rocks jut up from the ocean like massive swords, and in all my years I have never come across a crew brave enough to traverse it."

"'Tis a shame," Theron replied in a low voice as he gazed at the city. "Such a grand city should have a fine port to trade her wares. Instead, the men must travel for miles down the southern coast until they find the port city of Arleyard. Calmer tides grace her docks."

I could have marveled at the grandiose capitol city all day, but Theron had different plans.

"Come, we seek audience with the king," started the lizard as he began to walk toward the city. "With every passing minute, the Thundrians ravage the lands. We have no time to waste."

The four of us began to walk toward the city, and as we drew closer, I could truly admire the grand scale of the city among the barren environment. The main doors to the city, which were wide open, had to be at least ten times my height and had intricate curves and patterns of blue and gold etched into them. Twenty guards stood present at the gate, and after a quick conversation with Theron they moved aside and admitted us through the entry to the city.

Inside, the four of us stood in an open square with a circular grass knoll in the center. No snow was on the grass, and it was surprisingly green and well kept. At the center of the grass was a sizeable fountain with three ornate pillars arranged in a triangular fashion, spewing water forth. In the center of the fountain a large stream of water shot up and drenched the three surrounding pillars. A plaque was in front of the fountain, and Ariel began to read it aloud in her angelic voice.

"For those who may traverse these lands let it be known: at this site the holiest of treasures lies. Not a treasure worth its weight in gold, but one that will preserve the years. May no angel, man, or lizard behold it. Neither the tyrant nor the martyr may hold it beside their throne."

"What does that mean?" I quickly asked Theron. I figured if any of us knew the meaning of the plaque, it would be him. To me, he seemed more learned in the workings of this land than anyone else.

"None know," he responded as he stared at the fountain. "This city was built here for a reason. In the times of old, when settlers first scoured the land and sought a place to build, they came upon this fountain. Their people grew strong from its waters and could work faster after drinking it. Because of this new resolve, they chose to build their city here."

"Did these same settlers erect the statue?" I asked as I pointed to the statue of Lloyd that loomed above us to the northwest.

"Over two hundred years ago, that statue was made after a great battle was fought here," Theron explained in a mystified voice. He pointed to the peak briefly before adding, "When the tyrants of old times allowed slavery, one slave trader brought Lloyd and a group of outcast lizards into the city. The boy was forced to fight in an arena atop that very peak."

I had heard much of Lloyd's story in the lands of Alfras and Thundria, but never had I learned of his time in Finre or Drientus. I was quick to ask, "What happened to him?"

The lizard smiled a grand smile as he proclaimed, "Along with a great lizard companion, he broke out and freed the city. Together, they murdered the tyrant that lorded over the city and led a campaign across this land. As all know, that campaign led to the downfall of the wretched king who had stationed himself in the Thundrian capitol."

I looked at the statue of the angelic hero as Theron turned to me and added, "You should be proud to have his name."

"I hear that a lot," I replied as I averted my eyes to Mithias and Ariel, who had made their way to the edge of the fountain.

"So can we take a drink from the fountain?" asked Mithias as he peered into the waters.

Theron hesitated for a moment before replying in a hushed tone, "No. The king of this place... he does not allow it."

Before anyone else could talk, Theron declared, "Come, let us make for the palace atop the southernmost peak."

"Will he accept us into his court?" I asked as Theron began to walk away. Our lot followed him in step through the crowds of workers and traders as he frowned and turned around.

"He accepts all who seek him, yet few attempt to," said the lizard in a soft voice.

"Why is that?" Ariel asked before I could voice the same question.

Theron continued with the same frown upon his face. "This king, he is malevolent beyond all measure." His voice became nothing short of a whisper as he added, "He is known for being a full-fledged fool who knows nothing of honor or tradition."

Mithias was quick to ask, "How does such a man rule?"

"The same reason any king rules," Theron said as we made our way through the city. "His blood."

Before any of us could respond, Theron beckoned us onward and hurried his step. As we ascended the gigantic staircases on each level of the mountain it was obvious how the land was laid out. When we walked about the first level we beheld the sick and poor, who lived in shacks made from driftwood or worn brick. The constant clanging of pickaxe against rock could be heard until we ascended to the second level. The shanties gave way to the stone houses with the curved roofs I had seen earlier.

These houses got bigger and bigger as we ascended, and soon I found myself surrounded by regal homes that seemed to be infinitely larger than my village hut. We must have walked for an hour before we reached the grand castle atop the southernmost peak. My legs were tired and my ears felt as if they were going to explode, but finally we stood before the ornate staircase that led to the castle.

"All this wealth shadows the peasants," Ariel muttered as I took my first step on the staircase. Her words were more literal than I initially thought. I turned around for a moment to see that the castle shadowed parts of the city as the sun started its decline into the western sky.

"The minority who reside here hold the majority in the palms of their hands," replied Theron as he continued past the massive houses toward the castle. "The people of this city dare not rebel against their powerful leader. It is known all too well that he commands great power through his malice and greed."

"Wonderful," said Mithias, "The man we seek—the one who could stand up to Thundria—is a cruel dictator."

"We must take what help we can get," murmured Theron as he continued to lead us toward the great citadel. "Now let us compose ourselves. We must bestow upon him all our honors if we are to have a chance of receiving help."

Once we reached the top of the steps I beheld the full scope of the citadel. The castle was enormous, at least twice the size of my whole village. It stretched into the sky as if it were an affront to the Divine Two themselves and lingered about clouds that rolled by us where we stood. The guards who stood before the ostentatious entryway asked us to state our business once we were before them. After Theron stated that he was a prince and wished to see the king, they warned us of his ill temper before permitting us to enter the citadel. A single guard led us through a labyrinth of halls, which were deserted except for a single lizard. This soul was impossible to miss, and as he stormed by us toward the exit, I examined him thoroughly.

This lizard was like a wall and walked with a stride greater than all of ours. He was at least twice my size, maybe more, and carried a blade that spanned the length of my body in his right hand. From his head shot six finely polished horns that were quite long. His gold and diamond armor clanged as he bumped into me. His force was so great that he knocked me to the ground in an instant. He glared at me with crescent red eyes as he snarled.

"Watch your step, human!"

Once the lizard was past us Mithias helped me to my feet and remarked, "I didn't know they came that big."

Theron looked at the fleeing lizard with wondering eyes for a moment before stating, "There is something strange about that one."

After a short spell of silence, Ariel asked, "Theron? Are you okay?"

The ranger shook his head quickly before turning back to our lot and remarking, "Let us continue. We did not come this far to be distracted by such pestilence."

The maze of corridors eventually gave way to a massive scarlet door, which stood wide open. We entered the door to behold a chamber laden with gold and marble. The walls were carved tapestries that gleamed as torch fire danced over them. At the center of the gleaming riches and ancient artifacts sat a fat, dark man. In front of him was a massive table with a feast fit for twenty men. All types of exotic animal meat lay on platters about the table. Flies swarmed around the man's meal, but he paid them no mind as he held a flank of meat that he eyed as if it were gold. As we entered I saw him take a massive bite out of the meat and wipe his mouth with a stained rag.

He was a short, plump man whose face was coated with meat and grime. An amazing jeweled crown lay crookedly on his balding scalp. He had hair on the sides of his head that fell down to his neck, yet the top of his head was bare. The hair that fell all about him was greasy and shone against the torchlight of the chamber. The king's enormous belly was wedged up against the table, and I could see that his purple satin robe was stained with food. As he chewed with an open mouth I saw that he had lost half his teeth, and those that remained were tarnished.

To his right was a man whose skin was as pale as holy light. I believed that if he stood against the snow he would be nearly invisible, yet he wore a black robe that covered his whole body.

The robes were tied around him with a simple braided rope, and as we entered a sinister smile played on his face under his hood.

"What brings a tattered lot of peons to my hall?" the king asked as he slammed his hand down on the table and sent the meat flying. "Can't I enjoy a good meal in peace?"

I stood as Theron knelt down before the slob.

"Sir Gwain," Theron began with his face to the ground.

"You shall call me 'your majesty' while you remain in my court," the king shot back as he picked up the meat that had fallen. "None speak my name in these hallowed halls."

"Yes, your majesty," Theron replied in a somber voice as he raised his head. "I am surprised, though. You do not recognize me?"

The king swallowed another bite and briefly looked over Theron in his dirty clothes from our weeks of travel.

"The common folk hold no place in my eyes," he scoffed as he reached for a biscuit. The man's rudeness caused me to hate him almost instantly, yet I stayed my tongue. Ariel proved more vocal.

"Theron is anything but common!" she shouted.

Theron looked distressed as Mithias calmly asked, "You do not recognize a prince of your lands?"

"A prince? Of what province?" the king asked as his eyebrows rose.

Theron instantly replied, "Wercon, sir, to the southeast."

The king spat at his reply. A soggy, half-eaten piece of meat landed on the table before he spoke.

"Wercon?" he began in a menacing tone. He examined a biscuit and paid it more mind than he did Theron. After taking a bite he was quick to exclaim, "The village of rogue lizards that worship the creatures of the wood more than their king? The home of Finre's finest fools and foragers?"

Theron looked at the floor, and it was clear he had been hurt. I would not stand by as my friend was insulted. "We have not traveled across land and water to be snubbed like the good people of your kingdom. We have urgent news the likes of which you must hear!"

King Gwain quickly shot back, "Then out with it, boy! And mind your tone. If your voice rises so it echoes in this chamber

I shall eject your whole lot, and your fat friend would do well to maintain his temper."

Before Mithias could speak, Theron momentarily regained his composure and declared, "My king, Wercon has fallen to an army of the unknown. A great force threatens this land."

The king pushed his chair back and clumsily hobbled to his feet. He waddled around the table with difficulty and came to stand in front of Theron. He looked up at the lizard as his pale companion stood behind him. The king displayed a sly smile as he spoke.

"What would you have me do, lizard?" he asked in a menacing tone as he took another bite from his diminishing biscuit. The man chewed the bread with an open mouth so that crumbs spewed forth as he stood before Theron.

"I cannot advise a king, sir," Theron quickly stated.

Before the king could talk, Mithias bellowed, "But I can!"

Mithias approached the king and towered over him as he spoke with anger laced all about his heavy breath. "Theron has spoken highly of this kingdom. He says your shields are as thick and your blades are broad. Deploy your troops to the eastern wilds and take back the lands that were once yours!"

"Mind your tongue," the pale man shrouded in black garments behind the king quickly remarked to Mithias. "You speak to a king."

Mithias paid no attention to the man and stared down at the king to gauge his response.

"Lizard," the king began as he walked to the edge of his table. "What flag do these invaders bear?"

"The flag of Thundria," Theron said with the utmost confidence in his voice.

"Thundria? You would have me fight the strongest nation in existence?" the king asked in an annoyed tone. A slight smile appeared on his face. The conversation almost seemed to amuse the little fat man.

"This city is well fortified," said Theron. "I suspect that they are no ragtag group of sell-swords or deserters. Thundria has terrible, inhuman creatures at their disposal that ruthlessly slaughtered all the people of my village. They will come here, but from behind these walls we can hold them off before chasing them from our lands."

The king was silent for a moment as he turned to the remnants of the biscuit in his hand. The man eyed the last bite for a moment before tossing it aside. It rolled into the dark corner of his chamber, where he paid no mind to it.

"And if we did fight them," he began in a menacing voice, "and if by some instance we won, my city would lie in ruins and my people would be slain. The survivors would hardly give me the respect I deserve." He paused for another moment before declaring, "I cannot risk such a battle."

The pain Theron felt was clearly painted across his features and his whole face sagged. We all felt the same agony he did, but Mithias was first to voice his disdain.

"This is a force that has already destroyed Alfras and Wercon. Now they speed toward your walls! This battle will come whether you prepare or not. Have you not heard of the losses in the southern islands?

At this notion the king returned to his dirtied throne and paid no mind to the man's shouts. "Word of the rampage to the south has reached my ears, yet Finre will not fall to the same fate as the lawless ones to the south," he declared.

"Of what do you speak?" I shot back as he leaned back onto the throne.

The kings eyes met mine as he spoke. "I have heard much of you, Lloyd," he started before he motioned toward the cloaked man, who had moved silently to the side of the throne. "High mage Geno tells me much of the journey your company has endured."

Just as he said this, the massive blue lizard we had passed in the hall earlier walked into the room. His sword was sheathed, yet at his side stood a mass of at least twenty guards.

"You found Theron in Wercon, and now you are here in my courts," the king said to me with a smile. As he smiled, the wail of an eagle entered my ears. Within seconds of the noise entering my head, a grand eagle with a wingspan that matched the length of my sword flew into the room and perched on the extended arm the pale man who stood by the king. The doors slammed shut behind the bird.

"Eagles are amazing creatures," stated the king as he glanced at the magnificent bird. "The high mage employed by me has known this eagle since birth. One could say that the eyes of the bird act as his eyes."

"The eagle saw us," whispered Theron with dread as he stared at the creature that sat atop the dark man's arm.

The king placed both of his arms on the sides of his throne as he leaned forward and motioned toward the man in dark garb.

"You see, high mage Geno came to me just a week ago with news of the Thundrian invasion," he said with a deceitful smile. The pale man slowly nodded as the king continued. "He told me of our enemy's numbers, and told me of what became of Alfras. Then I was given a choice between life or death, freedom or enslavement."

"You wouldn't..." I began. The king smirked.

"I acted on behalf of my kingdom," he quickly spat back as he leaned back in his throne and clasped his hands together. "Why risk war when a simple surrender will end all battles and allow me to hold my throne?"

Mithias drew his axe and readied himself for a fight, yelling, "You're a coward who supports genocide and chaos!" Two guards quickly rushed Mithias from behind, yet their attempts to contain the giant captain were futile. Mithias took them out with a single blow and stood ready for a second wave. The guards instantly encircled our lot with their weapons drawn. Mithias circled like a caged animal trying to judge who would approach him next.

"The Thundrians are murderers! You must avenge the fallen!" yelled Theron. He still refused to draw his weapon despite the fact that Mithias, Ariel, and I all stood ready for a fight.

The king turned to the pale man to his right and demanded, "Geno, take them to the dungeon!"

Geno nodded to the lizard who stood like a giant. The eagle screamed as the colossal lizard rushed at Mithias. Before Mithias could raise his axe and prepare for a strike, the lizard smashed his claw into the man's chest. Mithias flew through the air for a moment before slamming to the ground, unconscious. The three of us attempted to run to Mithias' side yet were held back by the plethora of guards, who subdued us with ease.

"Marcus, hang these four at tomorrow's dawn. Let them be an example to the people who would question me," the pompous king declared as he looked the gigantic lizard in the eyes. He turned his gaze toward mine, and in a hoarse voice added, "Those who do not support the alliance between Finre and Thundria are traitors to the throne and the new order. This kingdom has no place for the likes of you."

"This is no alliance!" I shouted as two guards held my arms behind my back and began to drag me out of the room. "You are a tyrant and a coward!"

Before I could continue, a guard's armored fist met my face, and the last thing I saw was the blood-red rug beneath my feet before all around me turned to darkness.

CHAPTER 10

A flurry of obscurity enveloped my mind and time seemed to stand still while speeding forward faster than ever. This veil of darkness slowly changed to a welcoming shade of gray before giving way to foreign surroundings the likes of which I had no desire to experience. An immense throbbing pounded against my skull as light from an unknown source flickered against the corner of my eye. From the obscure darkness I heard a voice that echoed within the confines of my mind.

"You coming too, kid?" asked a familiar voice without a face.

My eyes squinted open and moved around for a moment, but everything before me was still a blur. I closed my eyes once more and wished for the sweet embrace of sleep to envelop me, but it would not, for the same voice beckoned me to remain in the land of clarity.

"Come on! This is no time to sleep," came the voice again.

I forced my eyes open to see Mithias standing to my left and looking down at me. He wore tattered rags, and as my head lolled to the side I noticed his belt with various knives and tools was missing. He grabbed my shoulders and sat me upright on a worn stone slab. As soon as Mithias moved me, a sharp pain rang out in my head and my right hand jolted to what I believed to be the source of the wound. As I rubbed it I felt a sticky, ragged surface against my palm. Once I put my hand back in front of my face, I noticed it was stained with blood. I slowly wiped it off on my dirty undergarments.

It was very dark, but from what I could tell I was in a small cell. Mithias grabbed the hand I had run through my hair and, after examining it briefly, looked at my head. As he did so I looked at the steel bars that kept us in our cage. The bars were thick yet tarnished with age. There were no windows anywhere around, so the only light emanated from a candle that sat to my right on the stone slab. Mithias' large head came into my vision as he spoke in a voice that caused my head to thump once more.

"You'll be fine," he stated with a nod. "The bastard gave you a good blow to the head, but I fixed it up."

I grabbed my head tightly with my right hand and turned to him as he slumped against the bars. I looked at the man who normally beamed with confidence and beheld a shell of this former self. His face was bruised and purple from the impact he had endured earlier and he looked more ragged than ever. One of his eyes was swollen and black and there was a massive scratch on his right arm.

"You look awful," I stated frankly.

Through his bruises, Mithias cracked a smile. "The same can be said for you."

Suddenly it hit me. Theron and Ariel were nowhere to be found.

"Where is Ariel?" I quickly spat as I rose to my feet. My head began to throb uncontrollably, so my body instinctively slumped back to the stone slab.

"Calm yourself," Mithias replied before he motioned to the bars. In dim candlelight emanating from the cell across from us I beheld Theron and Ariel. I grabbed my head and slowly stood up so that my skull would not pulsate again. I took two steps to the bars of my cage and in a loud whisper called my friends' names. Theron was the first to respond.

"Are you all right?" he asked as he pulled up his sleeve.

"I'll be fine," I responded.

Ariel approached the bars that bound her to the same cell as Theron. The angel looked tired, and her normally pristine blonde hair was ruffled and foul. She too wore peasant clothing, yet hers was especially dirtied and worn.

"It's good to see you up," she said with a weak smile forced across her face. Her angelic voice echoed through the chamber, and I realized that our cells must be in a larger prison corridor.

"Where are we?" I asked.

Mithias grabbed my shoulder from behind and maneuvered himself to the bars before he spoke. "Theron says we were dragged down here by the guards," he began as he looked out of the cell. In his left hand was the candle. The wax column was nearly depleted and it was clear we would not have the grace of light for much longer.

As the candle flickered, Theron spoke in a somber voice from his cell. "We are in the prison under the castle. Because I held my tongue, the guards simply hauled me down here instead of knocking me out."

"How could you not curse that man?" Ariel asked through a disgusted sigh as she sat down against the wall.

"He is of royal blood, Ariel. I cannot curse a king."

"Mithias didn't have a problem doing so," Ariel said as she looked across the hall at Mithias and me. "Neither did Lloyd."

"Yet you stilled your tongue," Theron shot back. "You cannot call me a coward without calling yourself one."

Ariel was about to spit something back, but Mithias bellowed a command for silence before the two could continue to bicker. His command fell upon willing ears, and within an instant all was silent once more.

"Now is not that time to bicker like idle children," he said, then turned toward me. "We are to be hanged for treason against Finre and Thundria by tomorrow's dawn."

As fear enveloped me I was quick to ask, "Would the public not protest the hanging of Ariel and me because of our age?"

Theron spoke from his cell as he shook his head. "The people here are no normal lot. The guards lust for power and the royals have fallen under a dark cloud that seems to have enveloped the whole populace. I would not be surprised if we were simply declared enemies of the state. By Thundrian law, those who go against the crown face certain death. If the king has adopted that law, as I'm sure he has, none will question his judgment. The poorer folk of the city may even praise a good hanging at the gallows."

"We cannot stay here," Ariel softly stated as she tried to run her fingers through her dirtied hair. It was to no avail, for her locks were terribly tangled.

"Can't you cast a spell to get us out of here, Ariel?" I asked as I grabbed the bars with both hands. She shook her head in disappointment.

"There is something within these castle walls that prevents me from using magic," she said with a frown. "I felt it when we met the king. The dark man behind him cast some sort of veil upon this place that stifles my abilities."

Theron nodded as I turned to Mithias. The normally verbose captain was strangely quiet, so I asked, "What are you thinking of?"

Strangely enough, a slight smile stretched across the man's stoic face. Without turning to me, Mithias sat upon the slab and declared, "Stay put. Once the guards make their rounds to check on us, we'll make our escape."

"How?" Theron and I asked at the same time. Mithias simply waved his hands and smiled as he comfortably leaned back against the stone I had slept on. The candle began to flicker wildly as it breathed its last breaths, but I paid it no mind. Instead, I stood in the darkness and looked on as Ariel took her candle to the back of her cage and laid down on the slab. Theron leaned against the wall and looked up at the ceiling, as if he were daydreaming, so I attempted to do the same, but it was to no avail.

I paced about the cage for three hours as Mithias sat silently on the stone slab. I had been trying to get him to tell me what his master plan was every couple of minutes. My constant questions seemed to wear the man down, and just as I was about to wheedle the plan out of him, I heard footsteps echoing down the hall. Our candle had burned out long ago and we sat in the darkness, so our ears were more attuned to the surroundings than before. The footsteps echoed off the damp dungeon walls, and a light that caused my eyes to squint soon followed their sound.

"It is time," Mithias whispered to me. He cracked his knuckles as he looked at me with a stern gaze and declared, "Forgive me for my silence, lad, but if I were to tell you of my plan you would have surely contested. Do not hold my actions against me, for I only do this to survive."

Before I could react, he quickly grabbed me and slammed me against the back wall with a force that caused my spine to throb. My wail was followed by questions but Mithias did not answer. Instead, he struck my left leg with such a force that it swept out from under me. Ariel let out a screech, and Theron screamed Mithias' name as I lay on the ground, cradling my throbbing leg. Mithias grabbed me by the collar and hauled me to my feet. He held me against the wall as if he were about to batter me again, but instead he waited until a voice rang out in the chamber.

"What's going on here?" demanded the lone guard as he approached the bars.

Mithias donned a look of sheer hate as he shot back, "Be gone with you, guard! This boy's actions have damned me to a swift demise, so by my power I shall end him here tonight!"

"Quiet yourself, prisoner!" shot back the guard. "The boy is to be hanged beside you. His death shall not be by your hand."

Mithias dropped me to the ground and approached the cell bars as he exclaimed, "It was by his order that we came this way! This worthless sack of flesh and bone, curse his name, will die tonight!"

"Enough," the guard said as he peered through the bars. He eyed me suspiciously as I cradled my leg, then he declared, "I will not have his majesty's prisoner killed before his judgment. This boy, along with all of you, will serve as an example to the people." The guard locked eyes with Mithias. "You will be brought to another cell for the rest of your sentence."

The guard's eyes slitted as he approached the bars that Mithias stood directly behind. Like an animal trying to steal food from its master, the guard cautiously extended his candle toward the cage bars. Just as the edge of the candlelight began to illuminate my figure, Mithias lunged for the guard and pulled his whole body against the bars. A look of shock came over the man's face as Mithias grabbed the guard's arms and pulled them through the gaps in the bars. The man opened his mouth as if to screech.

"Scream and I will rip them off," Mithias said calmly as he tugged at the guard's arms. Fear filled the guard's regretful eyes, but his mouth slammed shut. Mithias looked the man up and down before he found the item he sought. Without hesitation, he put both of the guard's hands in one of his and grasped a key ring on the guard's belt.

"Lloyd, if you are able, open the door while I entertain our guest," he said as he tossed the key ring to me.

Despite the intense pain in my leg, I sprang to my feet as hope filled my soul and picked up the key ring. I flipped through the keys and inserted each into the simple lock that held us in our prison. After four attempts, the lock clicked. I began to open the door as the guard walked backward with his hands still through the bars. Mithias held onto him tightly and walked forward with the door.

"Go free the other two," Mithias ordered as I ran to Theron and Ariel's cell.

In the unbearable tension of the moment, I struggled to still my shaking hands and ignore my leg, which pounded relentlessly. It took me a long moment to free my other two companions, but once I did I turned around to see Mithias maneuvering himself so that a barrier of iron no longer stood between him and the foolish guard. Once he stood before the guard, he released his grasp as he swiftly declared, "I want the weapons we entered this place with. Where can I find them?"

The guard shook in fear. "The... the end of the hallway. They are in unlocked wooden chests. All of the prisoners' belongings are stored there."

"Thank you," Mithias responded with a nod toward the shaking man.

In one stroke, he slammed his fist into the man's head and knocked him to the ground. The guard was out cold from the blow. Mithias grabbed the candle that had fallen and began to make his way down the hallway. He rushed forward and beckoned us to do the same. The few prisoners in residence around us begged to be released, yet Mithias granted them no such freedom. I felt bad that I could not help the others, yet I did not know who the scoundrels were or what crimes they had committed.

Some may have been innocent, yet there certainly were murderers and thieves in the bunch, so my soul did not weigh heavy with doubt as we continued forward. Within a brief minute we were at the end of the hall, where a wooden desk was located. Behind the empty chair at the desk were several great chests. Mithias quickly placed the candle on the table and began to rummage through the chest located directly behind the chair.

"Theron, this is yours," he said with a smile as he pulled out an intricate longbow. Its detailed markings seemed to glow in the candlelight and Theron's face brightened as he looked at his weapon. He quickly grasped it before Mithias handed him a quiver full of arrows.

"Mithias, Lloyd, your weapons are in here," said Ariel as she stepped back from an open chest. She watched as Theron strapped on his quiver before making a swift declaration. "We must make haste." Her eyes darted about.

We all agreed on this notion, but it was Theron who spoke up next.

"I can navigate through the myriad of hallways. They kept me conscious on the way down here. Let us rid ourselves of this place."

We all agreed that Theron should lead, so without another word the lizard strung an arrow and slowly ascended a narrow staircase nearby. The stairs were curved in a half circle that was dimly lit by several torches on the wall. We had to be wary not to let our steps echo on the cobblestone, so our progression was slow but our eyes were vigilant. After a moment, more light began to flood into our view and we met with a long hallway. A burgundy velvet rug stretched in front of us and curved around a corner that seemed very far away. Candles hung from the ceiling in between each reinforced door.

"The residents of this place sleep," Theron whispered. "We would do well not to wake them."

The four of us crept down the hallway and turned at the end to see a huge stairwell that continued up a dimly lit passageway. With his bow held taut, Theron led our lot up the staircase. As we walked up I felt a rush of cold air run through my hair and eventually overtake my entire body. Once we reached the top of the stairs, wind flew all about us as cold air slammed at our exposed bodies. I could only see about five paces before me, so Theron took a torch off the nearby wall and continued to press forward, out a door and through an intricate garden. As we walked down a path covered in a thin blanket of snow we found ourselves surrounded by massive hedges and finely crafted statues. We progressed through the gardens with hopes that salvation and freedom lay beyond the hedgerows. I truly believed that soon we would be rid of this place, yet my heart sank as I heard a faint horn in the distance.

"What is that?" I whispered to Theron as the horn continued to sound. He looked toward the walls we had escaped from and raised his voice in agony.

"The guards of the castle know we have escaped—make haste!" His voice bounded across the garden and weaved its way above the wall, where a handful of guards stood. One of them pointed to us while many more dashed down the stretch of the wall. In an instant, the four of us ran through the darkness, stumbling among the roots, weeds and flowers as the guards gave chase. Horns blared like the howls of mad animals as we disappeared from the guards' sight. Soon, we heard the clanking of armor from the walls we had exited. I believed that none of us had a plan of action until a light entered the corner of my eyes. Theron had dropped the torch, and it had quickly caught ablaze as it made contact with the dry, untamed shrubbery that was not coated in snow. Hedges and bushes were quickly engulfed in flame, and soon the whole garden behind us was ablaze. The guards slowed as they struggled to maneuver themselves around the fires, yet their wills were strong and they would not stop. My comrades and I ran as fast as we could before we stopped and came upon a dreadful realization.

We had been running on top of this mountain in the wrong direction. During our whole escape I believed that we were headed toward the colossal steps that would lead us through the city. Instead, we had been running about a courtyard that extended from the castle walls to the edge of a sheer cliff. A wall, a little shorter than Theron, halted our advance. Beyond this wall was a massive fall that led to the stone mansions below.

We stood on a huge circular section of path and looked over the wall as we each tried to figure how to safely get down. I contemplated attempting to climb down the cliff face but all plans of action were instantly repressed as a voice came from behind us.

"That's far enough!" it boomed as large flakes of snow whipped about us.

The four of us turned to see at least three dozen guards facing us down with their weapons. Some held arrows that were eager to escape their masters' grasps while others brandished shining swords that begged for blood. The same voice that had arisen earlier came to our ears once again as a single guard stepped forward.

"You will halt your escape here," declared an armor-clad man. Mithias held his weapon steady, ready to strike as the guard hastily approached. Theron and I took note of his stance and did the same. The soldier gripped his blade tightly as he anticipated a fight. I feared that this would be our final hour, but I was determined to stand strong before the forces that encroached upon us. The reaper seemed to be just over my shoulder until the most unlikely of voices dampened the situation.

"Stop this now!" a familiar voice came from behind the guards. The group of them opened up and a small, fat man strolled between their ranks.

"So you thought you would make it?" the man inquired with a smile. An awful taste came into my mouth as I recognized the stout figure that dumbly grinned at my lot.

"What is a king doing up at such an hour?" Theron asked the man, who paid no mind to his burning garden behind him. Flames rose behind the figurehead of Finre as he took a step toward us.

"Silence yourself, scale-skin!" he shot back as he approached us. He stood just a few paces from us and began to survey our lot with a smirk painted across his plump face. "You pitiful lot of wanderers have been a thorn in my side ever since you crawled before me."

I contemplated striking down the man before dying, but he did not remain within my reach for long. He turned and walked back to his troops and stood safely in their ranks before making a prompt assertion.

"I would have them wait for the gallows tomorrow so that they may serve as an example to the dissidents of my empire, but they are far too crafty to keep locked up. Kill them where they stand and let them rot where they fall."

He turned to walk away. The men who held their arrows began to walk before those who only held swords. In this moment, my body began to shake as my mind raced. A thousand ideas of how to survive the situation instantly flooded my psyche, yet I could not act. I stood like a statue as the archers began to line up before us. I felt the cold hand of the reaper upon my shoulder as the archers readied themselves. There was no doubt in my mind at this moment that I would die under the gentle snowfall of Eurtongard. My journey would end and I would soon join my parents and kin in the afterlife. My left hand felt a great pressure, and I looked to see Ariel squeezing it tightly. She turned to me with the greatest of fears in her reflective eyes. Her eyes almost begged me for salvation, and my heart broke when I realized I could not grant it. The darkest hour of our journey was upon us, and I thought it to truly be our last.

Yet luck was on our side that night, for a roar that brought alarm to even the strongest of men pierced the silent night sky as the archers donned looks of sheer terror. The unholy sound came from my back, and all who stood in the garden turned to look past me. Acting through instinct alone, I turned and beheld the source of such a noise with a gaping mouth and bulging eyes. As my eyes beheld that which I had never seen, I thought myself a fool for believing the illusion before me. I believed the sight was a holy being coming to take me away once an arrow pierced my flesh, yet I felt neither steel nor pain. The creature that had made this sound stood as a testament to sheer strength as it continued to let out a roar that seemed to shake the very mountain I stood on. Soon, four companions of the same kind swooped down from the heavens and landed between my party and the guards.

In all my years of living I had never believed that I would stand before such a creature. What my eyes beheld were five fabled dragons that gazed down at the dozens of souls who stood before them. I stood as if stone bound me, for creatures that were only rumored to exist now looked down upon my party. The largest one, who stood before all others, almost seemed to nod at me before he turned his gaze to the cadre of horror-struck soldiers. Some ran in fear from the fabled beasts, while others stood awestruck. I knew nothing of the nature of these beasts, and as I stared them down I believed that I was closer to death than ever.

The dragons around me were colossal beasts that carried themselves with a grace that was surprising due to their size. They were frightening beyond measure, yet beautiful, for as I beheld them in the torchlight I could see their scales glisten like the ocean at sunset. The one that landed first was the largest of them all—at least twenty feet high at the shoulder. The beast glanced at my group with wild yellow eyes that seemed to pulsate riotously, and then he turned to the soldiers behind us. Against the torchlight, the dragon's pale blue scales lit up my entire body with the radiance of the sun itself. Thousands of steel-like scales lined the creature from head to tail. The creature had to be at least forty feet long, and it dazzled me despite the fact that I was on death's doorstep. The dragon's wingspan was three times his length, and the webbing of the wings stretched as the dragon pushed them behind him. Two long golden chains were hooked onto the first dragon's scales and stretched from his shoulders to his knees. The chains, which were bound by four stakes embedded in the dragon's sides, flailed in the late night wind and echoed through the air with a strangely melodic sound. The few things I knew about the elusive creatures expanded in the next moment as a voice emerged from the dragon, who turned his gaze to the guards.

"Be away with you, peons of unholy accord," demanded the creature. Its voice was deep, like that of an old man, yet with it came unprecedented youthful power. The few guards who remained dropped their weapons and ran, making their way past the king, who turned around in a rage at the fleeing army. In an instant, his rage turned to terror at the sight of the dragons and he screamed. He rushed past his loyal guards and left the four of us at the mercy of the beasts.

Once all the guards of Eurtongard had gone, I looked in terror at the dragons who stared me down with plate-sized eyes. The dragon who first spoke turned to our party and examined us with glowing eyes that seemed to pierce through the darkness of the night. The creature was unknown to me, but I knew his presence had saved my life. I stood before him with feet firmly planted on the ground and listened to his next words carefully.

"Ascend one of my companions," he groaned as his four companions lowered their necks. With little choice in the matter, I scurried up the long neck of one of the dragons without hesitation as Ariel, Mithias, and Theron did the same. I used the scales on the dragon's neck as hand and footholds, and before I knew it I was on the beast's back. He did not so much as flinch as I did this. I noticed a leather strap tied around the base of my dragon's neck. The dragon moved his head to look at me and said in a stern yet benevolent voice, "Put the strap around your body so you don't fall, human."

I pulled the loop around me and tightened it with a small metal buckle. Not far beneath my knees I saw small footholds that resembled stirrups on a steed, so I braced my feet against them. Once I was secure, the dragon turned his head to the night sky, extended his wings into the air, and launched himself off the cliff. Within an instant we were shooting toward the heavens like an arrow. I held onto the strap for my life as both cloud and night rushed past me. A moment of sheer terror seemed to last a lifetime as we rose vertically away from all civilization below us. Finally, the dragon leveled himself off. The leather strap held my body in place and I hesitantly peered over the side of this beast to behold the vast kingdom below. The buildings that had once stood high above me were now mere dots across the snowscape below. I relaxed my grip on the leather strap and looked about me to see a dazzling display.

Soon the other four dragons flew beside mine, and the group of them formed a flying V. The dragons flew to the west, and the icy night air whizzed past me at such a speed that I could hardly bear it. I did not know whether the dragons were leading my lot to salvation or a fate worse than death, and as I held on for dear life I feared the toils of my adventure had just begun.

CHAPTER 11

I was separated from my companions for nearly half an hour as the icy wind battered my skin with such unrelenting force that I thought I would freeze at any moment. Just as I believed that my body could take no more, my dragon instructed me to hold on for my life. I did as the beast commanded just before he swooped down into a large clearing nestled between an endless sea of trees. Once we landed, the dragon did not hesitate to instruct me.

"Get off."

As I began to move, my bones moaned in the cold air of the night. I stepped off the dragon and sank into the ankle-deep snow. The freezing sensation cut into the soles of my feet, yet I did not notice this at that moment, for the sight of the five dragons before me held all my attention. My friends soon stepped off their dragons, and the four of us looked over the five beasts, who were illuminated by the light of the two moons. A moment of silence was all about us as a light snow drifted to the ground. The dragons looked to us as if we were foreign creatures, then one spoke.

"Are you sure this is the one?" the dragon Ariel had ridden asked the largest dragon, who had led the flying V. A smile seemed to stretch across this dragon's face as he nodded at me.

"I could not forget such a face," he replied as he looked me over with crescent eyes. "This is Lloyd."

Despite the fact that we stood before fabled beasts of myth and lore, Mithias could not quiet himself. "How do you know his name, creature?" Mithias asked in a defiant tone.

The dragon leveled a gaze at the man. "It seems you're as feisty as ever, Mithias," He scanned over all of us. "Your brows grow heavy and your lips are crooked. You long for an explanation, yes?"

I nodded, and my comrades agreed that we desired a proper explanation. The dragon held a distant gaze as he spoke.

"Alas, to tell you everything would bind you to your fate," he replied as his head lowered.

I inquired as to what the dragon's words meant just as I felt warm air from his massive mouth pass by me. He replied with haste.

"In time you shall know, Lloyd.... In time all shall become clear to you and your companions. I cannot tell you all I know, for you four must unveil your destiny on your own," the dragon replied in a drawn-out fashion. His words struck a deep chord within my heart, and as he spoke them I found my mind spinning. I looked at him with an unease about me that was clearly recognized in his deep amber eyes.

"You do not trust me?" he asked.

The beast who stared me down was a powerful creature who I believed could easily kill a dozen men in the blink of an eye. His breath was warm and his scales were built like plate armor, yet amid all this power he held an honest gaze. His crystal eyes lightened as I confidently declared, "No, I trust you, dragon. You saved my company from certain death. Though I know not of what you speak, were you an enemy you would have incinerated us by now."

As the last remnants of fear diminished within my heart, I bent one knee and lowered my head in respect before adding, "I thank you on behalf of my party."

I heard his elderly laugh echo off the trunks of the trees and dart through the surrounding woods as I knelt. Feeling the need to end his mockery, I stood up and faced him.

"You laugh at my gesture?" I asked innocently.

The dragon shook his head and let the laugh rid itself of him before declaring, "To see you bow before me is a strange sight indeed."

Before I could question the dragon once again, he spoke in a more collected voice.

"Lloyd and company... no more questions tonight. We shall rest until the sun hangs high in the sky. Once the time is right, we will take you southwest."

The dragon then turned sideways and sat down before extending his left wing. Through the forest, a fierce wind began to stir up, whipping my hair in front of my eyes.

The lead dragon, whom none of us had ridden, looked at his four companions and called, "Tartania, Yarcti, Heruon, and Jeauq!"

Each responded to its respective name instantly. All listened intently as the dragon looked toward us and said, "Shield the small ones from the howling winds of the northern night."

The five dragons encircled my company in a shelter of sorts, and the fierce winds died down as their warm bodies surrounded us. We were relatively warmer, but the snow that fell continued to chill us. The dragons seemed to notice this, for each dragon extended its left wing toward the center of the shelter they had made. Thus, we were provided with a relative amount of cover from the unforgiving environment. Soon we were warm from the intense body heat of the immense creatures.

"Do you think we can trust these beasts?" Theron asked as he eyed the bodies of the dragons all around us.

"If they wanted to kill us, they would have done so already," I softly stated in the hope that the creatures could not hear me.

Ariel was the first to nod at these words. She stretched out her pristine wings as she yawned and stated, "My mind is wary in the company of these beasts, but my limbs grow tired after our escape."

Surprisingly enough, her statement brought a wave of fatigue about me, and despite our remote feelings of fear we chose to sleep. My exhaustion led me to the long, thick tail of a burgundy dragon. Without thinking twice, I placed myself upon the tail and attempted to use it as a bed. The scales were uncomfortable yet warm and, despite my unease about these creatures, my body soon fell into the gentle lull of sleep.

Several hours went by before I was awakened. As I beheld the brilliant sun I instantly realized that it was midafternoon. The tail of the dragon I slept on was slightly shaking from side to side, so I sat up and looked at him with drooping eyes. He turned to me and said, "We must fly, human."

I stepped off his tail and noticed the other dragons were waking up my friends. It was strange to me that these creatures were all so tightly knit. They worked like a regiment of strong soldiers, each one waking up at the same time, and each one following orders from a superior officer who, in this case, was the aqua-coated dragon who knew my name. The beasts had been deemed elusive and savage by my people and most others all around the world, yet, as I watched them converse under the bright sun, I viewed them as wise and sophisticated creatures who exhibited greater manners than most humans I had come across. The lead dragon with two long gold chains adorning either side of his body approached my lot and spoke in a commanding tone as we drearily meandered about.

"Are you ready to depart?" he asked my group.

Mithias was quick to answer him. "What about food? We haven't eaten since yesterday."

"And you shall not eat again until late tonight," the dragon shot back.

"Two days without food? I shall starve before then!" Mithias said.

The dragon whose tail I had slept on smiled as he looked at my plump companion and remarked, "You'll be fine, human."

"Heruon is right," the lead dragon declared with a nod. "We must take flight now."

This dragon lowered his head to us as he added, "You will all mount me today. In the night I have put the reins of the others on myself. Danger is all about in these dark times, and I want to keep you close. My kin shall scout the skies all around us and make sure we are safe."

Having little choice in our fate, the lot of us fastened ourselves onto the leather harnesses and readied ourselves for flight. The dragon turned to his comrades, asked them if they were ready, and upon their confirmation, shot up into the sky. Once the trees below us became mere dots I looked toward the horizon and marveled at the landscape that stretched in front of me.

We flew over mountains, forests, and lakes at speeds I had never thought could be achieved. From atop the dragon, lakes seemed like puddles among patches of grasslike forests. Occasionally, bears or packs of wolves could be spotted hunting on the vast landscape, yet they seemed to blur as we rode on. Never in my wildest dreams had I believed that I would sit atop a dragon and survey the frigid landscape as if I were a god. I was uneasy at the might of the huge beasts that sped us to the southwest, yet the beauty of the day captivated me with such ferocity that it set my mind at ease even as the cold winds relentlessly battered me.

After many hours of flight, the sun finally vanished beneath the horizon, but within minutes of this occurrence I saw a thick smoke rising from the trees in the distance. The dragons began to descend into a patch of open snow amid the trees as a light snow began to fall once again. The beasts slowed their speed and descended as the source of the smoke revealed itself against the setting sun.

Nestled at the edge of the tree line in the clearing was a small cabin. The five dragons landed in front of it, and my company unfastened our leather straps before making our way to the ground. As I observed my surroundings, the dragon that we had ridden let out a great roar that could be heard for miles.

A single man emerged from the cabin. He was a grizzly old fellow with short, dark hair and a beard that stretched to his chest. His eyes were dark from age, yet muscles bulged from his arms and a warm smile stretched across his old face as he approached us. He wore a loose leather vest and thick cloth pants and beamed as he stood before the dragon.

"Mordikai!" he yelled at the feet of the dragon I had ridden. The man wrapped his hands around the dragon's neck in an embrace. As he did this, a woman emerged from the house with two boys at her side and an infant in her arms. The boys smiled as they beheld Mordikai and rushed toward him with youthful exuberance. Their innocence reminded me of my sister, and my heart sank as I thought of her. Instantly, a terrible longing fell upon my broken heart as a vision of her face overtook the environment around me. I knew I would not be seeing her for quite a while. I felt lightheaded and watched as a darkness crept into the corners of my eyes, but after a brief shake of my head I was able to pull myself back to the present.

The two children tried to climb the dragon's legs as they laughed, and this made the dragon release a warm smile the likes of which I had not seen stretch across his face before.

"What brings you here, friend?" the man asked as his wife came to his side.

Mordikai motioned toward my lot. "I am fulfilling an old duty entrusted to me by a long-lost friend."

The man's smile began to fade as he looked at the four of us. He slowly shook his head and let out a sigh amid the boys' celebration. He looked at the dragon with a stern, worried expression that stained his face as he spoke.

"Then this must be Lloyd?" he asked in a voice that bordered on a whisper.

"I am sure of it," stated the creature. The man then hobbled toward us. He greeted the four of us with a simple nod before ordering his wife and children inside. Once they were gone, the man began to walk toward his cabin as he spoke in a wise, old voice.

"You must forgive my rudeness," he began as the four of us took step behind him. "Your arrival begins a new cycle of events that I have dreaded for too long."

I was confused beyond words and wondered who the man could possibly be. I had never met him or the dragons before, yet they all seemed to know me, and now my presence was associated with dreaded events. The old man led us to a crude circle of logs on the south side of his cabin. He sat down on a log and motioned for us to do the same as Mordikai knelt beside him. The other four dragons sat in the distance, just within ears' reach. As I sat, I looked at my companions in a desperate attempt to quell my anxiety.

It was clear Theron did not feel as overwhelmed as the rest of us, for he turned to the head dragon and asked, "Mordikai is it?" The dragon nodded his head. "Can you tell us what is going on here?"

At this comment the dragon confidently replied, "I know much, yet I can tell you little, though I shall do my best to put your minds at ease."

I sat down on a large log and shared it with Ariel. Mithias leaned against the cabin as Theron stood in front of the colossal dragon who began to speak as he brought his eyes to mine.

"Lloyd, you went to the capitol city of Finre with your company to warn the king of Thundria's armies, correct?" he asked. I nodded, so he continued.

"And once there you discovered the king had sided with the enemy. He imprisoned you for not taking his side, is this so?"

"This is all true," I said as I straightened myself on the log and leaned forward. Curiosity overpowered my unease, so I asked, "How do you know all of this?"

"I can only tell you that a dear friend has informed me of these events," he said as the corners of his eyes squinted. "At the moment, for me to say otherwise would be devastating to your company. I know a great many things that would put your souls in a state of unrest, so, by command of a dear friend, I must be careful with my words."

Mithias was quick to state, "That doesn't sound very trustworthy." All eyes fell to him. He stood up straight and asked, "Who is this dear friend you speak of? How do we know you are helping us and not leading us into a trap?"

As Mithias asked this, the other dragons stirred in their positions across the clearing. It was clear that some were attempting to spy on our conversation, but Mordikai paid them no mind. Mordikai's next words quelled their unrest.

"This friend of mine is one you know but do not see. My friend will make his presence known to you when the time is right, but until then all I can say is that his words will guide you as they guide me. As for my reliability, I have ruled the dragons for centuries, and any dragon can tell you that I am trustworthy."

"But where are these dragons?" Ariel inquired. "Few have ever seen your kind, and to my knowledge yours is a race of sadistic beasts."

The dragon let out a sigh at this and looked to the sky as he spoke. "Harsh words toward my kind are newborn in this young world, little angel. Hundreds of years ago, there was a great war. My kin fought alongside those who wished to protect the virtues of freedom and liberty across the lands. In the battles that ensued, I watched my friends and family fall to steel and magic."

Theron was quick to ask, "Do you mean the great war against Thundria over two centuries ago? The slave rebellion in which the great hero Lloyd fought alongside your kin?"

"The very one," the dragon replied. His eyes fell to Ariel's as he added, "Though it was much more than a rebellion. The entire world was in conflict...."

"Then you must be over two hundred years old!" I remarked.

The dragon shook his head as he continued to speak with a compassionate voice.

"I am far over two hundred years old, child. My people see many more days than yours do."

Theron's wit continued to prod at the dragon's story. "If you helped mankind so long ago, why hide from them now?" he asked as he leaned forward.

The dragon shook his head. "Despite our strides in the Great War, my kind was slowly cast aside after the generation of soldiers who fought alongside our ranks perished from this world. Their children and grandchildren fell victim to gossip and fear. Before I knew it, the sons and daughters of those who had pledged friendship to my kind demanded that we no longer burden them with our presence. Many long, cold generations of man, angel, and lizard alike have passed since I instructed the dragons to never to converse with two-legged souls again."

Mithias stepped toward the dragon as he slyly stated, "Except for us."

The dragon nodded his head. "You four are special."

"And how exactly do you know this?" asked Ariel. "How do you know the names of Lloyd and Mithias?"

The dragon peered down at her and smiled. "I know all of your names, Ariel. You four are not so unfamiliar to my old eyes."

I searched deep within my heart as Mordikai said this. I believed that in my entire life I had never seen a dragon. My mother used to read me stories about their kind as a child, and she claimed she once saw one, but she said that was right before

I was born. She claimed that a dragon flew high above our village and the entire population hid in fear from the beast who could destroy us all. If I had seen a dragon, or even conversed with one, I would certainly remember it. I was not given more time to think of my past, for the dragon before me continued to speak.

"That is not important now," Mordikai said. "Do you know where you are going from here?"

I shook my head. Our goal had been to warn the king of Finre of the coming threat, but that had failed terribly. There was no place for us to go now, and it seemed that Thundria had taken all the land they wanted.

"So you thought me to be both a savior and a guide, old friend," the dragon said thoughtfully as his distant gaze turned to the tree line. There was a pause before he turned back to our lot. "I want you four to travel to the northwest, not far from the coast. You shall pass through the small village of Goltimn, the great oak of Snola, and the ice fortress of Ikai. At Ikai, take a ship to the continent of Drientus. Once on Drientian soil you must venture to the capitol city of Firius and warn her king of the coming Thundrian threat. Their armies are moving fast, and soon they will be rid of this land and onto the next."

Theron was quick to inquire, "Should we not warn those along the way of Thundria's presence here?"

Mordikai shook his massive head as he declared, "I know you wish to inform those in the villages of this danger, but you must not."

Ariel shot back, "Would you have us lie to those in danger?"

At this, the dragon shook his head and quickly replied, "I would have you say nothing at all."

This clearly upset my whole company, who shared in my disdain. Loud protestations arose from my companions, but the dragon silenced us all.

"If you are to make yourselves known, the one who seeks you will find his target," boomed the wise dragon. "The Thundrian lord has eyes and ears all about the settlements. If he finds you now, many more lives will be lost over the coming months."

Theron stood before the colossal giant in defiance as he asked, "So you would have us sacrifice innocents so that more may thrive in the future?"

To this remark Mordikai let out a low, drawn-out sigh. "I would have you move about the shadows for the safety of more lives than you can imagine."

After a moment of silence Mithias voiced his opinion. "I don't like this. What use is our journey? Drientus is closer to Thundria than Finre is! The armies of Thundria have probably pillaged and looted their lands by now. Besides, what guarantee do we have that their king will be more open to us than Finre's king, and why would Thundria cause such havoc?"

The dragon was quick to respond in all his wisdom as the old man watched in silence.

"Drientus is the only land that harbors as much power as Thundria. The tyrant of Thundria wouldn't dare invade that place until he has secured the rest of the world." The dragon looked at the sky, which was dotted with countless stars, as he added, "You should also know of the waters between the two lands, Mithias. Weren't you yourself once a ship captain?"

Mithias thought for a moment before slowly declaring, "The waters between Drientus and Thundria are the most treacherous in the world. A fleet of fifty ships could enter at one coast and only five would arrive at the opposite shore."

The old man who had embraced Mordikai sat up from his seat and began to speak. "Word will travel fast of the Thundrian conquests across the land. By now, Drientus has heard of their actions and has most likely secured their capitol city."

Mordikai looked at our lot as he stated, "As to the king of Drientus, he is a far more respectable man than the king of Finre."

"And Thundria?" prodded Mithias. "Why have they unleashed such horrors?"

"Thundria seeks one thing, and that is the pillars of old times," replied Mordikai after letting out a sigh weighted as if by a thousand sorrowful memories. The dragon donned a distant gaze. "The Thundrian king casts a dark veil over the eyes of his people and blinds them to the true horror of his army's advance. They praise him for his false promises of a new golden age that will come upon the lands once he holds the might of the pillars."

"He would kill so many for pillars of ancient legend? Devices that are myth among the people?" asked Theron.

Mordikai nodded slowly. "They are more than simple legend, Theron. They are real, and they hold a power the likes of which no man can realize. Time and space bend to the will of he who commands them. The dark one tells his people that he shall use the pillars for good, yet his silver tongue masks his cruelty. Make no mistake: he is an evil man who, led by a dark force, will stop at nothing to devour this world and all the people in it."

"So we must fight back?" Ariel slowly asked.

"You must stand at the Drientian capitol beside her king," said Mordikai. "My followers have matters of our own accord we must attend to, but I assure you we shall not desert this cause."

"So that's it, then?" Mithias asked with a hint of anger about his tone. "The world is being plunged into a war because of ancient myth and we must save it?"

"This is not myth, Mithias," shot back Mordikai, "and this shall be no ordinary war. This will be the defining conflict for generations, and the victor shall sow the seeds of the new world. The four of you must not waver, for with every wasted day the armies of Thundria grow strong. Your quest to defend the land has only just begun."

"And why the four of us?" I hesitantly asked as I took a step forward.

Mordikai almost smiled as he declared, "That, Lloyd, will become clear in time. For now you surely realize you cannot stay within the boundaries of Finre." Mordikai's gaze met my whole company as he added, "You four are escaped criminals. If you wait too long before venturing to the neighboring cities, warrants will be out for your arrest. If you stay here, the armies of Thundria will catch you. You must flee from this land right now if you have any hope of survival."

"It seems we have no choice in our fate," said Theron in a low voice after a moment of silence.

"What does it matter?" I asked him as I took several steps forward. "We must do as the dragon says. You and I have both lost all we hold dear to the Thundrians. I know you would not wish the same fate upon anyone else." My gaze turned to Ariel as I added,

"And Ariel, you would not be doing your people an honor if you were to desert us now. You know this to be true." Finally, my eyes fell to Mithias. "Mithias, so long as I breathe you have an oath to protect me. Would you leave me to this task alone?"

Silence did not linger in the air for long before a consensus was met. We knew what we had to do and we would not falter on our journey so long as our protector, the dragon Mordikai, held true to his words. Theron fought to avenge his family, so he was by my side in an instant. Ariel could not return home because of Thundrian expansion, so she vowed to continue on, and Mithias would not break the oath he had sworn to my late father. I knew I could not falter and let others suffer my same fate, so my decision to continue on came easily. Once we agreed to help him, the dragon smiled and turned to the old man as he asked, "Should you not introduce yourself, my friend?"

The old one donned a bashful smile and slowly said, "I am sorry, I forget my manners in these trying times. My name is Reig. You can sleep and eat at my humble home tonight. A stew is already cooking."

Mithias followed at the first mention of food. Mordikai suggested that we follow my comrade before Ariel and Theron politely took their leave of the dragon, but I could not follow them despite the fact that my stomach roared. I remained outside after Reig and the others left us and stared at Mordikai for a moment.

"You should eat; aren't you hungry?" the dragon asked as his eyes pulsated.

"Shouldn't we leave as soon as possible?" I asked.

Mordikai shook his head. "Thundrian forces are spreading, but you should be safe for a night. If I know the four of you as well as I think I do, a good meal and some rest will be necessary for the next leg of this trip."

I hesitated for a moment before asking, "Mordikai, how exactly do you know me?"

The dragon grinned slyly and slowly remarked, "You're just as inquisitive as when we first met, Lloyd."

I was silent as I awaited a definite answer, yet Mordikai refused to give me one. Instead, he declared, "I cannot tell you all I know

now, but you shall find out in time. As your journey continues you will begin to lead, but you cannot be any ordinary leader. You must hold great power while remaining dignified. You must be both strong and graceful. You must lead as I lead my people."

"And how is that?" I asked.

The dragon took a breath and his eyes narrowed as he said, "Through both might and majesty."

I thought of Mordikai's words for a moment before I asked, "And what should I make of you?"

"I am an ally now and forever," the dragon said. "Remember the date of your capture by Finre's king, and keep my next words in your heart." The dragon leaned closely toward me as he spoke his next words with a steady breath and a deathly gaze.

"Upon the steps of your demise, look to the setting sun with hope, for I shall split the skies as a shooting star falls from the heavens."

After he said this, he turned and approached his lot of dragons who had kept their distance. I wanted to ask him more, but soon the five dragons took flight and vanished into the night air. As I thought of his words, I realized that the date I was captured was just yesterday. I had not been keeping track of the days, but I believed that the day before was the sixteenth day of the second month. I shook my head in an attempt to silence my thoughts that swirled about like a hurricane. The chilly air was settling about me, so I turned and entered the homely cabin.

Warm air hit me as I stepped through the open door and began to examine my surroundings. A simple fireplace sat on the opposite wall, and it burned with a passion that spread deep warmth into my heart. Over the fire was an iron cauldron that was being monitored by the woman I had seen before. To her side were the two young boys, who played with wooden swords by the fire, and from where I stood they seemed content. Around the fireplace there were several chairs and a simple settee covered with animal skin.

To the right was a simple table set with five chairs. Mithias was already stuffing his mouth with bread so fast that he didn't notice me enter the room. There was a baby chair of sorts that was set upon the table, and in it I saw the infant, who looked to be a little over one year of age. The baby girl seemed transfixed by Mithias, yet he paid her no mind.

Across the table was a wall with two doors. In between the two doors was a chest that Theron was rummaging through with Reig. As they did this, Ariel came into the room through the rightmost door. Her rags were gone and she wore a beautiful outfit. The top was laced in the front and was white as snow with the exception of two crimson strips of cloth that ran in a V shape at her neck. She wore simple white pants that were rather baggy at the bottom, where I could see a new pair of boots fitted on her feet. Holding her outfit together was a pristine silken cord that was as pure as the snow all about us. She walked toward me, and with each step she took a slight thud could be heard on the wooden floor. As she approached, the scarlet red cloak she wore swayed from left to right.

"Lloyd!" she exclaimed with excitement once she was before me. "They have clothes for us!"

As she said this, Theron pulled out an outfit for himself. I did not take note of its design, for I found myself transfixed by Ariel.

My eyes did not seem to meet hers as I asked, "There are outfits for all of us?"

"Yes," she answered with a warm smile that I had not seen in quite some time. "They are in the chest. Put yours on and get out of those dirty traveling clothes."

I did as she suggested and rummaged through the chest until I found attire that looked like it would fit me. A black cloak and piece of worn chainmail were also in the chest, so I took both upon Reig's command. I entered the door Ariel had exited earlier and found that it was a child's room with two beds and a crib. Once there, I quickly changed into the sturdy brown pants, gray shirt and onyx vest, and even tried on the chainmail. The clothes fit perfectly and the chainmail shone. I could hear my companions in the main room, so I quickly pulled off the chainmail and went to join them. My friends were sitting on the chairs and couch in new garments as well. Theron wore a leather vest and cloth pants, while Mithias had received a massive blue coat and dark pants. I took a seat on the couch next to Ariel, who was blowing on a bowl of stew.

The woman approached me as I sat and asked, "Stew for you, Lloyd?"

I instantly nodded my head and she presented me with a hot bowl on a plate. Soon the two boys slowly made their way to the fireplace, where they remained as I began to eat my fill. Reig sat on a wooden chair and rocked back and forth while he gazed at my lot as his wife poured her own stew before sitting on the floor near the children.

"I have many questions I must ask you," Theron began from a chair adjacent to the couch.

The rugged man donned a reserved smile as he replied, "And I have much to tell you. Do you wish to ask your questions? Or shall I tell you what I know?"

"Tell us what you know," Theron replied with a swift nod before putting another spoonful of stew into his mouth.

"Very well," the man began. "My family and I have lived in this cottage for no more than a dozen years."

His gaze turned to the elderly woman, who smiled at him as he added, "Namt and I chose to escape city life and live off the land." He returned his gaze to Theron, as he continued. "In the fourth year of our seclusion, just after the birth of my second son, Mordikai flew into the clearing beside our house. My fledging family was filled with terror, for we had never seen a dragon. Yet our fears had no ground, for Mordikai soon spoke peaceful words to us and befriended my family through honest acts. The dragon brought us abundant amounts of firewood and animal carcasses without demanding anything from us. When I asked him what I could do to repay the favor, he had a single request."

The man looked toward me. "He told us that someday a group of four would arrive at our cottage. I asked him many questions about these four strangers, yet all he said was that your coming would mark a great change in the world."

As the cracking fire spread welcome warmth throughout the cottage, Ariel asked, "And you were fine with this?"

The old man shrugged his shoulders. "Mordikai proved himself to be a good friend of my family, so we had little reason to fret. The dragon simply told us to make clothing for these individuals and gave my wife general specifications as to what should be made."

The man scanned the room as the fire crackled. "I know not of what Mordikai speaks, but, seeing you all here brings my heart pain. His words make me concerned for the world."

There was a silence for a moment before the man shook his head and thoughtfully concluded, "Ever since he first arrived many years ago, he has come to visit us every so often. My family has become quite accustomed to the dragon. Needless to say, he is a valuable friend."

The only thing that could be heard in the room after these words was the cracking of the fire and the slurps Mithias made as he guzzled down the last of his stew. He wiped the soup from his beard with his sleeve, then sat on the couch next to me. The couch groaned as he pressed into it.

Ariel caught Reig's attention as she asked, "How does Mordikai know so much?"

The man shook his head and glanced at the ground before meeting her gaze once again. "I do not know, but he is both strong and wise. The dragon once told me he is over four hundred years old and fought in the Great War over two hundred years ago. I cannot be sure of this, but I know of no reason why he would lie to me."

"Four hundred years old?" Mithias sputtered as a droplet of stew inched down his chin.

The old man nodded as he declared, "Actually, Mordikai once told me that some dragons can live to nearly a thousand."

Though this fact astounded me, I was impatient to gain more knowledge of the here and now. I soon leaned forward on the couch and asked, "Is there anything else Mordikai wished for you to tell us?"

"He told me that I must make sure your company heads northwest, past the town of Goltimn to the grand oak of Snola. From there you must find your way through the frigid northlands to the ice fortress of Ikai," he said. "Once there, you must take a boat to the continent of Drientus and make your way to the capitol. He told me...." Reig began to trail off and repeat the words "He told me" several times.

"What did he say?" I asked as I looked closely at Reig. The light from the fireplace danced off his face as the man met my eyes and whispered words of dread.

"He told me your company will face a great trial at the capitol. He said that every fiber of your being would be tested in the heartland of Drientus," he replied as his deep eyes bored into mine. Namt brought the young ones away from our discussion as the man who ruled the house stood. He took a long pipe from the mantel and lit it before I voiced my opinion.

"Well," I began as my company turned toward me. "I think we should trust this dragon. Given the circumstances, I think it is best that we heed his words."

"You know what that means regarding your sister, right?" Ariel asked. I was silent as Daria's image crept into my mind. It pained me to know that I may not return to her for quite some time. Part of me feared that I would never see her again.

"She should be fine at Sacrimen," Mithias interjected.

I was quick to turn to Ariel and ask, "She will be fine, right?"

Ariel nodded and said, "My people will not leave their secluded den. She will be in safe hands until we return."

With that weight lifted off my already heavy heart, I contemplated all that had just happened. From what I could tell, Mordikai was a truthful and wise being who wished to help us. The dragon's words were veiled and strange, but we knew there was no returning from whence we came. As we agreed upon our next course of action, Reig wore a relieved smile on his face. He let out a billow of smoke from his pipe before speaking.

"Head toward Goltimn at first light tomorrow," the man stated as he stood up from his chair while regularly taking puffs from his pipe. "I will give you a wagon and the two horses we have, as well as a plentiful stock of food and drink. The journey to Snola will take you through a deep forest the likes of which few traverse. It should take half a month to make it to Snola by wagon, and another half to make it from Snola to Ikai."

"Couldn't we just fly there on the back of a dragon?" Mithias asked as he leaned back in his seat and rubbed his full belly.

Reig shook his head. "I believe Mordikai and his company have already left. They have other matters to attend to, but the dragon will probably return to you someday. He has a habit of coming around when you least expect it."

The man sat back down, and before we could speak his wife approached us.

"You all must be tired," she said as she approached with several blankets in her arms. Behind her, the boys carried goose-feather pillows. "I'm sorry we cannot offer you a warm bed. You will have to sleep on the couch or on the rug at the fireplace."

Ariel assured her that we were perfectly content with the lodging. The woman smiled and assured us that the embrace of the night would come quickly. Sure enough, it did. As soon as I lay down on the floor I became very drowsy and my bones seemed to ache with a warm tingle, yet sleep did not arrive soon. Not even Mithias could fall asleep and it seemed that all my companions were shifting uncomfortably underneath their blankets. After a moment or two, Theron spoke up.

"Are we really not going to inform the innocents of the coming storm?" asked the lizard, who looked to the rest of us for a response. The dying cackle of the fire was all that could be heard for a moment before Ariel made a declaration.

"We hold the power to save lives, yet the dragon forbade us from using it," she whispered. She looked at me from her place by my side and softly asked, "What do you think, Lloyd? The dragon seemed to like you the most."

"That is peculiar, lad," added Mithias before I could respond. "I am bound to you by an oath sworn to your father before his death, so I will follow you anywhere you go, but I beg of you, let us avoid mysterious dragons that seem to know a great deal about us."

Theron was quick to say, "Our path is still long, but Lloyd, I must know: will we not warn the people of their demise?"

My heart was torn, but I knew what had to be done. I hastily uttered words that pained my ears to hear.

"The dragon who saved us is both wise and strong," I began as my eyes stared at the ceiling. "As much as it pains me, I believe that we should heed his words."

"Then we let the innocents fall?" Theron asked.

I had not the heart to respond to this question, so after a moment of silence, Mithias whispered, "Aye."

CHAPTER 12

The plump king sat on his throne in dismay as he looked at the massive lizard warrior. The tall lizard had made his presence increasingly known after discovering that the valuable prisoners had escaped the grasp of the Finrean Empire. The king looked the beast in the eye and let out a curse before beginning to dig into the feast before him.

"Where were you the night my prisoners escaped?" the king inquired as small pieces of cooked meat flew from his mouth to the ornate tablecloth before him.

The lizard, Marcus, looked at the king in disdain and replied with a harsh voice.

"Previous engagements bound me." Marcus regretted not slaying the four he had thrown in the dungeon just two days prior. He knew trusting the king of Finre and allowing him his wish to make an example of the four had been a mistake, and as he gazed at the fat one he held deep-seated anger in his heart. He cradled his massive helmet in his left arm as the king continued to speak.

"That is not an excuse," the king barked back at the giant who stood his ground. "I have upheld my side of the agreement, yet you fail to deliver me my reward! What of your promises?"

"Promises?" the lizard asked as he casually stepped toward the king.

The round man stood up, holding a haunch of meat in his hand, and walked around the table as he spoke. "You told me if I embraced Thundria and brought the four adventurers to the jail you would immortalize me in gold and silver!" He took a large bite from the meat. With a full mouth he demanded, "Tear down that awful statue of Lloyd and erect one in my glory! Your king commands it!"

A smile stretched across the lizard's face. The lizard took another step toward the king, who had to arch his frame to look up at the massive creature before him.

As the lizard stared down at the round man, he spoke with a smirk across his face.

"I told you many things that only a fool would believe. Regardless, you failed to appease my master. The prisoners escaped."

The king dropped his food to the ground and raised his fists in an irrational fury. "A statue of gold shall be erected to immortalize my name! You dare insult a king who shall be immortalized as a god?"

The lizard did not hesitate to declare, "I only speak the truth, your majesty."

The giant turned his back to the small man. "The armies of my nation have flooded your city and your guard does nothing." Before continuing, the lizard turned back to the king, and in a soft and amused tone, asked, "Did you really think that I would reward you, even if you didn't foolishly let the prisoners escape?"

The king's eyes grew wide as he took several steps back. His backside hit the table and he called out for his guards, yet to his horror there was no response. The king yelled again and again until he was out of breath, but the only response was his own echo in the grand hall. As the echo faded, the lizard smiled, then yelled for the guards in his usual gritty voice. Half a dozen guards of Eurtongard flooded into the chamber before the echo from the lizard's voice could dissipate in the stuffy air. The king's heart maintained a steady beat for a moment as he approached the six soldiers who were covered in new, dark-tinted armor.

The guard's armor was black and red and shone in the light cast through the windows. As the king stood looking at the guards, the lizard turned and looked down upon their lot.

"Where has your Finrean armor gone?" the king inquired as his heart began to beat faster. No soldier bothered to answer, and instead all six looked at the large lizard. Marcus placed his worn helmet on the table then addressed them.

"Where is the bulk of my force?"

"They reside within the walls as we speak," said one of the guards. "They shall continue to flood the city for quite some time."

The lizard nodded slowly before asking, "What resistance have they encountered?"

The soldier who had initially spoke from behind his helm declared in a stately voice, "Rogue groups fight, but the majority have accepted their fate by the king's command."

"What force? What is the meaning of this, Marcus?" the king spat out in confusion.

The lizard looked down at the king with an unsympathetic expression on his face. He began to lean toward the fat man, who was trapped against the wooden table he dined from. The guards circled him and blocked any means of escape as the lizard drew his massive blade and spoke.

"Tell me, king," the lizard began as he ran the palm of his right claw along the smooth edge of the blade. "What do you value?"

The king was quick to answer once he beheld his reflection in the blade.

"My life and my honor!" he yelled as sweat began to pour down his face. His gaze was transfixed upon the blade as he screamed, "What are you doing?"

"You are a blind fool," the lizard shot back. "I have threatened both since my arrival yet you embrace me with open arms, and for what? False promises of riches and glory?"

The king shook in horror as he declared, "You seek to betray me, Marcus?"

He attempted to scuttle away from his aggressor, but two former Finrean guards quickly grabbed his arms. The king screamed and thrashed about like a child as he yelled, "You shall never take this throne from its rightful owner!"

The lizard was quick to ask, "Its rightful owner?"

He began to laugh at this notion, yet as he did so his deathly gaze never diverted from the king. Suddenly his laughter ceased in a single expiration as the guards stood in silence like statues. The lizard then knelt down so that he only stood a foot above the king. He grinned at the king, and with a hand that did not hesitate or falter, he thrust the thick blade through the king's chest. The blade pierced just below the king's heart, and in an instant the screaming man was reduced to a limp being who desperately clung to life with each breath. The king's face was frozen and his breath began to quicken and thin as his eyes met the lizard's. The king could not stop uttering the lizard's name as his wide eyes looked at the blade.

"The very blood that lays claim to your throne now stains the kingdom that would follow a fool to the grave," the lizard whispered before he twisted the blade.

The king's gaping mouth changed in an instant as the lizard removed the blade from his enemy. Blood soaked the regal carpet as the king collapsed. By the time the servant of Thundria had sheathed his sword, the foolish king had wheezed his last breath. With his dark deed complete, Marcus turned to the soldiers.

"Former captains of Finre, lords of a dying kingdom," yelled the lizard as he turned to the six soldiers who had witnessed the murder. "Tell those who once followed this fool that he died by his own blade in an attempt to escape his duty. Let his cowardice immortalize him! As for those who will not lay down their arms, slay them where they stand and let them rot where they fall."

Without a word the soldiers filed by their master with expressionless armor covering any human qualities they had once held. The lizard hastily exited the room and nearly collided into a woman in scarlet garb standing before him. The woman watched as the lizard scrambled to honor her.

"Isalia!" the lizard exclaimed in shock. He went down on one knee and bowed his head.

"Stand, Marcus. This is no time for formalities," she responded with disgust in a voice that would befit a frigid demon. The lizard shot to his feet and looked down on her as she asked, "Has the king been taken care of?"

The lizard smiled and exposed his blade from its sheath to show her that it was still wet with fresh blood. The woman did not share his glee and simply nodded her head as she turned from him.

"Walk with me," she said as she started to move through the chambers of the castle. Marcus sheathed the massive blade and took step beside her in silence before he broke the awkward air.

"Lady Isalia," he said in the most honest and honorable of voices, "I did not expect you so soon. Have the plans been going as expected?"

She nodded her head and turned a corner. "They have been perfect. I personally saw to the ritual in the middle of the Alfrasian islands. Now that our duty is complete there, all of Finre will be occupied in just over a month. It shall take our troops some time to reach the towns on the coast, but once they are there, all hell shall be unleashed upon the unsuspecting peasants."

The woman emerged from the castle and looked down on the once-tranquil city that now burned. Human and beast soldiers alike raped the city of all its beauty without regret or remorse. Those who had suffered by the foolish king cursed his name as they were slain or bound in chains. Families were torn apart by iron and steel and forced to watch as all they once held dear turned to ash. The woman in red looked at the carnage without expression as she stated, "Now it is time for us to move on to the next step."

"Production and creation?" the lizard asked as he, too, looked over the devastation.

"Of course," she said with her eyes fixed on a man and young boy who fought for their lives against overwhelming odds. The boy was slain and the man went into a short-lived rage, just before she added, "It is by His command that we power the pillar."

The lizard looked down to the city as the pristine streets began to run red with blood. As he witnessed this, he asked, "Will it work as He says?"

With her eyes transfixed by the primal carnage, the woman declared, "It did on Alfras, so why not? This city harbors more than enough citizens to invoke the pillar. With it raised, our armies shall continue to multiply."

The woman turned her dark stare to her follower. "We shall require many men, women, and children for this task, Marcus. Many souls."

The lizard turned to his master and asked, "When will there be enough blood for the summoning?"

"Right now," the woman responded without hesitation. She turned and left the lizard looking down at the city. Screams of desperation rose to his ears, and he let loose a sly grin.

As Isalia walked back into the castle she was met with a dozen old men in robes who had been very close to her since her dark ritual had been completed at the seas of Alfras. She looked at each before slowly asking an important question.

"Are you ready?"

The oldest of the lot, who was far past the years of any natural man, stepped forward and responded in a dark and gnarled voice. "I feel the divine column begging for rebirth at this very moment. Once it is raised, the transformation of the remaining inhabitants shall be carried out with ease."

Isalia nodded and took leave of the men so that she could continue to examine the sight that she had not been able to view in Alfras. Hers was a duty of necessity, but on this occasion the woman rejoiced in the fact that she could view the moments leading up to her dark ceremony. Her eyes lit up and she smiled as the statue of Lloyd that sat atop the second of two mountains in the city fell to the ground.

CHAPTER 13

I slowly awoke and drearily looked over to see that Ariel was still fast asleep. Her body was close to mine, and her right arm was delicately draped over my chest. I carefully picked up the angel's limp hand and placed it on the floor before cautiously standing to observe my surroundings. A brown blanket covered Mithias, who slept like a log on the couch. Opposite him lay Theron, who nestled his head against a pillow on the rocking chair where he slept. I looked back down at the angel and noticed that a blanket was at her waist. Before going anywhere, I pulled it up to her chest so that she would keep warm in the cabin. A slight smile befell her face and I felt a distinct rise in my spirits as she continued her slumber. I quietly walked across the room and turned to the kitchen.

Reig and his kindly wife, Namt, were preparing breakfast for my lot, and soon the sound of clattering dishes and the scent of fresh food brought my companions to the table. All of us ate a hearty breakfast, and just as the sun began to rise over the trees, Reig brought around a simple wagon led by two old but sturdy horses. Once a small ration of food was loaded onto the wagon we were ready to depart. The couple who had helped us wore smiles on their faces all morning and insisted that we take several coins of gold just before we left. After thanking them for their kindness we bid them a fond farewell from the wagon. Mithias sat on the driver's bench and flicked the reins lightly, which signaled the horses to move out. With a sudden jerk of the wagon we were on our way. Once the cottage was behind us, we headed

189

northwest through a trail in the snow-drenched woods for an easy week until the woods gave way to a deep valley.

This valley harbored the town of Goltimn. It was a beautiful sight, for as we emerged from the woods, a fog that had encased us for some time released us from its grasp so that we could see clearly once again. In the valley a great waterfall fell into a lake, around which the entire town was built. Small stone houses with thick, smoking chimneys graced the shore. Through a thinly veiled fog that had cast itself upon the valley, I saw people moving about. Candlelight flickered in windows against the sunset and the whole village seemed to have a benevolent glow about it. Without hesitation, Mithias maneuvered the wagon down into the valley until we found ourselves in the heart of the simple town. Mithias guided the wagon through town, looking for an inn, as I looked out to the lake to see people fishing in simple canoes. As I took in a deep breath of the crisp, cool air, I beheld a familiar sight.

Upon the lake I saw a man fishing with his son. Their canoe gently rocked back and forth on the still lake as the son tugged on a thick fishing pole that shook and bent. The father encouraged his son to use all his strength to reel in the creature that violently pulled against the line. The boy had a deep determination about his eyes and nearly squealed with excitement as the catch broke the surface of the tranquil lake. He used all his strength, but it was clear even from this distance that his strength was wavering. The father could see that his son needed help, so in an instant he placed his hands around his son's and began to assist the boy. Together, the father and son brought the catch to the floor of the canoe. The two cheered and smiled as I looked on from the wagon. I found myself smiling sadly as I thought of my own father. Our times at sea had been less exciting, but now, as I ventured deep into foreign territory, on the run from the wrath of an entire kingdom, I longed for simpler times. Despite my longing I could not falter on my journey. With a shake of my head my attention turned from the two who rejoiced to the town before me.

This town was like something out of a children's storybook. A lightly spread fog was all about us and flowers of all shapes and colors grew in the grass, which was occupied by the village's youngest residents. The children laughed and frolicked under the setting sun as if nothing were wrong with the world. Their innocence of youth was something I admired, but I knew that all too soon that innocence would be robbed from the children. With Thundria at Eurtongard, it would not be long before they secured the many towns scattered across the frozen land. I could not bear to look at the damned children for any longer, so I set my sights straight.

We soon found a shanty with many people heading in and out of it, so we hitched up our horses and left the wagon outside. I felt a distinct pain in my legs and realized that I had been sitting in the wagon all day. I had not taken the time to stretch my legs, and now I paid for it with terrible aches and pains. My lot walked inside the structure to discover that it was a wild bar. Angry, drunken men could be heard arguing and yelling throughout the place. The warm stench of malt liquor and gin lingered in the air as we walked toward a rough-looking man behind the bar. He was more than welcoming when he realized we had money, and after a quick exchange of coin we were upstairs in our own room. Theron and Mithias returned to the bar to share a drink while Ariel and I decided to explore the town. Our aimless conversation was lighthearted despite the recent events, and with Ariel beside me I found momentary peace before we returned to retire for the night.

Before drifting off to sleep I prayed for light feet to guide me toward the king of Drientus. I hoped that I could reach Drientus before the Thundrians decimated this peaceful village and that all could find life elsewhere. If Drientus chose to act against Thundria, my sin of silence would truly have to be forgiven. With that hope in my heart, I drifted to sleep.

I awoke to find that only Theron was in the room, reading a book. He told me Ariel and Mithias were already eating together downstairs. That the captain would eat beside the angel was a welcome thought since he had once cursed her race so vehemently. I glanced at the book Theron held.

"What are you reading?" I asked him after stretching my arms and legs. As he spoke, I stood and began to equip myself.

"Ah," he began as he turned a page and looked up. "Just ancient tales."

"What is the myth about?" I asked him as I put on my boots and leaned against the ravaged wall behind my unkempt bed.

At this question Theron looked away from his book and smiled as he sarcastically asked, "You want me to read you a story?"

In all honestly, I replied, "If you're up for it. It's been a long time since I've been read a story."

Surprisingly enough, the lizard was more than happy to read the familiar tale out loud as I prepared for the day. Theron began to tell me the all too common story of a God and Goddess from long ago. Despite having heard the legend countless times before, I listened intently to Theron's each word so that I did not have to think of my current task. Theron told me they had created all life and created three pillars that led to the heavens across the land. A great war was waged between the forces of good and evil long ago, and just as evil was about to slay the last of the good people in the land, the God and Goddess had wept tears of redemption. These tears cleansed all life from the land and destroyed all that once was. Finally, when all was lost under the new ocean, two baskets were found. One held a baby human boy and one contained a baby angel girl. The God created two lizards to save the two children in the baskets, and the Goddess created a land where they could live. After doing this, both fell to the seas in utter exhaustion before their creations began to rebuild civilization.

The book must have been angelic, for it claimed that the Two now lived through all the glory of the natural earth. Once Theron had concluded, he closed the book and turned toward me.

"Quite the fable," I announced as the lizard looked on. At this remark, the lizard shook his head and dropped the book onto the table with a thud.

"Utter rubbish, if you ask me," Theron stated as he leaned back in a chair that wobbled with every minute movement he made.

I leaned forward from my less than comfortable spot on the bed and softly asked, "Why's that?"

With his learned gaze cast on me, he sarcastically asked, "An evil army of creatures rising from the depths?"

"Many say it is just a story. Mere fiction," I replied.

The lizard shook his head as I said this and was quick to declare in an irritated tone, "Not all agree on that fact. My kind does not see things as the angels do. All this nonsense that The Two are still alive in the lands today; it is rubbish. My kind nourishes the land and takes only what we need from it while the angels flail their magical abilities about left and right. This magic uses the very essence of the land, and through it they chip away at the natural earth. They have no regard for the planet all around us, just like the humans."

"They angels claim they receive their magic from the Two who are within the world," I replied, remembering what Ariel had told me. "They treat it as a gift."

"They worship the land while taking from it," replied Theron, "You, Mithias, and Ariel are good people, but I'm afraid I can't say the same for humanity and angels as a whole. Both humans and angels slaughter animals and take resources from the land without hesitation. For every tree the lizards of my village destroyed, three more were planted. And every animal consumed was given to us by the creatures of the forest."

After a pause, I attempted to cool Theron with a simple statement.

"There are many different people in this world," I began with the greatest intentions. "We must accept that now more than ever in this hour."

There was no silence between my words and the lizard's.

"I know this to be true." The lizard stood up and made his way to the sparse bookshelf. "Yet my disdain for those who plunder the beauty of this world is deeply rooted across countless generations. To think that I would be questing with humans and angels...." Theron let out a slight chuckle before adding, "My forefathers would dub me a fool!"

The lizard glanced my way before adding, "I do not mean to offend you, Lloyd. Though I speak words of animosity toward both your races, you are a friend."

"Think nothing of it, friend," I said as my mind wandered elsewhere. It seemed that deep down Theron had as much contempt for other races as Mithias, but I was not about to try to change his mind; not this early in the morning.

Before I went out the door, Theron declared that a bath had been drawn. I sighed and took off the clothes I had just put on after the lizard kindly remarked that he had forgotten to tell me earlier. I took a quick bath and made sure to wash the two stubs that shot out from my back so that dirt would not accumulate about them. It was common knowledge that angels had to keep their wings clean so that they could easily fly, yet half-humans like myself generally only washed their stubs once a month. Crust and grime would build up where the base of the stubs met my back, and attempting to scrub it away was both tiring and painful.

It was embarrassing to have the stubs protrude out of my back. I never seemed to fit in. I was rarely ridiculed for them, but with my stubs I felt distant from both humans and angels, for I was neither. Adults would give me a passing glance before whipping their heads away, as if to make me believe they thought me to be an equal. All the while, their children would stare and ask questions if they had not been exposed to my kind before. My comrades had never brought up my stubs and looked past them, and by all accords I believed them to consider me a human despite my deformity. Had they ever even thought about the fact that I was a half-human? This question lingered in my mind until I emerged from the bathroom to a quiet room.

After a hearty breakfast our lot continued on our way to the north. A simple dirt path led us away from the beautiful village that seemed so peaceful during a time of such strife and tragedy. The town was one of the most beautiful settlements I had ever seen, but I could not bear to look at it was we rode away, knowing that it could all be lost to Thundria. The dragon Mordikai had warned me not to tell anyone of our path, but as I looked at the town that shrank as we continued on our way, I wanted to scream and get as many people to safety as possible, yet no words escaped my breath. With a heavy heart and few supplies, we entered the boundaries of the frigid forest that stretched for miles to the north.

CHAPTER 14

Isalia was once again perched atop the bridge that overlooked the capitol of Finre. It had only been a week since she had arrived, but already her evil had overtaken the city. The once beautiful city had faded away by her hand, and now only a shadow was left in its place. She stood with her back to the ruined statue of the great warrior, Lloyd. All that remained of it was the golden base that was slowly being chipped away. Further behind the statue was the great southern mountain of Finre, where the castle lay. Of late, a terrible ring of smoke had set itself around the mountain and blotted out the sun from most of the city. The female menace descended a staircase and began to walk through the streets that encircled the dark and foreboding mountain so that she could behold the full extent of the evil she had wrought.

The highest streets used to contain massive mansions made from the finest stone and marble that displayed the power of their owners. These homes bore expensive items and beautiful gardens. Now, as Isalia walked the streets, she saw these houses turned to ruin before her eyes. Fires engulfed some buildings while people who were drunk with power looted others. Isalia smiled as her minions frolicked about the flames, for the ones on this level of the city were closest to her and had earned the right to pillage what they willed. The screams of those who lived in the homes had long since vanished, for all residents of the mansions had been stripped of their clothes and belongings and led to the lower district.

Within several minutes the woman found herself in the middle district. She had ordered the middle and lower districts to be combined into a terrible industrial mess that spat forth rancid fumes and constantly burned as production of weapons and armor continued through the night and day. This hell was where the lower ranks of her army worked on crafting great armor and weapons. Isalia watched as swords were created from hot steel in mighty blazes that warmed her pale face. The sound of hammers clashing with the hot steel could be heard for miles all day and all night, for her army of beasts and men never stopped to rest. Once complete, swords and axes were tossed aside into huge piles. Chain mail and armor that bore the mark of Thundria was also crafted by blacksmiths deep in the district, then tossed into similar piles. Isalia didn't pay attention to this terrible marvel of industry, for she was headed for the lowest level, where her army continued to grow.

It had been a long process, but Isalia had nearly completed her new army. She smirked as she filed through several lines of dirty peasants who stood in a loose formation and shuffled forward while guards watched them carefully. The innocent ones wept and cried out to the fallen Two, but they could not escape the fate that awaited them at the front of the line. At the front of each line was an old angel. Each angel wore a dark cloak with a golden outline of the two moons etched into its breast piece. Under their hoods, their golden eyes pierced the darkness with the radiance of distant stars. The lot of robed angels called forth soldiers to hold each peasant in front of them, and then they began to chant. Theirs was an unholy, deep chant that gradually rose above the hammered steel and grunts of furious blacksmiths at work. As the mages chanted, they each raised a hand in the air and began to move it toward the peasant who stood before them in sheer terror. No matter how hard the victims struggled, their faces met a mage's cold hand, which felt as if it were dead and decayed.

Once flesh touched flesh, the restrained individual would begin to flail about as if possessed by a monster. Terrible screams of the damned could be heard as the prisoner wailed, and within seconds all knew why. The peasants thrashed and screamed until their bodies blurred to those around them. White streaks emanated from all portions of their bodies, and soon these streaks gave form to an entity that slowly floated into the air. This formless apparition was, in fact, the soul of the peasant, and the mages watched as the soul began to separate itself from the peasant and inch away from the body. As the mages continued their dark chant, they pointed their fingers at the apparition. This gesture caused a mind-numbing shriek to span across the whole district and, combined with the echo of the blacksmith's hammers, the malicious melody that had lasted for days continued. Each apparition dissipated into thin air and the body of each peasant went limp. Like clockwork, the next man, woman, or child was brought forward to meet the same fate as the bodies were hauled away.

The process that Isalia had so adequately named "Rejuvenation" was now half complete. The lifeless bodies of the peasants were then loaded onto a horse-drawn cart that made its way past grieving slaves who could do nothing to assist their fallen friends. The bodies were brought to another group of mages, who took on the task of creating monsters from the flesh and blood that once was. These mages resided in a red tent nestled between the ruins of two shacks. They sang a chant similar to the one the previous mages had sung, yet theirs had an entirely different purpose. They chanted and touched the fresh corpse as darkness greater than any natural night crept about the tent. As the mages chanted, the lifeless bodies on the cart began to twitch in a horrific fashion. Arms and legs flailed about and bones snapped as the bodies struggled to make their way off the cart to stand before their masters. The foul stench of death swept through the air of the tent as the once frail and starved bodies began to bulge and pulsate with new muscles that broke through their thin and rotting flesh. Skin tore and black blood spewed from the cracks in their skin as their raw muscles continued to overcome who they once had been. Finally, the face of each poor victim would melt away as the face of a beast emerged from within the body to take its place. Once the beast had ripped out of its cage of flesh, the creatures were led from the tent farther down into the depths of the city. These creations were no longer human; instead, they were mutated slaves of contorted flesh who obeyed their master's will to the end.

Once they had left the rejuvenation area, they were taken to the piles of armor and weapons to be suited for battle. The creatures that Isalia's mages had created were clad in hastily-made gray armor. This armor was not buffed or shined, but instead clamped onto the monsters as soon as they approached it. The only distinguishing feature of the armor was the smeared image of the Thundrian lightning upon the breast.

Isalia had mounted an army of thousands a mere week after the fall of the Finrean capitol, and that number was steadily growing. These beings rarely ate and never slept. Once they spotted Isalia, thousands of dutiful soldiers took rank and stood waiting for their orders in a tight formation. As Isalia strolled before the strongest lot, the creatures stirred and their grunts grew louder and louder before she made her way to the formation. She began to walk in between their ranks and survey every few she came across. Their breath was rotten and air from their nostrils could be heard blowing past the disarray of muscles and boils that had accumulated on their horrid, scarred faces. After taking many steps into their ranks, Isalia turned and walked outside the group before surveying them one last time.

"Beings that have since graced this world," she yelled as she stretched out her arms. "Too long have you been confined! Too long have you lingered in the hearts of weak beings!"

From the ranks a dark ovation rang out as the creatures raised their weapons and clanged them together like toys. Isalia smiled as they cheered, yet soon held her hand for silence among their ranks. It was instantly obtained.

"Forced to hide behind the souls of men, forced to comply with their will! You are Hate in the flesh, and you have every right to rule!" she screamed.

Another roar echoed through the walls of the lower complex.

"Yet there is a kind that would stop you," Isalia yelled as she thrust her hand into the air. The unholy celebration quickly came to a halt as she returned to walking through the now disorganized ranks. Each creature she passed turned toward her as she continued.

"You surely have heard of what I speak," she began in a sly and seductive tone. "Those from whom you came—the races of human, angel, and lizard—all harbor your brothers and sisters in their hearts, yet they suppress them. Rip apart their cages of flesh and I shall set Hate free!"

Wild shouts and cheers erupted again as the creatures began to pound their feet on the ground.

"You shall not know fear! You shall not know hardship!" Isalia screamed over the chaos. "For you are Hate, and you shall extend the rule of Thundria across the world!"

The creatures, which now encircled the woman, erupted in a wild wail that could be heard far past the dying forests around the city. Isalia smiled as she pushed past them to exit the chaos. Once she found herself out of their ranks she noticed Marcus standing in full shining armor with several lizards behind him. He quickly took step next to her as they walked away from the mass.

"Your orders, my lady?" he asked.

Without turning to her inferior, the woman barked, "Take your troops and our king's wolf legion to the southern shores of Finre. Travel fast and rest rarely, for every moment you spend resting is one that He frowns upon."

Marcus quickly asked, "What of the new soldiers of Hate incarnate? Shall they accompany me?"

Isalia smiled as he mentioned them. They could still be heard cheering behind her as she added, "No, not them. They will travel west across the plains, sweeping this land clean of those who would not follow us while you do the same in the south."

"Then what?" he inquired. "Surely an army of thousands is not needed for that simple task. The western villages are few and far between. The people who inhabit them will easily die."

Isalia stopped dead in her tracks and turned toward the lizard with a stone grimace on her face. "You must think on a larger scale, Marcus." She turned away from the lizard and took two steps away from him before casually stating, "Once your army is on the southern shore and mine is in the northwest, we shall set sail for the lands to the west. We shall spearhead Drientus with your forces from the southeast and mine from the north; the armies of Thundria shall converge on the capitol of Firius with a strength this world has never known."

For a moment, the lizard looked out at the city as he recalled an order from the highest seat of command in Thundria.

"Will we need an army to take Dreintus?" asked Marcus. "He claimed that the people of the land are blinded by our nation's trickery."

Isalia shot him a glare before she snapped back, "There are those who could bring light before the fools of that land. Our leader knows this and is not willing to take chances. If the people see past our ruse we will hit them hard so to root out any resistance. You would do best to silence your tongue before I speak ill of you to his highness. You wouldn't want our king to relay a message of your disidance to, Him."

Marcus began to sweat and quickly offered apologies before he asked, "From where do the deformed ones depart on the northwestern shore?"

"In two days they will march to Goltimn," said Isalia. "A Thundrian fleet will come in from the far north and transport my bestial army west once they reach Ikai. The two armies will be at Drientus in a pair of months." She looked into the massive lizard's eyes as she added, "Take your troops south. You must reach the shore in four weeks. I will make sure that vessels are there to carry your army west. The waters are dangerous and I expect you to take two more weeks to cross the ocean, then your march to the capitol will take the last two weeks. Can I trust you to lead an army of thousands?"

"Of course, my liege," he quickly responded as he took a knee toward the woman so that they met eye to eye. Once they did, Isalia nodded and patted the lizard's head as if he were her lapdog.

"Excellent," she whispered after this action. She turned from the lizard, then called over her shoulder, "The wolf soldiers of his majesty's own creation will follow you and your veterans into battle, but delay bloodshed too long and they will demand meat. Do not be afraid to supply them with the weaker ones in your lot."

Marcus hesitated before slowly asking, "But what of you? Shall you march with the troops that head for Ikai?"

Isalia continued to walk away. "I shall convene with the troops of Hate when they are near the capitol. First I must venture to the homeland and meet with his highness."

"Why is that, my lady?" Inquired Marcus.

Isalia turned. "Organize your troops, Marcus; you leave at dusk."

She walked off into the distant reaches of the town, leaving Marcus to gather his troops and force their march. Without a personal guard or friends of any kind, the mistress of darkness made her way toward the outskirts of the city where her mount stood. Without thinking twice, she jumped on the wild creature and rode to the southeast. The rider and mount vanished over the horizon as the neverending eruption of desperate screams and clanging metal slowly faded at her back. It was not long before she reached her private vessel and set sail for her homeland. She smirked as she set off, knowing full well that her king would be proud of such progress.

CHAPTER 15

I looked at the trail behind me with Ariel by my side. The beaming sun shone down upon us as Theron drove the two horses onward. Mithias sat at his side and hung his head low as he snored heavily. For ten days of travel on the wagon, each sleep was worse than the next. We stopped for eight hours a day to collect food and water from our surroundings and catch some sleep, and then we hopped back on the wagon and prepared for sixteen more grueling hours of travel. During our journey my infrequent slumber was often interrupted by a bump from the rutted dirt trail we followed. The steeds hated us, for they only got eight hours of rest each day, and we only stopped to feed them twice during the light. Yet this did not concern us, for we knew that we had to make haste to Drientus.

The woods looked like a bleak portrait of death that followed us wherever we went. Each tree was covered in snow, which also dusted the ground all around us. Light and snow rarely reached the ground, for both became entangled in the maze of branches above us. The foreboding and unlivable landscape, however, instantly changed to one of wonder as I beheld the city of Snola.

In front of us stood a tree of legendary proportions. The trunk stretched high before us like a wooden wall. As I looked up to the sky I could see no end to the great trunk, for it breached the clouds as it rose. Foliage grew about thousands of branches that were thick as a fishing boat was long. These stretches of oak twisted through the air and cast a shadow so large it seemed to entrap the forest we had traversed. Leaves the size of my torso were beginning to grow on the desolate branches that slowly came to life. The path we had followed for so many days ended at the base of this tree, where we could see a grand archway cut into the trunk. We drove our wagon through the arch in the tree, where we instantly found ourselves among lizards and humans of all shapes and sizes.

Once my eyes left the inhabitants, I realized these races had carved a utopia the inside of the tree. The wagon began to roll over a stone ground that had been laid down inside the tree long ago, for it was worn and uneven. The oaken homes around us had been carved from the very insides of the tree and stood tall around our wagon. As I looked up I could see a wooden ceiling of sorts far above me. Through the streets I saw lizards and humans going about their daily business. None marveled at the vast array of flowers and vines that grew in all places about the oak, yet I could not take my eyes off them, for their vivacious colors and entangled beauty were simply astounding and a welcome site after the frozen forest we had traversed. The walls were coated in a rainbow of flowers that seemed to encroach upon every inch of the tree. Theron pulled the horses to a halt at the side of the stone street.

As we stepped off, I continued to look about me in awe. Intricate designs were masterfully carved into the structures that had been cut out of fine oak long ago. The few sections of wall I could see beneath the vast foliage were jagged and almost looked alive due to a vibrant shade of cinnamon that shone in the soft blue light that emanated from numerous torches about the city. The vast space amazed me and, try as I might, I could not take in the full scope of my grandiose surroundings. I kept quiet as I looked about in awe, but Mithias could not contain himself.

"It's magnificent!" he exclaimed. He had never before gotten excited about architecture or civility, yet it seemed the beauty of the city could capture even the most powerful man's approval.

The wooden ceiling was laced with long, thick vines that were tangled together to form an intricate tapestry of green life. Some even hung down onto roofs of wooden buildings and crept to the stone floor below us. The luscious, foreign flowers that coated buildings and walls seemed to be very much alive despite the freezing air outside the tree. The astounding surroundings looked like something out of a fairy tale one might read to a child, and they captivated me as Theron began to speak.

"Only once have I ventured this far north," he began as he surveyed the magnificence all about him. "Only once have I seen the beauty of Snola before my eyes, and now that I see it again I believe it to be twice as amazing as when I saw it last."

The rest of our lot was silent, for we had never seen such natural loveliness pass before us. The buildings had ornate spiral columns and arched roofs the likes of which I had never seen. Each one harbored many souls, who bustled in and out of them. I could have stared at the city for hours, but as fate would have it, Theron kept our duty close to his heart.

"I'm afraid we will not be staying on this level," Theron stated.

"What level?" I inquired.

With a smile Theron pointed to the distant ceiling as he said, "You notice there is a roof above all who dwell down here, yes?"

"Of course," I responded as I turned to him.

"This tree is both wide and tall," stated the lizard, looking all about us as he spoke. "The lizards who carved it out so many years ago left a thick slab of the tree untouched every one hundred feet. Each slab serves as a floor for buildings built upon it."

"Just how tall is this whole tree?" Ariel asked as she turned toward him.

"There are dozens of levels, all leading up to the top where the king resides," he responded after turning back to the angel.

Mithias politely stopped a lizard walking by who carried an infant on her back.

"Might you tell me where we can find a decent inn?" he asked.

"Of course," she responded as she stopped her stride and turned toward the great man. She spoke in a polite and soft voice. "If you head up one level you will be able to spot an inn named The Gentleman's Rest by a fountain."

"Thank you," Mithias said as he nodded his head. The woman did the same before leaving us.

"How do we make our way to the second level?" I asked.

With a grin, Theron replied, "You must use your eyes, Lloyd."

Theron pointed across the crowded streets to a huge spiral structure that stretched up to the ceiling. This structure was a double helix of sorts, and on each side of its two platforms I saw inhabitants either ascending or descending the gradual incline. The spiral had a very gradual incline and circled numerous times before it disappeared out of sight onto the next level. Theron turned to me and spoke as I looked at the grand spire in awe.

"That is the great helix, the spine of the tree," Theron said. "It is used by all to access the multiple levels of the city. It has been carved at such a infinitesimal incline that carriages and steeds can use it."

"What are we waiting for, then?" Mithias quickly spat as he hopped back onto our wagon. "We need supplies for the trip ahead."

"And a guide," Theron added as he joined Mithias on the wagon. "I'm afraid there are no trails that lead to Ikai. We will need someone who knows the way to take us there. Let us find the inn before making such preparations."

We got back in the wagon and set off through the crowds. Once we arrived at the helix, our horses hesitantly ascended the ramp, which was riddled with small notches so their hooves would not slip. On the thick ramp, we passed by crowds of civilians who casually walked up and down the great helix. I was awestruck as we ascended to a point where I could behold the full breadth of the first level, yet the inhabitants seemed to pay no mind to the splendor all about them. In a short while we were at the second level, where the helix continued on. We led our wagon off the helix then looked about our surroundings once more.

This floor resembled the first, for it was just as glorious. Great buildings of fine oak lined the solid wooden streets. Because we were inside the tree, no natural light shone in, yet the innovative people of this city had learned how to capture the light. Lining streets, buildings, and the very inside trunk of the tree were torches that shone bright with a light blue flame. The flame danced around the wood it was placed against instead of spreading through it, and unlike normal flame, it lit much greater areas.

We soon came across the inn that was mentioned to Mithias. It was an astounding building with large columns supporting an arched roof. After hitching our horses and wagon outside we walked up several steps and pushed open two grand wooden doors. A sizeable marble foyer was laid out in front of us, containing dozens of velvet chairs where well-traveled merchants and traders sat and discussed coin and distant hearth. As we entered the massive hall, a lizard dressed in full livery approached us. After a quick exchange of words and coin the lizard left the four of us standing in the grand foyer. Had my duty not bound me to travel, I would have liked to explore the sanctuary of oak, but my fatigue was getting the best of me so I voiced a question.

"When will we depart?" I asked as I turned to face my friends.

"Tomorrow morning," Theron said. "I will find supplies and a guide in this city."

Before he could leave, Mithias declared, "I won't let you go alone. I'll handle the supplies, you just get us a guide."

Theron began to protest, yet Mithias waved his comments off as he walked back toward the great doors. Ariel asked the two to tend to our steeds before they left but they simply waved her off as they left the room while bickering like children. Once Ariel and I were alone, I turned to her.

"I guess we can wait in our room, then?" I asked Ariel.

She smiled and nearly yawned as she declared, "I could use a warm bath."

And so our evening was set. Ariel and I bathed and cleaned our clothes before we had a chance to relax. In our grand room I found myself talking to Ariel late into the night, despite the fact that my body begged for sleep.

It was easy to talk to her, and when we talked my soul did not seem so weighed down, so I talked with her about lighthearted times until Theron and Mithias returned. Theron had found a guide for us who expected our presence in the main square of the first floor at noon the next day. Mithias had found sufficient supplies, so the four of us made several trips from the first floor of the inn to the second to move crates of provisions to our quarters. After some bedside banter, the four of us fell into the momentary serenity of sleep, where we remained until morning.

The next morning we awoke just before noon and rushed to get out of the inn with supplies in our arms. When we emerged from the inn we quickly unhitched our worn steeds before leading them down the ramp opposite the one we had ascended on the helix. Once on the main floor we found ourselves amid the bustling crowds once again. Theron led the wagon forward to an alley between two buildings, where a burly lizard whose scales were a mix of gray and gold emerged. He wore a simple eye patch over his left eye, and when he spoke his tone was much deeper and more gnarled than any of ours.

"You're late, Theron," he declared as he placed his hand on his hip. He began to gently tug at the short horns on his chin with his other hand as he added, "You told me your arrival would be timely."

Mithias was quick to shoot back, "He told you we would try to get here on time. We never made a guarantee."

"Mind your tongue," Theron said after he put his box on the ground. The lizard foolishly added, "He's the only guide we could get."

When the lizard with the eye patch heard this I could see his eyebrows rise slightly. A small grin appeared on the corner of his mouth before he spoke his next words.

"I hate to tell you this, Theron," he slyly said as he paced forward. "But I'm afraid I cannot take you up north any more."

"Why not? We had a deal!" Theron exclaimed.

"Heading north is a danger," stated the rogue, who continued to emerge from the shadows as he spoke. "During this time of year, bears twice the size of men wander in packs and hunt any foolish enough to wander into their domain. Mind you, their domain is one of ice and frost in which very few survive. Not until the summer sun rises will the path north be safe."

"You told us that you had traveled north many times," Theron asserted.

"Aye," responded the lizard before pausing for a moment. "But never have a I traveled during this season for such a price."

"Spring will soon be upon us, Johan," Theron remarked as he stared the lizard in the eyes. "The weather will be fair."

"That means all manner of beast will be coming out of hibernation. I have seen the beasts of the north in my travels, and let me tell you they are big enough to kill a man with a single swipe, and fear neither steel or flame. Now that spring has arrived they will be looking for food," Johan shot back.

"What will it take for you to take us north?" asked Theron.

"One hundred gold pieces," he declared from his safe spot in the ally.

"One hundred?" Theron yelled. "We agreed upon thirty yesterday!"

"Times change," responded the lizard. He extended his hand and asked, "Will you pay the fee or not?"

"We don't have that kind of money on us!" Theron shouted in a voice that drew the attention of a few passers. "This is insane! You cannot raise such a price in one night!"

Theron grew angry and Mithias began to weigh in on the argument that unfurled. Johan held his disposition despite numerous threats from both my companions, and it seemed as though we would not receive passage to the north if this continued. I knew the solution to this dilemma, and spoke my mind despite coming upon the realization that the swindler would be receiving far more than his fair share for this journey.

"Silence!" I yelled above the three. They slowly stopped arguing as I walked over to the steeds that led our wagon and looked the rogue lizard in the eye.

"Johan, is it?" I asked the lizard, who nodded as I grabbed the our horse's rein. I looked the rogue dead in the eye before asking, "What if we give you our two horses in exchange for your services?"

Johan was silent as he passed Theron and Mithias, who eyed him with contempt. The lizard approached our horses and looked them up and down before placing his claws on the creatures' hind legs and bellies. After a moment of examination, he swung around to me.

"So," he slowly began as he approached me. "I can take the horses into my company at this moment if I take you across the tundra?"

I nodded, and after a moment of anxiety I confidentially voiced my thoughts.

"Do we have a deal?" I asked as my whole company turned toward the lizard. The burly creature looked at me with a smile.

"You drive a hard bargain, kid," he stated before extending his claw toward my hand. He looked me straight in the eyes as he declared, "I'll take it."

I looked at his claw then back to his face. I did not shake his claw, and instead replied, "We'll shake hands once you deliver us to Ikai safe and sound."

The large lizard let loose a great laugh and called for an assistant. A small girl emerged from the shadows of the alley, unhitched the horses from the wagon, and led them into the shadows. Johan demanded that the girl bring forward two mantises for the journey, and his small companion carried out his order without hesitation. The girl guided two of the strangest creatures I had ever seen from the shadows. I had heard of the mantis before, but this was the first time in my life I had ever stood before one. I looked at the two creatures with trepidation.

Each beast had a leaflike back that was slick and smooth. This back was connected to four thin but muscular legs that propelled the monster forward. The mantis had a long, bright-green neck that was very thick at its base. From the base of the neck sprouted two enormous claws that were held in front of the creature. The claws looked like thick, inverted arms that could be used for movement if they were folded in, or combat if they were opened. The beast I was looking at extended its two arms in the air, and I clearly saw rows of barbs emerging from the clawlike arms. The protruding, globelike eyes of the creature were several times larger than my hand and were strewn with hexagonal shapes. In each hexagon on the creature's darting eyes I could behold my reflection, which seemed to pulsate and distort itself as if it were a reflection in a calm brook. In between the eyes were two long antennae that violently lashed at the air as the beasts twitched about. Below the eyes and antennae I saw a small opening for a mouth. Around the mouth there were four mandibles of sorts, and each moved independently in and out as if the beast were trying to stuff something into its small chops. After several seconds of looking at this beast, I took several steps back in disgust and fear. Ariel joined me at my safe place as Theron and Mithias walked toward the dangerous-looking creatures.

Mithias placed his hand on the torso of one of the beasts that eyed him suspiciously. Despite being so close to the creature, Mithias calmly spoke to Johan.

"It's been quite a while since I've seen someone with the guts to own a mantis," said Mithias as the creature made a hissing noise. Mithias instantly jolted back from the creature. At this, Johan laughed and approached the creature. He shushed the monster before patting its underbelly with the palm of his hand. Strangely enough, the mantis calmed itself and made a slight clicking noise.

"Mantises are the only beasts perseverant enough to make it to Ikai," said Johan as he turned away from the creature. "The cold will set into most horses, but mantises, they are strong." His eyes ran over the creature as he added, "They persevere for their masters."

All through their conversation I could not keep my eyes off the little girl. Ariel must have noticed, for as Johan was talking about the superiority of the mantises she whispered, "She kind of looks like Daria, doesn't she?"

The resemblance of the little girl to my sister was uncanny, and as I looked at the little girl, Mordikai's words rang through my head. He had ordered us to not cause any commotion in the surrounding cities, and by his word we had to keep our knowledge of the Thundrian presence on Finre a secret. I was bound by Mordikai's command, but as I looked to the dirty and weak little girl I could not remain silent.

"Johan," I hesitantly began as our guide spoke to Mithias and Theron. He turned toward me as I looked at him and asked, "Can you do me one small favor?"

"I'm doing you many big favors by taking you north as it is, boy," said the lizard. He must have noticed my lingering gaze on the little girl, for he quickly added, "You taking a liking to little Priscilla there?"

He took several steps to the little girl and placed his claw on her head as he added, "She's a good helper. Small, too. So small and average that just about everyone passes her by, except for me. I need average children to do my work, for the ones that exceed in more... traditional fields refuse to stoop to my level."

211

"And what level is that?" asked Ariel intently.

Johan's sly smile stretched across his face once more as he replied, "There's a lot of coin carried around these cities. My little helpers pick up all the gold that is misplaced in the day."

"Pickpockets," said Theron.

"For lack of a better word," Johan shot back. He stepped before the little girl as he quickly added, "Be wary of your attitude toward my business. Remember that I am the only one you could find to take you north on such short notice."

I hardly paid any mind to his words and, with my gaze set on the little girl, I declared, "While we are gone, I want her out of the city."

"Lloyd," Mithias began.

Before he could finish, I turned to Johan and said, "Is there some place she can go outside of the city while you are gone?"

Johan looked me up and down suspiciously before slowly asking, "What exactly is your angle, boy?"

"My reasons are my own," I firmly declared as I took a step toward the rogue lizard. "Our horses are far more valuable than the extra seventy gold you demanded of us. Make up the dividend by putting this girl out of the city in a safe place."

Johan seemed to be taken aback by my directness, if only for a moment, but he quickly regained his calm, sly composure.

"You hold no sway over me, human," he stated. He stepped forward with his devilish smirk stretched across his face. "But I like a man who is bold, and you, my young friend, are nearly bold to a fault."

"So we have a deal?" I asked.

"I'll grant you this favor," replied Johan. "But you four better not cause any trouble on the road, and I swear by the Divine Two if anyone starts to sing when boredom sets in upon the icy stretch I'll leave your lot for the bears."

Johan then turned to the girl. "Priscilla, go home to your parents in that hovel just outside of town. I'll be gone for a month, but once I return a bird will be sent for you."

The little girl almost cracked a smile as she glanced at me before she scuttled away. Once she was gone, Johan turned back to me and said, "Her family lives in a slum just a mile west of here. That safe enough for you, boy?"

I nodded my head. The gray and gold lizard scoffed and declared, "Then enough of this nonsense! The sooner I get you four to Ikai the sooner I can return home. There's money to be had in this old oak, and I don't plan on dawdling about in the wastelands with the four of you."

Theron shot me a worried glance, but I paid him no mind, for as I saw the little girl disappear through the city streets I knew she was safe, and in a way I believed that Daria was now safer.

Wasting no more time, Johan hitched his mantises to his wagon after we loaded it. Once we were ready, he lightly touched his monsters with the reins. The mantises slowly made their way through the city streets and past all those around us before we found ourselves outside the ancient oak once again. I sat on a cushion of hay in the back of the wagon and watched as we rounded the tree and began our journey north. Several hours went by before we found ourselves leaving the forest we had traversed for so long. I looked about at the ice-laden wasteland with a grimace as the mantises propelled our wagon forward at a greater pace than the steeds we had once owned. We now followed no path as the stranger led us through the cold barrens that stretched about us. The cold air set itself upon me and I huddled under fresh blankets and kept close to my companions to keep warm. The next leg of our journey was sure to be a miserable one the likes of which I hoped would come to pass speedily.

CHAPTER 16

The armies of Hate incarnate continued to head west at frightening speeds. For five days they had not seen battle, and they longed for the taste of fresh blood. Their desire for death drove them on with such force that the legion of beasts neither slept nor rested. Their ranks were disorganized, for Isalia dared not appoint a leader, yet they remained together, for the same ends drove all. Theirs was a force that sought only to consume life and destroy civilization. If the armies hungered, the weakest soldiers in their ranks were slaughtered and eaten. If they needed water, they drank the blood of the weak and left them rotting in the forests. They knew nothing of companionship and sought a single goal: the blood of those who opposed Isalia and the Thundrian Empire.

Their unholy wish for blood would soon be granted, for they had entered a great forest just two days earlier and could now see a great trunk extending high into the sky through the woods. The smell of fresh flesh was in the air and the soldiers knew that their reward for over a week of perseverance would soon be within their grasp. The scattered armies took a bottlenecked formation as they funneled into the archway cut into the base of the massive oak. They let out an unholy shriek that pierced the ears of all who had the misfortune of hearing it as they rushed into the tranquil city. The force overwhelmed the few guards who met it, and within an instant the dark masses flooded the streets and killed any soul they set their sights on. The armies of Hate easily laid waste to all that stood in their path. The streets of the first level were quickly stained with blood, and now they prepared to ascend the tree. The archway into the tree was blocked by the cruel army, so civilians and soldiers alike had nowhere to run but up. The richest noble and the poorest commoner ran side by side from a force that could not discern between the two. To the army of Hate, each man, woman, and child of any race was simply a delicious meal.

The army ascended each stage and decimated the levels one by one while people on the higher levels waited in fear. Men and young boys took up blades and bows in an effort to protect their friends and families, but against the odds they faced their terrible fate was sealed. As the army continued up the dozens of levels, it ravaged the city and feasted on the flesh of those it felled. Those who awaited their fate wept as the sound of steel-toed boots slammed into the grand helix.

After countless lives were lost, the armies finally reached the highest level of the tree. Those who did not have the right to be there set their eyes upon a sight that few had ever seen. An ornate wooden palace stood in front of the grunting force, yet this palace was not simply made out of the wood from the tree. The finest gold and brightest silver was inlayed into the wood and caused the palace to shine against the blue torches around it. The soldiers of Hate ran past their reflections in the metal walls and rushed the front gate without paying any mind to the splendor on display. A young soldier stood on a balcony in the main tower and turned to his sovereign with a shaking figure and deep eyes as he spoke.

"My king!" he yelled. He was a young lad who had seen too few summers to meet death, and he quivered madly. "They have reached our walls!"

The old king, whom very few had ever seen, sat in his throne room, which overlooked the gate to his palace. The wooden doors had been shattered by the rampaging masses. An ornate courtyard of vines and greenery was instantly trampled as the beasts rushed toward the flesh they so desired. Hate stormed into the castle like ants into an anthill during a storm, but the king did not stand to watch this. Instead he held a distant gaze that worried the nearly two dozen soldiers about him.

"Your orders, sire?" asked another soldier in a leather jerkin as he tightened his sweaty palm around his lance.

The king remained silent and stared into the distance, his eyes aflame with fear and remorse. He sat on his throne, garbed in the finest of silks, wearing a regal crown and holding a scepter, facing down a swarm of soldiers who sought only death. He looked like a king from a painting or picture in a storybook, yet his royalty did not set him apart from any other man who had been killed by the horde. The king turned his heavyset eyes to the soldier who prompted him and quietly declared that his door should be barred.

The twenty-some soldiers did not hesitate to rush the door that separated them from the approaching beasts. As they braced it with any furniture they could find, the king walked in a ghostly fashion to a table near his throne, where paper and ink lay. He grasped a quill and wrote on the paper as the door began to rumble. The king hastened his work and began to write in a sloppy manner, for his hands trembled more with every passing impact against the door. The door began to pulse and crack, and the few guards left in the palace desperately pushed their weight against it. The king averted his gaze from the note to the door as he wrote, and beads of sweat started to trickle down his forehead and onto the parchment. After what felt like an eternity, the king let out a sharp whistle consisting of several notes, and within seconds a falcon with the wingspan of a man swooped over the enemy soldiers that littered the courtyard. The magnificent falcon flew from a perch high in the ceiling of the trunk and rushed through a nearby window. Once in the room, the great beast landed on the king's outstretched arm. The king whispered to the animal as he tied the note to its leg.

"It has been a pleasure knowing you, my friend," said the king as he stroked the majestic creature that looked at him with darting, confused eyes. The king sought to waste no time and quickly whispered to the bird, "Take this to your master in Ikai. Let your wings carry you to her frigid gates with a haste unbeknownst to men. King Triden must behold what I have written."

The doomed king then lifted his arm, and the falcon set flight back into the trunk. As the falcon shot down the double helix, flying past the thousands of beasts at incredible speed, the door that separated the soldiers and the king splintered and broke, and the malicious army pushed through. Soldiers of Hate annihilated the few guards who stood between them and the ruler, and then set their sights on the prize. Soon, the king's wail echoed through the tree's chambers as the falcon shot past the aggressors all about him. The bird glided in and out of the mass of soldiers who continued to ascend the helix to the top, and before long the intelligent bird had made its way out of the confines of the trunk. With a screech that rushed through open air, it flapped its wings with great force and vigor as it turned to the north.

The armies remained in the great tree for the rest of the day and set out at nightfall after they had feasted upon all who had resided in the trunk. After sweeping the place for rogue survivors, they chose to do the unthinkable. Without remorse or hesitation, Hate set fire to all reaches of the grand trunk, yet the soldiers did not stay to watch the destruction they had caused. Smoke poured out of the old oak as the army, content after its feast, moved north to continue its dark task. Sometime in the night the tree fell to the ground with a blast that could be heard for miles. With the morning light, snow began to fall and drape the scarred remnants of the city in a blanket of ashen sorrow. Thousands had fallen in the city, and their corpses would forever be lost among the ruin of their utopia.

CHAPTER 17

"Ikai is in sight!" yelled Johan before he slowed the two mantises he controlled. "Best you stir and behold her full glory!"

Mithias and I slept in the gleaming sun, yet our sleep ended at Johan's words. When my eyelids parted I saw the vast snowfields that shone with a great intensity from the blazing sun. Today was an unusually warm day on the plains, for the majority of our trip north had been marred by a freezing cold like I had never known. On this day, however, the sun sparkled off the snow and caused my eyes to tingle with an uncomfortable feeling of great pressure, yet I kept them open to behold the sight I had been searching for over many days. My companions and I turned to the north and beheld the city of Ikai in its full splendor.

We had been traveling for two weeks in the wagon before our eyes beheld any glimpse of civilization, yet once we did behold what little civilization the barren plains had to offer, we were overjoyed. Perhaps it was simply the fact that we had been kept in the wagon like prisoners being taken to the gallows for the past two weeks, or perhaps it was the fact that we had not had a decent meal in many nights, but the city that beckoned us was the warmest sight I had seen in quite some time.

Johan slowly led the wagon forward as each of us looked at a colossal wall that stretched from the distant coast to the tall northern mountains. The wall was neither stone nor timber, and as we approached I beheld its thick ice in full splendor. This barrier was so thick that we could not see through to the other side. Instead, we could only see the warped reflection of ourselves in the sheer ice as we approached. On top of these walls marched guards in bright red armor, which stood out against the blue lands and overcast gray sky. There was no gate to the city, simply a large arch that revealed the inner workings of our destination. We could not see into the city as we approached the arch, though, for many guards blocked our path. Once we drew closer to the arch, we met with a plethora guards who drew their weapons upon seeing us. One of the guards stepped forward to our lot and demanded that we halt as soon as we were in range of his lance. Johan calmed his beasts at this order.

"What brings your company to the walls of Ikai?" the guard demanded as he and several other guards held their lances toward us. They held stone gazes that caught my attention as I fumbled over words.

"It would seem Ikai is not as open as it once was," remarked Johan before I spoke.

"We are simply travelers seeking a vessel to Drientus," I responded, making sure to secretly keep my hand on my sword's hilt. No guards advanced at this statement, and the one who had previously spoken released his tongue again.

"Travelers?" asked the guard. I nodded before he slowly added, "The lands are too frigid to traverse in these months. Travelers could not make it this far north."

"I have guided them," remarked Johan as his keen eyes met the guard who spoke. "I am a seasoned traveler of these lands who has seen far colder seasons in my years."

The guard shook his head as his men held their weapons steady. He glared at us as he declared, "Darkness hangs high above us in this late hour. A terrible storm has been unleashed in the south and our king demands that we keep a look out for spies that serve the mighty hand of Thundria."

"The south?" asked Theron. "Do you mean to say Thundrians have been spotted in the frigid wastes of this land?"

All was silent for a moment as a cold wind set around us. The guard who had spoken initially soon hesitantly said, "Your eyes are earnest, but I cannot trust you in this tumultuous time. Our king will determine your fate."

Before any of us could speak, the guard turned to his men and demanded they strip us of our weapons. As the guards approached us, Mithias drew his axe while Johan brandished a dagger. The guards encircled them and thrust their lances mere inches from the necks of my two companions. I contemplated drawing my weapon but chose not to, for as I glanced at Theron, the lizard slightly shook his head. All was silent for a tense moment, until Ariel broke the thin air with words of wisdom.

"Stop!" she yelled to Mithias and Johan as nearly fifty guards poured out from the city and surrounded us. "These people are allies of the old Finre; if we fight them we are no greater than our enemy."

"So I should just let them take us into custody?" spat back Mithias as he looked into the eyes of the soldier in front of him. His axe was still readied and he looked prepared to spill blood as he stared at the guard. "I have once been imprisoned by a king in this land and I do not plan on returning to a cell."

"At this time we have no other choice," said Ariel as she placed her hand upon Mithias' axe. "Would you pit us against all Ikai?"

Mithias looked at the guards who held lances to him, and then back at Ariel before speaking in a calm voice brought on by realization. "No, you are right."

He then dropped his axe to the ground and watched as two guards struggled to drag it away. We reluctantly handed over our weapons and stood still as our hands were bound behind our backs. I glanced at Ariel as my hands were bound while a single soldier who did not fear the mantises led our wagon inside the gates. I could easily tell Ariel was trying to hide the fact that she was nervous. Once her eyes met mine, I simply nodded at her as if to tell it was okay, but even I did not know if our journey would end here or not. The guards hauled us through the front arch and we beheld the city before us.

Simple wooden houses dotted the streets and overlooked a valley that met a dark shore. The water was murky and seemed ominous, unlike the crystal clear shores of my homeland. The water was tinted with such a shade of blue that it almost looked black against the snowy shore. The smell of salt entered my nose as we continued to walk through streets that were filled with people frantically running about. They moved as if death itself followed them, but the guards who led us paid them no mind. We soon found ourselves in front of a cliff that gave way to the grand valley below us. On either side of the valley the ocean waters crashed against jagged rocks, yet in between these rocks sat a port with many fine ships in stable tides. The able vessels looked as if they were ready to depart, and several massive ships already dotted the distant waters. I turned my eyes away from the strange sight and beheld the fortress to which we were being led.

The valley curved into a crescent and great stairs led to the base of the valley. At the bottom level more houses sat, but within the crescent of the valley sat a mighty castle which jutted out from within the rock. The massive keep was adorned with banners that flew violently in the wind. Each banner had a large white bear standing strong against the blood-red background. My eyes were stuck on the scarlet banner that stood out against the city, but my ears picked up something far less grand.

My eyes followed my ears and caught a great mass of panicked residents frantically gathering supplies. Some carried boxes while others carried their young down into the valley. At the shoreline I could see the imposing vessels being loaded with people and supplies. These ships begged for departure while the people of the village crowded onto their decks as if their very lives hinged on their presence aboard the crafts. Once we descended into the valley, our group was bumped and bashed by fearful citizens running toward the shores. I could not stay quiet as commotion and chaos enveloped the city.

"What chaos has descended upon this place?" I asked the guard who held my hands behind my back.

"Silence yourself, lad, or I'll have to silence you myself. Your innocence seems legitimate, but it is said Thundrian spies are the greatest liars in the land," shot back the young guard over the bustle of the people in the town. I found myself growing angry with him as he continued to push me onward.

"I tell you, I have no intention of harming your city! I am not a threat!" I yelled back as a woman carrying a small child bumped into me. She shouted some insult then disappeared into the panicked crowd.

"The king shall decide that," replied the man over the chaos as we continued through the streets. Soon we had made our way down the stairs and found ourselves outside the castle that was built into the concave area of the valley. We were rushed into the main hall and through a maze of corridors until we found ourselves in an imposing chamber. It must have been a chamber underground, for the walls were moist cave walls and no windows lit the chamber. The only light we could see was that from two candles next to a throne, where the silhouette of a lone figure sat. We were thrown at the feet of this figure, which did not move as we slammed to the ground.

"My king," said one of the guards as he took a knee. The echo of his armor buckling echoed off the moist walls. "These individuals just entered our kingdom. They claim to be travelers, yet they arrive at such a dark hour that we thought otherwise."

The silhouette at the throne stood and walked to his right. His royal shoes clicked on the solid rock floor, and his silhouette darkened as he left the candle light. We quickly heard the scraping of metal, and soon another figure emerged from the darkness, yet this outline was not human. The second looked like a massive bird, whose large yellow eyes gleamed against the light. Once the king walked into the light, the second silhouette revealed itself to be an enormous falcon that soon perched itself on the arm of the king's royal throne. It was larger than any bird I had ever seen and had a wingspan the length of Ariel or I. The bird cocked its head and curiously surveyed our company as we made our way to our feet before the ruler.

The sovereign was garbed in purple silk, the finest of the lands. He wore an intricate crown with a large blue crystal in the center. The king's beard was gray, almost silklike, and it stretched for nearly a foot. His head was balding but the greasy, combed-back hair on the sides of his head seemed to reflect the candle-light nearby. His blue eyes seemed lifeless, and as he opened his mouth his lips cracked with such force that I thought they would bleed. As he spoke, his coarse words echoed through the chamber.

"I do not need guards to watch over me like a vulture," he said in a harsh old voice as his diluted gaze flew over them. "Go back to town and assist the villagers, and give these individuals their weapons back! We are not like the Thundrians, who strip the unknown of all they have."

"But sir!" yelled one of the guards. "They could have come to kill you. Perhaps they are enemy scouts, or spies of some sort."

The king looked into my eyes, then glanced at the others for a moment as the candlelight flickered against his frail figure.

"No," he said. "Not this lot."

After a moment of silence, he firmly declared, "Leave us be."

The guards reluctantly unbound us before presenting us with the weapons we had carried. I snatched my sword from the guard who presented it to me and quickly sheathed the blade. The group of guards who had escorted us to the chamber reluctantly left their king to his own devices. Once they had gone, I turned to the king, who no longer held the falcon. The creature hopped to the floor, moved toward my company, and began to eye us suspiciously. I glanced down to the refined-looking bird before the king began to speak.

"You must be confused in this hour," moaned the king while he stood as still as an old oak in a derelict forest. I was still heated from being treated harshly for no reason, so I voiced my opinions as calmly as I could.

"Being called the enemy of a village which I have never seen is not the greatest show of hospitality," I responded as the king's stone vision pierced my eyes.

"The people here flee as if death is pursuing their every step," said Ariel. "What is going on here?"

The king walked back toward his throne and picked up a parchment that had fallen to the ground when he stood. He handed it to me, and my four companions gathered close to read the text.

"*My dear friend. I write to you in my final hour, for an army has ravaged the halls of my grand oak and now threatens my palace. They bear the mark of Thundria and have wiped out all that my kingdom has. Their strength is tremendous and their will to kill is unsurpassed. I do not know their full intentions, but I fear their bloodlust will bring them to your doorstep, so I beg of you, use your great navy to evacuate your village. Do not attempt to hold your kingdom, for the armies of both Snola and Ikai combined could not put a dent in their unrelenting force. Flee as soon as this reaches your eyes, and return only when you know more about the force that will end my life."*

It was simply signed, "Heront." Once I had finished reading the note aloud, the king spoke once more.

"Heront and I have long ruled our kingdoms through peace and trust," said the king as he stepped to the falcon and began to run his hand against the animal's feathered head.

"We found this falcon wounded and abandoned during a hunt in our younger years," he continued as the falcon ruffled its feathers. My eyes met the sovereign's. "The two of us took it back and raised it. Over the many long years of existence, we both ascended to places of great power in our neighboring cities. Shortly after we became rulers, we agreed to use this falcon as a means of communication during only the direst of situations. Now, in this hour, I fear my childhood friend has lost his home to an army that now marches toward my kingdom."

At this news, Johan was clearly devastated.

"Do you mean to tell me Snola is gone?" he asked in desperation.

The king nodded slowly. "Heront's words seem hastily written. The note does not lie."

Johan said nothing as he donned a distant gaze of both shock and remorse. Surprisingly enough, Mithias drew his arm around the lizard and attempted to console him. Johan would have none of this and shook the man off as Theron spoke.

"In the letter, it said they bear the mark of Thundria." The king nodded his head. "We have faced this enemy before in Eurtongard. Had we not escaped their clutches, we would be rotting on the gallows by the king's command. Trust me, sir, we are not your enemy."

The king jolted in surprise when Theron mentioned the capitol. "So then my theory is true...."

"What is that?" Ariel asked.

"I have suspected as much for months," the king stated with distant eyes. "The one who resides over all of Finre is a weak and pompous man, and my most trusted allies know this. Those loyal to me in the capitol recently reported that a towering lizard from Thundria visited him just over a month ago. My spies whispered of dark dealings between the two and warned me of the lizard's malice. Never did I believe, though, that such devastation could be wrought on the land because of our foolish king."

"The ruler of this land was weak," said Mithias as he stepped forward. "He tried to kill us in the name of Thundria."

"So he has truly fallen to Thundrian influence," said the king in a slow voice that waned as he continued. "If they have taken the capitol as you say, then they are deploying their troops from there."

He sat on his throne and let out a deep sigh as he added, "My hope was that the reports were false, but your presence here confirms my greatest fears. All of Finre could fall."

There was silence as all looked to the king for his next words. He did not meet any of our eyes. "You cannot be my enemy and know this much... I can feel the honesty about your tone."

Although I was relieved, a deep concern grew for one I loved as my heart sank.

"All of Finre?" I asked. I thought of my sister far to the east and turned toward Ariel. "What of your tribe and my sister? They could be in danger!"

It seemed like a lifetime passed before Ariel responded in a cool voice that calmed my heart. "Nonsense. None know of Sacrimen. It has been a safe haven for my people for generations."

I was still not satisfied. "What if the armies were to discover it? My sister could be murdered just like my family!"

"Calm yourself, Lloyd," Mithias quickly declared as he placed his hand on my shoulder. He forced a glance Ariel's way as he added, "Ariel speaks the truth. You and I both saw how secluded that place was. Even if the sanctuary is discovered, do you truly believe any mortal could pass by the watchful gaze of the guardians?"

I surveyed the two, then quietly apologized even though my mind still raced. Ariel nodded, but Mithias quickly got back to the business at hand, for he was quick to believe that we did not have much time to bicker.

"We came here seeking passage west," he said. "We are seasoned in the arts of combat and willing to lend you our blades if you can take us to Drientus."

"We are headed that way," responded the king in a surprisingly calm voice. "The long arm of Thundria has yet to cross the sea of sand and grasp the northern forests of Drientus. It is there that we will seek salvation from the coming storm. If you are to lend your strength to our cause, we will take you alongside us."

"Wait just a minute," Johan butted in before the king could say more. The lizard's face seemed ridden with grief and fear. His next words were slow and his tone escalated as he spoke. "I never signed up for this," he began in a broken tone. "I was just supposed to get you here, then leave. Now my life is in danger and my home is gone?"

"I'm afraid none of us signed up for this," Theron responded as he took a step toward Johan and placed his claw upon the rogue's shoulder. "Yet here we are. You can stay if you wish, but I doubt the armies of Thundria will show you any mercy."

"Besides, Johan," said Ariel, "Had you not come north with us, then you may have experienced the power of Thundria firsthand. You should consider yourself lucky."

Johan let out several curses under his breath. I could tell that he did not fully accept the situation, but he knew what had to be done, for he soon asked the king if he could load his mantises onto a vessel. The king granted the man that favor, but before he could conclude his words the doors behind us burst open.

A guard ran to the king and slid to a halt before him. "They have—they have come, my lord Triden," he gasped. "The enemy marches toward our city now."

The king shot up from his seat in surprise.

"Already?" he yelled in an anger that a man of his stature did not normally hold. "Heront's words reached my eyes only hours ago! Can these forces of evil move with such speed?"

The guard answered, "Their forces blanket the frigid plains and move like a swift ocean breeze."

"What of the people in the town?" shot back the king, who hastily paced toward our lot with the guard at his side. "Have all made it to ships?"

The guard looked up to the king with fear-laden eyes as he whispered, "I do not know. Many are out at sea, but there are many more still evacuating. Some seek shelter in their homes and refuse to leave, while others struggle to make it toward the shore."

The king's eyes lit up with horror at these words. He pushed past the guard and walked toward the door as he continued to speak in a booming voice. While he talked, he extended his arm and the falcon perched on it. "Get to the top of the valley and drag any citizens you can to the ships. Have the vessels depart instantly! We must get as many as we can to the ships!"

The king burst through the main doors with all of us in tow. The guard kept pace behind the king, who walked at a speed that men half his age would have had trouble keeping pace with. The king dashed through the castle as he shouted orders at any guard his eyes fell upon. We followed his lead and soon emerged outside, where our mantises and cart sat. The guards urged the king to rush toward the shore, but he would not leave us without a few parting words.

"I need not warn you of the coming storm, for you have seen its power firsthand," he said with a sharp glance. "There are those who will not make it to the shore, but I pray that your company will."

The king paused for a moment before he slowly uttered, "To think, if your words are true, the army that you fled from lay just behind you all this time."

"You do not trust us?" asked Theron.

The king was taken aback for a moment. "Your eyes are earnest, but my gaze has failed to recognize feigned friendship before. If you truly oppose Thundria, you must prove it, but now is not the time. Make haste to the coast, travelers."

With that the king was ushered toward the shore by a platoon of guards. Each guard scanned the city for any signs of those who would harm the one they were sworn to protect. I watched the king vanish into the crowds as Theron fearlessly approached one of the mantises that was hitched to our wagon. I turned to see him unhitch the creature and mount it without hesitation. Johan looked to him in disbelief.

"Where are you going?" he asked as Theron held onto the beast with all his might.

"You heard the king," stated the lizard. After settling the mantis he calmly added, "There are those who stand defenseless against the coming storm. We cannot leave them behind!"

Just before the lizard rode off, Mithias jumped onto the back of the mantis with him. The two left us screaming for them to return. Theron rode the mantis against the waves of people who rushed toward the shore, with Mithias sitting right behind him. I watched as they rode the creature up earthen steps and began to make their way to the top of the valley, where more houses lay. I looked at the other giant green creature, which looked back at me with beady eyes, before turning to Johan.

"Can I ride it?" I asked the lizard as fear of the creature enveloped my heart.

The grief-stricken rogue looked at his creature and slowly took two steps toward it. Once he stood by the giant bug, he whispered something in its ear before patting it on the side and turning toward me.

"She is a willful mantis," said the lizard as crowds rushed all about us, "but she will support you so long as you trust her."

I nodded my head and hesitantly moved to the creature that stared me down. Before I could mount it, Ariel stopped me and asked, "Do you truly seek to ride closer to the Thundrian army?"

"We must get Theron and Mithias," I stated as I mounted the creature and extended my hand.

Ariel was quick to grasp my hand and mount the back of the mantis. I hadn't the slightest clue of how to control the creature I sat on, so Johan yelled to the beast, "Follow your brother, girl, and then bring these two back to me when they please!"

With these words, the creature let out a wail and rushed toward the stairs we had descended. I struggled to hang on as the mantis shot past the villagers. The intelligent creature masterfully weaved about all those who fled and made sure not to bump any who sought salvation at the shore.

Once Ariel and I arrived at the top of the valley we beheld Mithias and Theron, who had stopped in a stone clearing between several grand houses not far from the arch leading into the city. The lizard's mantis bucked slightly, but through the prince's finesse the animal was quieted. Not knowing how to stop the mantis I rode, I yelled for the creature to stop. Amazingly enough, it did. From where we were I could see the arch in the great wall and the barren snowy plains beyond it.

Yet these snowy plains were no longer barren, for an army clad in tarnished gray armor marched toward town. Soldiers in the middle of each platoon had a crimson being of some sort under them that led the platoon forward. Through the screams of those around me I heard and felt the enemies' boots slam against the ground with such a force that it caused the to land tremble as if an earthquake were occurring.

Mithias took out his spyglass and peered through it before letting out an exasperated exclamation. "By the Gods!"

"What is it?" I asked him, now by his side. He shoved the spyglass in my arms and I quickly peered through the lens.

Through the glass I could see the banner of Thundria wavering in the wind. I moved the glass down to see soldiers in the platoon carrying it, then moved the spyglass right to see what had shocked Mithias. The beings of a sunset tint that were under several soldiers were in fact the same type of ravenous mantis we rode, yet they were so large they made our mounts look like newborns. After several seconds of looking at the advancing swarm, I dropped the spyglass out of my hand, for I never wanted to behold such a sight again. Luckily, Mithias caught the delicate piece of equipment before it hit the stone ground, and placed it back on his belt.

"What are we to do now, Theron?" Mithias barked. "Those mantises could descend upon the city at any moment."

All were silent until Ariel caught a glimpse of a child standing on a sidewalk. The boy wept through wide eyes and wildly looked about like a lost animal. Upon viewing this, my angelic companion instantly jumped off our mantis and rushed over to the young boy. The lot of us followed her as she knelt down to his level.

"Boy, where are your parents?" she asked as the child raised his eyes to her. "You must get out of here!"

The boy had a distressed look about him as swarms of civilians fled all around us. Amid all the pandemonium the boy wiped his nose and shook.

"I never knew them, fair lady," he said in between gasps for breath before his eyes met the angel's. "I am an orphan."

As Ariel looked at him I raised my eyes and noticed the building he stood in front of.

"Ariel!" I shouted. "Look!"

I pointed up at a tattered sign, which simply read "Orphanage." Without thinking twice, I hopped off the mantis and approached the young boy. Strangely enough, the mantis remained behind me as if it awaited my next course of action.

"Are there others inside?" I asked the young child as I knelt down to his level.

"Yes sir," he replied as he wiped streaming tears from his face. "I have four friends inside. The adults left us here when they caught sight of the bad men, and we have no where to go."

Upon hearing these words I shot to my feet and ran toward the building. Without thinking twice, I rushed inside as the ground began to tremble with even more power than before. Behind me I heard Mithias yell for me to return, but I could not bring myself to do such a thing. Right before I burst through the door, I took notice of Ariel's urgent words to the boy.

"Follow me!" she yelled before her steps followed mine.

Once inside the derelict building I found myself in a deserted room with a desk before two wooden staircases. The door behind me slammed shut as Mithias and Theron bolted inside behind Ariel, who held the boy in her arms. He was no more than four or five years of age. Once the door slammed shut, Theron yelled above the disorder that plagued the city.

"Is there anyone in here?" Theron's voice echoed through the chamber, which was riddled with dust. Despite his booming voice, there was no response. He turned toward the rest of us and quickly barked orders.

"Search for them quickly!" he declared over the turmoil from whence we came.

We did as he said and scattered through the immense foyer. I swept along the wall to my left while looking under covered tables and chairs for the children. All the while the ground shook with greater fervor and that increased with every passing moment until it felt as though the whole building were shaking. Within seconds of searching I came across a wooden door in between several tables and crates. Behind it I heard weeping and heavy breathing, so I leaned on it.

I whipped the door open to see two young children staring at me with deep, tear-filled eyes. As light entered the broom closet, they both let out a loud scream and the older of the two lashed out at me. I grabbed his hand before he could punch me in the gut and pulled him close as he wailed.

"Calm yourself, child!" I yelled before the lad of less than twelve years could throw another punch. The child reared back when he caught a clear look at my face. He cried as my friends rushed over to my side.

"We found one!" said Ariel as she looked to the two I had just found.

Mithias walked over to the pair of children and picked up one in each of his arms as the third child hopped onto Theron's back. After scanning the room for a brief instant, Ariel asked, "Where is the last one?"

Just as she finished her sentence I heard a chair topple over behind me and turned around just in time to catch a glimpse of a small figure darting up the stairs. I gave chase. As I darted up the stairs Ariel begged me to return, for the growing thunder from the approaching force could now be felt all around the orphanage.

I continued to run up the stairs, jumping two stairs at a time, as I shot back, "I'll get her! Take the others to the coast!"

I bolted to the top of the steps just as the child disappeared down a hallway to the right. Once I rounded the corner I saw her backed against a good-sized glass windowpane. Her resemblance to my sister was striking, and for a moment it felt as if my heart skipped. She held her back to the window and shook as I stared her down. I shook my head quickly and approached her slowly with a hand outstretched as I lowered myself to her level.

"Do not fear me, child," I said in the calmest voice I could muster. "I am here to help you."

The child cried out in fear, so I murmured words of encouragement. I steadily approached her with an outstretched arm, baiting her toward me all the way. Finally, I was in arm's reach of her, and I pulled the child toward me. To my surprise, once I pulled her in she held himself close to me and repeatedly apologized as she wept. Before I could comfort her, I heard the distinct ring that came from metal smashing into metal outside. The child flinched and spun herself around in the direction of the sound. I darted to the window and peered out to see that the army of my enemy had reached the arch. Before my eyes I beheld their broken ranks rampaging through the city. The city's soldiers were scattered and disoriented, and most guards didn't fell even a single enemy before rushing for the shore. A few brave souls in the streets had banded together in hopes of delaying the enemy's advancement. These men, who exhibited more courage than all their peers, formed a line before the oncoming force and did their best to delay the inevitable. Their efforts were in vain, for a single volley of arrows unleashed by the raging enemy troops mowed down the few men who stood strong against Thundria. Many villagers were safely at the port, but those who had been foolish enough to stay behind were soon slaughtered in the streets like wild animals. Men, women, and children of all races and sizes were ripped from their homes and murdered without cause or mercy. After a quick moment of observation, I covered the child's eyes and took the girl in my arms, then ran back to my comrades with light feet. I descended the stairs in an instant and darted out the door. Once outside I frantically looked about for my mantis, but it was nowhere to be seen. I desperately searched through the chaos in an attempt to find the creature, but it had gone. I turned to the advancing horde and was about to draw my weapon before a terrible realization hit me. It was at this moment that I realized we were facing no ordinary men.

Each soldier was bigger and stronger than any I had seen, and the skin on the hands that tightly gripped their weapons seemed to be decayed and worn. Their exposed muscles on their arms tore through the skin that bound them and all across their armor I could see stains of dried black blood. Blood and puss seeped from their disgusting muscles, yet this did not seem to slow them.

One in the bunch was not wearing a helmet, and as I looked onto his face I felt as if my eyes were going to melt out of their sockets.

The creature had the body of a man and a head of a monstrosity that lurked on the edge of children's nightmares. His scalp was cracked and had rogue dry hairs hanging down before his face. His face was barely visible under layers of muscle and skin tissue that seemed to pulsate as he rushed toward me. Across the layers of flesh and muscle I could see numerous scars. As he opened his mouth to scream, he revealed to me his foul, decaying teeth, which looked as if they were about to fall out. They were stained with blood and cracked to such an extent that their very image repulsed me. The enemy's piglike nostrils, which I could hardly see under his mass of muscles, flared as I met his terrible, soulless eyes. These eyes were not like human eyes, for their colors were opposite of a normal human. The pupils of this beast were as white as snow while the rest of his eye was covered in the darkest shade of black. In the face of such evil, horror rushed through my spine.

I was about to put down the girl I held and draw my sword but suddenly several streaks of flame smashed into the enemy troops. The fire came from Ariel, who appeared behind me.

"Mount up!" she yelled from atop the mantis as she struggled to control the beast. Ariel had a single lizard boy on the back of her mantis. The boy held onto the angel's frame with all his might as the mantis wildly thrashed about. I quickly followed Ariel's orders and placed the girl I had saved upon the mantis as the advancing horde let out howls. The mantis stopped bucking as I mounted her. As screams emanated from the devils behind me I attempted to cover the ears of the young child who bore a striking resemblance to my sister. Arrows flew toward us as we darted away from the Thundrian aggressors, yet none hit their mark. Soon we were out of reach of the horde and shooting past the rest of the fleeing civilians. We descended the earthen steps toward the few ships left in dock with throngs of people all around us. The pier at the end of the valley only had four ships left, and all of them were about to join the fleet that sailed toward the horizon. We urged our mantis to the end of a pier, where a ship was filled with sailors and people who recklessly tried to cut the ropes that connected it to the dock.

The four small legs of the mantis flew across the wooden dock as we spurred her onward toward the ship. I watched as a sailor madly cut the last rope on the vessel we approached. He yelled for the ship to begin movement, and rows of oars emerged from the ship and slammed down into the cold water with a great splash. In unison, the oarsmen all rowed and the ship slowly pushed off from the dock. Ariel spurred the mantis on faster and faster as the oars penetrated the water again and moved the ship away. The ship's gangway was dragging against the wooden dock, for in their haste, the sailors had not taken the time to raise it up. As the plank scraped against the dock, it splintered and tore yet still stayed attached to the ship, and I knew that it was our only hope of reaching safety. Ariel spurred the mantis even harder as the gangway continued down the dock toward the open sea. My eyes were trained upon the loose plank as Ariel screamed for the mantis to move faster. When the plank was just inches away from plunging into the ocean, the mantis leapt onto it. I gripped the small girl tightly as my body violently rocked forward. The mantis used its innate sense of balance and control to dart up the plank and onto the deck just before the plank ran out of dock and plunged into the dark, freezing water. The realization that I was alive did not dawn upon me until the mantis stopped its movement and turned toward the shore. In my daze I caught sight of bands of enemy troops flooding onto the docks and roaring toward the three remaining ships. It was then that I realized I had escaped death once more.

I panted heavily in pure exhaustion that I had never known as I looked to the shore to see what evils had been wrought upon the innocent city. The houses overlooking the valley were ablaze and many unfortunate souls still ran for shelter from the power-hungry enemy. Bloodcurdling screams filled the air as people of all kinds were dragged out into the streets to be killed. I beheld horrors as I watched the beasts of muscle and flesh bite into their victims. They leapt onto civilians like a wild dog leaps onto a piece of meat, and from where I stood I could behold the terrible consumption of the living. My stomach churned and I nearly vomited as the Thundrian beasts claimed their prizes of war.

I could also see innocents running in utter desperation for the docks that no longer held ships. Some broke down in tears as they watched their salvation abandon them, while others plunged into the ocean in an attempt to swim away from their fate. The Thundrian soldiers showed no mercy as they wildly eradicated any form of life in the city. From where I sat on the mantis aboard the ship, I could behold all the darkness of the massacre before me.

Deep hatred stewed within me as I looked at the devastation. My mind wandered into the lowest and darkest corners of my subconscious, the likes of which I never wished to recognize. I wished that I could brutally destroy all those who benefited from such bloodshed. I longed for the day when I could march upon Thundrian soil and spill every last drop of the blood of their people. My deepest desire was to murder all men, women, and children who called themselves citizens of Thundria, for the feast that I briefly beheld went against all codes of men and gods alike. Hate enveloped my heart to an extent I had not believed was possible. As my blood boiled I felt that nothing could cool me, yet a familiar, melodic voice flew about me and I found myself able to breath once again.

"Look at that..." said Ariel as she pointed toward the distant horizon. As I looked toward the devastation with hate, she appeared to look toward salvation with graciousness. She turned my attention toward the sight that had calmed her so, and as I beheld it I couldn't help but thank the memory of the Two for such a sight.

Dozens of ships bearing the flags of the village were sailing out to sea alongside and in front of our vessel. Each ship's deck was filled with villagers and guards while men rowed the oars below deck. Ships that were farther away from the chaos no longer rowed oars. Instead, they let the wind take up their sails and guide them to a safer place. The people on the deck of each vessel had few possessions, and despite the distance between us I could clearly see that most were weeping, but all seemed to cherish the fact that they could still draw breath. I turned back to see the flames of the village rising, then heard Ariel's breath mutter some angelic prayer on the wind. I began to look around frantically while still sitting on the mantis with the orphan before me. The other three in our company were not with us.

"Where are Mithias, Theron, and Johan?" I inquired as dread set into my heart. Just as fast as fear had entered me, it left as a voice rang true through the air.

The voice stated my name, and I turned to see Theron approaching me from between the masses on deck. In an instant I hopped off my mantis as both Mithias and Johan approached from behind the lizard. The children who we had found in the orphanage had been saved, and each meandered around our company in a daze brought about by the terrible events of the day. From a distant place on the crowded deck, the king of the fallen village looked onto us with a nod of approval.

All our company embraced and shared in a fleeting joy as the ships continued toward the horizon. Few words were said as we turned toward the fading shore. We could say nothing in the face of such death. I looked at the smoke and flames with doubt and fear about me, but these emotions passed quickly, for the strangest, yet most welcome act was performed in that very moment.

I felt a tight grip encase my right arm and, without looking down, I clearly knew the one who held me. Ariel, who I had traveled with for so long, tightly grasped onto me with a grip I had not believed she could produce. I looked toward the village of darkness before my eyes caught the light that shone upon the fleet of survivors. With Ariel holding my arm, a warmth that purged my mind of dark thoughts entered my body and cooled my emotions. I did not know how this warmth entered or why it remained, but I did not care, for the slightest hint of bliss returned to my soul. Our lot of four plus the brokenhearted guide stood on the deck and stared in silence toward the shore of flames until it was but a flickering speck against a rolling sea of dark blue. I do not know how much time passed as Ariel held my arm tightly among the weeping and brokenhearted, but I discovered that the moment experienced on deck between the two of us seemed to be one of the longest moments of my short life thus far. Evil thoughts that I had not believed I could ever conjure left my mind, and I was once again prepared to move forward.

CHAPTER 18

It took nearly four weeks, but the army that the lizard commander Marcus led finally made its way to the southern coast of Finre. Marcus stood on the shores that graced the cool coast and looked out to a sea infested with ships bearing the Thundrian flag. As more and more bestial, human, and lizard troops formed rank on their appropriate ships, Marcus paced the shore. Each rank of soldiers filed onto the decks, where they met with savage sea dogs who ordered them to the oars.

Marcus found his way to the lead ship, which bore a red Thundrian flag edged in a black and gold border that shone in the midmorning light. As Marcus stepped across the gangplank to the deck he could feel that his boots had become worn in the past month. His army had traveled at a swift pace and stopped for only a handful of hours each day. By now those who were not bestial slaves began to grow weary of their plight, yet no one spoke their minds, for those who were not creatures bound to the nation feared those who were. All lizards and humans knew that if they were to speak out or act against their orders they would meet a quick end at the hands of the beasts they served beside. Despite this fact, few soldiers let thoughts of escaping the army flood their head, for most remained bound by pure bloodlust. The majority of the troops who still had the ability to conjure emotions carried out their evil actions with smiles across their faces.

Once Marcus was on board the mightiest vessel in his fleet he gave orders for the ships behind to begin departure into the dangerous waters before them. The sun slowly disappeared behind a thick layer of scattered clouds as the ships made their way out toward the ocean that separated them from Drientus.

* * *

The ship that I had been on for the past two weeks was now on the eve of its voyage, for with the morning light would come the coast of Drientus. Through the last weeks I had been given reports on the kingdom and learned that it was made up mostly of humans who made their living tilling the fields and growing crops with their families in small communities. Like all continents of the world, rogue angelic tribes were scattered throughout the wilds, yet most kept to themselves. The greatest monument in the land was the capitol that sat in the center of a flowing basin. A mighty river forged into the land from the eastern sea and made its way down the continent. It split apart midway into the continent and wrapped around a great mountain to form a gigantic island that sat in the middle of the land. It was on this island that the capitol city of Drientus, known as Firius, resided.

The men of this land had built their great city around the volcano Rabaul. One manuscript described it as "A glowing vessel of light which shines through the brightest day and darkest night." No manuscripts ever recorded an eruption occurring, yet all who described the volcano said that deep within the peak tumultuous magma stirred. The heat exuded by this terrible inferno caused few to venture near its rim. During the journey I was also presented with several maps and renderings of the city that various merchants had brought with them from Ikai. In several drawings, artists depicted the royal palace of the city. It was carved out of the side of the volcano and barred with iron and stone. The drawings depicted great halls and elaborate chambers that spread throughout the stronghold. The castle exterior resembled a colossal tower that rose high above the peak of the volcano on the southern side of the mountain. The keep that stretched high into the sky looked over many ornately designed marble buildings. I studied beautiful sketches of the city for hours as my eyes took in all the pictures had to show. During the voyage, I spent the majority of my time acquiring all the knowledge I could about the land we approached; yet, on the sixth night of our two-week voyage I had a unique moment during my frequent solitude.

On this night I sat in the small quarters assigned to me. It dark except for the small amount of light given off by a dying candle that shortened more with every passing minute. I wanted to learn all I could about Dreintus so I studied everything from detailed maps of the landscape to information about the capitol's layout. If I hadn't known better, it would seem I was planning an attack on them and not seeking their kingdom on the advice of a dragon. I had all the information I needed to attack them if I held the army. It was alarming to me that I could gather so much valuable information in a mere week, and it made me wonder how much information the Thundrians had acquired over generations. I was about to read a red, dusty old tome when suddenly my concentration was shattered. I heard a soft knock against my door, so I slammed the book shut and placed it back on the table. I softly answered the knocking in a low voice and beckoned the individual on the other side to enter my chambers. Soon my eyes were graced with the sight of the angel who had been by my side for nearly five long months. She was clothed in a translucent pristine robe that had been presented to her by a woman on the ship. Her golden strands of hair stretched down the back of her garment, and her face wore a slight smile as she entered the room.

"What do you want?" I asked briskly. She looked startled, and I quickly shook my head and corrected myself.

"I'm sorry, Ariel," I said in a whisper so not to wake the others in the numerous crowded rooms around me. I was lucky enough to secure my own room, but Ariel had to bunk with Theron and Mithias. "I've been immersed in these papers for days now. They seem to be sucking the life out of me."

She smiled at my apology and replied, "It's okay." The angel slowly shut the door before she added, "You have reason to be upset. We journey onward into the night after being chased away by an army of thousands. All the while we speed toward a distant land none of us know much about."

She glanced down at the red book I had placed on the table. Her sharp angelic eyes caught minute specks of dust stirring from where the book landed.

"We—" she began as she brought her gaze to mine "—Theron, Mithias, and I, thank you for your diligence. Mithias knows the most of the Drientian landscape, but even he is insecure about our next passage. Your temperament is understandable in these cruel times."

"Thank you for understanding," I said as I made my way toward my bed and sat on the straw stuffed mattress. "I want to gain knowledge of Drientus, for I feel that when we arrive on her shores we will plunge into chaos again."

Ariel let out a soft sigh that most men would not catch, but my eyes soon met hers. I could instantly tell by her distant gaze that something was amiss.

"What troubles you?"

At this the angel met my gaze with somber eyes and she suggested, "Perhaps we could leave this dank room and go on deck. The sun has just begun to rise and the sky is filled with its glory."

I did not realize I had been engrossed in information all night, nevertheless I held a joyful disposition at Ariel's request. As a grin slowly crept across my face I replied, "That sounds like a great sight to behold. Let us depart."

I followed Ariel out of my cramped, musty room and into the hall. Small chandeliers with candles in them gently swayed back and fourth and lit our way until we emerged on deck. There, we were battered by a cold wind, but this did not deter me, for the sight on the eastern horizon caught my gaze. The tip of the radiant sphere was just above the stretch of ocean and the two moons were barely visible as the coming dawn slowly turned the sky to cerulean blue. We made our way to the eastern edge of the ship's bow and leaned on the worn wooden railing. As we stood there and watched the sun rise I could hear the gentle brush of the waves against our vessel, which lay on the northern edge of the fleet that slowly moved forward. The cold northern winds slowly gave way to a more temperate air that warmed my skin as I took in a great breath of fresh air. In this moment I felt more alive than I had in the past week.

Now that I was no longer in the confines of my room, my mind began to wander. As the sound of the waves caressing the mighty vessel echoed in my ears I began to think back to simpler days that seemed to have passed a lifetime ago: days when I was trying to make my father proud by simply reeling in a good catch; days that were filled with the laughter of children in my simple village; and days when my sister had two brothers and not just one. In those days I had known only the small village I had thought I would forever inhabit. As I thought to those days, I thought of what a fool I had been to wish an end to them. I had found an adventure that children dreamed of, but with it came hardships the likes of which no man should ever face. As I became absorbed in the essence of my thoughts, a voice that soothed my racing mind rang against the soft waves that brushed against our boat.

"This morning is one of great beauty," Ariel announced as she stared across the stern. "Despite all the chaos of the world, this sunrise remains."

She told no lies, and I responded after a moment.

"It's odd," I stated with a smile as memories rushed back to me. "We met on the deck of a ship halfway across the world months ago, yet now here we stand." I did not avert my gaze from the calm waters. "And it seems that both times we were fleeing from the damned Thundrians."

Ariel turned to me with a raised brow. "Do not let hate of them fill your heart, Lloyd."

I looked at her in confusion as I bitterly declared, "How can you not hate them, Ariel? They have taken everything from us!"

"I hate what they have done, yes," she said as she turned back toward the ocean. "Yet there are those in their kingdom who only wish for peace. The king's quest for domination surely does not hold favor with every last soul."

"How can you be so sure?" I asked in an irritable tone as I thought back to the massacres on my island and Ikai. "You saw the Thundrian dogs murder all those innocents in the city behind us. How could the people of a nation stand by and do nothing as such slaughter occurs in the name of justice? Do not pretend to know our enemy!"

As my last words escaped my breath in an irate flurry of disdain, Ariel whipped around to face me with anger twofold greater than mine.

"You should not feign such confidence, Lloyd!" she spat out in a voice I would not have believed the small angel could muster. As she continued in a low tone, she shot me a stern gaze. "Let me tell you this. I know this enemy better than you, for my people have dealt with them before. Though it was rare, angels of my island would venture to Thundria under the guise of travelers so that they could acquire technology and wealth in exchange for using healing magic on the sick and weary. In all their travels they met with no conflict from the Thundrians. Most were kindly folk who opened their households to us and treated us with every respect. Who are you to damn every last child of the Thundrian Empire? Who are you to speak against the word of one whose tribe does not thirst for war in the same way you humans do?"

I was baffled, and my tongue stayed itself, for Ariel had rarely taken such a tone with me, yet her words held truth within them. Aside from our initial encounter, her kind had always been peaceful, and never in any story had I heard of an angel acting out of malice or hate. Ariel stood looking out to sea and breathing heavily after her tirade against my nonsense. In an instant I wished I could retract my foolish words, but I knew that what had passed could not be changed.

I cautiously placed my hand upon Ariel's shoulder as she looked away from me. "Forgive my harsh judgment of the Thundrian people, for my blood still boils from the massacre at Ikai. Seeing those sights took a terrible toll on my riddled mind, and these sleepless nights are not easing my patience."

After a moment of silence I placed my hand onto the railing of the ship once again. I feared that my attempt to remedy my unwise words had failed, but just when my heart seemed to sink to the deepest depths of my soul, Ariel brought it back to a content resting place with kind words as she slid her hand onto mine.

"We have gazed into the very heart of evil, but we cannot let it consume us," she responded before looking at me. Once she met my gaze she slowly added, "If we sink to the level of our enemy, we are truly as lost as they are. If we blindly hate those before us, then we might as well have died in Ikai."

I contemplated her wise words and pondered whether or not I should offer an apology again. I chose not to and instead thanked the angel for her patience with me. Ariel still seemed on edge, so I attempted to change the subject to an idea that had been weighing on my mind for quite some time.

I pulled her gaze toward mine as I turned to her and said, "The dragon Mordikai confuses me."

"How so?" replied Ariel in a calm voice.

"He told me that he had met us all once before, yet as I search my memory I cannot recall ever meeting a dragon. I doubt few people have had the privilege of meeting such a sacred beast."

"Perhaps he met us when we were children?" Ariel replied.

I shook my head at the suggestion. "That cannot be." My eyes rested themselves upon the dark, rolling waves. "Had a dragon come to Alfras, the whole village would have known about it."

"My village would have stirred as well."

It was clear that neither of us had an answer to this question, so after a moment of quiet contemplation she simply declared, "Mordikai is an enigma, but he saved our lives, and for that we owe him our trust."

As I contemplated her words, I declared, "Most people believe dragons to be extinct. If Mordikai would show himself to us, we must be important to him in some way."

To this Ariel said, "I suspect he has greater things in store for our company. It is by his word that we have traveled so far westward. His word put us on this path."

With heavyset eyes on the eastern horizon I solemnly replied, "And I pray this path shall not be our last."

* * *

As I began to stir on the dawn of the fourteenth day, I thought fondly of our time together on the deck that morning. As I made my way to the deck I looked about at the sight I had beheld for so many mornings. Men began to fish for another meal such as that which we had been eating for the past weeks, and the children ran about the ship laughing and playing. Throughout the day I met with Mithias, Theron, and Johan, who all longed for the shore. A great deal of our journey had been spent at sea, and as the sun slowly arced across the sky I found myself greatly desiring stable ground to stand upon, for despite all my time spent at sea, my land legs still proved to be more stable.

It was not until the sun began to set in the west that the shoreline of Dreintus became visible. The white shore was spread thick with crystal clear pebbles that washed in and out with the gentle tide. Beyond was a magnificent forest filled with large leaves that sprouted off thick, sturdy trunks. The air had become much more temperate as we continued to travel across the sea, and it was now clear that we were in the tropical region of Drientus. As the ships in front of our formation began drop anchor and ferry civilians to shore, Ariel and I made our way to the small rowboats that took us to the beach. It did not take long before the majority of the passengers were standing on stable ground again. Once on shore, Ariel and I looked across the stumbling crowds for a brief moment. She coolly grabbed my hand. then walked farther up the beach as members of the timid and confused crowd meandered about. Due to her delicate body and great dexterity, she began to navigate the throngs of refugees with ease, yet as I followed I bumped into various civilians. Ariel and I had taken a boat without our companions in it, so the angel wandered to higher ground in an attempt to find a familiar face. Suddenly a loud voice was heard above the clamor. I turned to see Mithias pushing through the mass to get to Ariel and me. Behind the man were Theron and Johan. All five of us converged in the middle of the assembly, and Mithias quickly begot a benevolent smile.

"We've been blessed with quite a fine evening, Lloyd!" Mithias bellowed as he tightly grasped my shoulder before looking down at my hand that lay in Ariel's. His merry smile turned sly.

"It seems you two have sure warmed up to each other."

Ariel quickly released my hand from hers and blushed as the teasing man laughed. She was quick to exclaim, "We were simply looking for you!"

"Of course," Theron responded with the same smile painted on his face. He covertly glanced to Mithias before adding, "We didn't assume otherwise."

"Come on, you two," I slowly began as heat crept across my face. Despite the fact that my friends jested at my expense, it felt good to be in their presence on dry land once again. The momentary laughter was a much-desired escape from our current plight.

Several soldiers approached our group on some of the few horses that had been taken aboard and were quick to interrupt our jests. The masters stopped their steeds before us and a single rider surveyed our group. After a moment of brief examination, one of the soldiers spoke.

"The king has requested that the guard take your mantises for the time being," he informed us. Johan instantly donned a look of disdain, but Theron was quick to speak calming words.

"That is fine," said Theron as he stretched his legs. "It has been too long since we've walked on dry land."

"Hey! Those are my mantises and I think I should have some say in who rides them!" Johan yelled.

The guard frowned at him before Mithias quickly pulled the lizard aside. "The guard can put them to better use than you or I," said Mithias in a low but powerful voice. "You can meet up with them later."

Johan was about to argue with Mithias but the hefty man turned back to the guard.

"Guard, where are all these people heading?" Mithias asked.

"Well," began the guard as his steed's tail flew into the air and the horse pawed at the ground, "the king has ordered that we take all to the small settlement to the west in the deep woods. Rumor has it our king has an ally in these woods who will shelter our people."

The guard paused for a moment, then turned to the a second mounted guard beside him.

"Do you remember what the place was called?" he asked.

"Chigo, I believe," responded the other guard from under his helm.

The first man sighed. "I fear his majesty is making a mistake. No line of trees shall stop the advancing Thundrian forces."

"Yet perhaps the cove will," said the second soldier. The first was quick to hush his friend after glancing at us.

Mithias couldn't contain his curiosity. "You would hide something from us? The ones who saved orphans from your own village?" asked Mithias as he advanced.

The second man turned to the first and declared, "It will do no harm if they know."

The first sighed and then mumbled, "There is a cove on the northern shore. It bears a great system of caves that the people burrowed and developed long ago. Our king will consult the leader of their small village and request that both towns seek shelter in the caves."

"He shall not continue south with us toward the Drientian capitol?" inquired Ariel.

"He has a great many people to lead, my lady," responded the lead guard, "and these matters weigh heavily on his troubled mind. He will need a place to collect his thoughts and protect his people. Besides, to lead so many famished and broken souls through the great desert to the south would be folly. Half would die in the dunes, and the ones that made it to Firius would be sick and exhausted."

In an instant I could tell that Ariel was distraught by his words. Sure enough, she gave words to her feelings of frustration.

"But Firius is in danger of falling," she pleaded, "Can he not send aid?"

The second rider slowly shook his head and averted his eyes from the angel as he uttered, "I cannot speak for him, but I know his priority is his own people. After losing our homeland he is not going to risk putting his people in any more danger. I'm sorry."

All was silent for a moment until the first guard declared, "Once we reach the safety of Chigo you can address him with your plea, but do not hold hope close to your hearts. The safety of his people will guide him on his path."

I started to express my concerns, but the first soldier quickly cut me off. "We have duties to attend to," he said. Before leaving us, he extended his hand, which held two torches, and added, "You'd best take these, for our journey to Chigo will take us through the night."

After we were given our instruments of light, the two guards left us without saying another word. The refugees who had traveled with us slowly began to walk to the west in tattered ranks that we joined without a second thought. We trudged through the forest for five exhausting hours with only a few tired guards to guide us. There were no clear-cut paths through the tangled brush and massive trees so we were forced to follow the handful of guards who seemed to know where they were going. We traversed winding rivers and muddy shallows in between dense thickets, but in the end we found lights splitting through the trees from the village. More than a thousand of us shuffled into the clearing of a small, silent village that almost seemed uninhabited.

Simple homes made of rot-ridden wood held inhabitants who awoke to watch as our tattered and tired lot shuffled in. Dark whispers could be heard as the sound of over two thousand feet penetrating the muddy ground echoed through the warm night air. As my lot continued in the ranks of brokenhearted souls, we were suddenly brought to a halt. Before our group was a single house that was bigger than all the others around it. From where I stood in the crowd I could barely make out a figure standing in front of our assemblage. The figure spoke to the king while all the disheveled souls stood like statues. I awaited any command, but Theron would not sit still.

"We should get closer," he began as he attempted to look over the sea of heads in front of us. Before I could interject, the lizard started to weave his way through the masses. Mithias followed him, and then Johan chased after the two. Ariel and I followed the trio through the tightly-packed crowd as we broke through all those who stood before the king.

The king spoke to an old, weak looking man who was illuminated by the flickering light from a soldier's nearby torch. His hair was white and tangled like a mangled cobweb, and his face was saggy and old. He wore simple cloth pajamas that looked dirty, and he fumbled for eyeglasses in his pocket as he looked at the king. Once he put the glasses on the man nearly stumbled backward. His eyes instantly increased in size and he stuttered for a moment before speaking.

"It really is you, Triden?" he exclaimed in disbelief as he approached the king and arched his head up.

The king looked down to the odd little man and replied, "It is, my friend. I only wish I were seeing you under better circumstances."

The old man adjusted the side of his shining glasses before he looked past the king. After he beheld the plethora of dirtied and battered refugees, he turned back to the king and lightheartedly exclaimed, "Do you bring your whole kingdom with you on this unprecedented visit?"

No laughs were had over the frail man's comment. Instead, King Triden placed his feeble old hand on the man's shoulder and let out a long sigh.

"Can those at my back find shelter?" he asked. Before the elderly man could speak, the king of Ikai added, "They have been through hardships the likes of which none should ever endure."

The squat, aged man instantly changed his witty smile to a look of concern. He glanced at the ranks of men, women, and children who wore dirtied rags. A deep frown stretched across his tired old face and his brow crinkled. After a short examination of the crowd, the elder turned to two young men who stood behind him.

"Awaken your brothers in arms," he ordered with a distressed look about him. He held a firm gaze as he added, "Tell the people to open their hearts and homes to these folk. Make sure every soul in Triden's party has a roof over their head tonight and be sure to treat them as you would treat your own."

The soldiers reacted instantly with nods and rushed away to the houses behind them. The king turned to us.

"This lot came to my village just before the attacks," Triden said as he waved his arm before us. "My force believed they were of the enemy, but I watched as they risked their lives for a handful of orphans who nearly died in my city. Though they claim to be simple travelers, I believe a greater fate is in store for them.

I want them by my side as we discuss the terrors that have been unleashed in the east."

The old man nodded, then hesitantly asked, "Just what exactly brings you here?"

Triden lowered his eyes to the man as he raised his arm toward the house and stated, "Perhaps we should speak of this in private, where the light of a warm fire can hear the tale."

It was agreed and we were led inside. The house was deserted and had a tarnished and muddy wooden floor. We stood in a dark room large enough to fit many men. In the dark I could barely make out a small spiral staircase that allowed one to ascend higher in the home. As we entered, the old man lit a fire in a small fireplace then lit a candle and placed it on a big table beside the entrance. Per his instruction, we pulled up chairs and sat as the man spoke.

The small man introduced himself as Ainsly. It was explained to us that King Triden and Ainsly had met nearly five decades ago when the young prince was visiting Drientus. According to the king, Ainsly was a scientific genius of his time whose knowledge had enthralled all those around him. The two shared a love for science and magic and had become fast friends who wrote to each other on many occasions. The ability to sustain a relation-ship through letters alone astounded me, but I could not ven-ture to ask the two of their past. Instead, I listened closely to the Finrean king as he spoke to his old friend.

For nearly an hour Triden discussed the Thundrian attack on his kingdom. Once he had finished he requested that my lot tell of our journey. We told of how we had come to be involved in the conflict between Thundria and the rest of the world, and by the time we were done, both King Triden and Ainsly were leaning forward in their chairs. Once we concluded with our arrival at Ikai, both the King and the scholar wore looks of sheer disbelief. The king let out a long sigh once the story was over, and Ainsly's hands began to shake on the table. Ainsly put down a pipe he had lit midway through our story and let out a small billow of smoke before speaking in a faint tone.

"So they attacked Alfras," said Ainsly as the smoke that escaped his breath rose about us. "Then they must have sailed north and attacked Finre, and from there they probably seek to spearhead Drientus."

"What do you mean?" asked the king, who wore a look of sheer perplexity before his friend continued.

"The king of Thundria is not dumb, Triden," stated Ainsly as he walked to a drawer and pulled out a thick piece of paper. He ordered us to clear the table, and we promptly did. Once the table was clear he set the paper down and we realized it was a map of our world.

"Look here," he said as he pointed to the continent held by Thundria. "They would not dare attack Drientus first, for Drientus has a military force twice the size of Alfras and Finre combined. Besides, the waters between Thundria and Drientus are notoriously turbulent. Thundria would not dare sent a fleet directly to Drientus."

He then pointed to Finre with one finger while keeping another on Thundria.

"With Thundria in the west and Finre in the east, Thundrian troops can converge upon this land. One party could depart from the port of Ikai in the northwest of Finre, and another could depart from the port of Cheron in the southwest. Upon landing on Drientus, they could follow the mountain passes and fertile grounds. By doing that they will spearhead Firius from the northeast and the southwest" he declared. While he talked he began to move both fingers closer together toward Drientus. His fingers wove between mountains and across great plains until they both hit the capitol of Drientus. I looked at our destination with dread as Ainsly spoke.

"Thus," he said, raising his eyes to the lot of us, "They shall arrive in the capitol from both sides at the same time."

The room fell silent as all stared at the map. I analyzed all that the man had said before coherent words escaped my breath. "The walls of the capitol are thick, and Drientians number in the thousands." I remembered this from the logs I had read on my passage to Drientus. "Wouldn't the people of Firius be able to withstand a direct attack?"

The man shook his head.

"No, not now," he stated before taking off his glasses with trembling hands. "The southern wall of Firius is not fortified in the least. Gaping holes in its base just big enough to allow a crawling man through were made to allow sewage to exit the city. Besides that, the southern wall is riddled with cracks. The force that descends upon Firius from the south could easily enter her walls with a single siege device." After a moment he added, "Besides, Thundria has surely grown after the fall of Eurtongard."

"Why does that make any difference? Would Thundria not have lost troops in the attack on the eastern lands?" Ariel asked as the man examined his frames for a moment before resting them on the bridge of his nose once again. The air around us was still as the man frowned and turned toward Triden.

The man was silent until Triden turned to his friend and said softly, "I feel they should know."

There was more silence until Theron asked, "Know what?"

"Only the royalty is supposed to know!" Ainsly shot back with a fervor that had previously not befallen him. "Telling them would break generations of silence!"

King Triden looked down at his friend as a smile broke across his face and declared, "Royalty and curious scholars who meddle in the affairs of the aristocracy."

Ainsly turned away from Triden. The old king drew in a deep breath.

"They must know, Ainsly." Triden turned toward my company. His eyes scanned all but Johan before he announced, "These four... they will change things. I can feel it in my weary bones."

Ainsly looked at the five of us, then back at the king, and suddenly stood up. "This is madness," he said before scratching his head and arcing his brow, "but what my friend says is true."

He maneuvered his short figure around the table and stared up at me. "If you five are to hear this, then you must promise me you shall do everything in your power to stop the Thundrian forces."

"We already are," I responded with great confidence. All but one in my lot shared in my courage. Johan lowered his eyes as Ainsly scanned us. Ainsly caught Johan's hesitation and approached him.

"You are not ready for this task," he said. The short man studied Johan's quivering eyes. "You never have been."

Johan raised his heavily hung head to Ainsly and muttered, "I was a guide and nothing more. What little I had in life has been taken from me, and now I find myself without direction." With a stern gaze the lizard added, "The Thundrian Empire took everything from me, but I am no fighter."

"Yet his tongue is sharp enough to kill a man," said Mithias. "He slyly took a great deal of commodities from us in exchange for safe passage. He is not utterly useless."

Johan watched as Triden approached him and asked, "So you have no skill with a blade?"

With a quick shake of his head the lizard replied, "Very little." His hands rose before his face as he added, "These hands have stolen, but never killed."

"Now they shall be used to take innocents to safety," declared Triden in a stately voice. "Those who linger in this room will hear a secret that shall burden them with a daunting task. If you wish to avoid such a fate, lend your hands to Ainsly and help get the innocents to safety in the coming days."

Johan glanced at us, then back to Ainsly for affirmation. After the short scholar nodded, the lizard looked back at my lot and spoke in no more than a murmur. "It has been an adventure living with all of you, and a nightmare, yet I cannot continue." His tone mixed roguish pleasure and childlike fright. "With Snola destroyed there is nowhere I can go, and as much as I would like to thrust a knife into the gut of the one who did all this, I have not the resolve or training to do so. I am sorry, but I cannot continue."

"We understand," Ariel responded. "Right now your place is not on the battlefield, it is helping those off it."

To this Johan smiled sadly. He had lost his home, possessions, and old friends, yet he forced a smile. The only remaining lizard in my company brought up an issue that must have lingered at the back of Johan's mind.

"I'm sure your mantises shall be returned to you," Theron said as he looked at Triden for affirmation. The king nodded.

Theron added, "We would not try to steal what is yours, especially after you lost so much."

Johan looked at Theron with a truly benign smile, the likes of which I had never seen on the lizard, before turning to the king and stating, "I will take my mantises only if these four are given steeds for their journey toward the Drientian capitol."

Triden looked at Ainsly, who quickly nodded and stated, "I would have your four friends travel no other way, Johan."

The rogue lizard turned back at us with an expression of both relief and grief impressed upon his features. A deep, drawn-out sigh escaped from his yellowed teeth before he hugged the four who had employed him over a month ago. After he released me, the last of the four he hugged, I spoke truthful words that emerged from my heart.

"We all thank you for your assistance," I declared. "Without your help we would have arrived in Ikai too late to continue on and met our demise."

The king then rose and placed his hand on Johan's shoulder. Triden spoke in his usual stately voice as he said to the lizard, "Go find my guards and tell them I have appointed you as an Ikain guard. Assist them in whatever way you can."

Johan nodded, then looked at us one last time before saying, "Stay safe, my friends. May your trials be few and your tasks be fair."

The lizard then walked out the door. Once Johan had left our presence, Ainsly turned to us once again.

"Now that the room is brimming with courage, let us continue," said Ainsly. He sat down in the chair and lowered his eyes toward the map with dismay as Triden began.

"You have no doubt heard the story of the war between Gulinthor and the Divine Two," he said quietly. I could not imagine someone not hearing that tale, for some form of it had been drilled into the minds of most people on the planet.

"Have you ever wondered why the pillars were sought by Gulinthor?" asked Triden.

"He wanted to kill the Divine Two," said Ariel. "The trio of pillars held a power that would have allowed Gulinthor to reach the heavens."

Ainsly shook his head. "That is all the commoners know of the story."

"There is more that is known only by the greatest royalty and a few scholars," said Triden. "All of us have been sworn to secrecy, yet if you are to combat Thundria, then you must know of her king's intentions."

Excitement and fear rose in my heart, and all fell silent before Triden continued.

"In truth, there was a fourth pillar. One that stood in the middle of the kingdom. This pillar was said to have magical powers the likes of which not even the Two holy ones possessed. None ever fully realized this power, but after years of studying ancient texts salvaged from the most unlikely places, Ainsly has come across a terrible revelation."

We looked at the short old man as he said, "The pillars were exploited during the great rebellion led by the hero Lloyd and during the war of old times, no more than a dozen generations before your birth. At one point long ago, a great thinker, a lizard named Daedalus, wrote that only great bloodshed could truly activate their power. It was my hypothesis that the pillars, which until recently lay dormant under the earth, could be raised through great bloodshed."

"But why raise them?" asked Theron.

"The ancient lizard Daedalus once noted that those with greater magical prowess could use their eyes to transcend events of the past. I believe that if one with enough power beheld the fourth pillar while the others still stood, that person, too, would be able to view events far before the present time. With all four pillars raised, one with extraordinary power may even be able to transcend time and perhaps alter history in ways none could ever predict. The full extent of the pillars' power is unknown, but one thing is certain: if an evil one with extraordinary power raises all four, terrible things will happen."

Every hair on my body stood at this new revelation. The power to transcend time was something I was sure none of us had ever imagined possible.

The candle sputtered, then caught flame again as Ainsly continued in a voice that sounded like a deep moan. "Gulinthor wanted to see the Divine Two dead. He believed that he could take his form to the past and overthrow the Divine Two before they created the world. Therefore, he sought to travel back in time to steal their powers before life was ever created. With this power he sought to craft his own dark paradise of fire and steel that would extend across the bounds of existence. His hell would continue for eternity, and none would ever stop it."

King Triden intervened. "We can only guess what his intentions were after capturing the four pillars, but thank the Two, he never reached his goal. The Two divine ones drowned the land in tears and washed away all life before he could accomplish this task. As you know, the races they left behind slowly built their numbers and constructed kingdoms and diplomacy. All of that has led to what we have today, yet below our feet lie the four pillars, which wait for awakening."

Silence filled the room. Words escaped me and my mind was blank. Manipulation of events long since past, infinite power, all of it seemed so far above my head. The only thing to be heard for several moments was the flicker of the flames atop the candles. After several moments, Theron finally broke the silence with a simple question.

"So, how are the pillars to be raised if they are so deep within the earth?"

"One does not need to physically pull them up from their depths," said Ainsly. "As I stated, a great amount of magical prowess and bloodshed is needed to complete that task."

I was quick to ask, "Does our foe have the ability to raise the pillars?"

Triden shook his head but spoke in unwavering words. "Thundria's armies have threatened all the lands and shed so much blood throughout, yet we do not know of the magical properties within the dark king's employ."

Theron seemed to uncomfortably twitch as he asked, "Does Thundria's king know where the pillars lie?"

Ainsly nodded his head in dismay and Theron donned an anxious grimace.

"I believe that the three races of the world naturally flocked to the locations of these pillars without knowing it due to our subconscious desire for strength and power," stated Ainsly. "You have surely heard that within the great cities of the world there are forbidden fountains. Only the richest may drink from their life-giving waters."

I remembered hearing this fact from Theron back in Eurtongard when I beheld the beautiful fountain in the middle of the grass knoll. Ainsly concluded, "It's not farfetched to believe that the pillars lie near each capital city."

King Triden turned away from his friend and declared, "Ainsly and I believe Finre and Drientus have capitols that were built over their pillars. Alfras' pillar is likely in the middle of her three islands, so it cannot be built over, yet its energy can be felt by the strongest mages."

"How do you know all this?" I asked.

Triden answered, "The royalty of this land has known the secret for countless generations. Thousands of years ago, great kings and scholars sought out the pillars and employed the greatest mages to try to pinpoint the location of their power. After generations of study, they hypothesized that the reason people felt so empowered by the natural water in the capitol cities was that the pillars themselves gave power to the populous. Ainsly has followed up on these studies all his life and has taken the same vow of secrecy that bound the mages and researchers before him."

Even the largest of my companions seemed moved by these statements. Mithias asked in his familiar bellowing voice, "Why not come forward with this knowledge?"

To this, Ainsly quickly said, "Think about it."

Mithias looked perplexed until Ainsly explained, "If everyone knew of the prospect below them and the idea of seemingly infinite power, the entire world would be up in arms seeking out the pillars and the ingredients needed to achieve domination. The populous would blindly scramble to this power and abandon all that holds this world together. We cannot allow them to know, for greed would overtake this world."

"Look at what is happening now," added King Triden. "One cruel king knows the location of the pillars and he is using their dark power to take over the world. It only takes one dark heart to ruin this world with the power of the pillars."

There were many questions that I could have asked, but Triden was quick to declare, "Do not concern yourself with the details of this legend now, for it is not the time to ask questions. You must know of the king's plan and act."

Ainsly pointed to the heartland of each nation across the world on his map as he said the names of the country in which they resided.

"Finre, Drientus, and Alfras. If we draw lines between them, it will form a triangle," Ainsly drew an imaginary line with his finger, and it was clear that a skewed triangle connected each one.

As we all looked at the map, the scholar asked, "Now, do you notice where Thunder's Highseat, the capitol of Thundria, lies?"

It was within the triangle, though it was not within the center.

"The fourth pillar was in the center of the ancient utopia," Triden declared as I looked at the capitol of Thundria with wide eyes. He was quick to add, "Though over time the lands have shifted and the position of the pillars has changed."

"Regardless, the fourth pillar cannot be activated without the other three," Ainsly stated as he leaned back in his chair. "The Thundrian king sits on top of the one thing he desires, and he knows it. Once the pillars across the three capitols have risen, we do not know exactly what he will do with the fourth. All we know is that he will hold more power than any being has since before the flood that washed out all of civilization countless millennia ago."

Triden looked up at us with heavy eyes as he slowly declared, "We must stop him from acquiring this power. Drientus must not fall into the hands of Thundria, for if the pillar is raised it is only a matter of time before the king of Thundria gains ultimate power."

All were silent for a long time as the first rays of sunlight began to breach the trees and creep into the windows of the room. Our tale had taken a long time to tell, and only when the morning sun began to grace the village did I realize how much time had passed.

The silence was soon broken as Theron spoke. "Why have you told us this?"

There was a pause before Ainsly stood up and looked at the four of us. His old bones cracked with every movement. "You must go to Firius and make sure it does not fall. This kingdom holds the last pillar which Thundria has not taken."

"That is what Mordikai wanted," said Ariel as she glanced toward me. Upon hearing this word, Ainsly perked up and interjected himself into the conversation.

"Mordikai?" he asked as he scuttled toward Ariel. "How do you know that name?"

Ariel shot back, "I could ask the same of you. Dragons do not make themselves known to the people of this world so frequently."

"Mordikai and his band of faithful dragons are the ones that have found many relics of the ancient world for me to study. They have visited me for many years, and every time they come they bring more texts from the ancient world. I ask them how they acquire such things, and to this Mordikai explains that an old lizard friend he knew during the great rebellion hundreds of years ago studied the essence of the pillars alongside him. Mordikai speaks fondly of this lizard, who went by the name Daedalus. According to Mordikai, most of the texts brought to me were written by this learned being."

Ainsly looked back at us as he declared, "If the dragon wants you to go to Firius, then I suggest you make haste. He is a shadow who makes himself known only when he must, but with his rare presence comes a vast amount of invaluable knowledge."

"We will leave now if we must," said Mithias, despite the fact that our lot had not slept in quite some time. "The sooner the better, right?"

"Of course," replied the king without hesitation. Ainsly went through some drawers in his desk and soon pulled out a compass, which he handed to Mithias before he spoke.

"Head south through the forest," he declared. "You will have to make your way out of the woods, yet in four or five days you will find yourself in a barren desert. Once you hit the sands of the desert, head southwest for two weeks until you find a lone tree that shines with the radiance of the sun. From that tree, head southeast for two more weeks until you emerge on a grassy field before a great mountain range. Follow the river you meet there through these mountains until it parts. At the part you shall see a great bridge that will lead you onto the island where the capitol is located. After an hour of travel on the island you will find the capitol."

"Thank you," I said. I retained all the vague information he gave me and hoped to the Two that it would suffice. The four of us slowly stood up for the first time in hours and stretched our legs as the king stood as well.

"You will not remember all of that," King Triden declared. Before I could speak, he whistled and the falcon that had first carried a message of warning to the man swooped into the hut. It landed on the table. Triden said, "Take this falcon with you. For many years he has helped me, and now he shall guide you."

Mithias stiffened his brow and looked to the bird, which was preening its feathers. The great man asked the king, "Does that bird follow you everywhere?"

To this the king laughed and declared, "He is a loyal creature who stayed by my side during our travel. He knows the way to the capitol and will find his way to my side once his duty is complete. Follow him by day, then send him out over the sands to find food for you by night."

"So the four of you shall go toward the capitol and warn them of the coming threat," Ainsly murmured.

He continued after several seconds of silence, "To think... only four individuals with the knowledge of the truth possess the courage to fight the legions that threaten us all."

"Do not fret," Triden said as he stood between Ariel and me and put a hand on each of our shoulders. "These four are strong and shall not fall easily."

Ainsly collected himself and turned away from us. He walked over to a small stove and stated, "I shall have a hearty breakfast prepared for you, then I want you to leave this place and make haste to the south. With every moment you delay, the Thundrian horde gets closer to its goal."

We were served a hearty meal of grains and fruit as the sun broke through the foliage all around the small colony. We ate while Ainsley wandered around town, giving directions to the people who prepared to leave and head north. By his command the villagers would depart to the safety of a northern cove along the coast. Triden explained to us over breakfast that he hoped to escape the Thundrian forces and keep his people safe within the cove until the evil had passed.

Once we had eaten our fill, Ainsly returned and escorted us to the southern edge of the town, which was bordered with thick foliage. When we stood before the thin dirt path through the foliage with the four steeds we had been granted, I placed my hand on Ainsly's shoulder and thanked him for his help. Few words were exchanged before the small man released the falcon into the air. The bird flew up to a high branch and looked down upon us as we prepared to set off.

"He has been instructed to lead you," said Ainsly. "Fear not for his well-being, for the bird is both strong and wise."

I held the my horse's reins in my hand as I stood and looked up at the falcon. After watching him flutter his wings from the branch, I turned toward Ainsly. "Your aid in this troubling time will not be forgotten, Ainsly. Stay safe."

"And to you, Lloyd and friends," Ainsly responded with a grim expression, "I would pray for little hardship to come your way, but you and I both know the dangers of the path you must take. I hope that you four can brave the extraordinary trials and emerge unscathed."

I turned with the rest of my company, led by Mithias, who cursed under his breath as the mighty sun bore down on him. The ride before us would be long, but in my heart I knew that with Ainsly's guidance and Triden's falcon we would arrive at Firius. I longed for the chance to right the wrongs done to me by the Thundrian army, and deep within my heart I hoped that revenge and justice would be carried out once my lot reached the capitol. I did not hold onto this hope for long, though, for the sun shone with such intensity that even the shade beneath the canopy above was uncomfortably warm. It felt as if we were already in the desert. Under such heat I could not keep my thoughts straight, so I simply kept my eyes forward as Mithias led our group through the dense brush, cursing all the while.

CHAPTER 19

After a long month of travel, Marcus found himself on the grey, sandy shore of Drientus. He stepped onto the soft sands with his metallic boots and indented the grains with each stride. During the weeks of rough seas and violent winds, the lizard's troops had become rowdy and thirsty for battle. They hurried off the ships and onto the shore as fast as their legs could carry them, and soon rank after rank of soldiers stood under the blazing heat of the infant summer's sun. The lizard general strode between their rowdy lines, and once he reached the head of the ranks he looked across the verdant plains in silence. The army of thousands stood still, and not a single sound could be heard about the landscape except for the whipping of the Thundrian flags in the wind. Each rank had a designated flag bearer who held his banner high as the wind wisped about. As the lizard looked across the plains, one of the ship captains quickly walked through the ranks with two soldiers by his side. Once he reached the goliath of a lizard he tapped him on the highest part of Marcus' body that he could reach. The lizard felt a slight tap on the back of his torso and spun around to see a normal-sized man looking up at him with a smile.

"What is it, shiphand?" the lizard asked.

The captain would have normally scolded any man who called him a mere shiphand, but due to the size and rank of the lizard before him, he shot back no angry comment. He simply told the lizard the great news that he had learned of long before he had picked up the army.

"Isalia told me to tell you of a gift," the captain informed Marcus. Before the lizard could reply, the ground began to tremble. Rocks on the shore shifted toward the sea and the soldiers struggled to hold their positions within the ranks. Some fell onto each other while all wondered what could cause such a sound. Marcus drew his weapon and his troops began to do the same as the source of the rumbling emerged from beyond a distant hill.

"Sheath your sword, Marcus," stated the captain. "The king of our great nation has sent his best to aid us."

The lizard's face lit up with terrible joy for the first time in weeks at the news. He ordered those behind him to sheath their weapons as he did the same. The trembling began to increase across the vast plains, yet the soldiers held their ranks. Soon the heads of those who approached the Thundrian ranks came into sight over the curved plains, and the smile on Marcus' face widened.

"With these weapons, the weak walls of the capitol will fall like a house made of straw in a windstorm," remarked the lizard as he began to walk toward those who approached him. Their new force would be unleashed upon the capitol of Drientus, and by all logic, they would slaughter the few soldiers who sought to stand up against them. Marcus hailed the Thundrians that approached him before donning an arrogant and childlike grin.

* * *

The falcon screeched as he swooped down onto the sands where we all slept. Each morning, the falcon brought us desert creatures such as sand worms, which ranged from a foot to three feet in length. They were disgusting and pale creatures that roamed under the sands and survived off moisture deep underground. According to Theron, they came to the surface late at night to feast on the small bugs that pestered my company during the day. This was when our falcon would strike them down. Their taste was horribly unique in that it was very dry and stale, kind of like burnt seafood, only far worse. Each night I found myself picking fine grains of sand out of my teeth after eating one of the horrendous creatures.

As the falcon swept down into our camp, Ariel used her magic to start a fire in the sands and we began to cut a fresh worm into several pieces. Brown, mudlike blood spilled onto the sands and slowly seeped between the grains until the surface was no longer moist. Once Mithias had finished cutting the creature into several pieces, I took one of the pieces of meat and threw it to the falcon that lingered behind me. The astute bird caught the piece in his beak and flew a good distance away from our party.

While Ariel used simple magic to balance the meat above the flame, I lay down on the sand with my head against my horse. The mare turned her head to look at me while I leaned against her, but soon turned back to look out at the sands while her tail swatted a fly. Each night, we slept close to our horses and each other for warmth, for even as we entered the warmest months of the year, the desert nights threatened to freeze us. Despite the cold of night, the low-lying sun scorched us whenever it came into sight. With dismay, I looked at the meat that began to smell of death.

The acquisition of food was not an issue for my company, but the small amounts of water we had stored in various pouches from the forest was all but depleted after two weeks of travel through the rolling sands. I opened up a pouch and lifted it to my lips, yet strangely, not a single drop of water graced my cracked grimace. The desert had a way of killing any emotion within my heart, so as I put my pouch away I felt neither worry nor fear. Deep in my mind I knew that if we did not come across an oasis we would all meet our end, but exhaustion from the relentless heat caused my mind to not wander about such worrisome topics. Fortunately, the falcon had a way of guiding us to sanctuaries of pristine vegetation nestled between the endless sands just when we ran out of necessary supplies. I hitched the pouch to my waist, then mounted my horse while the animal still sat and gently pulled on its reins. As our horses got to their feet, we waited for the falcon to guide us on our way. The bird meandered around for a moment, curiously looking at us as if to see if we were ready to go, then took flight to the south. As the falcon flew away from us, I nudged the sides of my horse and rode off into the distance with my company by my side.

The day was no different than any day among the waves of sand. The sun beat down on my brow with an intensity no words could describe. My skin was worn and felt like leather as it broiled in the relentless, undying heat. The words of my company were few and far between, for to speak a single sentence under the great blaze seemed harder than climbing a mountain. As I gazed toward the boundless horizon, I noticed a thick haze obscuring my environment. This haze was malevolent, for on more than one occasion it had tricked me into seeing salvation that was not before me. In silent hesitation, I sat atop my horse as we continued across the stoic barrens. Luck would prove to be on our side during this day, for deep in the distance I beheld a sight so grand I thought it to be an illusion.

A sizeable willow tree stretched high into the desert sky under the afternoon sun. Its healthy trunk was strong and at least four times the length of my body. The tree's leafy branches swayed in the almost unnoticeable breeze. Against the tree such a light was cast that I could hardly look at it head on. To gaze at its pristine glory was to gaze at the sun, and I could not look upon it for long without my eyes burning. I knew this was where my company would make their turn to the southeast, yet for a moment I did not care.

Although the tree was a marvel, I paid little mind to it, for beside the tree was a large body of sparkling water that looked more marvelous than the richest wine in all the lands. My company picked up speed, and the waters of life drew closer and closer. The short amount of time it took us to reach the water seemed like hours, yet that time seemed like a blurry memory once I reached it. I forgot about my journey and company for a few brief moments as I drank the water and splashed it onto my soiled clothing. Mithias, Ariel, and all of the horses drank deeply, and I could only assume Theron was drinking the water like the rest of us. After smothering myself with water until I was satisfied, I heard the falcon screech. I paid the bird no mind as I drank the water. One of my companions took a short break from gorging himself to complain about the ear-shattering noise.

"Someone quiet that creature!" yelled Mithias after the falcon let out several more piercing cries. While he yelled, he continued to drink water from the basin like some sort of wild animal. He continued drinking with a smile on his face until our glee was shattered by an unknown voice from behind us.

"Perhaps you should pay the bird more mind," said a voice that sounded young and arrogant. I turned my head to the side while water dripped from my mouth and hair and stared at the direct tips of two arrows. For a split second, I squinted as the sun glinted off their sharp metal points. Their owners could not be seen against such blinding light, but I was positive that the arrows were held taunt in bows. As I squinted against the sunlight the same voice beset me.

"Rise to your feet."

I kept my eyes upon the arrows as I rose up and attempted to discern those who stood before me. In my drunken haze brought on by the relief from the water, it was hard to make out clear images before me.

"What brings four travelers across this wasteland?" asked one of the individuals who held a strung arrow.

In an instant Theron raised his hands and hesitantly replied, "We seek passage to the capitol."

No silence lingered in the air, for another voice came to me as another person strode up near us. "From what land do you hail?"

Mithias remained calm as he replied while holding his hands in the air. "The boy is from Alfras. The angel is from a remote island off the coast of Thundria, and the lizard is from the forests in eastern Finre."

"And what of you?" asked the first voice as my vision began to clear.

"I am a ship captain, orphaned in my youth," replied the burly man in a low tone.

Silence lingered as nearly a dozen arrows were pointed at my company and me.

"Enough," boomed a third voice that echoed louder than the two before it.

Footsteps brushed against the sand, and what came into my sight was an angel, who placed his hand on the shoulder of a comrade as he added, "They do not flinch at the large man's declaration. A truth is being told. If they simply seek passage to the capitol, we have no right stop them."

The haze that had been brought on by my deprivation was lifted as I heard these words. My eyes focused on the figures before me, and in an instant I realized that all were angels. Dozens stood in front of me and hundreds more were perched upon the peak of a sand dune behind them. Most sat atop sturdy steeds that could clearly catch us if we sought to run. They were garbed in thin cloth that was colored to match the shade of the sands, and as they sat atop their steeds I could see their garments flapping in the wind.

"Put down your weapons, comrades," demanded the angel who stood in front of me. "These four will do us no harm."

To this, an angel who still held his bow ready asked, "Can you be so sure, Godfrey?"

The angel who spoke in a soft yet powerful voice nodded. "Besides, if they are foolish enough to strike us, they will be filled with arrows in an instant. There's only four of them."

Retracting bows all around followed his nod. Once all had ceased their aggressive stances they filed past us toward the spring. Many shot us strange glances as they did so, yet my eyes focused on the angel who had saved us as he spoke.

"You must forgive us," stated Godfrey as many other angels walked past him. "We have been wandering this desert for quite some time.... It seems to have taken a toll on our manners."

I was still shaken from meeting the tip of an arrow, yet Mithias seemed unaffected and began to speak.

"You angels would do well to know when to keep your weapons down," he rudely remarked.

The angels who were close to us glared at Mithias as they walked past him toward the great spring that provided sustenance for the whole throng of them. The angels flocked to the spring like weary animals, yet they held some sense of humanlike quality as they calmly filled their pouches rather than gorging themselves in the heavenly delights of the spring. Mithias held a glare on the angel who remained before us.

"Again, I offer my apologies," stated the angel, who clearly noticed Mithias' disdain. He held out his hand as he continued. "My name is Godfrey, and I lead these angels."

Godfrey looked to be many years my senior, but he was not past his prime. His wings were tinted with a deep, dark blue, yet his skin was as fair as a cloud. Most angels I had met had worn pristine clothing, but he and his companions wore dirtied garments that had been ravaged by the desert. His graceful, flowing hair seemed very similar to Ariel's in tint and length. Godfrey had a very kind and caring face despite the fact that upon his back was a sharp and shining blade fit for battle. The angel's soft but chiseled face held a smile as he extended his hand toward Mithias.

Mithias looked down at the angel's hand with dismay and refused to shake it due to his primal disdain for the creatures that stemmed from a place unbeknownst to me. Ariel immediately jumped in front of him and shook the angel's hand firmly. Theron and I did the same, but Mithias busied himself by filling his canteen with water.

"You're probably wondering what brings this host of angels into the desert," said Godfrey in a voice that was both gentle and accepting.

"Well it's not every day that you find hundreds of angels lingering about a barren waste," began Theron in a calm voice. "Why are you here?"

"I have asked myself that question many times over," responded the angel as he began to walk toward the water's edge. "Firius has changed in the past few months." Godfrey's gaze was fixed upon all his company as he declared in a somber voice, "Our kind is no longer welcome in the capitol."

"What do you mean your kind?" asked Theron. It was clear he could not believe the words he heard, for his voice rose as he asked, "You mean angels?"

Godfrey turned to Theron as he blatantly replied, "Of course."

"That cannot be true. An entire race exiled from a capitol?" asked the lizard. "What would drive the king to exile all angels from his city?"

"Oh no," said Godfrey as he turned back toward us. His next words were mere whispers on the wind. "Not all angels, only those who refuse to obey him."

"Why would all of you refuse to obey him?" asked Theron as he stepped toward the angel. "Any angels who leave their village and take residence in a city must swear allegiance to the throne. He is your king, and therefore you must give him your service and loyalty."

Before he spoke again, the angel let out a low groan under his breath. "This is true, but something has changed about the king. He used to roam the city streets and directly mingle with the people, but now he spends all his time in the highest tower of his keep. He no longer graces the people, who now live in fear of his next orders. The benign and honest man I swore to serve is now but a shell of his former self."

There was a pause, and we said nothing, so the angel continued.

"It was two months ago when he announced several new laws which affected the angels," said Godfrey after glancing back to his pack. "My kind were given curfews and were not allowed to be seen in public with lizards or men. They were taxed heavily as well, and soon my people were struggling to live on scraps. Being a knight captain of the royal army, I entered the castle to seek out the king, yet was exiled to the desert with all those loyal to me in tow."

"Why has he changed all of a sudden?" I asked.

Godfrey took a drink of water from his canteen. "I cannot be sure, but ever since he was visited by a Thundrian steward many months ago, he has changed."

"A Thundrian steward?" Ariel asked.

Godfrey nodded. "A man by the name of Grosovner. I do not know what conspired between the two of them, but I fear my king has been tainted by the man, who has since left this land."

Upon hearing the name of the nation that had damned my whole company I glanced at Ariel, who returned my gaze with one of dread. Theron watched as Mithias turned toward me with a stare of uncertainty about him before he spoke up in an unusual tone.

"How have you survived this desert for so long?" asked Mithias in an inquisitive voice. "We've been in this wasteland for only a couple of weeks, and on more than one occasion we have come close to death."

"We have not strayed far from this spot," responded Godfrey as he knelt by the spring and began to fill his canteen with water. "This is the only water above ground for miles, so many animals flock here. Their meat has tided us over for these two long months, and this spring has yet to dry up, yet we are unsure of how long we can survive the relentless desert."

The angel took a swig from his canteen before wiping his mouth and asking, "So the four of you are heading for the capitol?"

"Yes," I answered. I was still unsure how much I could trust this angel, yet the bars around my heart wore thin to his plight, and I awaited one of my comrades' voices to assist me. I wished that someone in my group would speak of Thundria's conquest of the known lands. None did, so after an awkward spell of silence the angel spoke again.

"What business do you have there?" he slowly asked with an amused yet perplexed look about his features.

I hesitated, as the others went silent. I did not fully trust Godfrey, but apparently the angel in my company did. Ariel stepped toward him and softly said, "Perhaps we should discuss it in private."

Godfrey laughed for a moment and stretched out his arms as he stated, "Not a single person in my company has seen a moment of privacy in two long months. There are simply too many angels around for us to talk in private. Now tell me, what is your business?"

"We best trust him," said Ariel as she turned toward us. Godfrey's eyes met mine and seemed to bore into my soul. As the angel turned back to Ariel, a minute discomfort arose within my stomach as she added, "We both fight against the same enemy."

Not a moment of silence lingered about the air before Theron stated, "She's right."

He turned toward Godfrey then and began to speak briefly of the Thundrian threat that could lie beyond the nearest horizon.

He quickly told the angel of Thundria's advances across Alfras and Finre. Mithias added that we had been told by the dragon Mordikai to go toward Firius and warn the king of the Thundrian advances. We chose to leave out Ainsly's words about the power of the pillars, for fear and uncertainty bound us to his royal secret. As we concluded our tale, the angel donned a look of disbelief and resentment.

"Do you take me for a fool?" he yelled in a voice that drew the attention of several angels around him. The four of us stood dazed and confused before the angel as he asked, "A dragon?"

"Our story is unbelievable, yes," I started as I slowly advanced toward him. "Yet it all happened."

"What proof do you have?" shot back Godfrey in a voice as hot as the desert sun.

In a rare display of charisma, Mithias added, "Does it matter? You can choose to believe us or not, it won't stop us from going toward the capitol. A message was entrusted to us, and we plan to deliver it. You should consider it a great honor that we would share such information with a stranger."

The human and angel stared each other down for several tense moments that seemed last on forever. Finally, Godfrey averted his gaze from the strong man's eyes, turned away from us, and looked out over his unorganized company in defeat and silence, yet Mithias was not done.

"But perhaps our meeting has meaning," Mithias stated after a moment of silence. The angel turned his head toward us and Mithias continued with his hand upon the angel's shoulder. "Our meals have been few and we were out of water before we came upon this oasis. Each member of my lot knows that death could reach our limited number at any moment. The company of those with food and water would be much appreciated."

"Are you suggesting that we come with you?" asked Godfrey.

"I'm suggesting that your company escorts us to the capitol, your home," remarked Mithias.

To this suggestion the angel instantly spun around, "Are you insane? I was exiled upon pain of death! If I were to return with my company, the king would send his guard against us. They would think me to be leading a coup."

"Are you so sure the guard would attack you on sight?" asked Theron. "You said you were knight captain of the guard. They must have some respect for your word."

Ariel was quick to add, "The fact that you have been expelled from your homeland just after the arrival of a steward from Thundria is suspect. There is something beneath the surface of what you see, and surely the people of the capitol think so as well."

"What are you suggesting?" shot back Godfrey.

I spoke up. "The king of Thundria uses dark devices to achieve his goals. Do you find it mere coincidence that your kind are damned to this desert after a Thundrian steward arrives in your kingdom? You know now that Thundria is slowly engulfing all the world in chaos, so would it not be wise of the Thundrian king to rid the Drientian capitol of her knight commander and those loyal to him before an attack?"

The angel stumbled upon words for a moment before uttering a sentence laden with grief brought about by loving memories.

"I was the most adorned and cherished commander in that city," stated the angel with a distant gaze. Godfrey almost held a smile as he added, "All praised my name, and the king himself looked to me as a valued friend. I was sworn to protect my homeland at all costs."

"You are still sworn to protect Drientus," Theron commanded in a stern voice. "March into the city with us and reclaim your rightful place in Firius. Hold the banner of Drientus high as you go toward the castle. The people of your homeland have been blinded and do not know of Thundria's might. Bring vision to them once more."

Mithias was quick to add, "Besides, if the city loves you as you say, your march will not be hindered."

"Then what would we do?" asked Godfrey as a glimmer of hope sparkled in his eyes. Ariel was the first in our lot to speak proud words.

"If your king cares for Drientus in the least he will act to defend it from the Thundrian forces," she said. "We will confront him with all your forces inside the castle hall."

"Besides," I added in a voice that pulled all attention toward me. "Your capitol is at risk of falling to evil. If you still have any loyalty for your land, then surely you do not want to see your kingdom succumb to steel and flame."

Godfrey confidentially raised his head toward all of us, his eyes aflame with great passion as a sly smile befell his face. He yelled with a force and vigor that brought the surrounding angels toward him.

"All right, then!" he said with a youthful enthusiasm from years long past. "The veil that has been cast over my home shall not remain! We will ride to our home and uncover the truth for our people!"

Few words were said to the angel after his passionate affirmation. Godfrey rounded up his legion and declared that we were friends of his company and were to be treated as such. He declared that the nation of Drientus was in danger. After adding that all those in his company were sworn by oath to protect their nation, many agreed to follow their captain. The few who still hesitated to march back into the city that had exiled them eventually agreed to return, for they knew that surviving in the desert forever was not a realistic possibility.

And so it was that we joined company with Godfrey and his legion. Each angel in his group rode a powerful steed and formed ranks upon Godfrey's command. The four of us mounted our horses and joined Godfrey in front of his ranks as he galloped to the southeast with great anticipation. The falcon screeched as it shot through the southeastern skies toward our destination.

For many days we rode alongside Godfrey. During the day the hot sun pounded down upon us, and during the night the frigid cold threatened our very lives, but in Godfrey's company we felt much safer than before. The four of us soon befriended the proud angel, and through our frequent conversations, my company and I grew to appreciate Godfrey for his playful banter and wise disposition that seemed far past his years. Our remaining time braving the hardships of the desert was well spent in such welcoming arms.

When we found ourselves back on grassy plains that were graced with a mountain range before them, I was overwhelmed by a feeling of relief. We crossed the mountain range by way of a simple path and followed a serpentine river that swiftly flowed north for another day before we finally saw it split. Ainsly was accurate in his directions, for as the river split we beheld an imposing bridge that crossed onto the land on the other side of the great waters. Our lot of hundreds crossed it with the banners of Drientus held high in our ranks as the distant peak that stood in the center of the capitol city became visible on the horizon. It was in this city that we would finally make our stand against Thundria.

CHAPTER 20

Isalia had traveled many long weeks before she finally found herself standing in the halls of her fortress once again. She stood in the highest hall of the highest tower, where her king sat alone in darkness. Before him there was a simple table with a mirror on its surface. Planted upon the mirror was a globe of whisping shadow that watched as she slowly entered the room. As Isalia knelt before the dark figure, he leaned forward to see her in the ring of light cast by numerous torches that hung on the wall.

Isalia began to stand up as she stated, "I have traversed the seas and flown to your halls with the utmost speed. Now please, grant me the honor of hearing your wisdom."

"You have progressed through Alfras and Finre quite well," responded the shrouded figure. Isalia was about to give him thanks for his kind words, which were all too rare, but he added, "Marcus' troops have set down on Drientus and met up with my reinforcements. The army of Hate that swept up the western coast of Finre has landed in Drientus and will be upon the capitol soon. The fires of war will come to the Drientian capitol in the coming days."

Without a moment's silence Isalia smiled and said, "I plan to join the army of Hate after our time concludes. We will take hold of Firius with ease."

The shrouded man fell silent and let out a sigh of discomfort. The mysterious figure glanced at the orb before him with unease about his heart. After a moment of contemplation, he looked up at the scarlet lady. Isalia picked up on her lord's unease and took a step toward the table with the mirror on it. In dismay she asked, "What troubles you? Drientus will not oppose us. Your hand has shadowed their land for months; now all you must do is tighten your grasp."

"You think it is so simple?" the man asked as he glanced down at the orb that seemed to hold a lightning storm within its confines.

Isalia hesitantly shifted her balance. "Do you doubt your own plan?"

"There is reason to bring such force to the capitol, even when the people are blind," he said in a gritty, inhuman voice. His pulsing, crimson-tinted eyes met Isalia's as he slowly added, "A thorn lies in my side as of late."

The scarlet woman became angered by her lord's vague speech, but she held her composure as she asked, "Of what do you speak?"

The man looked at the general with a sinister gaze as he spoke in a deep voice that did not seem to be his own. His crimson eyes flashed and turned pale white. The king was not himself as he continued to speak.

"Isalia," he began in an almost demonic tone, "I want you to bring someone to me. Too long has he traveled without my guidance. Too long has he lived under the misconception that I must be destroyed. Bring him to me so that I may, enlighten him."

"Anything, my lord," stated the lady without hesitation. "Who is he?"

The king motioned for her to look into the orb on the table, and she scuttled over to it like a rat to cheese. The king watched as the orb before him projected images of the one he wished to see onto the surrounding walls. The images moved and danced about and mirrored the actions of the young man through his tumultuous journey. The dark lord gave Isalia the name and location of her target before the image upon the wall faded.

"He is of great importance to me. Harm him if you must, but do not send his soul to the other side, for there he will be lost to me. If that happens, you will join him in the afterlife."

"Of course. It will be easy to claim him," she stated with confidence as she took a step back. At this, the being who spoke in a demonic tongue asked, "Will it?"

Isalia looked at the king in fear and confusion. He snapped, "Through this orb I have seen him escape you many times. He was on the eastern island of Alfras during your attack, and he even evaded that wretch of an underling, Marcus, at Eurtongard."

Isalia was quick to reply to the man's anger with soothing words that reeked of overconfidence.

"Rest assured," began the lady, who did her best to hide her panic. "He is my priority."

The stern king looked her over as he sat down. He let out a groan as if he were an old man as he sat on his wrought iron throne. His muscles settled and his eyes returned to their former tint once more. In a humanlike voice devoid of any demonic tone he declared, "Do not let your pride get in the way of duty, Isalia. The commands of the one who has granted us such power must be met. If you cannot bring me the boy, he will end you without hesitation."

Isalia quickly nodded, bowed to him, and exited his chamber. She hustled down the stairs of the great tower and emerged on the walls of his castle. The night air was thick and blew her short blonde hair all about as she glanced down at her quivering hands. After she stilled her shaking hands she made haste down the steps and across the castle drawbridge to where her charcoal steed waited for her. She mounted the animal and sped off through streets that were filled with soldiers who patrolled day and night. The lady knew nothing of the young man she had been told to apprehend, yet her resolve did not waver. Lloyd would be brought to the dark lord, of that she was sure.

* * *

The company of fallen angels with my lot in their ranks arrived in Firius at dusk. The guards who stood at the northern gate had not yet lit their torches for the evening. A night watch stood in two rows in front of the gate, which we steadily approached on our mass of horses. I hardly paid any mind to so few soldiers, for the capitol was a marvel before my lolling eyes.

It was built around a dormant volcano that expelled a thin ribbon of smoke at all times of the day and night. The peak emitted a soft ginger glow in the dusk, and as we rode forward it looked as if the horizon itself bent to the will of the massive peak. The city was built in levels of white marble streets that encircled the volcano, which reminded me of the layout of the Finrean capitol. Unlike Eurtongard, however, there were no slums within the city, and each level exhibited a grand image that did not wane as my eyes scanned the city. Also, the city walls did not enclose Firius in a simple circle; rather, they jutted out toward the plains then shot back to the city at an angle. During my studies on the way to Drientus I learned that the walls formed a seven-pointed star. The walls themselves were massive and built in stories so that one could stand within them and view the surrounding lands through small arrow slits. As if the arrow slits were not enough, beneath the few gates to the city were numerous murder holes.

The main palace was easily visible from where I sat on my horse, but from a distance I could not behold its full grandiosity. It had many high towers that rose far above the mountain's peak. These towers found their resting places above the clouds, and as I looked at them I wondered just how far they stretched into the heavens. The buildings upon the mountain made it look as if marble spikes shot out from the earth itself. Once we reached the closed gate and the palace became hidden behind the wall, roughly two dozen guards held spears to our company.

"Halt!" yelled one of the guards in a nervous voice upon seeing our mass. Godfrey rode his willful horse to the front of our thunderous legion and looked at his former underlings. When the guards saw Godfrey, a stunned look came upon their faces and murmuring broke out in their ranks. Soon, one of the younger-looking guards spoke.

"By order of the king," stated the child, who looked to be a few years my junior, "all angels that follow the former knight captain Godfrey are to remain in exile upon pain of death."

Godfrey's massive steed stirred at these words, yet the angel quickly calmed the beast and glared at the guard as he spoke. Godfrey's eyes glistened as he looked at the young man. He was clearly pained to be in such a position. As Godfrey spoke, the child listened intently, as if he were the angel's son.

"Hans, is it?" he asked the young guard. The boy looked at his friend by his side for some sort of reassurance. When he got none, he slowly turned back to Godfrey and nodded his head. The angel said, "I have trained you since you were old enough to stand on your own and hold a blade."

Hans was silent and brought his gaze to the ground at Godfrey's words. Godfrey then looked at the older, more experienced-looking man to Hans' right. "Jacob Blacksin. You and I fought side by side in the battle of the Steeped Soldiers not five years ago."

"That we did, Godfrey," the man replied.

"How many barbarians did we manage to slay that day?" asked the angel.

"In the fray I counted twelve by my blade and sixteen by yours, but time has skewed my memories," the man softly replied.

After a short nod, Godfrey looked at each guard and recited his name. Following the name, he said a sentence about how he had helped that guard sometime in his life. He had helped some hunt, others had received wise words, and one man had even had Godfrey's assistance in delivering his firstborn child. Godfrey recited all he had done for the lot before asking, "Is it truly a crime to let your friend talk to the king?"

After a moment of hesitation, one of the guards pointed his spear in the air and placed it by his side. The others soon did the same in silence as they averted their eyes from their former master. Godfrey proudly nodded his head and rode his horse forward.

I was right behind Godfrey when a single soldier looked at him and whispered, "Be wary, master. Although we choose not to fulfill the law, there are soldiers within the walls who will. The king has brought those who have fallen from your grace to his side."

"Praise be to you for your wise words, friend," Godfrey responded as he set his sights upon the distant palace and spurred his horse forward through the gate with my company and his soldiers not far behind. The thick city streets were populated only by a handful of humans, all of whom looked worried and frightened. As we rode on, most of them looked at Godfrey and his loyal knights with surprise on their faces, yet their surprise turned to warm smiles after the initial shock of seeing an angel in the streets once more wore off.

The streets themselves were far better maintained than those of Eurtongard. Each building that lined the street was a marvel of modern architecture. Homes for families no larger than mine were five, sometimes ten times bigger than my former home on Alfras. It did not cross my mind to wonder why no lizards roamed the streets, yet Theron could not keep himself quiet as he noticed this.

"Where have all the lizards gone?" asked Theron as we rode.

Godfrey frowned at Theron as he replied, "It would not surprise me if the curfew now applies to both."

The streets encircled the volcano and slowly ascended to the peak in a massive spiral that was lined with houses. The road we traveled was cut from the mountain itself, and every building past the ground level was embedded in the side of its rocky face. It took us a great deal of time to reach the fourth and final level of the city. At this level we found more guards in the streets than civilians. These guards gave us uncomfortable stares and nothing more, yet I hardly paid any mind to them, for my gaze was fixed elsewhere.

The fourth level of the city was still far from the peak of the volcano, but from where I rode I saw two ways to reach the volcano's rim. One was by ascending scattered and worn earthen steps engraved into the side of the volcano. Because we were so far from the peak, I imagined that ascending these stairs would take a great deal of time and strength as opposed to the second method of reaching the peak. The palace we were steadily approaching had three large spires arranged in a triangular fashion with a fourth, taller spire in the center. The tallest of the four spires stood in the middle of the other three and stretched past the distant rim of the volcano. As this spire ascended into the sky I could see a thick bridge connecting the rim of the volcano to the tip of the spire. The bridge had marble supports embedded in both the spire it emerged from and the rocky face of the volcano it spanned to. As I continued to gaze at my surroundings, our whole company rode past guards who watched us diligently as we approached the fortress.

The palace was built in front of the north side of the volcano. The four towers that spanned high into the sky were each grand with massive curved spikes coming out of their sides and numerous man-sized windows lining their walls at every story. These spires did not cast a shadow down upon the city, but rather they shadowed the radiant volcano that tinted them orange. Once we approached the gate before the magnificent palace, a handful of guards stopped us. After some talk, Godfrey was able to convince them to let us into the castle due to his former status. Before he progressed, they warned Godfrey of the newest members of the royal guard who stood by the king, and Godfrey gave them the same thanks he had given the guards at the main gate to the city. The angel commanded his legion to wait as he took my company and five other guards into a lavish courtyard. We dismounted from our steeds as the falcon that had saved us from starvation numerous times swooped down into the quad and perched on a low-hanging branch. Per Theron's request, the falcon stayed behind while Godfrey approached the tallest spire to the north. The angel was about to enter the main building with a handful of his guards, but my company would not stay in the courtyard so we quickly followed him into the massive tower that could instill primal fear in the most stone-cold hearts.

Once inside, Godfrey commanded that we follow him closely and quietly. Any guards who stood before us stood awestruck as their revered captain calmly but hastily walked through the gigantic halls of the tower. Soon we found ourselves in a hall with many columns on either side of an ornate rug that stretched a long way down the hall. Guards stood in front of each column and drew their weapons as Godfrey continued past them with a grand stride. Godfrey's stride did not falter until two foolish guards came between him and a pair of intricate double doors. Both wore simple leather garb, and when one began to speak, Godfrey donned a look of rage.

"By order of the king," began a guard who held his hand before Godfrey, "none shall enter the throne room."

Godfrey was about to speak until the guard looked to him and declared, "Any angel, even one of your former status, shall be killed if you attempt to enter."

To this, Godfrey sneered at the man and stated, "So you are the one the others now loathe. Would you really deny me, Kalias? Would you deny your leader?"

The man did not fall victim to Godfrey's charisma. He held his left hand extended as his right brushed the hilt of the blade that rested in his scabbard. As he did this, he looked at Godfrey with contempt and declared, "Don't make me kill you, captain."

Godfrey smirked at the thought, and after a moment, he replied, "I'd like to see you try Kalias."

In a flash of movement Godfrey latched onto the guard before him with a single hand. Using a strength that did not seem to befit him, the angel threw the guard to the side. Suddenly, a multitude of guards flooded the room and rushed toward us. I was rushed by a soldier with a pike who did not hesitate to thrust his weapon at me, but I nimbly avoided the blow before pulling the weapon out of the guard's hands. Once I held the pike, I slammed the back end of the instrument against the soldier's face with one swift move and knocked the man unconscious in an instant. Before his body even hit the floor I had whipped the pike around to face another guard. Through instinct alone I parried a blow from his sword with the pike before slamming the wooden pole into his face. He hit to the ground with a thud and entered the unconscious realm alongside his friend. I whipped around toward Godfrey, expecting more guards to rush me, but to my surprise all but two had been dispelled. My companions and Godfrey's guards all looked frazzled, and it was clear to me that they had each dispelled the attackers that threatened us all. The two guards of the king's employ who remained exchanged a worried glance before dropping their weapons to the floor and kneeling to their former captain. I dropped my temporary weapon to the ground. Godfrey strode past the cowards and barged through the doors as my company followed. Godfrey ordered the five soldiers who had come with us to guard the door and make sure no one passed as we strode into the throne room.

The room was grand and laden with gold columns on either side of a single long rug at our feet. At the end of the rug sat an old, weak king who looked far past his youth. The king was adorned with pristine scarlet robes, countless jewels, and numerous lesions and boils upon his wrinkled skin. Once we entered, he stood up from the throne and looked at the five of us with dismay as Godfrey swiftly approached.

"Godfrey!" His voice boomed through the chamber with a power unimaginable for his small figure. The old man raised a pale finger toward the approaching angel as he shouted, "How did you enter this place?"

"I have decided to return, my king," responded Godfrey without breaking his stride. The pale king stood among four guards who frantically turned to Godfrey as he approached.

"You have been exiled upon pain of death!" yelled the king in a wavering tone.

Godfrey continued his unhindered approach. "I have decided to return and take my chances."

The king turned toward the guards at either side of him and shouted, "Kill them!"

The guards approached us with their weapons drawn, but I refused to draw my weapon against them. My comrades and Godfrey did the same and held their ground. The first enemy to approach me grabbed my collar, but I skillfully pushed him backward and he lost his grip. Another guard approached me from behind and tightly wrapped his arms around me before I could evade him. His grip soon loosened, though, for Mithias hit the back of his head and the man fell to the ground with a thump. The one I had pushed to the ground struggled to stand up in his armor, but stopped once I kicked aside his sword, which lay on the ground near him. I drew my blade on the innocent man and held it to his neck as my company incapacitated the remaining soldiers. The king slowly stepped back as the angel advanced.

Godfrey paused when he was just out of arm's reach of the king and donned a look of sorrow.

"Why have you done all this, my king?" he begged. "Why impose such laws upon your people and exile those most loyal to you?"

The king staggered toward a curtain behind him and grabbed a blade from a hidden weapons rack. His left hand quivered as it held the blade with the point directed at Godfrey's throat. Godfrey looked at the fearful man for a moment before he glanced down to the king's hand. It was then that his tightened brow loosened and his eyes softened.

"My king," he began slowly before raising his eyes from the king's left hand. "You have always been right-handed."

The king remained silent as Godfrey scanned his features for a moment before adding, "And the scar above your eye that you received when hunting boar as a lad is gone. By all that is holy, how did I not notice this?"

The king sweated profusely and the blade loosened in his grip as Godfrey took a step forward and yelled, "Who are you and what have you done with my king?"

In a flash the impostor disappeared behind the curtain. Godfrey ran after him as I heard the sound of footsteps clamoring against stone steps. I lifted my sword from the frightened guard and followed Godfrey and my companions, who rushed up the stairway. We hustled up the spiral stairs to a hall that became narrower and narrower as we progressed until it was too thin for us to continue side by side. At the end of this narrow hall, Godfrey watched the king burst through a thick wooden door. The angel was hot on his tail with my company close behind in a single-file line. The old king traveled faster than any senior I had ever beheld, and he breathed heavily with the might of a valiant youth. Once past the doors, he attempted to close them, but Godfrey sprinted toward his destination with all his might and reached the doors just in time to slam his weight against them. The angel burst through the doors and knocked the king to the ground before the rest of my company joined him in the room. As soon as I entered the room, my eyes beheld a sight so surprising that I almost could not believe that which was before me.

A slowly rotating, diamondlike structure that held a translucent tint in its sky-blue walls was before us. This structure hovered several inches above a stepped, circular golden basin. Upon this basin were countless engravings of strange characters that I did not recognize. The crystal spun very slowly in a clockwise direction as I took it in. The structure seemed benign, yet upon closer inspection I discovered the disturbing reason why it was tucked away in this room. Within the confines of the device I could see an old man floating with his arms extended and his eyes closed. He looked exactly the same as the king who had fled from us and was dressed in the same attire.

"What type of trickery is this?" whispered Godfrey as he put his hands on the side of the crystal.

Before he could examine the structure further, the impostor emerged from behind the door that Godfrey had swung open. The man was bleeding from his skull after having the door slammed into his cranium and let out a wail as he brandished the small blade. He shot toward Godfrey's back and revealed gold-tinted teeth as he brought the knife down upon my newest friend. Had Godfrey not seen the man's reflection against the strange crystal, I fear he may have died, but luckily the angel's astute perception caused him to see the attack. In a heartbeat, Godfrey whipped around and grabbed the man's arm. Godfrey rushed him to the wall, where he slammed the suffering man into the cold gray stone.

Godfrey was but inches from the fiend's face as he screamed, "What have you done to my king?"

The sneering pretender firmly declared, "You'd best take your hands off of me before my guard arrives."

Godfrey let out a primal scream as he threw the helpless fraud toward the spinning crystal. The impostor slammed against the golden basin with a force that surely broke one or more of his ribs. Upon impact, the trickster howled in pain and lurched away from the gold basin that had broken his bones. Godfrey lifted him to his feet and slammed him against the wall once again.

"Get him out!" Godfrey yelled in the face of the impostor. As he said this I started to hear footsteps echoing through the narrow corridor beyond the doors. Mithias and Theron grabbed the two open doors and pushed them shut. Together, they brought a large plank of wood down against the doors just before they began pulsate inward. The two held the doors shut as angry banging came from the other side. Godfrey didn't even glance at the door as he held the impostor against the stone wall in between two small windows.

"Mithias!" he yelled as he tightened the grip on his victim. "Use your axe to break the crystal!"

Mithias glanced at me for assistance, so I ran to the door and put all my weight against it. Mithias then left his place and ran to the crystal with his massive axe in hand. Before he could strike the crystal, however, the force of the door crashing inward caused me to fall onto the ground and I watched as several guards flooded in with weapons drawn. They rushed in with swords in hand but came to a sudden halt once they saw the king in the crystal.

"Guards!" yelled Godfrey as he held the false king against the wall with one hand. "This man deceives you! He is not your king."

The guards said nothing, but angrily looked between the impostor and Godfrey. Godfrey was quick to exclaim, "His majesty has been imprisoned by this vagrant who seeks to undo us all!"

Not a moment of silence passed before the rat in Godfrey's grasp spoke.

"No!" squealed the false one in a sharp voice. Godfrey instantly punched the impostor in his bloodied face with his free hand before he yelled, "Mithias free him!"

The guards did nothing as Mithias raised his axe high into the air. Ariel, Theron, and I looked on as the sharpened axe struck the spinning crystal and shattered it into a million miniscule shards that rained upon the ground. In an instant the king's limp body fell to the golden base with a loud thump. Godfrey dropped the bloodied and beaten charlatan before rushing over to his king. Once by his side, the angel delicately cradled the frail old man in his trembling arms. Godfrey raised his ear to the king's mouth and listened for air as the whole room fell silent. The king's eyes were shut and no breath escaped his mouth. All feared the worst until salvation came to the formerly imprisoned ruler. The king coughed many times as his eyes lit up with life and his body convulsed madly. Godfrey continued to hold him as the king's eyed darted about the room before landing back on the face of his angelic captain. As his coughing slowly subsided he looked up at Godfrey.

"Is that you, my friend?" he whispered before more coughs broke through his breath. Godfrey paid no mind to those around him as he smiled to the king.

"It is, King Tiam," Godfrey responded as several guards rushed over to the king and slowly lifted him off the ground. The king lifted his right arm in the air then dropped it to his side. He did the same with his left as Godfrey and two soldiers helped their fragile leader up. The old man looked down while he was raised, but once the soles of his feet graced the ground for the first time in months, he looked up at Godfrey. The king's eyes widened with fear as he looked over Godfrey's shoulder to see a terrible image.

"Look out!" he yelled raspy in a voice laden with fear.

Godfrey turned around just in time to see the impostor rushing at him with his knife draw. The angel whipped around and grabbed the false king's hand then skillfully twisted it around so that the knife plunged into the villain's gut. The cold steel pierced the fake one's flesh and caused a look of utter shock to appear on the man's scared face. Godfrey pushed this fraud over to the window and slammed his back against the glass with such a force that it cracked. It was then that the true identity of the impostor was revealed.

The impostor's skin changed from beige to a light brown as the gray hairs upon his head began to fall to the ground. The old flesh that adorned his muscles turned young again as his face began to fill with color. His hair fell out until only a tan and bald scalp could be seen. The deep blue eyes that once looked at Godfrey with contempt turned to a dark shadow of brown as the impostor's once-wrinkled features vanished. Once the true identity of the man was revealed the true king began to speak.

"Grosovner?" the king asked as the man struggled to remain in the world of the living. "Is that you?"

The man gasped for breath as Godfrey whipped around and asked, "Grosovner? The steward from Thundria imprisoned you?"

The old king murmured, "Yes, it was he who stole my likeness just before locking me away in my own tower. He was the one who nearly killed me."

In an instant Godfrey picked up the dying man and slammed him into the cracked window that looked out over the magnificent city.

"What did you hope to achieve?" yelled Godfrey before he slammed the man against the glass again. "Why did you manipulate this kingdom?"

In the face of certain death, Grosovner managed to crack a smile after coughing up profuse amounts of blood.

"This is a mere setback," said the broken man, who smiled a bloody grin after his trite statement. "The armies of my land shall burn this place to the ground whether they are allowed entry or not. My death changes nothing."

Theron looked at the steward with disdain as he uttered, "He imprisoned the king in this chamber to benefit Thundria."

Godfrey yelled in a terrible anger, "This man was going to open the gates for the invaders under the authority of the king!"

After a moment of rage, Godfrey collected himself and tightened his grip on the steward. Godfrey continued to hold the steward against the window with all his might as his eyes met the king. The benevolent ruler looked at the steward, who gasped and coughed with every passing breath. Godfrey donned a malicious frown before the king swiftly nodded.

Godfrey turned back to the steward with a sly grin upon his face as he spoke his final words to the fallen man. "You may be able to shape shift, but let us see if you can fly."

Without another word, the powerful angel shoved the wide-eyed man through the glass window. Glass shattered and flew down toward the ground as Grosovner wailed in terror. On his way down, Grosovner's legs smashed against a stone awning and instantly shattered. The man's scream brought all eyes to him as he plunged down the side of the spire toward the city streets far below. As we stood atop the spire, we heard his scream abruptly stop after a soft thud echoed in our ears. A second later, an exclamation from the general public could be heard echoing up from the streets below as civilians flocked to the smear of flesh and blood that had formed just outside the castle walls.

"Good riddance," Godfrey stated after he leaned forward to look out the broken window and wiped his hands together. After his deed was done, he calmly walked over to the king, who stood with an arm around each guard beside him. The guards easily propped his weak bones up as he spoke in a broken and fragile tone.

"Grosovner trapped me in the crystal months ago…." The old man struggled to speak. "He used the guise of friendship from our Thundrian neighbors to gain my trust, and through his darkness I was trapped. For so long I could do nothing as my waking mind heard all the horrors he unleashed upon my fair land in my image. He nearly destroyed all I sought to create as king."

Godfrey honorably bowed his head. "And he has met a fitting end for his actions against Drientus."

The sovereign nodded his head at this, and after letting out a brief moan, declared, "Take me to my throne, Godfrey. Let us unravel the evil that has settled upon this place."

The sun had set and the light of two great moons could be seen entering the windows on the fortress walls. The guards we had previously beaten shamefully carried their king down the stairs and through the curtains that led to the secret chamber. The five of us quickly followed them into the throne room, which was still littered with unconscious soldiers. Once the king was seated upon his throne he ordered his loyal soldiers to take those who had been knocked out to the castle infirmary. As his men followed their orders he looked at Godfrey with a playful smile on his face despite the severity of the situation.

"You really did a number on these men," stated the king with a smile.

Godfrey let out a hearty laugh. "It seems I did not train them as well as I hoped."

After sharing a brief laugh that only old friends could share, the king looked at my company with gratitude and spoke in a soft and thankful voice.

"Through my prison my attuned ears could hear all the workings of the castle. Beside Godfrey I heard four others fighting to save me. I know now that it was you four. I must thank you all for your efforts." He leaned against his throne. "Yet I do not know your names."

Godfrey introduced each of us and then the king nodded and thanked us once again for our help. Before he inquired about anything else, he asked, "What is the full extent of the evil that has been wrought upon my lands? How do the people of my land suffer?"

Godfrey struggled to speak as his face donned a look of dread. After some time, the angel hesitantly told his old friend of the terrible laws enacted by the steward and how he had been exiled. Upon hearing the full extent of the impostor's evil, the king shot up in his chair and yelled to the few remaining guards around him, "Go through the streets and spread the word that the real king is back! The curfews and laws against my people are abolished, now and forever. Let this kingdom be rid of Thundria's oppression."

The few guards in his company quickly exited of the throne room, leaving the five of us where we stood. Once again the old man slumped back on his throne and asked, "By the Two, how could this have happened?"

None of us could answer that question, so after a moment the king's curiosity got the best of him. He turned his attention to the four of us and asked us what business we had in his kingdom. I took the liberty of speaking on behalf of my friends.

"King Tiam, we have been told to warn you of an attack by Thundria."

"Thundria truly wishes to attack? During my incarceration I assumed they were planning something devious, but I did not know they would truly wage war." He paused for a moment and averted his eyes from mine as he added, "So Tulinthor has finally decided to expand his borders."

Theron perked up and asked, "Tulinthor?"

"The leader of the Thundrians, yes," the king declared.

I turned to the lizard beside me and noticed his look of utter confusion. After traveling with the lizard for so long I knew when his thoughts were swirling about, so I asked him to speak his mind. The lizard glanced at the king before he spoke.

"It was my knowledge that a man named Relinthor Lightningsong ruled Thundria," stated Theron, who looked to the king for correction. The king was quick to enlighten us.

"His reign ended nearly a year ago," said the wise man. "His son, Tulinthor Lightningsong, now continues the line of Lightningsong kings."

Before I could ask about this ruler, the king gazed into the distance and spoke of the one who he believed wished him dead.

"Tulinthor has a dark heart. I could tell from the moment I met him over a year ago that he longed for chaos. His desire for darkness would turn anyone from his presence, yet the impostor informed me that he still controls his kingdom. In fact, I was told that his people love him."

"How can that be?" I asked. "His empire is slaughtering innocents all over the globe. Their army lays waste to women and children!"

I could not believe that any sane man or woman would support a man who wrought such despair. My mind could not comprehend a nation willing to follow a master who unleashed his armies upon innocent women and children. I resented Thundria even more as the king began to speak once again.

"I cannot be sure of each Thundrian's belief." The king sighed. "But the steward talked of Tulinthor as if he were a god, and it is said that the people view him as such."

Godfrey appeared to grow annoyed with the conversation and was quick to interject. "Perhaps we should focus more on the matter at hand. If what these four say is true, we cannot idly question our enemy as they approach our gates."

King Tiam agreed and asked once again why his kingdom was under attack. I revealed the story of our journey and how Thundria had slaughtered all those before them. Though Ainsly and Triden had told me that all the royalty of the lands knew of the fourth pillar, I chose not to tell the king that Tulinthor sought the power of the pillars. He appeared weak from his trials and I knew that the coming battle wore heavily on his mind. If we survived the upcoming battle I would speak to him in private about Tulinthor's true intentions.

"We don't know why they have started attacking," I said. "Yet we know that all of Alfras and Finre have fallen to their might. Now they march toward your city."

"By the Gods," whispered the king as he slumped in his chair. "I have failed my people…. Grosovner sought to incapacitate me so the armies of Thundria could march into my city. He sought to open my gates and watch as my people were slaughtered."

"Yet he did not succeed," asserted Godfrey. The angel glanced at my company and waved his arm toward us. "These four are giving us a chance to redeem ourselves and defend our kingdom." Godfrey turned toward me. "How long until they attack?"

I shook my head. "I cannot be sure, but I have it on good authority that with each passing moment they move closer to these walls."

"Just wait for the ground to tremble uncontrollably," added Theron. "Their armies shake the very earth as they march. Vile, dark creatures the likes of which only the most shadowed corners of your nightmares can imagine will descend upon this place with a malice and cruelty unbeknownst to men. These creatures, summoned by the darkest magic, march under the banner of Thundria toward these hallowed halls."

The king moaned. "You seem to know more of our enemy than I. How do you combat such a force?"

"They may outnumber us," I said, with my knowledge of the city I had acquired on the ships to Drientus in mind, "but we hold the city. These walls haven't fallen for a thousand years."

"Their forces shall smash against my walls like ocean water on a cliffside," said the king.

"Yet like a mighty cliff, we shall not move," added Mithias as he stepped forward and met the king's eyes. "We shall fend them off with all our might."

The king looked up at Mithias with confidence in his face and began to glance over the room, briefly pausing at each of us as he met our eyes.

"Yes," he nearly whispered. The king shot up from his throne and looked at all of us with a newfound confidence. "They are strong, but so long as we hold the city, we hold the power necessary to overcome them. We can defeat them!"

Godfrey released a grin and bowed his head before the king. "It is good to have you back, Tiam."

The old man approached the kneeling angel with a smile upon his face. "Rise, Godfrey. If it weren't for you and these four travelers, I would still be in that prison."

"But—" started Godfrey, who was about to utter some formality.

The king raised his hand for silence and continued to speak. "But nothing. On this day you shall not bow to me." The king turned to our company as Godfrey reluctantly stood up. "Are you all sure you don't have any idea when they will attack?"

"You know as much as we do now," stated Theron. "They could come in a day, or they could come in a week. Our guide told us that we should travel to your halls swiftly, though, for the army would descend upon this place with a great speed."

"Wait, Theron," said Ariel. "They sacked Ikai right as we left...."

The angel approached the king and asked for a map. The king led our company to a side table near his throne. After spreading a map of the world out on the table, all eyes turned to Ariel. She put her finger on Ikai and moved it south to the ocean between Finre and Drientus. "These waters are dangerous, correct?"

"Of course," stated Mithias. "Jagged rocks and wild waters make it nearly impassable."

"So they had to sail their ships from Ikai to Chigo like we did. That would mean they are traveling south through the desert," stated Ariel in a soft voice that slowly rolled past her crimson lips.

"So they're still right behind us," I replied in a similar voice. A shiver rocked my spine as I came upon the realization that the Thundrian plague had probably followed us through the shifting sands of the desert.

"Then they shall be here soon?" asked Mithias.

"Probably," Ariel stated. "We do not know their pace, but the mass flies quickly by the will of its master."

Godfrey turned back toward King Tiam. "My king, a handful of my men and I could watch the bridge to the north. When we catch sight of the enemy we could ride back and warn of the attack."

The king shook his head. "You have done far too much for me already, Godfrey."

"No," Mithias replied as he turned toward the king. "Let him go with our falcon. The creature will fly into the desert and come back when it has caught sight of our enemy."

"I will take the bird to the desert," said Godfrey. "My duty to this kingdom is far from over."

The king reluctantly nodded. "It is up to you Godfrey." All of us turned toward the angel. "Send word of the coming attackers at first sight."

"It will take me a handful of hours to find my strongest brothers. We shall ride out under the moonlight and return upon first sight of the enemy," Godfrey concluded before leaving us.

The king frowned as Godfrey left the five of us in the room. His grimace turned to a look of hope as he laid his eyes upon my company.

"The four of you have done a great deed." He slowly made his way back to his throne. "If we make it out of this, I shall personally see to it that you each receive a great title within my kingdom."

The four of us said nothing, for in a time like this the last thing we were concerned with was obtaining rewards. Our survival was once again at stake, only this time death seemed so much closer in the face of the advancing horde.

The king suggested that we sleep in the guest quarters of his palace for, according to him, we would need our rest because our attendance in a war council the following day was to be mandatory. Our weary bones thanked him before he called an escort into the room. As we left the chamber, King Tiam told our escort to spread word of a coming attack on the city.

The escort led us down a maze of corridors and up a flight of stairs before we found our quarters. At the end of a spiral staircase we came upon a wooden door that was unlocked and opened for us. The marvelous room was located near the peak of one of the four towers. Four large beds lay against the left wall, and bookcases sat on either side of a fireplace across from the beds. At the end of the room, two glass doors stood open and gave way to a view of the southern part of the city. Mithias plopped himself onto a bed as Theron and Ariel began to peruse the multitude of books. I walked out to the balcony and leaned against the stone railing as the escort left our company. My thoughts swirled about as I looked over the marvelous display of civilized society before me, yet I feared that it would all be lost in the coming days. I took a deep breath as the events of the day played in my memory and prepared myself for the coming terror that would descend upon the beautiful lands all about me. Try as I might, I could not bring myself to remain calm and majestic during such times. I lay awake in bed for hours that night in hopeless anxiety before ultimately giving up on the hope of sleep.

CHAPTER 21

We had done as Mordikai had asked, and now we found ourselves trapped within the walls of a city on the verge of war. I could not sleep as my mind swirled about in an endless hurricane of senselessness, so I went to the terrace adjoining our small room that overlooked the city. The terrible tide of bloodshed had not yet reached the walls I stood behind, and for a moment I allowed myself to look over all that could be lost in the coming days.

From my place atop the high balcony in the massive tower I could see the full, unobstructed majesty of the southern city drenched in moonlight. The dormant volcano lay behind me, and in the westbound wind I could not smell any of its ghastly fumes. The city stirred in the night as the guards moved from house to house, spreading word of the coming battle. Upon hearing the terrible news men could be seen making their way to armories all around the city. Tears and harsh words flooded the city as news of battle came, yet no one could do anything but prepare for the onslaught that would soon come.

I saw Godfrey and several other angels riding out of the eastern city gates and onto the plains. The falcon flew after them as their horses galloped across the plains to the distant river that surrounded the land. In the night I could only clearly make out their lit torches, which shot across the plains like shooting stars in the dead of night. The city the gates were shut behind them and locked in place by nervous guards. I looked at the scene before me with dread in my heart as I contemplated the words of the king.

I could not comprehend why the Thundrians would follow a leader such as Tulinthor. By all accounts, he seemed a monster bent on destruction, yet according to the impostor Godfrey had killed, the people held him up as if he were divine. I feared the mad resolve of an army led by such a fanatic, and as I gazed across the city my thoughts became dark and clouded until a voice pierced them.

"It's terrible isn't it?" I turned to see Theron approach from behind and stop to look at the city as I had been doing.

"If we do not stop them here, all is lost," I replied in dismay as the lizard leaned against the stone divide on the edge of the balcony.

He nodded. "Yet, if we can stop them, this conflict may finally turn in our favor. This is our chance to stand against the force that has robbed both of us of our families."

I looked over to him and noticed that the light from the two moons reflected against the scales on his skin, which shimmered. I remembered the horrific day when he had lost his family. His anger, while terrible to others, had seemed normal to me, for it was the same rage that had enveloped me upon seeing the corpses of my family. Theron was a good soul who had been through the same hardship as I, and hearing his confident words brought strength to my weary soul.

"You are right, my friend," I responded with a smile as I leaned against the stone that separated my body from the city.

"Come now, Lloyd," said the lizard as he stood up straight once more. "I only awoke to use the chamber pot, not talk late into the night. The sun will not rise for many hours, and for us to stand here and wait for it would be folly. We need our rest."

Soon Theron was back asleep and I was in my own bed. Sleep did not come easily, but when it arrived it filled my mind with nightmares and terrible images of both past and present. Finally I awoke in a cold sweat and could not sleep again, so I turned to my side and noticed that Ariel was not in her bed. I frantically sat up and began to scan the room for her, but there were no signs of the angel. I silently but quickly stood up and turned to see a winged figure standing out on the balcony I had stood on earlier. As I approached the doors I beheld the angel in her full splendor. She wore a nightgown she had taken from a dresser in our room and looked out over the city that would not rest. Her full blonde hair whipped to the side in the wind, and her fair hands clutched onto the stone divide with great might. She looked out toward the people who would find no rest as the battle encroached upon Firius. Soldiers worked on fortifying the walls as best they could, but it was clear that even the thickest walls on the northern side of the city were weak from years of neglect, while the southern walls were marred with gaping holes. Past the city I could see only darkness that stretched into a star-laden sky that glowed in the light from the powerful volcano. The two moons were full, and the greater of the two cast its light with such a luminosity that it seemed as if it were not so late in the night. I knew that we still had hours before the sun rose and gave the city light during the dark times.

The door made a slight creak when I nudged it open, and this caused Ariel to quickly turn and look over her shoulder. She looked surprised, but when she saw me the look dissipated and gave way to a warm smile. The night air was still and cool as I walked up next to her and looked out over the plains.

"What brings you out here?" I asked as the angel kept her gaze transfixed on the city.

She let out a slow sigh before softly declaring, "I can't find any rest."

"Neither can I," I said, still looking out over the plains. "It seems that all we once held dear has left us, and now we stand beside the reaper. His cold grasp tightens ever more these days, and I fear we will be taken from this dismal world long before our natural time."

There was silence for a moment, then Ariel spoke. Her words had a certain sadness to them, the likes of which brought further sorrow to my heart. "This is the way things have to be, Lloyd. We must fight, even if that means losing all that we care for."

A southern wind began to blow against me, and I soon felt Ariel's grasp on my arm. Without thinking, I wrapped my arm about her and held her tight against the chilly breeze that shot about us. The air soon calmed, yet the angel still held my arm very tightly. I looked down at her and beheld a single crystalline tear rolling down her pristine cheek.

"What's wrong, Ariel?" I whispered.

She looked up at me and said nothing as the tear fell to the stone floor. Her grip on my arm tightened and she slowly leaned in and buried her head in my chest. She did not sob or speak as I held her; instead, she simply clung to me tightly, and I found myself returning the embrace. I looked down at her and her soft face soon looked up at mine. The beautiful blue eyes that I had admired for so many months gave rise to feelings the likes of which I had never known. In an instant, our lips met. I held her tight as she raised her soft hand to my cheek. For a single brief moment, we kissed and entered bliss against the dark landscape all about us. The cold air of the sinister night seemed to dissipate as the warmth of her body spread all through me. I am not sure how long the kiss lasted, but when it was over, I wished it had continued for a lifetime. I looked down at the angel and raised my hand to her face so that I could wipe away the remnants of her sole tear.

"Ariel," I said softly as I looked down at the creature who had enthralled my heart. "So long as I draw breath I will protect you."

"And I you, Lloyd," she responded as she remained in my grasp. I looked out over the plains with her in my arms and dreaded the coming storm even more. My life wasn't the only thing I was concerned about now; I had to protect the angel that I had come to so greatly admire. The two of us remained on the balcony for hours until the sun rose in the eastern sky. I could not think of anything but the angel beside me as I watched soldiers emerge from barracks and armories far below us. Most carried chain mail in their arms and wore their weapons on their backs as they walked past those who could not fight. Mothers and wives alike wept in the morning light as fathers gave their children last words of goodwill. As I looked down it was obvious some of the soldiers were only boys, just a few years younger than I. Ariel and I walked back into our room, hand in hand, and noticed that Mithias and Theron were still sound asleep. My eyes began to feel heavy, so I hugged Ariel tightly then moved to my bed and watched as she went back to hers. Mine was a rare sleep of unmarred content until I found myself being ripped out of my dream world and into reality as Mithias' voice flooded my consciousness.

"Get up, kid!" Mithias yelled just a few inches from my face as he shook my shoulders. I jolted awake and sat up so fast that my skull nearly slammed into Mithias' head. Luckily, the hefty man pushed away just in time to avoid a collision. I began to look about the room in confusion, but when I saw Mithias still in his normal garb I felt fine. Had he been dressed for battle I would have feared the worst and prepared myself for a fight. Instead, I calmly sat against the back of the bed and looked at my friend.

"We have visitors," he said as he walked to the door and pushed it open to reveal the spiral flight of stairs that had led us to this room. In front of the stairs was a small slit that served as a place archers could aim their bows during battle. Upon Mithias' request, I got out of bed and made my way to the small vertical opening in the wall. I peered down to the southeastern end of the city, where a great deal of commotion took place. The gates of the great city were being opened for a multitude of humans in tattered garb. In front of their scattered ranks rode a well-armed man on a snow-white steed.

I took my eye away from the scene and turned to Mithias just as he declared, "The king has requested that we meet with him while he greets these villagers."

"Who are they?" I asked.

"A guard told me they are from a southern village," Mithias said as he leaned on the side of the doorframe. "They saw Thundrian forces land not far from here and made haste for the capitol."

I looked back through the slit before asking, "How close are the enemy forces?"

Mithias shrugged before he suggested, "Why don't we find out now, lad?"

I nodded, then quickly slipped out of my nightclothes and into my usual garments as Mithias waited outside the door. Once I had my cloak on, I fastened my scabbard to my side and slid my worn yet sturdy sword into it. With Mithias leading the way, I rushed down the stairs to the courtyard below where I discovered my friends waiting for me on the stone pathway. It must have rained early in the morning, for the sky was overcast and the stones beneath my feet were slightly damp. As I approached Theron and Ariel, the lizard turned toward me.

"It's about time," remarked Theron as Ariel smiled shyly. My eyes fell to her as a grin emerged on my face.

"Lloyd sleeps like a log and remains as silent as a corpse as he dreams," said Mithias as a smirk spread across his broad face. The lizard and man began to chuckle slightly, but I did not mind, for laughter during such dire times was a relief. Nonetheless, Ariel intervened.

"Enough. He's here, so now we can go," she commanded.

The four of us made our way down to the first level on the southeastern side of the capitol, where we were met with a procession of worn humans who shuffled into the confines of the city with defeated looks upon their faces. They looked to be poor and carried little but the clothes on their backs. We pushed our way to the front of the scattered line to the man who sat atop a snow-white steed. The man held a deep frown on his scarred and war-torn face as the natives of Firius eyed him and his lot with fear and suspicion.

"Sir!" I yelled to him as he rode his horse forward. He paid me no mind and continued on, thus forcing me to tread up beside him and repeat myself. The man glared down at me with a cold stare from jade eyes between his thin jet-black hairs and yelled, "I shall speak to the king and the king alone, boy."

"Then speak swiftly," came a voice from behind us. I turned around to see the king walking forward with several guards by his side. The man who had spoken rudely to me instantly dismounted his steed and bowed before the king.

"King Tiam," stated the man with his head still bowed. He looked up as he continued his speech in a deep and powerful voice. "We come from the southern villages that serve your flag. An army of thousands set down on the southeastern shore near our village of simple farmers. Their ranks bore the mark of Thundria, yet they had terrible soldiers that were neither human nor animal alongside the men in their ranks. I myself witnessed their bloodthirsty masses shake the very earth. Upon seeing their ranks I returned to the village and ordered all to evacuate."

"The soldiers were neither human nor animal?" asked the king. These words brought fear to the surrounding mass, so the king stayed his curiosity for the moment and simply asked, "Is what you say true?"

"As true as the sky is blue, my lord," replied the ranger as his horse pawed the ground.

"We have much to discuss, then," said the king after nervously glancing my way.

"Guards!" he yelled to the lot that followed his steps. "Take all men who can fight from this lot and equip them for battle. Bring the others to safety on the fourth level."

As dreadful commotion began to spark in the crowd of simple farmers and workers, the king turned toward the four of us and quickly said, "You four will come with me."

We followed the king and the mysterious rider back up to the fourth level of the city and into the king's tower once again. He returned to the map he had laid out the day before, which detailed Drientus' every forest, mountain, river, and village.

"You claim they come from the south, ranger?" asked the King. All eyes turned to the unknown rider as the king circled a small area south of the capitol city on the map.

"Yes," said the ranger, whose face was adorned with old scars from battles long since fought. "I witnessed thousands hit ground, then a legion of nearly a thousand more join them with mighty siege weapons. These siege towers were many stories high, and each held a massive battering ram capable of easily destroying these worn and battered walls. On top of that, they were pulled by," the ranger paused to clear his throat, "the southern beasts."

The king met his eyes with a fiery gaze. "The beasts from the south? Are you sure?"

"Yes," replied the ranger. The two looked at each other with deep stares. I interrupted and asked what the southern beasts were, as my company had no knowledge of them.

The ranger turned toward me. "The black mantis. A beast twice as strong as any normal mantis. This monster bows to few masters except the strongest men." The ranger took several steps toward my company as he added, "It can slice through a man's torso in the blink of an eye with razor sharp claws. The body of this creature is muscular, and its hide is thicker than armor fashioned by the greatest blacksmiths. On top of that, I beheld terrible beasts in the ranks of men and lizards. These beasts bore the head of a wolf and the body of the human. Their howls still haunt me to this very moment, for through their cries I could discern a terrible thirst for blood. They are ravenous and hold the Thundrian banner high as they march this way."

Silence fell about the room as the king slumped in his great throne. His defeated gaze fell to the floor as he spoke in a distant and desperate voice. "We cannot win." The king looked at his map in dismay.

"My king?" the ranger said.

"It's all too much," stated the king as beads of sweat formed on his worn brow. "Their numbers are vast and their ranks are filled with horrors the likes of which inhabit the nightmares of only the darkest man. They ride black mantises and wheel their siege devices toward my tattered walls." King Tiam rose his head. "If we hope to live, we must surrender."

"Do not speak in such a way, old man!" Mithias yelled. The ranger glared at him and quickly strode over to Mithias.

"Respect your king!" he spat.

Mithias stepped toward the ranger with a stare of contempt and rage. "My king? I have no king, ranger, and you would do best not to assume otherwise. In all my long years I have killed many and seen many more fall to cowardice, but never did I think a king would slump so low." Mithias turned his fiery eyes to the king. "I have not traveled through frozen tundra and shifting sand alike to lay down my arms before an army of beasts that have taken so many from the world."

"Mithias!" yelled Theron before the ranger could get a word in edgewise. All eyes turned to the lizard as he stated, "Calm yourself."

Mithias continued to stare down the king, yet made no attempt to speak again, for another soon graced us with his presence. Godfrey walked into the room, and a foul aroma sifted through the air. He wiped several beads of sweat from his brow as he approached the king.

"I have news of the coming horde," he stated after glancing at my company.

The ranger turned toward Godfrey. "You are Godfrey, the knight captain of the Firius forces, correct?" Godfrey nodded his head, and the man quickly extended his hand and exclaimed, "It is an honor to meet you."

Godfrey firmly shook the man's hand and asked, "And who might you be?"

"My name is Pailo," said the ranger with pride. "I come from the southern village of Lilieon, which borders the swamps. I spotted Thundrian forces make landfall several days ago, so I evacuated my people."

"By the gods," said Godfrey as his gaze became obscured. "They're already at Lilieon?"

Pailo nodded before Godfrey slowly said, "That would mean they are not far behind you then."

Godfrey tightly gripped his forehead with the ends of his fingers as his eyes squinted shut. All watched him for a moment before he released his forehead and slowly stated, "I came back to say that the falcon has spotted them half a day's march away from us. I suspect they will be here by sundown."

For a moment Pailo looked confused. "Wait, there are two forces descending upon us?"

"My king, we must take action now or we will be caught off guard," Godfrey demanded without paying any mind to Pailo. The king said nothing as he stared past us all.

"My king?" Godfrey asked as he took a step forward.

The king snapped out of his daze and shook his head in confusion before looking around the room at the familiar faces before him. Several beads of sweat began to drip down his face and accumulate on his chin before they fell onto the ground as one. Once the single bead of sweat splashed onto the floor with a very minute sound, the king spoke.

"Our enemy holds the numbers to wipe us out by dawn." He looked at all of us and shook his head. "Is there no way to avoid such bloodshed?"

There was silence until I spoke amid the still air in a booming voice that cast all eyes upon me. "They have us by the north and south. To the east and west lie continents that are controlled by Thundrians. This city is the last ray of hope we have against Thundria. We must defend it with our lives, or else the world will burn."

Godfrey glanced at Pailo as he asked, "What do you know of the southern forces?"

"Their troops number in the thousands, and along with black mantises, they have siege towers capable of ripping through our feeble walls if they reach us," replied Pailo.

Godfrey shook his head in disbelief before turning back to the king and declaring, "We will stay behind both walls and attack the forces that threaten us."

Instantly I remembered all I had learned on my voyage to Drientus, so I quickly chimed in.

"Godfrey, we cannot hide behind the southern walls." The angel was quick to ask me why before I explained, "The northern walls may be weak, but the southern walls have massive grates within their bases to allow sewage to flow out of the city. These grates are rusted and worn from the mass amounts of sewage flowing through them. If a battering ram were to slam into the few man-sized grates, they would easily be able to shatter them. We could barricade them with sandbags or lines of pikes, but nevertheless it would not be difficult for a handful of enemies to push through one of the many grates in the wall."

"Then what do you suggest?" asked Godfrey.

I turned back to the king. "The capitol has a handful of catapults and ballistae used to defend it. Let us roll these siege weapons to the southern wall to combat the siege towers."

"But that will not be enough," said Pailo. "They had over a dozen towers, each more armored than the last. We cannot hope to destroy all of them with siege weapons."

I was at a loss until Mithias exclaimed, "Then we ride out to meet the southern attackers. We station troops outside the walls and ride forward against their masses. We must risk everything to keep the foot soldiers and the siege towers from reaching those drains. This city was not built for such an invasion from the south, so we must ride out to meet our enemy head on."

Mithias was able to smirk before adding, "The best defense is a good offense."

"Are you insane?" shot back Pailo. "To rush a legion of thousands is certain death!"

Mithias turned toward Pailo. "If you have any sense about you then you know our words are true. If Lloyd says the drains in the south will allow the enemy to get in, then we must do everything to keep the Thundrians from them."

Pailo did not reply, and a spell of silence lingered in the air for a moment. The ranger knew the terrible truth of the matter and reluctantly agreed to my idea.

"And what of the northern reaches?" asked Godfrey as the king remained seated.

"We should send all but the most skilled archers to the northern walls," Theron suggested. "Arrows will do little against black mantises and siege towers. Archers will be best used if they fight normal mantises and foot soldiers from the northern wall."

No objections were voiced to the plan, and silence lingered in the air. All turned back to the silent king, who looked as if he were in a different place entirely. His eyes were empty and his body was still as I spoke.

"Lord Tiam, I have witnessed the forces we face slaughter men, women, and children of all races and creeds. Their might blankets the land and blots out the sun as they tear through village after village. My company and I have suffered for many moons to reach this place and make a stand against them, and we plan on doing so whether your forces support us or not. We cannot lay down our arms, for if we do, the Thundrians will engulf this world in an evil the likes of which none could ever imagine."

No response came from the stoic king, so Godfrey made a stand and spoke.

"We cannot wait here." The angel turned toward us. "Our enemy outnumbers us and our options are few, so we best—"

"Enough, Godfrey," came the king's voice before the angel could finish. All turned toward him as he rose and declared, "You believe the enemy will be here within the day, correct?" Godfrey nodded "As much as it pains me to say, we must prepare for battle if we wish to see the rising sun." The old man turned his gaze toward Godfrey as he let out a deep sigh before softly declaring, "Any man, or woman, who can hold a blade must be brought to the front lines."

"You can't be serious, my liege!" objected Godfrey. "We cannot bring women into this. They have served as handmaidens and wives all their days and know nothing of combat!"

"And what would you have me do, Godfrey?" shot back the king. "You said it yourself: we are outnumbered and have little choice in our next course of action. If this battle must be fought, I will do anything to win it."

"Would you have me removed from the fight, Godfrey?" Ariel asked irritably.

Godfrey was quick to reply, "You have traversed the unrelenting desert of the north and proven yourself as one with exceptional will. You are not like the pampered women of this city."

Ariel snapped back, "We face the greatest force to threaten this land in generations with thin numbers and worn fighters. I am willing to take power from where you see none and, whether you like it or not, you know you need all the forces you can muster."

Godfrey would not be pacified, and instead shouted, "We are talking about mothers and daughters! We will rob children of their fathers as it is, but must we take from them their mothers as well?" Godfrey turned back to his king as he added, "Would we sacrifice the honor of our land to save our lives?"

"We will have no honor to hold if we lose our lives," said Mithias. The large man stepped between Godfrey and Ariel as he added, "Would you have the women rot on the highest level of the city when they could kill the enemy and save this city?" Before Godfrey could answer, Mithias harshly added, "Do not let your petty grievances lead to the destruction of this place."

Godfrey was still clearly irate, so Pailo approached the captain and spoke somber words. "I shall take it upon myself to ensure the safety of those who have no experience with a blade. They shall not be put on the front line."

The angel slowly looked Pailo up and down before declaring, "Let them guard the archers who will take to the northern wall. They will see little action so long as the Thundrians do not scale our walls."

Pailo nodded before Godfrey turned his gaze toward Ariel as he reluctantly added, "If the worst does occur, we can only hope their deaths will buy the seasoned archers time to retreat to higher ground."

Theron took a step forward. "Then my place will be on the northern wall, alongside the majority of the archers." The lizard as he turned toward Ariel, Mithias, and me. "The rest of you can take to the southern plains."

Mithias instantly grinned and shot back, "Oh no you don't!"

I looked at him in confusion before he placed his hand on the lizard's shoulder and added, "When the Thundrians make it up the northern walls, and they will, you'll need someone to protect your tail. I'm not about to leave that task to a handmaiden."

"Very well," stated the lizard in a hesitant tone.

"I, too, will join you on the northern wall," Pailo added as he stepped toward Theron and Mithias. "And I will make sure the soldiers of this city know where their talents will be put to the best use. Archers on the northern wall, cavaliers and men at arms on the southern plains."

I nodded as Pailo bowed before the king and took his leave.

Godfrey looked at the ancient king. "I shall take it upon myself to make sure the villagers hidden within the confines of the buildings on the fourth level are safe. Once that task is complete I will make my way to the southern plains."

Tiam approved this statement and the angel took his leave, leaving the four of us alone with the king. The king let out a sigh and slumped farther into his chair. His disoriented voice did not fit his status.

"What am I to do?" asked the king of no one in particular. I remained silent at this, yet for some reason Mithias grew angry.

"What are *you* to do?" Mithias yelled. "Is that all you're concerned about?"

"Calm yourself, Mithias," Ariel said as she put her hand on his shoulder.

"For a king, you don't seem very noble!" yelled the warrior as he gestured toward Tiam. "Are all the aristocracy of this land as cowardly as this?"

Ariel attempted to calm him, but it seemed to be to no avail. Instead, Mithias' irate behavior caused the king to shoot up from his throne.

"What would you have me do, then?" shouted the king.

Mithias was silent as Ariel released her grasp on his shoulder. He looked at Theron, who shrugged his shoulders as the king awaited an answer. The king watched as I approached him with a frown upon my face.

"You are too old to fight," I said as I placed my hand upon the king's shoulder, "But you can calm your people. The presence of their king among their ranks would calm them before the storm batters us. When the time comes, seek shelter with those who cannot fight and reassure them with your presence."

There was a moment of silence as we all looked at the king, who looked back at the four of us. He looked at us with a renewed sense of confidence as he slowly whispered, "I can do that."

"It is decided, then. We must make haste to our positions," I said without a hint of uncertainty in my voice. "The battle will be upon us soon whether we are ready or not."

And so the four of us took our leave of the king, who vowed to follow my advice and assist his people before the coming battle. As we entered the streets of the fourth level we looked down to the other levels and witnessed thousands of individuals running to the northern and southern walls. We heard the sound of children crying as mothers and fathers alike were ripped away from those they had brought into the world. Those who had never seen combat were given worn bows, while others were given dull swords the likes of which I doubted would prove their worth on the battlefield. Regardless of their weapons, their fates were clear because of their fear and inexperience. The four of us came to a halt when a stairway leading down to the third level presented itself. Theron and Mithias would make their way down the steps while Ariel and I would continue around the volcano until we hit the south side, where we belonged. I knew that my presence on the northern wall would do no good, and Ariel knew that her magical abilities were best used on the battlefield. At this point of separation, the four of us split into groups of two and looked at each other with remorse. A heavy silence befell our lot.

"I guess this is goodbye," said Ariel as she looked at Theron and Mithias with dismay. I found it hard to make eye contact with my friends, so I looked north to where the plains were clear as the grass blew in the gentle eastern wind. As Mithias began to speak, I held my distant gaze.

"No," Mithias declared in a soft tone. "We will see each other after the battle is won, that is for sure."

I knew in my heart there was no guarantee of my own survival, let alone the survival of all my friends. A battle of such great magnitude would claim countless lives, and I could only hope that my friends would not be among the dead or dying. As I thought of my own destruction and the loss of my comrades, Theron spoke words that calmed my mind.

"Though we have our differences, you three have been the closest thing I've had to a family since my loss." There was a long pause as I reflected on my time spent with these three before the lizard added, "Let us vow that we shall meet in this same place once the battle has finished. Let us vow that the morning light will cleanse us of all of the evils we encounter."

The four of us agreed to meet in the same sun-drenched spot once the battle was over. Though I still had a great fear about my heart, I reluctantly turned away from the only family, aside from my sister, I had left in the world. Ariel and I walked away from Theron and Mithias in silence until we came to the worn and ragged southern wall. Once there, we went into a guardhouse where we suited up for battle. We watched for the next two hours as soldiers exited the grand southern gate. On the field, men and women alike were packed into close formations that stood as still as stone. Each one of those who stood shoulder to shoulder seemed lifeless in their armor and looked out over the empty plains with a certain fear of death. The collective lot of thousands awaited a force bent on destroying all the light in the world.

I stood next to Ariel in silence, for I found that I could not conjure words as I awaited the reaper's cold hand. For the next several hours, I found that my hands trembled and my mind raced. The sun would set on a bloody battlefield, and I prayed that I would live to see the horrible aftermath.

CHAPTER 22

Four hours had passed since I had positioned myself outside the deep southern wall. The blazing heat scorched the ranks of soldiers who were frequently brought water from brave civilians who refused to seek shelter in the fourth level of the city. I turned and looked at the few archers who meandered about the walls above the closed gates in dreadful anticipation of the dawn of battle. Because the walls were built in levels, archers were positioned on each story. The archers in the middle sections were safest, for they could only fire through small arrow slits while the ones atop the four-story wall only had a line of waist-high rock to protect them from any projectiles. The main gate in the junction of two segments of wall was directly behind me, and to get into the city the attackers would have to pass under several murder holes between the plains and the end of the gate. The gaping sewage holes in the walls on either side of me had been plugged with sandbags, but with enough effort the enemy could break through them and crawl into the city. Because of this, we would charge the enemy and do our best to prevent them from reaching the tattered walls. Six other gates were positioned around the city, but it seemed most likely that the enemy forces would come toward this point. If they chose to attack another gate or spread their forces, we were ready to react accordingly.

I stood on verdant grass that slightly swayed in the gentle breeze as I looked to the west where the sun lay in the sky. From the position of the sun I assumed that we would only be graced with light for another hour or two. It was suspected that our enemy would arrive at any moment, but with every passing moment of peace I found my mind tricking me into believing that there would be no battle on this day.

I stood in at the head of a rank twelve men long and eight men deep. Each soldier wore typical Firiussian armor: worn chainmail underneath a leather-studded breast piece. Some soldiers were lucky enough to have two-piece suits of armor consisting of light steel, but most wore studded leather that could not likely withstand a single arrow. The soldiers also had leather or, in some cases, steel greaves that were tightly clasped around their legs. Each soldier in the ranks held either a spear, axe, or in the case of those in our ranks, a firm broadsword. Some had simple helmets that had three distinct points on the top in triangular fashion, but most wore no helmet. There were at least forty ranks identical to mine standing before the wall, and it seemed that they stretched infinitely down the field.

In front of me stood a rank of horsemen that were ready to charge upon command. Leading the numerous ranks of riders positioned before the footmen was Godfrey, who sat atop a grand brown steed clad in armor. Godfrey wore light raiments that set him apart from the other soldiers who sat atop their horses around him. The angel rode his horse tirelessly back and fourth before the ranks of men as his keen gaze studied the south. A grimace of cold command was painted across his face as he once again raised his simple helm and looked toward the southern sky. Next to me stood Ariel in her normal attire, yet underneath her cloak she wore shabby chain mail. Both garments were light and allowed her to move freely about the field, yet the mail clearly had not been used in battle for sometime. My wandering thoughts were interrupted as she spoke.

"I don't like this," Ariel said.

"Of what do you speak?" I asked.

"There is a wall many feet high behind us." She turned toward me. "Yet we are out here in the open waiting for the enemy?"

"Look at the drains," I said as I nodded toward one of the many man-sized drain holes that led into the city. I went on to say, "Even if we put a multitude of spearmen or archers at the other end of that drain, the enemy would still have access to the inner workings of the city. We must attack them head on to make up for the poor architecture employed within the walls."

Ariel silently nodded her head as a remorseful frown fell upon her face. A deep sigh escaped her breath as she turned toward the great fields before us.

Without thinking, I grabbed her hand and turned her gaze toward mine. "Remember, we are going to protect each other and meet our friends on the sun-soaked roads of the capitol by tomorrow's dawn. We promised."

After a brief moment of silence, Ariel reluctantly smiled. The air was still for a moment before I spoke once more with a light-hearted tone. "It could be worse." Ariel turned to me in confusion. I returned her perplexed stare with a smile. "It could be raining."

* * *

On the other end of the battlefield, Theron stood in his usual attire with a thick layer of chainmail underneath his shirt. He paced the ground above the northern wall in dismay as both Pailo and Mithias sat on two boxes and played a game involving dice and coin. Theron had been pacing about for the past twenty minutes, stopping every few moments only to glance out into the open fields, mumble something, and then continue his senseless walk. This childlike unrest had caused Mithias to yell at him several times before the lizard went back to his usual routine. Just after the lizard mumbled something to himself, Pailo looked up at him with an irritated demeanor.

"Would you sit down?" Pailo whinned. Theron shot him a deathly glare then continued his pacing. This stare silenced the ranger, but the captain would not hold his tongue so easily.

"For the sake of the Gods, relax," Mithias commanded. "Your pacing will not bring the fight to us any sooner."

"We've been waiting for so long," remarked the lizard with a frown as he continued to pace.

Pailo stood up from his crate and walked over to the wall that rose to the base of his breast. As he did so, he placed his hand on the lizard's back and looked across the fields in dismay.

"Don't worry, Theron," he said with a heavy frown. "The battle will come."

"Look at us," Theron said as he raised his arms to the sides. Mithias looked at the lizard, but Pailo fixed his gaze across the plains. Pailo squinted as the nervous lizard continued in a voice that brought the attention of many soldiers around him.

"Everyone is pacing about, waiting to face the reaper," stated Theron. "If he doesn't come soon, I'll die from boredom."

Pailo paid no mind to the lizard's words, for his eyes had widened as he looked out over the plains. The sound of metal thundered into his ears as a faint dark mass breached the distant horizon. Pailo quickly picked up Mithias' spyglass from the box by which they sat. His line of sight was only slightly improved, yet through the glass he could see a black, almost pulsating mass making its way forward at a steady pace. Several flags protruded out of the tangled mass, all of which bore the mark of Thundria. Pailo nearly dropped the spyglass to the ground as the earth began to pulsate ever so slightly.

"What is it?" asked Mithias as he stood and approached the edge of the wall.

Pailo said nothing. The ground continued to quake more with every passing moment. Soldiers stopped roaming about and quickly made their way to the edge of the wall, where they leaned forward in an attempt to see the obscure mass in the distance. Theron quickly came up beside Pailo and looked out to the fields in fear, yet as Mithias watched the mass come toward him he simply picked up his axe and stood ready at the top of the wall. Pailo thrust the spyglass at Mithias and began to run down the northern wall, shouting orders all the way.

"Soldiers of Firius to the wall! They have arrived! Steal away any fears that mar your consciousness and ready your weapons, for soon they shall penetrate both flesh and bone!"

Archers and fighters alike ascended the inside stairs and took their posts along the many levels of the northern wall. On the top level they formed two lines against the wall, one that stood directly before the wall and another that stood right behind that line. Theron and Mithias watched as the mass continued to march toward them and take form. The two looked on as their hands tightened around their respective weapons. Soon their skills in combat would be put to the ultimate test.

* * *

As the ground began to rumble, Ariel and I attempted to see beyond the ranks of horses in front of us. Between the horses we could make out a multitude of gray and black far off in the distance. It had no shape or form and pushed forward like a dark cloud on the eve of a thunderstorm, yet as it slowly moved closer it began to unfold before my eyes. The mass had several dark spires that stuck out of it. Upon closer inspection, these were the grand siege towers of which Pailo had spoken. They were a couple of stories taller than the city walls and adorned with blackened steel. Spikes lined their lower sections, and above the spikes were numerous slits for archers to fire their arrows through.

"What could move such colossal spires forward?" I asked of no one in particular.

A soldier by my side was quick to reply, "The black mantises are more powerful than you can imagine. Their great ranks can haul the towers for miles."

Lines of mantises, black and green alike, began to fill my vision between the horsemen who held their posts despite their fear. I found my eyes turning to the towers, which stood many stories tall. At their bases I saw mighty battering rams that were strung back and ready to be released upon the weakened walls at my back. I intently studied the towers, which could easily ransack the city. I could not see the black mantises that were feared by so many, but apparently several men around me did, for they began to tremble and speak of death as their eyes beheld the dreaded sight. Godfrey quickly maneuvered his horse around to face his comrades as the ground continued to rumble. His wild mare bucked and pawed at the ground as Godfrey addressed the soldiers with a booming voice that brought all eyes to his.

"Soldiers of Firius!" he yelled over the distant rumbling. The war drums of the distant soldiers crept into my ears as Godfrey maneuvered himself before us. Some soldiers blew horns as the army slowly came in sight over the horizon, and this sound penetrated my ears to such an extent that I felt a terrible vibration move through my stomach. The soldiers stirred as their captain continued to speak.

"As the darkness to the north and south closes in, fear not death!" shouted Godfrey as the horns and drums fell short of his voice. With a booming tone that raised above all else, the angel yelled, "Fear not suffering, and fear not loss! Show the valor which Drientus has harbored for generations, and unleash the might of our great nation upon the wretched beast before us!"

A cheer went up from the soldiers all around as Godfrey's voice echoed across the fields. Ariel wailed at the top of her lungs as all those around us did the same. I unsheathed my sword and joined in the battle cry of my comrades as I raised my blade high in the air. Over the shouting, Godfrey declared, "To arms, my comrades! To arms, my friends!"

The sound of thousands of weapons being unsheathed and raised into the air was heard through the ranks. This, alongside the shouting, made for an unholy echo that flew across the fields toward the ears of the enemy.

* * *

Marcus rode a grand black mantis and was coated in thick red armor. The massive creature brought fear into the hearts of his own troops, both human and beast alike. Upon hearing the distant wail of his foes he pulled back on the reins and brought the towering beast to halt. The entire army behind him ceased its march in an instant. Marcus listened to the roar from the troops across the plains as he coolly scanned the opposition. The lizard raised a clenched fist to call for the drummers to cease their pounding. They did as they were commanded within an instant.

A lizard approached Marcus from behind and stood next to his mantis with a frown painted across his face.

"It is as our Lord at Thunder's Highseat told us," stated the lizard as he looked up at his superior. "They are ready for us. Grosovner has failed."

Marcus did not return his gaze, but spoke in a gritty and deep voice. "It is no matter. They will meet their fate by the end of the night."

The small attendant to Marcus' side asked, "Should we not separate our force and attack multiple gates at once? If we flood into one we will suffer heavy casualties."

Marcus looked at the small steward with disgust. "We have no lack of battle-hardened soldiers. Do you really think a ragtag group of rebels can stand up to the might of our bestial followers?"

The young lizard had no answer, so he simply lowered his head.

Marcus brought his mantis forward and the mantis riders in his ranks followed him. The ranks of troops that marched behind Marcus turned around and began to march toward the back, while lines of mantis riders moved forward and made a line to either side of Marcus. The line of mantis riders was deep and loud as human, lizard, and bestial soldiers alike prepared for battle. The soldiers in the formation roared with a great bloodlust as they awaited their commander's signal.

After a moment, Marcus was handed a large, twisted conch shell, and with one swift blow on this instrument, mantis riders down the line drew their instruments of war. Marcus tossed the shell aside, drew his nine-foot blade, and held it high in the air as his mantis began to make its way forward. The rest of the mantis riders followed in his step, and soon their pace quickened to a devastating gallop, rushing across the fields toward Godfrey's troops at unprecedented speeds.

* * *

Once Godfrey heard the conch shell he knew the battle was upon him and began to move his horse forward. He strode out toward the enemy, slowly at first under the blazing sun of the late afternoon. All the riders behind him did the same and kept pace as their trot evolved into a gallop that pushed the very limits of speed a horse could achieve. The two sides wailed in a sick battle cry as they rushed toward each other across the beautiful fields. Wild screams engulfed the once-tranquil field as steel and soul alike rushed toward one another. The distance between the two forces was short, and within moments the two armies collided with a great velocity.

Horses slammed into mantises, and riders from both were thrown to the ground. Spears instantly impaled several men and beasts while others were brought to the reaper by the mantises' claws. Only those with a great deal of skill and luck managed to survive the initial clash. Godfrey was one of the lucky warriors. The angel skillfully drove his steed past the dangers and found himself deep within the mass of mantis riders. A select few troops with similar luck found themselves by his side, but none fought as well as the knight captain. Using all the force he could muster, Godfrey swept his sword across the neck of a lizard on a mantis to his left. That lizard fell to the ground and became trampled by the creature he had once controlled as thick green blood spewed from his jugular. Godfrey paid no mind to this, for he had already lopped the arms off the beast that was half wolf and half man to his right. The angel wailed as he forced his blade through the neck of a mantis, which let out a screech before falling to the ground. Godfrey was covered in his enemies' blood by the time he killed his fourth and fifth victims, yet his resolve did not waver. The angel desperately killed all those around him as the battle to the north began to unfold.

* * *

On the opposite end of the field, the black mass that approached Mithias, Theron, and Pailo came to a halt nearly four hundred yards away from the wall. A single line of mantis riders faced the wall and raised their spears in preparation for a charge. Because they were so close, the soldiers of Firius had a clear view to the army of Hate incarnate for the first time. To see the inhuman, muscular creatures up close for the first time brought fear into the hearts of all those who had sworn to protect the city.

"By all that is holy, what are we facing?" asked Theron of no one in particular as his eyes scanned the mass of muscle and flesh before him.

"Some sort of black magic has morphed these creatures into what they are now," stated Pailo as he cracked his knuckles. "Let us banish them from this world and send them to the great beyond where they rightfully belong!"

As the last words escaped Pailo's breath, the mantis riders began to charge the wall while letting out a ghastly howl. Archers of Firius unleashed a volley of arrows that flew through the air and swiftly met their unfortunate targets once they were within range. Despite suffering heavy causalities in the first barrage of arrows, the will of the enemy riders did not waver. The mantis riders charged in a fit of rage toward the wall with their foot soldiers right behind them. Archers rained arrows down upon the mantises, but many found it difficult to hit targets that sped toward them so quickly. Theron readied himself for battle as he strung the first of many arrows that would fly true before the sun set.

He caught sight of a particularly strong-looking target within the mass that rushed toward the wall. He released his grip on an arrow, and the projectile pierced through the air and hit the target on the shoulder. This type of wound would take most men down to their knees, yet the creature merely flinched as the arrow made contact. Theron quickly drew another arrow and fired at the same target. The arrow impaled the target through the chest, causing black blood to spew forward onto several enemy troops. Despite this deathly wound, the soldier of Hate simply grasped his chest, broke the arrow, and continued to charge forward in a fit of rage. Theron hesitated, for he could not believe what he was seeing, but then drew a final arrow and hit the target again in the chest. This was the wound that finally brought the creature down. Theron blinked and focused on the raging mass as it trampled over its fallen comrade. The lizard's courage wavered, yet despite his uncertainty, he drew a fourth arrow and aimed for a second target.

By the time Theron had killed a single enemy the mantises had reached the thick wall. Each mantis had two thick ropes tied around its back legs; these ropes dragged in the fields as they ran. Once the beasts reached the wall, their riders swiftly jumped off of their mounts and landed on the ground. When the mantises were free to move on their own, they grasped onto the stone bricks with their front claws. These claws dug into the stone like shovels into the soft earth after a light rain. The creatures used their claws to scale the wall as their back legs scuttled on the wall to find places where they could gain footing. Archers shot numerous arrows at the heavily armored creatures as Mithias looked at the beasts with anticipation all about him.

"This is where I come in!" Mithias yelled as he readied his axe. Suddenly, a mantis sprung up before him and quickly swept its sharp claws over several archers. These archers met a quick end as the deadly creature's claws severed all flesh they met. The two ropes attached to the creature's hind legs tightened as Mithias ran toward the beast. He narrowly avoided losing his head to one of the beast's razor sharp claws. Mithias ducked and rolled under its legs and quickly slashed his axe across the creature's under-belly. The mantis' dark and moist insides spewed fourth from its belly and stained the battlements it stood on. Mithias quickly rolled away from the gore and watched as the mantis fell to the floor in a pile of bile and entrails.

Mithias looked upon his fresh kill with a confident smile, but his glee did not last for long. He turned back to the wall and peered over it as the battle continued, only to discover that the enemy was using the ropes dangling off the felled beast's legs to ascend the steep wall. The legs were protected by a thick layer of flesh and muscle that could clearly not be cut, so Mithias slammed his frame into the mantis and attempted to push it away. It was to no avail, for the dead beast was too heavy even for Mithias to move. Thinking quickly, the captain rushed over to the two ropes and attempted to cut them with his axe, yet once again he was unsuccessful at halting the enemy's plans, for the ropes were woven tightly with thick threads Mithias had never seen. The weave was so tight it seemed as if Mithias' axe was meeting unshaped steel instead of thin fiber. The enemies quickly scuttled up the ropes and made their way over the wall as best they could, yet only a select few were lucky enough to avoid the tip of an arrow to make it so far. After desperately trying to cut the ropes that seemed to be blessed with a strange type of magic that made them stronger than steel, Mithias readied his axe as rogue enemies successfully made their way to the platform where he stood.

* * *

I turned toward Ariel in dismay. Godfrey's mounted troops were being stormed by the enemy's ground forces, and they struggled to keep them at bay. Only two massive siege machines had been disabled. The rest continued forward at a steady pace despite the efforts of Godfrey and his followers. The signal for our charge would sound from Godfrey's trumpet once he felt enough mantis riders had been felled for a ground force to advance safely. We waited anxiously for this horn, yet we also dreaded it, for its sound marked the end of many men's lives. I knew all too well when I was supposed to charge, but my heart strained itself as my eyes watched the slaughter in the distance. Ariel and I stood frozen in fear, waiting for the dreaded sound to usher us toward our doom.

Finally, the loud blast from the horn shot through the air, and we knew it was time to meet the battle head on. In an instant the troops around us began to rush toward the battle with a battle cry of their own. The distant bloodbath beckoned all to their demise, yet not a single soul wavered in its resolve. Soldiers, farmers, housewives—all rushed past me, eager but afraid to join the carnage in the distance. My heart grew heavy as soldiers wailed ever louder and madly rushed forward. My very soul seemed to quiver as the forces of light plunged toward the darkness before us. I held my ground as horror overtook me, but then a familiar force purged my fear. A warm hand clasped mine and I turned to see Ariel looking at me with a halfhearted smile of both terrible realization and hope. She glanced my lips with a single kiss before rushing forward with the crazed mass of troops. With a deep, newfound resolve I ran forward and let out a deathly scream that rose with the chaos of the entire force. The distant screams and clashing steel in the devastating disarray became overwhelmingly loud as I came upon my foe.

Amid the chaos I found my first nameless and faceless target. The man before me wailed as he swept his sword vertically toward my skull. Through untrained instinct alone I quickly raised my blade and blocked the advancing steel. Sparks danced in the air and rained down upon the grass as men fought and died all around me. I rushed my foe and then swept my blade against his torso without a second thought. After the man slumped to the ground, I turned to my left and witnessed a terrible inhuman beast impaling a frightened woman with a spear. I ran through the chaos and stabbed the beast in the back of the head before he could even see me. I pulled my bloodied blade out of the fallen fiend and turned to see a black mantis rushing through the troops. The thorn-laden creature stood strong with a grand, muscular build that made it appear invincible. It batted away our troops as it rushed through the chaos straight toward me.

The creature stood nearly ten feet tall and raised one of its barbed front claws in the air then brought it down upon me in an instant. I rolled to the beast's side and slammed into its other claw, which had buried itself in the ground just inches from my belly. Then the claws retracted from the ground and came at me from both sides. The beast attempted to grab me, but I was quick to jump over the scythelike arms. For a single moment I was in the air before the creature. Its beady eyes watched as I thrust my sword into the underside of its neck. The creature reared up in pain as thick dark blood began to spray the ground. As the beast fell, so did the rider that was neither human, angel, nor lizard. I quickly ran over to the dazed rider before he could regain his bearings and sent cold steel through his furry chest. With another kill under my belt, I turned to survey the chaos about me for a brief second.

The battle was nothing like a conflict in fantastic stories. No brave knights in gleaming armor defeated throngs of foes from atop their snow-white steeds. No valiant men banded together for the greater good. What I saw around me was pure insanity. The battle had no organization to it, and after the initial clash it had evolved into an all-out brawl. Races of all kinds madly attacked any enemy they came across. Steel swept through flesh and bone, causing thick crimson life to spray into the air. When swords or axes were broken or knocked to the ground, men and women of all races clawed at their enemies. Those who were restrained kicked and bit their enemies while the thick stench of blood rose into the air. Screams and wails of the damned and dying mixed with the song of clashing steel to form a terrible orchestra of death. The combatants fought with their fists when they had to, and every body was covered in a thick layer of sweat and blood. Through all the madness I could see Ariel fending for her life.

She stood in the middle of a circle of humans and lizards who approached her with weapons drawn. They wore wicked smirks on their face as they closed in around her. Without hesitation, the angel extended both arms into the air and raised her ethereal wings to the heavens. A blaze of blinding light empowered her body as she began to conjure small spheres of flame in her hands. Ariel then propelled the spheres at all who were foolish enough to take her for an easy target. Once she had disposed of her immediate threat, she turned toward a mantis running toward Godfrey's back while he finished off another enemy. Ariel gracefully took flight and landed on the back of the mantis, next to the rider. In the blink of an eye she had shoved the bestial soldier off his mount and grabbed the reins of the flailing beast. Using all her strength, she pulled on the left rein and caused the creature to veer to the left and release a squeal of pain in the process. The mantis plowed into a handful of Thundrian soldiers as Ariel pushed it forward. The beast eventually reared up and threw her to the ground, but she was quick to get back on her feet and continue dispatching any Thundrians about her.

Thirty minutes of this chaotic mayhem went on without change, but it seemed like a lifetime. We continued killing without remorse or thought as the sun slowly retracted behind the distant mountains. Amid the battle I counted a total of fifteen siege towers, ten of which had been brought down after relentless attacks and lucky shots from catapults and ballistae on the wall. Five were now upon the walls we had fought so hard to defend as the Thundrians pushed us back ever closer to the city. Troops poured out of the moving fortresses and onto the upper wall like ants. Once on the wall they brought ruin to all they came upon. They flanked us and ruthlessly slaughtered everyone in their path. In this moment of desperation I looked back to the city after felling an attacker with pure fear about me as enemy ranks closed in to the rear. With enemies on both sides I feared for my life, but still held a dying hope for Ariel and my friends on the northern side of the city.

* * *

Mithias and Pailo found themselves back to back, facing down at least a dozen inhuman Thundrian soldiers. The beasts had made their way up the ropes at alarming speed and the archers were overwhelmed and low on arrows after a half an hour of carnage. Mithias and Pailo dealt with the problem as best they could, but the battle had taken its toll on their mental and physical states. Two beasts rushed Pailo with great momentum, but the experienced ranger quickly pulled two arrows from his quiver and strung them on his bow. Upon release, the arrows slammed into the skulls of the evil beasts and sent them off the wall. They slammed into a soulless sea of their comrades below as more continued to threaten the captain and ranger. Mithias cut through three beasts that charged him, and then whipped around to meet a wall of soldiers. Behind him, four friendly soldiers ran forward and engaged the enemy creatures in blind fury. After wiping sweat from his brow, Mithias wailed and rushed to aid the four soldiers, who were clearly ill equipped for the fight.

Meanwhile, Theron found himself at the second level of the wall inside the city. He had been forced down the steps by the overwhelming enemy forces and now fired his arrows through the arrow slits so he could stop the Thundrians from coming farther into the city. The lizard continued to fire from his bow as best he could, yet he knew very well that the forces on the northern wall could not hold out much longer. Each arrow he fired hit its mark in an instant, but many inhuman soldiers could survive several arrows before meeting their fate. The lizard watched as the enemy scaled the walls and breached the city like water breached a dam in a flood. Theron glanced to the south for just a single moment and prayed that his allies were fairing better.

* * *

Across the chaos all about me the words I had dreaded reached my ears.

"Retreat!" yelled Godfrey from the middle of the fray. He stabbed an inhuman soldier through the cheek before he yelled for retreat once again.

He repeated his words as he continued to attack all those who came around him. Using all his might, the grand angel staved off his attackers, and by his word the battle we fought turned into a mad dash for the city. Soldiers from both sides madly rushed all about me as arrows from unknown archers whizzed all about. I stood in horror for a single moment as a rider emerged from the fray. Atop the steed sat Ariel, sweating profusely and covered in blood, but she did not hesitate to order me onto the steed. I did as she commanded and soon the two of us were speeding toward the city as Godfrey's voice continued to call for a retreat. As we sped through the crowds of allies and enemies, Godfrey's call was cut off midsentence. Ariel stopped then, and both of us turned to see what had caused his shortness of breath.

From where I sat I could see nothing but a sea of blood and faceless soldiers. I frantically looked about the crowd until my eyes fell upon the proud angel who fought with unprecedented power. Godfrey stood before the enormous blue lizard who had passed us in the halls of the Finrean capitol prior to our sentence by the tyrant king. The lizard commander must have been nearly fourteen feet tall, and his glowing eyes shone through his armor like stars on a clear night. The lizard held a blade much longer than my height. He swung it at Godfrey, who ducked to avoid being hit, yet Godfrey's skill only took him so far. In a display of sheer power over the blade, the lizard whipped his weapon back from the direction he had first swung it. The blade cut through the air and met Godfrey's shining blue armor with a slam that echoed far across the plains. The angel flew through the air and slammed into the ground from the impact. On the ground his breath seemed to leave him and his eyes frantically danced about the heavens.

All time seemed to slow down as I called out to Godfrey in sheer desperation. Through the multitude of people running toward the city, I watched as the lizard calmly approached my friend and looked down at him with dissatisfaction. I could not see Godfrey's eyes from where I sat, but the lizard who stared him down smiled as his foe looked toward him. As blood began to seep out of the angel's armor, the lizard grinned widely and raised his blade. With a single strike he embedded his weapon in the dense chest plate that Godfrey wore. With a laugh of horrendous pleasure, this terrible creation watched Godfrey's last breath escaped him. Godfrey became nothing more than a corpse as his face turned up into the now-orange dusk sky in shock.

A scream escaped my breath and I attempted to whip the horse around so that I could face down the one who had killed my friend, but Ariel yelled, "No! It is too late for him! We must go!"

I looked at her half-turned head, then back at the lizard who slowly strode toward the city. Godfrey's body lay limp on the ground, and I couldn't begin to fathom such a loss. Hate enveloped me as Ariel spurred our steed on, so in a flash of fury I madly slashed away at any enemy unfortunate enough to be in the vicinity of our horse. My blind rage made me lose all sense of time, and before I knew it Ariel and I were before the open city gate. Our soldiers flooded into the city with the enemy in hot pursuit. Most Firiussian soldiers had made it back to the city by the time boiling tar was poured through the murder holes, but the thick liquid did turn a good handful of Firiussian soldiers, who were too slow to make it back to the city, into burning pitch. As some soldiers fought to hold the gate, we made our way to the steps that connected the first and second levels. In an attempt to bottleneck the enemy forces, our lot of hundreds stopped at the steps. I looked up to the fourth level of the mountain and vowed to protect those who lay inside for the sake of my fallen friend as the enemy slammed into our compact ranks with an incredible force.

* * *

Pailo and Mithias hit the ground with a thump behind Theron, who stood his ground at the base of the steps leading up to the castle wall. The two men had slid down one of the many massive ladders leading to the top of the wall when they realized that they were overwhelmed. Pailo was quick to recover from the fall and turned toward the wall that was slowly being filled with Thundrians. Pailo helped Mithias to his feet before firing another arrow at the encroaching enemies, who began to flood the highest level of the wall. The ranger, who held a great deal of command about him, was quick to realize that if his forces remained around the wall much longer their lives would be in jeopardy.

"To the second level of the city!" yelled Pailo as his men desperately fought off the ruthless force. As Pailo looked to the overrun walls, he added, "We must retreat!"

Pailo began to move backward through the city and continued to yell his commands as Theron leapt from the second level of the wall and rolled once he hit the ground. The lizard turned to his friend and nodded before releasing an arrow upon a man who had nearly struck down a Drientian soldier on the highest level of the wall. Mithias ran behind Pailo with Theron at his heels. As the lizard ran, he fired his arrows back at the oncoming enemy in an attempt to protect the hundreds of brave Drientian soldiers who had lasted so long. Only a fraction of the original force remained, and those who still drew breath now fled toward the second level with great haste.

Once at the grand steps, Mithias spun himself around and grabbed two retreating soldiers. He pushed them back around and held his axe steady on the long steps as his eyes became inflamed with rage. His voice boomed over the battle as he yelled, "We must hold them here!"

Pailo was quick to realize the genius of Mithias' declaration, for the ranger noted that the north-facing grand stairs would force the attackers to jam together as they advanced. Pailo turned to the soldiers who continued to retreat up the stairs as he made a declaration.

"Form ranks!" yelled the ranger as he took position behind Mithias and drew his bow over the man's shoulder. Many swordsmen soon formed a line in front of a row of archers, who shot at the Thundrians that emerged from the city streets and rushed up the stairs. The blockade held for a good while, but it eventually succumbed to the enemy force that seemed to have no end. Once the wall was broken, another retreat was sounded until the soldiers madly dashed to the fourth and final level. It was here that old friends were reunited.

* * *

By Godfrey's final order, Ariel and I had rushed into the city with frightened allies all about us. With their angelic leader gone, many men frantically rushed to whatever hole or safe haven they could find. It was only by the commands of a few brave soldiers, Ariel, and me that most men followed us up into the city. Archers took their places on the second and third levels and began to fire down upon the evil force that did not waver in the face of our volley. The enemy force continued forward and pushed the Drientian forces all the way back to the fourth level of the city, where I reunited with my comrades. The five of us convened with soldiers rushing about on either side of us. Together we took the surviving troops to the only stairway that led to the fourth level and formed one final blockade against the unrelenting swarm.

Only a few hundred soldiers remained in our ranks, and they were tasked with holding off the thousands who threatened us. The city was being torn apart by invaders who ransacked everything they came across. From where I stood, I could easily see the dark mass engulfing the entire city like a swarm of flies over a day-old meal. I knew that if we lost our hold on the final steps, all the innocents that sought shelter in the ornate homes behind us would fall. Against all odds, we valiantly made our stand against the force that sought the destruction of all.

A line of shields was made at the top of the fourth-level steps in order to stave off the invaders. The strongest men in our ranks held their bodies against these shields as the enemy slammed into them like a wave of water on a crumbling rock. From behind the shields, archers attempted to take out as many enemies as they could, making sure to quickly kill any mantis riders before they reached the line. Theron was one such archer, who took his place behind Mithias as Ariel cast spells of destruction upon individual soldiers who threatened us.

I grasped my sword in my bloodied and blistered hands and jabbed it between two shields that separated me from the horde. I heard a squeal from an enemy before I pulled it back to my side. I successfully killed a number of soldiers on the other side of the wall before my arm pulsed with a splitting pain the likes of which I had never known. My eyes bulged as they shot down to my shoulder, which was oozing blood. When I looked back up at the chaos before me, I noticed a spear coated in my blood retract to the other side of the shields. In this instant, all time slowed and I realized the mistake I had made. My arm had lingered in place for too long, and in this time an enemy soldier had thrust his lance into my shoulder. The spear tip had torn my flesh and muscle, and from the newfound wound, a terrible, burning pain was unleashed. Blood seeped down my arm and onto the cobblestone below me. As soon as my shoulder ripped open I let out a howl the likes of which I had never sounded before. The wound throbbed with an unbearable sweltering pain, and I stumbled backward in the ranks and slammed into Theron as he was about to string an arrow. He turned toward me with an expression of ghastly horror as he looked at my wound.

"Ariel!" he yelled as he grabbed my shoulder. His claw tightened around my wound and I wailed and watched as blood spewed onto the ground. To my surprise, Ariel quickly emerged from the mass of people and ran toward the two of us. Theron looked at her in desperation and horror.

"Lloyd is hurt!" he said in a booming voice as he strung another arrow.

My dutiful friend had let loose his arrow and strung another one by the time Ariel knelt by me. She looked down at my shoulder is disbelief, then grabbed my good arm and pulled me against the high wall of the volcano, which stood against the city streets. I slumped against the wall as she conjured swirling flame in her hand and declared, "Hold still, Lloyd; this will help."

Her hand covered my wound, and in an instant a searing fury of pain enveloped my whole body. My muscles shook, my eyes streamed with tears and I screamed a scream that could be heard above the chaos before me. I had never felt a greater pain, and it seemed as if my whole body were on fire. My eyes darted to the wound and, while the skin was torn and burnt, the gaping hole in my shoulder was sealed.

I slumped down against the rock and looked toward the sky, which had become very dark since the start of the battle. The sun had almost vanished, and as I looked at the tip of the life-giving orb, I feared that I would never see it again. The sweet allure of sleep beckoned me, yet it would not come, for Ariel continued to call my name and begged me to stay awake as she examined my wound. A crystalline tear rolled down her check as she wrapped a cloth around my wound tightly and looked deeply into my eyes.

"You'll be okay, Lloyd," she whispered. Her soft voice wavered against the chaos of battle. Her eyes seemed distant as the forces of evil continued to smash against our barricade with the power of thousands of men. I glanced at the horrid sight before looking back to her clear blue eyes.

"Ariel," I muttered as I grabbed onto her shoulder and held it tightly. I struggled to speak in between deep breaths as I declared, "I don't think... I don't think we're going to see the dawn together."

Ariel looked at me as a tear rolled down her cheek and pooled in a cut below her right eye. She glanced back at the line, which was now breaking because many soldiers who held shields were falling victim to the enemy's power. Death was behind the angel I so adored, yet she refused to meet it. With a somber stare brought on by pain-laden eyes, she pierced my very soul. Her hand pushed my hair away from my face as she gently caressed my cheek. My heart pulsated with both horror and delight as I looked at the angel, who remained silent as screams from the dying entered my ears. My grip on Ariel's shoulder tightened as I awaited the reaper, and my greatest regret in the moment was not being able to save her. It was in this moment of complete desolation that the tip of the sun vanished before the horizon. Darkness shrouded the damned land and I believed all hope was lost.

But suddenly, a grand roar broke above the land. My eyes fluttered and I believed that I was in a dream for a single moment before I came back into reality. Memories of old times flooded back to me as if I had experienced them yesterday, and all became clear in my mind for a single moment. I spoke the same words that had reached my ears months before, spoken by the mysterious dragon, Mordikai, who had saved my life.

"When the sun dips below the plains and a dark foe encloses upon the light," I said in a whisper that danced through the air. The words of my elusive ally rang true in my mind as I continued, "look to the north for aid."

Ariel looked at me with tear-filled eyes as if I were delusional. Using all the strength I could muster, I extended my hand and pointed to the northern skies with the slightest grin upon my face.

From the north came the salvation I had been promised long ago. A dozen dragons rushed toward the chaos as they let loose a cry that brought fear to both friend and foe. In their lead was Mordikai in all his divine glory, racing toward the battle that raged all about us. The dragons swept down upon the steps and grabbed many enemies in their claws and teeth. Mordikai himself landed in front of Ariel and me and faced the enemy, who surged forward on the steps. With a screech, he reared his head back then faced our foes, who could not believe the sight before them. From the dragon's mouth came a stream of searing flame that slammed into the Thundrian soldiers and turned their bodies into smoldering crisps and fireballs that madly flailed about.

The other dragons landed in the center of seasoned enemy ranks and swiftly dispatched them with ease while others slammed into the siege towers with enough force to ruin them in an instant. Neither man nor beast could harm the creatures as they ruthlessly slaughtered all those who swore allegiance to Thundria. All eyes turned toward the dragons as mine rolled to the distant castle. It was in this moment that I caught sight of a small rank of Thundrian soldiers disappearing into the castle.

A rogue group of enemies rushed past the chaos toward the castle with great fervor. In the middle of these forces ran a woman with shining blonde hair and crimson garb. Soldiers of Firius began a counter attack on the enemy as the dragons scorched all Thundrian life, but the woman somehow had made her way past all the insanity with a small guard about her. Ariel still stood by my side and watched as I wrenched to my feet and looked at the scarlet woman and her company as they entered the unguarded castle. Without thinking, I clutched my wound with my left hand and gave chase to the band with my sword dragging across the ground in my right hand. Ariel ran behind me and beckoned me to stop, yet I continued to follow the Thundrians into the castle with a speed I had never known I had. With Ariel in tow, I entered the castle and followed my enemy, who always seemed just out of reach. The beasts rushed through the horrified civilians and killed all who stood in their way. Most retreated, but there was one foolish old soul who sought to make his stand against the enemy.

I was in the courtyard of the main keep with Ariel behind me when King Tiam emerged from a group of freightened civilians. He beheld the band of Thundrians rushing through his courtyard and swiftly grabbed a dulled knife. I hardly had time to think of how foolish he was before he rushed toward the lady with a speed unprecedented to his figure and let out a garbled yell. Before the Thundrians took notice of him, he managed to thrust his blade into the still-beating heart of a bestial soldier. As soon as he had performed his deed, he was impaled by the platinum-haired woman and left to bleed out in the courtyard. Civilians encircled their king in an instant as the dragons continued to wail against the burning city. Though I wished I could remain by his side, I knew I could not stay with the king to discover his fate. I knew I had to continue in the wake of the crimson-garbed woman.

I do not know how many halls crowded with frightened civilians I weaved through in my daze, but eventually I arrived at the great bridge that spanned between the tallest spire of the castle and the rim of the volcano. Something deep within my soul propelled me toward my enemy at a great speed. I reached the rim of the volcano and stood many feet away from the woman as Ariel caught up to me.

From where we stood I could see a group of angels garbed in onyx robes start some sort of chant that wavered through the air and rose to the heavens. An armed soldier in this lot of nearly a dozen whipped his head around and looked at Ariel and me. He began to growl, yet before he could charge, the woman in red caught sight of us and spoke in a sharp voice that pained my ears.

"Do not attack!" she commanded as she turned around to face us. She paused and looked at us carefully after taking several steps toward my frail frame, then smiled and remarked, "So, you're still alive..."

I clenched my wound with all my strength as I attempted to hold my sword in the air, but it was to no avail. The woman before me laughed at my struggle.

"Be gone from this place, fiend!" Ariel shouted as she took a step forward. "Or suffer the searing pain of dragon fire!"

The ghastly woman before us let out a quick laugh before she replied in a sinister tone, "I have work to do, my dear."

Ariel became irate and was quick to shoot a sphere of flame at the woman, yet to her surprise the globe dissipated into thin air before it collided with the evil woman's skull. With a menacing grin, the mysterious enemy looked at my hand, which was clasped in Ariel's, and she lowered her brow. The scarlet-garbed woman laughed as she extended her arm and opened her palm. There, a small, translucent orb of light was formed. The air around the miniscule globe seemed to rush toward it as the woman reared back her hand. In one fell moment, the woman threw the strange sphere of light at Ariel, who stood like a statue as the projectile hurtled toward her. Time slowed in my mind as the spinning ball of light rushed toward Ariel. Using all the force I could muster,

I darted in front of the ball and let it slam into my chest. Once the orb struck me, my body became limp and a thick purple mist enveloped my vision as I slammed to the ground. After a single moment of struggle, my limbs stopped moving and all went black as the darkest night.

* * *

Ariel looked down at the paralyzed, almost lifeless body of her friend, then back at the woman, with hate in her eyes.

As she tightened her fists she screamed, "What have you done?"

Before Isalia could so much as smile, Ariel rushed toward her with fire forming in her hands. The angel was just a couple of feet away from the evil woman before an earth-shattering rumble overpowered the continuous chant of the angelic mages. This rumble sent Ariel flying off her feet and onto the ground as the woman smiled and the angelic mages nodded.

"So it is done," she remarked. Her gaze then met Lloyd's stiff body as the ground shifted and began to crack. Amid the rumbling, the mysterious woman rushed over to Ariel's dear friend and placed her hand on his freezing skin. Lloyd's stiff body began to move and elevate itself into the air near the terrible woman before she whipped back around.

"Get us out of here!" she shouted at the mages. The group of old angels began to chant as both Theron and Mithias emerged at the bridge and began to cross to the volcano. Once they reached Ariel's side, they saw the woman in red standing over Lloyd. Theron drew an arrow and quickly released it. The steel tip of the arrow was inches away from slamming into the woman's dreadful smile when suddenly she, and all those beside her, vanished into nothingness by way of a lingering violet mist. After that, neither Lloyd nor the lot of nearly a dozen Thundrians remained. The only remnant of their deed was the rumbling volcano that angrily stirred in the young night.

After several attempts at standing, Ariel was finally able to make it to her feet, where she swayed amid the quaking ground.

The angel stood up in disbelief and searched for Lloyd's body, yet she could plainly see that it was gone. She believed that her eyes deceived her, so she called the name of her friend as both Theron and Mithias rushed to her side. Deep within the volcano, magma began to bubble and jump. Two dragons landed on the volcano's rim before Mordikai joined their ranks.

Once he landed, a fellow dragon turned to Mordikai and said in a defeated voice, "We are too late."

"No, my friend," Mordikai said as he centered his vision on the quaking rim of the volcano, "we have arrived just in time."

Mordikai quickly let out an earsplitting roar that brought all his companions to his side. Thousands had died by the dragons' fire, yet none of the dragons who stood beside Mordikai seemed to waver in their resolve. Mordikai glanced at his friends for a moment before looking at the rim of the volcano once again.

"We must contain it," he yelled as his eyes met the dragons all about him. He turned back to the center of the volcano before he added, "All shall be lost if we fail."

Before taking any action, Mordikai looked at Ariel, Theron, and Mithias and yelled, "Make clear of this peak as fast as you can, or you will die!"

Theron and Mithias did not hesitate to raise Ariel to her feet and attempt to usher her toward the bridge, but she would not be moved so easily. Ariel released herself from the her comrades' grasp and turned back in a fit of rage and sorrow.

"We cannot leave!" she yelled as the dragons about her began to encircle the rim of the volcano. "I do not know where Lloyd is!"

Mithias quickly grasped the girl's arm and pulled her alongside him as he yelled, "We do not know where he has gone, but if we stay here any longer the three of us will meet the reaper!"

The angel continued to resist the great man until Theron declared, "If we die here, we are doing him and this world no good!"

With these words, Ariel's momentary lapse of reason had left her. The angel nodded, then followed her two friends across the crumbling bridge that led to the tallest tower of the castle. The three moved as fast as their legs could carry them across the collapsing bridge before they headed through the maze of corridors in the spire. With such swiftness, they soon emerged on the fourth level of the city, where no Thundrian enemies remained. Dead and dying bodies were scattered all about as the rumbling from the heart of the volcano continued with a passion that threatened to destroy the remnants of the city. The shaking ground began to bring down ornate houses and rogue parts of the castle from which the three had just emerged. The quaking made a roar louder than any dragon as the ground swept from side to side. In sheer desperation, Ariel looked toward the peak.

From the volcano came a holy light the likes of which no eyes could behold. All shielded their vision as the light shot straight through to the heavens. Dragons screamed as the night turned to day and the rumbling grew louder. The brilliant radiance extended beyond the reaches of the city before it vanished just as quickly as it had appeared. Suddenly, the holy light dissipated into the blackness of night in the same instant that the furious earth quieted her rage. The surviving forces turned to the formerly desolate peak to behold a gleaming marble column that parted clouds as it continued through the dark sky as far as the eye could see. All soldiers stared at the monument in wonder and awe before a single voice made itself known.

"Mordikai..." said Mithias in a whisper that sounded like a scream against the still air. Before anyone could say another word, Mithias dashed toward the earthen steps that led toward the peak. Theron and Ariel were quick to follow him up the uneven earthen steps. After a great deal of running and climbing, the trio arrived at the rim of the volcano, where each dragon lay dormant about the rim. Of all the dragons collapsed on the cold stone, only one stirred. This dragon looked at Ariel, Mithias, and Theron as they approached him with deep suffering in his plate-sized eyes. The three were upon him in an instant, and despite the fact that the dragon had trouble breathing, his body remained unscathed. Theron looked at the creature, who hacked and coughed with pain.

"Mordikai!" Theron yelled as he placed his claw upon the searing hot scales that graced the dragon's front left leg. He retracted his claw in an instant as it filled with terrible pain. Before any could speak, the grand dragon let out a final voice in the night.

"These dragons..." he said through fits of terrible coughs. Mordikai raised his eyes to his two-legged friends. "They are alive. We shall wake with coming light and my words of wisdom will return."

The massive dragon then fell forward and nearly landed on top of the three adventurers, who jumped out of his shadow at the last moment. For a single moment, pain was about the three, who looked at the body of the dragon, yet Mordikai's nostrils soon flared and sucked in air. Mordikai drew a steady, uninterrupted breath as if he were in a deep slumber. Just like Mordikai had said, all the dragons were alive, but enthralled in a deep, near-lifeless sleep. The three turned from the dragon and watched in silence as a single figure darted up the earthen steps. This figure revealed itself to be Pailo once his features took form.

The ranger panted deep breaths and didn't stop to survey the scene as he raised his head to his new friends and made the single declaration they so wished to hear.

"All but a handful of Thundrians were scorched by the dragons. The few lizards and humans left who serve under the Thundrian banner now flee to the southern swamps," he said between broken breaths. The man was able to utter one more statement through his exhaustion.

"We have survived."

CHAPTER 23

The city was ravaged, but not destroyed. Throughout the night, innocents were taken from the homes on the fourth level to the ruined city. As freightened civilians exited their safe havens, they were met with the dead and dying. The dying were taken away to be tended to or put to rest, but those who had died were left where they fell until the dying could be properly tended to. No one cleared the streets, for not a single soul had the strength to even begin such a task. The gates to the city were closed and barred once again as the remnants of the scattered enemy force fled to the distant southern swamps. Both the northern and southern fields outside the city were laden with death, but it was clearly the southern plains that were the more scarred of the two. The grasses that had swayed gently in the wind just hours before were trampled, muddy, and littered with bodies of both friend and foe while the north held mostly corpses of the fiendish nightmares created by Thundria.

Ariel, Theron, Mithias, and Pailo made their way into the crumbling fortress on the fourth level after the dragons collapsed. Once inside the tower that had sustained the least damage during the fray, a servant was quick to deliver the news of the king's death. After being impaled in his desperate attempt to stop the crimson-garbed lady, he had quickly bled to death. Despite the news, Pailo shed no tears and simply ordered the guards to tend to the wounds of the three adventurers. It seemed that for the moment the king-less city turned to the seasoned ranger for guidance, so by his command troops secured the walls while civilians cleaned the streets.

Ariel, Mithias, and Theron were tended to through the night, but sleep came to none in their lot. At dawn, the three adventurers and the ranger Pailo reunited on the steps of the fourth tier, where the stench of death was not as strong as it was on the lower levels. Each exchanged praises for survival, yet their joy proved to be fleeting. They turned to the streets with heavy eyes. Soldiers who had survived the encounter and retained their will through the night began to collect the bodies of the fallen and take them to proper resting places, whether that was a fire for the enemy or a fresh grave for a friend. As the four looked down upon the dreadful scene the three adventurers could not speak.

"So we have achieved victory," began Pailo. At this comment, none nodded in agreement. Instead, Ariel spoke solemn words.

"Victory?" asked the angel, who stared down at the ground. She looked up at Pailo and pierced his gaze as she spoke. "No, Pailo. Today we have simply dodged death. We did not achieve victory by any means."

A mad look overtook Ariel for a passing moment as she motioned to the infinitely high pillar that had emerged from the volcano. In a voice that was not her own, she exclaimed, "For the love of the Two, the ancient pillar now stands and Lloyd and Godfrey have been slain!"

Pailo was at a loss for words despite his great longing for a good sentence.

"Hold your tongue, Ariel," stated Mithias before Pailo could speak. The powerful man turned his eyes to the girl as he declared, "Lloyd's corpse does not mar the battlefield. He is lost to us, but he may still live."

"If there is any chance that he lives, we must find him," shot back Ariel as a fiery determination enveloped her heart. There was a pause for a moment before she added, "Though, I do not know where to start looking for him."

Before any of the fighters could speak, a loud thud was heard on the rocks behind them.

"I believe I can help," came a familiar, wise voice. The lot turned to see Mordikai standing before them. The frame of the grandiose creature seemed to sway against the gentle wind as the dragon stretched his massive wings. Mordikai's eyes were slanted as if he had just woken up, and his body seemed bruised and worn. Despite the severity of the situation, Theron could not contain a small bit of childlike excitement upon seeing the dragon who had saved his life on two occasions.

"Mordikai!" exclaimed Theron with a smile. "You stir once more."

"Of course, child." The creature spoke in a voice that seemed to stretch itself as he declared, "My company is all accounted for, but it seems yours is missing its keystone."

Ariel perked up at these words and was quick to speak. "Do you know where we can find Lloyd?"

"That I do," stated the dragon, who still struggled to stay afoot. "He has been swept away from this place by the scarlet devil."

Mithias took a step forward. "So he lives?"

Mordikai nodded and eased the hearts of all those who cared for the boy. To know that Lloyd was alive calmed the company for a moment, until Mordikai spoke his next words.

"He lives, but he suffers more than you could imagine." Mordikai's voice became heavy and distant. "The woman who took Lloyd seeks to present him as a gift to the dark lord who is the catalyst for all this chaos."

"Why?" asked Theron.

Mordikai let out a drawn-out sigh. "Though all of you are great warriors destined to fight the darkness of the land with a force that surpasses all men, Lloyd holds a higher destiny than any before my eyes. Though the entirety of his fate is veiled from my old eyes, for me to reveal all I know would confound you in a time when clarity is paramount. What you must know is that the dark one known as Tulinthor realizes Lloyd's vast strength and seeks the boy for his power. The crimson-garbed woman is merely an agent of his evil."

Before anyone else could speak, Ariel inquired, "How can we get to him?"

The dragon raised his eyes as he looked toward the southwestern skies. His nostrils flared as his eyes closed and he breathed deeply. A cool southern breeze soon flowed to the dragon, who stood like a statue against the winds. After a moment of silence, he spoke once again.

"The foul scent of the woman is to the southwest. Lloyd is in her company, and they are in a cold place."

Pailo said, "There are mountains to the southwest that separate the mainland from the coast. They are freezing, and traversing them would risk death. Besides, nothing lies on the other side but remote villages and waters crowded with jagged rocks the likes of which few ships can pass."

Not a single muscle in Ariel hesitated as she declared, "We must give chase to her!"

The dragon let out a sigh. "Though I agree, I cannot offer my assistance."

"Why's that?" asked Mithias.

The dragon looked back at the rim of the volcano where his troops stirred in the morning light. "My company and I have more important matters to attend to."

"Matters that are more important than Lloyd?" shot back Ariel. The dragon turned to her, not in anger, but rather, in remorse.

The cerulean-scaled beast looked down at her with a heavy brow. "There is a grand scheme of things that is unfolding in this world, and though I may be leaving you now, do not damn me, for I shall return when the time is right. You must trust me now as you did once before."

Ariel looked into the deep eyes of the one who had saved her life with a newfound realization. Though her heart begged her to be infuriated with the beast, she could not harbor such emotions in the moment. She solemnly nodded to the dragon before he turned to the ranger who had assisted the warriors.

"You will give these three the finest steeds you have," he said. "Then you will help rebuild this place."

Mithias looked between the dragon and Pailo before asking, "He will not be joining us?"

Pailo shook his head and replied, "My place is with the people of Firius. With no king to guide them, the capitol is on the verge of anarchy. I shall remain and lead the reconstruction of this place if the people will it. Only once our borders are secure will I consider the next step against the Thundrians."

Despite their longing for further assistance, the three could not argue with Pailo's reasoning. Once the matter of the capitol's reconstruction was settled, the dragon spoke again.

"Shall you rest for the day?" asked Mordikai as he looked over the three, who looked as if they were going to collapse at any moment.

"We cannot wait any longer," Ariel declared impatiently. "With each passing moment Lloyd grows farther away."

"We shall leave at once and take with us all we need," added Mithias.

"Take all you desire," replied Pailo. "You have done much for this kingdom, and I'm sure if Godfrey still drew breath he would demand that you leave this place with only the best supplies."

Mordikai looked down at the three determined adventurers with a steady gaze as he said, "Make haste, my friends, for though the battle for Drientus may be over, the war for domination of this planet has only just begun."

At these words, Theron turned from Pailo and entered one of the few standing towers after bidding him and Mordikai farewell. Mithias and Ariel did the same, and all began to prepare for their journey across the rugged mountains to the southwest. Through the preparation Ariel gazed out a broken window with longing eyes and a fast-beating heart. Though her vision could not reach Lloyd, she knew deep in her heart that wherever he was, he was waiting for her, waiting for his only salvation.

CHAPTER 24

The three who proved their strength through their unity sped across the plains as the dark king sat atop his tower in Thundria and viewed their progress from the crystal before him. Tulinthor looked at the three who had defeated his forces with his usual stoic features as they rushed to their demise, yet as he watched them something deep within him came to light. For the first time since taking his rule, the man felt the twist of anxiety and fear within his heart. He batted the crystal away in an instant and watched it shatter as it hit the marble floor of his wicked tower, yet the mist within the orb remained. This mist formed behind the tyrant and tightly grasped his shoulder as it looked into the mirror to behold the boy that was ushered toward him. His gaze fell back to the plains of his defeat as Ariel, Theron, and Mithias sped across them with an unwavering resolve.

* * *

Ariel sat atop her horse and looked across the southwestern fields with dismay. The smoking city was behind her as the almighty sun rose high in the sky to display the aftermath of the battle. Pailo's directions rang in her ears as she looked across the empty fields. She had to follow a winding path through the mountains to reach the western edge of the empire of Dreintus. Pailo had warned her of hostile angelic tribes who held residence about the peaks, yet this did not frighten her in the least bit. Her resolve to find Lloyd overpowered all other emotions within her heart. Her steed restlessly stamped his feet in the mud formed from battle as she looked across the field that was littered with decomposing bodies and empty armor.

Theron rode to the right of her and looked across the field with the same disposition. "So much death," he stated.

As the sun shone down upon the corpses of all races and sizes, a terrible sizzling noise could almost be heard against the wind as flesh burned under the relentless light. Theron could barely stand to the sight.

Mithias approached him. "Yet it is just the beginning," declared the commanding man as he rode his steed to the right of Theron.

Ariel looked about the fields with neither disgust nor remorse. "We have ruined the Thundrian forces on this land at the cost of many lives," she said as her eyes scanned the tainted landscape, "yet now Thundria knows of our power and resolve. With the three pillars standing, it will only be a matter of time before the power to these devices is unlocked and used against us. The fourth pillar will rise beneath Tulinthor's kingdom."

"We will not let that happen," remarked Mithias as he turned and faced Ariel with a hopeful smile. He held this disposition as he added, "We will stop the dark lord of Thundria from obtaining the power and bring him to justice, and we will find Lloyd, wherever he may be."

"Or we will die trying," Theron said.

The three spurred their steeds off across the fields as fast as they could. Storm clouds began to roll in from the west as they rode, blanketing the sky above their destination. The sun began to fade as the storm clouds rolled above the plains, and it was in this moment that Ariel realized the true trials of her journey had just begun.

ACKNOWLEDGEMENTS

I would like to thank several individuals for greatly contributing to the creation and publication of this book. The making of this book was no easy task, and had it not been for the help from the following individuals I doubt it would have been published.

My grandparents, Roy and Nancy Mitchell extended their generosity to me and funded this project to a great extent. I wrote this entire novel while attending school and didn't have anywhere close to enough funds to produce this book. They kindly gave me the funds needed to produce this novel through Createspace and because of them the book could be edited, illustrated, and produced.

My own parents, Sherry and Jeff, were incredibly supportive of this project as soon as I began writing. Both were always there for me and ever since I began to take a passion for writing they have supported me wholeheartedly. My mother was instrumental in refining my writing style from a young age while my father introduced me to a variety of quality novels and video games that gave me a great love for the fantasy genre.

Amelia Langford, my illustrator, needs to be given recognition as well for her beautiful illustrations of my world. She took several pages of my scribbled maps and turned them into something clean and beautiful. Her artwork is quite simply amazing, and I am honored to call her my illustrator for this book and my friend.

Finally I would like to thank my incredible team at Createspace for working with me to create the book. Their talented team of editors, interior designers, and cover designers did an amazing job making the book into something wonderful. Their service was always fast and reliable and I am happy to have published through them.

ABOUT THE
AUTHOR

Sean Mitchell was born and raised in northern Virginia. From a young age he became obsessed with fantasy adventure through numerous video games and books and his passion for fantasy only grew as he aged. His early experiences with fantasy fiction through various forms of media led him to explore writing. At the age of eighteen he began drafting the full Might and Majesty trilogy on a whim, but over the next four years writing the series enveloped him. He is currently a sociology major at Virginia Commonwealth University where he continues to develop his writing and hopes to someday have a catalog of best sellers.